"I don't want to be your wife."

Nora turned to leave, but Christian blocked her way in two strides.

"No power on earth can undo our marriage."

"I'm not a fool. Not all husbands and wives live together. You may live as you please, and so will I."

As she spoke, Nora saw Christian's expression harden. Contrition vanished, and he examined her from head to foot.

"Who has taken my place?"

"What do you mean?" Nora backed away as Christian began to stalk her.

"Did you seek comfort from some other man?"

Christian asked the question calmly, but his chest rose and fell, as if he couldn't get enough air in his lungs. Nora backed away, but he kept coming.

"I think your wits have turned to mud," Nora said as she tried to avoid her husband.

"No one else will ever touch you."

"I want no one else."

"Ah!"

Christian swooped at her, and Nora jumped back only to fall against a tree. He was on her in a moment, bracing his arms on either side of her and pressing her between his body and the tree.

"There is hope if you want no one but me."

Lady Gallant

Bantam Books by Suzanne Robinson

HEART OF THE FALCON
LADY GALLANT

Lady Gallant

Suzanne Robinson

BANTAM BOOKS
NEW YORK • TORONTO • LONDON • SYDNEY • AUCKLAND

LADY GALLANT
A Bantam Fanfare Book / January 1992

Grateful acknowledgment is made for permission to reprint the following:
Excerpt from THE POEMS OF CATULLUS translated by Peter Whigham
(Penguin Classics, 1966), copyright © Peter Whigham, 1966. Excerpt from
MEDIEVAL LOVERS: A BOOK OF DAYS, Poems selected by Kevin Cros-
sley-Holland. Copyright © 1988 by Phoebe Phillips Editions. Used by per-
mission of Grove Press, Inc. Excerpts from THE OXFORD DICTIONARY
OF QUOTATIONS (3rd edition 1979). Reprinted by permission of Oxford
University Press. Excerpts from CATULLUS translated by Sir William Mar-
ris (Oxford 1924). Reprinted by permission of Oxford University Press. Ex-
cerpts from SIR THOMAS WYATT: THE COMPLETE POEMS edited by
R.A. Rebholz. Reprinted by permission of Penguin Books Ltd. Excerpts from
THE MASTER BOOK OF HERBALISM by Paul Beyerl. Reprinted by permission of Phoenix Publishing. Excerpts from BRITISH LITERATURE FROM
BEOWULF TO SHERIDAN by Hazelton Spencer. Reprinted by permission
of D.C. Heath & Company. Excerpts from OVID translated by J.H. Mozley.
Reprinted by permission of Harvard University Press. Excerpts from EV-
ERYDAY LIFE IN MEDIEVAL TIMES by Marjorie Rowling. Reprinted by
permission of the Putnam Grosset Group and B.T. Batsford Ltd. Excerpt
from LIFE IN ELIZABETHAN DAYS by William Stearns Davis. Reprinted
by permission of HarperCollins Publishers.

ISBN 0-553-29430-X

Published simultaneously in the United States and Canada

PRINTED IN THE UNITED STATES OF AMERICA
RAD 0 9 8 7 6 5 4 3 2 1

DEDICATION

To Lois Ann Womack Heavener.
A woman of courage.
A survivor
And loving mother.
All my books are yours.

Introduction

The world of *Lady Gallant* is a world of intrigue and danger. This historical romance takes place against the backdrop of a struggle to the death between two women; a struggle for control of the kingdom of England and the hearts of its people; the struggle between Mary and Elizabeth Tudor.

When Mary Tudor ascended the throne of England in 1553, she brought with her a legacy of pain, tragedy, and survival. Her father, the infamous Henry VIII of the six wives, had treated her at various times as his golden child, a nuisance to be ignored, a stubborn and inconvenient heir, and an enemy to be subdued and destroyed.

Henry needed a male heir, for he believed no woman could hold England together against her own powerful nobles and the mighty threats of France and Spain. He asked the Pope for a divorce from Mary's mother, Catherine of Aragon, only to be refused. After years of maneuvering, he lost patience and dragged his kingdom out of the mainstream of Catholicism by establishing himself as the head of the church in England. Suddenly, Englishmen were no longer to follow the Pope, as they had for centuries. Henry gave himself a divorce, cast aside both Catherine and Mary, and married Elizabeth's mother, Ann Boleyn.

Mary turned to her faith to help her survive, as she watched her father drive her mother to her death by neglect, persecution, and heartbreak. She watched him tear down the bulwarks of her childhood—the Catholic Church, its monasteries, nunneries, and abbeys. Thousands of religious people were uprooted and displaced, just as Mary was uprooted and displaced.

Yet Mary survived, and when at last she came to the throne, she considered it a miracle wrought by God so that she could restore England to its proper state of grace within the true faith. She reestablished the Catholic faith, brought back the monks, priests, and nuns, and tried to make her people change. One of the ways she did this was by punishing Protestants if they refused to return to the Catholic faith. Throughout England Mary's bishops searched out heretics. Tragically, most of those who were caught were too uneducated or not powerful enough to protect themselves. Hundreds of Protestants died, and many of those who perished at the stake could not even read. They died because they couldn't repeat the right words in the right sequence, and the more people who died, the more Mary was hated.

Mary did not understand that England had changed forever—intellectually and spiritually. Too many powerful people owned former church lands; too many people looked forward instead of backward. One of those people was Elizabeth, the daughter of the woman who had ruined Mary's life.

Elizabeth was Protestant. She had to be, for according to the Catholics she was a bastard with no claim to the throne. Educated, intelligent, wily, Elizabeth represented everything Mary did not—the new religion, wide-ranging intellectual curiosity, youth, and beauty. Elizabeth was a threat to all that Mary was trying to rebuild.

Unfortunately, Mary was childless. Married to Philip, King of Spain, she suffered from his indifference and from her own inability to conceive an heir who would carry on her life's dream to re-create the golden kingdom of her childhood. Aging, desperate, fearful, Mary's mind began to weaken beneath the terrible burden she'd taken upon herself. Faced with the prospect of Elizabeth succeeding her, Mary had to make a decision: to kill her sister, or to surrender her dream by allowing Elizabeth to succeed.

A tragic dilemma wrought in an age of great progress and great suffering, the struggle between Mary and Elizabeth is the stuff of human drama. Come with me now back to a time when faith and life, love and politics intertwined, when—as Christian and Nora discover—to love the wrong person could cost you your life.

Chapter
I

Nuns no longer went in fear of their lives, as they had in old King Harry's time, and one had broken her journey to her convent at the royal manor of Hatfield. Her shaking, mittened hand closed the door of the Hatfield chapel. The nun tucked the hand back inside the sleeve of her habit and turned to face the central aisle. Hunched over with age, misshapen by a crooked shoulder, the old woman squinted at the only inhabitant of the chapel.

At the altar rail knelt a young woman dressed in satin with a black French hood set upon a waterfall of red-gold hair. The nun hobbled up the aisle and knelt beside the lady, then folded her mittened hands, enclosing a cross within them, and rested them on the rail. The red-haired woman kept her gaze on the cross before her. The nun bent her head in prayer, and Latin words filled the chapel. The nun sneezed and dropped her cross. Her quivering fingers unfolded as if to search for it.

In a whiplike movement, the young woman brought her white hand down over the hand of the nun. Long, tapered fingers gripped the old woman's hand; they snatched at the mitten and pulled it off. Stripped of its covering, the nun's hand lay still beneath the woman's. It was larger than the one that held it

prisoner. Smooth, golden skin stretched tight over long bones, and a signet ring of gold encircled the third finger.

The nun sneezed again, and the young woman laughed under her breath. "Serves you right, Lord Montfort. God punishes you for this disguising by giving you an ague."

The nun straightened. The crooked shoulder righted itself, and the body seemed to grow and stretch. Christian de Rivers, Lord Montfort, son of the Earl of Vasterne, rubbed his itching nose and peered at the woman around the edge of his black veil.

"Your Highness," he said. He dipped his head in an approximation of a bow, then sneezed again. "This habit is musty."

Princess Elizabeth smirked at him before turning her gaze back to the altar. "What tidings of my sister?"

"The Queen is ofttimes mad and all the time dying."

The princess sucked in a breath, but she said nothing.

Christian studied the altar rail. "She has given up the fantasy that she is with child and believes that the swelling is dropsy. But she swears Your Grace will never be queen, that you are—"

"A bastard. The fool. She can't set aside our father's will. If she does, the next heir is the Queen of Scots."

Christian pulled the mitten back over his right hand. "The council argues constantly. A few favor the Queen of Scots; most uphold Your Grace's right. All want to be rid of the Queen's Spanish husband and this stupid war with France."

The two black-veiled heads inclined toward each other as Christian detailed the latest maneuverings at court to the princess.

"And what of yourself?" Elizabeth asked. "Have you killed Luiz de Ateca yet?"

"Your Highness knows I cannot kill an envoy of the Queen's royal husband."

"I know you're not supposed to," Elizabeth said. "But you forget we've known each other since we were four, and convention never stopped you from doing as you please. Now tell me why you and de Ateca lust for each other's blood."

Christian wriggled his nose. "I refused Ateca something he wanted, Your Grace."

Elizabeth turned to Christian and lifted her brows. Christian sighed when he saw that she wasn't going to leave the topic.

"I denied him my . . . company."

"Your company."

"My friendship, one might say."

Elizabeth chuckled. "One might say, if one were a squeamish virgin maid. Oh, don't close yourself up like a comfit box. I understand. But Christian, no duels with King Philip's man. Ateca is dangerous, and I forbid you to risk your life any more than is necessary."

"Yes, Your Grace."

Somewhere a door banged closed, and Elizabeth's head jerked up. She looked over her shoulder, then back at Christian.

"You must go. If you're discovered, I lose my best intelligencer."

Christian shrank into himself until he resumed the bent and quivering form of the old nun. "Have no fear, Your Grace. I've no wish for the Queen to discover that one of her Catholic lords is a heretic who serves her sister."

"If she does, you'll be lucky if you end up in the Tower. If she suspects you question the old religion, she'll burn you at the stake. How many have died since Mary restored the laws against heresy? Several hundred, I trow."

Christian grinned at the Princess. "Your Grace hasn't heard the opinion of Lady Johanna and Lady Jane Dormer. I can't be burned because my heart and soul are made of ice."

A pale finger flicked the tip of Christian's nose. "You will ever be my Lord of Misrule."

He took her hand and kissed it. "I will ever be Your Highness's servant. I pray for your safe delivery from your enemies, for England needs you. We are bankrupt, starved, and tortured. And our deliverance is in the hands of old King Harry's daughter."

"God make me deserving of the love of the people," Elizabeth said.

"And may He protect Your Grace."

Christian hobbled back down the aisle and out of the chapel. The princess turned back to the altar. Neither looked back.

Christian avoided an encounter with the princess's guardian-gaoler by going directly to the stables for his mule. After giving the stable boy who'd cared for his animal a penny and a pat on the head, he lumbered down the road and off the grounds of the manor. It was a day of rare April sun and biting wind that turned his cheeks crimson. Having to sit in a hunched and skewed position, Christian was soon praying for sight of the fork in the road that would take him to London.

At last it appeared with its old stone marker, whose carving was so faded, it was impossible to read the signs. Christian slid off the mule, and looked around under the guise of inspecting the animal's hooves. A squirrel grubbed in the dust of the road. It was the sole occupant of the highway, which was no more than a dirt track. To either side of it lay narrow strips of cultivated fields. Beyond them loomed the pale green line of saplings that marked the beginning of the forest.

Christian pulled himself upright, hauled at the reins, and dragged the mule across the fields and into the trees. Deeper and deeper he plunged into the forest until he came to an ancient oak twisted and gnarled with disease. He tied the mule to a half-dead branch, then, sneezing, tore at the nun's headdress. It slid off to reveal luxuriant hair the color of an eagle's feathers. He tossed the veil aside. Without looking up from untying the girdle at his waist, he spoke.

"Come out, my angels. Lucifer wants company."

Rocks grew heads. Trees sprouted arms and legs. A thin stalk of a body dropped from the ancient oak. The owner of the body, one Inigo Culpepper, cutpurse and highwayman, hit the ground, rolled under the belly of the mule, and popped up to bow before Christian. He had staves for legs, hollow shoulders, and the movements of a frantic weasel.

Inigo pulled himself upright and grinned at Christian. "Liege."

Christian ignored the man as he stepped free of his black skirts. Something was wrong, he knew, or else his band of cutthroats and wastrels—would not all be gathered around like this. Wearing only his hose, Christian turned as Anthony Now-Now, a man with the bulk of a castle drum tower, approached him, carrying his soft riding boots. Behind Anthony was Three-

Tooth Poll, swishing over to Christian and holding out his voluminous lawn shirt.

"Oh, deary," Poll said, licking her lips, "you do grow wide and long." Her smile revealed the three teeth she'd managed to save during her life as a wandering peddler, thief, and whore.

Inigo swatted her hands from Christian's bare shoulders. "Away with you, bawdy basket. You'll not soil our lovely Kit with your poxy hands."

"Sod you," Poll said with a leer.

Inigo would have replied if not for the polar stare his liege gave him. He shut his mouth under the contemplation of a pair of eyes that looked as if someone had poured ice shards into purple ink.

"What are the lot of you doing clustered about like a heap of rotting fruit?" Christian asked. He didn't wait for Inigo's reply. "I see. Decided to make it easy on the constables and the hangman and let them catch you all at once."

Inigo paled. Poll skittered away, and the giant Anthony hid behind the dead tree. Several fake beggars busied themselves gathering firewood.

"Now, liege," Inigo said.

Christian shot his arms through the sleeves of his black doublet and fastened the silver buttons down the front. "If they catch you, I won't bribe them again. I'll dance at your execution and throw posies at your dead carcass."

With the suddenness of a thunder crack Christian whirled around and snatched a belt and sword from the man standing in silence behind him.

"I do so detest," he said with a snarl, "repeating myself like a schoolboy nattering over his books."

The victim of this strike of venom only blinked. He was dressed as a gentleman with sword and dagger at his belt.

"My lord," he said, "they wouldn't tell me."

For a moment longer Christian eyed Edward Hext, the man who had been his protector since he was a youth. Hext sighed with relief when Christian swung away from him, freeing him from the younger man's gaze. Leaping up onto a rock beneath the dead tree, Christian held out one of his hands and softened his voice to a siren's melody.

"Thomas, my bit of marzipan, come here."

A toddler in a dirty smock peeped at him from behind Poll's skirts. Christian opened the black and silver pouch at his belt and withdrew a drawstring bag. He dug in it, then withdrew a sugarplum. Thomas picked up the hem of his smock and trotted over to Christian. A dirt-blackened hand opened for the sugarplum. Christian held out the sweet but didn't release it.

"What brings your mother here, Thomas?"

Inigo made gasping sounds. Christian silenced him with a cutting motion of his free hand.

Thomas swirled his pink tongue around his lips. "Jack Midnight," he said, then snatched the sugarplum and ambled away.

A stillness settled over the group ranged about the dead tree, but only for a moment. Christian launched himself at Inigo, and the cutpurse went down with his straw-thin legs tangled around Christian's torso. In less time than it took to slice a purse from a belt, the blade of Christian's dagger was against Inigo's neck.

"I will ask this question once," Christian whispered. "What of Jack Midnight?"

Inigo swallowed, and the tip of the blade jumped with a convulsion of muscles. "They passed by not an hour since, him and his crew. I heard them speak of a party with a lady riding pillion. We couldn't go out till we were sure he'd left the area."

"And you weren't going to tell me until he did," Christian said. He slid the dagger behind one of Inigo's ears. "Shall I play butcher with your face to teach you obedience? The whores at the Cat and Fiddle will still open their thighs for you, but sweet Annie Turnstile might not."

"If you waste the time, you'll lose Jack Midnight."

Inigo was freed as quickly as he'd been taken. Christian sprang for the horses Edward Hext was already leading from their hiding place in a shroud of bushes. Inigo scrambled to his feet and leaped out of the way as Christian spurred his mount past him. Staring after the riders, he wiped the sweat from his upper lip.

Poll strolled over to him with little Thomas on her hip.

"I told you not to hide it from him," the bawdy said as the sound of pounding hoofbeats faded. "He's a Gypsy fortune reader about secrets, and he's wanted Jack Midnight's head on his lance since he was little bigger than my Thomas.''

"Piss on it," Inigo said. "Don't I know that? Don't I shiver like a naked priest with the sweating sickness over the last time he chased Jack Midnight?" Inigo stuck his thumbs in his belt and shook his head. "There's few in this world I fear for our Kit with, and Midnight's the first on my list. But the liege would follow Midnight to the edge of the earth and into hell if he could."

Inigo shook his head again and cursed. All he could do was hope Kit didn't find his quarry before he reached London. Deadly as his master was, Jack Midnight might just be deadlier. The highwayman possessed the sword skill of an Italian mercenary and the depravity of a witch's familiar. And with Midnight, Kit was undercut by his past to the point where Inigo wasn't sure the younger man could contain his rage.

Christian jumped his horse over a dried mud hole that looked to be as deep as a cistern. Between him and the next village was a stretch of twisted road with no cultivated boundary. The old forest crept to the edge of the path, encroaching on the packed earth. At one point the trees grew so close, their boughs formed a green roof that shrouded the traveler in gloom. It was a favorite spot for highwaymen.

Ignoring the protests of Hext and the pounding of the man's horse behind him, Christian rode on until he heard a woman's scream and the ring of swordplay. He drew his own weapon as he slowed his horse, then turned off the road to skirt the area from which the sounds of fighting came. Hext followed.

Christian threaded his way among trees and vines until he saw movement. In the narrow road, five men-at-arms in green and yellow livery stood against nine bandits. All but one man had been unhorsed. This man fought from his mount, and behind him clung a woman riding pillion with a basket slung over her arm. Two maids cowered on the ground, screaming. Christian's eyes searched the melee for a head of black and silver curls and a sword that moved with the speed of a hart in winter.

There! A man in green and yellow went down, skewered by a sword. The weapon was pulled free and swept up to catch the dappled sunlight. Christian spurred his horse forward. The stallion leaped into the road and barreled through four bandits. The men yelled and flew in all directions to be engaged by men-at-arms. Christian kept his attention on the man with the shining black hair painted with silver. The man turned at the noise of Christian's entrance. His eyes widened, and his shout of exultation exposed white teeth. He braced to meet Christian.

Leaning sideways in his saddle, Christian made a pass by his quarry and sliced his sword at the man's head. At the last moment he pulled his body erect to avoid the sword point that darted at his torso. It was a challenge, that first clash, and nothing more. Christian swept by, loosened his right foot from the stirrup, then turned and slid off his horse. His opponent was already running after him. Around them the fighting surged and ebbed. At his back, Edward Hext kept guard.

Christian hit the ground and pointed his sword at the man who faced him. ''Jack Midnight.''

His voice held nothing of the maelstrom that had taken the place of his wits. He looked into the black eyes of the man he'd wanted to kill since he was eight. The eyes looked back with gloating pleasure.

''Kit.'' Midnight laughed and made a circle with the tip of his sword. ''Well met and welcome back. Come be my slave again.''

Christian answered with a jab of his sword. The blades met, slid. Hilts locked, and Christian shoved with both arms. Jack Midnight jumped back, then swung and sliced at Christian's chest. They circled in a brutal dance with the cries of fighting men for accompaniment.

Dodging a movement he barely saw in time, Christian lunged and felt his sword jab into leather. Midnight cursed and hurled himself backward. He glanced at the cut on his upper arm.

''I'd forgotten the puppy has turned wolf cub,'' he said, then dodged another swipe of Christian's sword.

''I, too, have longed for your company,'' Midnight went on. ''You are my creation, son of an earl and apprentice of England's finest highwayman.''

Christian kept silent in spite of Midnight's taunts. He closed in on the man, backing the thief toward the man and woman on horseback. A yard away from the mounted pair, Midnight abruptly halted and he whistled. Something flew through the air and hit the man on the horse. His body jerked, and he slumped forward over the neck of his mount. The woman behind him sat unmoving and stared at the wounded man.

Unwilling to leave off his pursuit of Midnight, Christian shouted at the woman, "Get off and run, lackwit."

The woman jerked around to face him, but before she could respond, a human arrow flew from a bough above her and knocked her from the horse. Midnight blocked his way as Christian rushed toward the pair.

"Ah, no, my devil's urchin. There is someone I want you to meet." Midnight kept his sword pointed at Christian, but swept an arm in the direction of the thief holding the woman. "Kit, my love, meet Blade, your mate, my consolation, the second verse in my couplet. As you can see, he has earned his name."

It was the mention of consolation that finally spurred Christian to look. The first thing he noticed was a shining knife pressed against the woman's throat. He followed the angle of an arm encased in patched leather, faltered at a dark brown curl nearly the color of his own hair, and moved on to a face of innocent savagery. A young face with unlined skin and a jawline that angled high. Gray eyes regarded him with polite disinterest.

"Blade could impale lightning and carve a star," Midnight said. "Call the men off or I'll let him practice on the girl."

Christian looked back at Midnight.

"Let him. All I want to do is slice your gut."

Midnight nodded at Blade, and the youth grasped the yoke of cambric that covered the woman's chest above the low neck of her gown. He jerked, and the material ripped and fell from his hand. At the sound, Christian glanced at the white flesh Blade had exposed. The tight, square neck of the gown cupped the woman's breasts into two mounds, and Blade's arm pressed them upward so that they almost came free of their covering.

The girl hissed, and for the first time Christian looked at her face. He swore. God's blood, it was that mouse Eleanora Becket, one of the queen's women. "The plague take you, Midnight," he said, "Let her go."

"So you do care what happens to her." Midnight edged over near the woman and caressed one of her breasts. "Shall we tup her? Let's turn her from a dell to a doxy. You and I will share. It will be a new experience between us. Blade won't mind. He doesn't get jealous."

Christian strode over to Midnight. "You made me into an infant Caligula. You'll have to provide more interesting sport to distract me from my purpose. Let her go so that I can kill you."

He followed this request with a stab at Midnight's heart, which the highwayman quickly parried. Christian kept up his attack until a scream from the woman pulled him up sharp.

The youth called Blade had switched his grip on Eleanora. One arm pinned her to his body, and he now held the knife to her breast. The tip sharply dented the pale mound. During the whole encounter he had spoken no word. Christian caught his gaze and held it.

"Leave off. You don't have to obey him."

Straight, dark brows came together, and Christian was pleased to see confusion twist the hawklike features of the young thief.

Jack Midnight laughed. "By the devil's arse, are you trying to corrupt my novice?"

"No," Christian said. "I was waiting for Hext."

As Christian said the name, Hext ran the last few feet to Blade, raised the hilt of his sword, and rapped the youth on the back of the head. Blade fell to his knees. As his arms dropped, Eleanora scrambled free. At the same time, Christian sprang at Midnight. The highwayman was already running into the forest. Christian pounded after him, only to be halted by a cry from Hext. He swung around to see his man fall with a dagger embedded in his shoulder. Blade pounced on him, another knife in his hand. Christian was running even as the youth straddled Hext. Leaping the last few feet, he caught the boy with his shoulder, grabbed the wrist poised above his victim's heart, and crushed Blade under his full, hurtling weight.

Blade let out a muffled gasp composed of most of the air from his crushed lungs. His free hand winnowed between their bodies and came out filled with yet another knife. The tip slashed at Christian's eyes.

"God's teeth."

Christian grasped both wrists. Yanking them up over the youth's head, he rammed them into a rock. The weapons fell. The boy bucked, nearly throwing him off, then spat in Christian's face.

"Blue-blooded sod," he said, "I'll carve your prick and serve it to Midnight on a silver plate."

Pinning Blade's arms to either side of his head, Christian laughed. "By the saints, you sound just like me."

"Hoary piss-prophet, pig-tupping spawn of a Gypsy whore."

Christian brought the youth's wrists together and held them with one hand. "Careful, you tempt me to lesson you in manners."

"He told me about you, you bloody whoreson."

"Blade, my lad, your tongue is going to rot off." Christian kept his balance when Blade heaved up again, trying to throw him off. "Damnation if I'll leave you to be Midnight's fruit sucket."

At this, Blade arched his body and shouted, "No!"

Christian muttered an apology and hit the boy on the chin. Blade went limp, and Christian released a sigh. He shoved himself off the youth and went to Hext. The man was sitting on the ground, holding his arm. Next to him was Eleanora. Two of her men-at-arms were left standing. One hovered over the girl while the other gathered horses and looked to the wounded and to the hysterical maids.

Kneeling in front of Hext, Christian peeled away the man's torn doublet and shirt, then pried back his fingers to inspect the wound. Blade's accuracy had saved Hext's life. The dagger had pierced sinew and muscle, nothing more.

"I'm sorry, my lord," Hext said. "I didn't hit the boy hard enough."

Not trusting himself to speak, Christian wiped his hands on Hext's doublet, cupped them around his mouth, and emitted a cry that imitated the call of a hawk.

He dropped his hands and transferred a dissecting gaze to Eleanora Becket. "God deliver me from the imbecility of women. Don't you know how to kick? Next time make use of your feet and your legs instead of ensconcing yourself in the middle of a fight like a maypole with tits."

Eleanora crouched before him with one hand resting on her breast. He glanced at the translucent flesh of her breasts, glistening with perspiration. The sight of it somehow made him angrier. He stooped to help Hext to his feet, and the man leaned heavily against him.

"Easy, we're going," Christian said.

"My lord," Hext said. "The lady."

"Leave her to my pretty geese. They'll be here soon enough."

"My lord, you can't leave a woman to that lot."

"So she has to pay them for their help with a ride or two. Some good vagabond seed up her might turn her from a worm into a tigress."

Hext pulled his arm from Christian's shoulders. "Your father would cut off my right hand. I cannot leave a lady to Inigo Culpepper and his brigands."

The smile Christian gave his bodyguard usually turned a man's guts to ashes. As it was, Eleanora's man-at-arms backed away from him. Hext only set his jaw and waited. He had to endure Christian's frigid gaze for less than a minute, though, for the lady in question stood up and put her small hand on Christian's forearm.

"I'm sorry I didn't help," she said. "You're right, you know, I'm a coward, and I should have done something."

Christian turned his glare on her, and his silence made her lips tremble. As he continued to stare, from amid the trees emerged Inigo, Three-Tooth Poll, and their comrades. Hext slipped away to give them orders.

Christian spoke at last. "Is that hand over your breast meant to call attention to it or to make you resemble a madonna?"

"Neither."

He wasn't listening. He snatched her hand away. Beneath, like a red silk thread on white damask, a cut slanted across the girl's chest where it began to rise into the mound of her breast. Glistening trails of blood worked their way over the swell and disappeared into the valley between her breasts. Christian said nothing. Drawing a handkerchief from his sleeve, he wrapped it around his hand and feathered the soft material across Eleanora's flesh. She jumped, so he grasped her arm to hold her still.

"Poll, bring water," he shouted over his shoulder. He was

soon bathing the wound clean in spite of the girl's protests. When he finished, he wiped her face and hands, then dropped the cloth into the bowl Poll held for him. "I don't suppose you have one stitch of clean cloth about you, Poll?"

"Me petticoat."

"Give us a bit of it." Christian handed the rag to Eleanora to use as a bandage. While she stuffed it into the neck of her gown, he slipped out of his doublet. "Put this around you."

He adjusted the heavy garment, but the shoulders were far too wide. She vanished into the folds as if he'd dropped her in a privy, and it was then that he noticed how small she was. Snatching the doublet back, he exchanged it for the cloak on his saddle. She pulled it closed around her neck and stared up at him.

The French hood she wore was askew. Christian dragged it from her head with impatience. Long, dark curls tumbled out and rained down her shoulders.

His lips curled into a mockery of a smile. "Oh, Poll, look. It's a starling. No, a magpie, all black and white." He turned away and started toward his horse, snapping orders to Eleanora's two men-at-arms who were unwounded to follow him. Mounting, he walked his horse back to Eleanora Becket. She had picked up her basket and was cradling it in her arms.

"Don't gawk at me, woman. Who else will you ride with?" He swept an arm to indicate the dirty and lewdly joking thieves who were helping her men-at-arms while directing covetous glances at her and her maids. "Give me your hand, or I'll leave you to accommodate my pack of kittens."

A small hand shot out. He grasped it, disturbed at the feel of her delicate bones. Annoyed with his reaction, he hauled the girl up in front of him. She perched there as if she expected him to push her off at any moment. Fastening both hands about her waist, he pulled her back into his lap. It proved to be an error in judgment. A soft, swelling pressure settled over his loins. She wriggled in her embarrassment and ignorance, and with a voice that held the warmth of a snake's hiss, he warned her to be still.

A sudden breeze whipped black curls into his face. Christian swatted at them, and Eleanora twisted around to look up at him. Overly large brown eyes questioned him. He lifted his brows and sneered at her full lower lip. She turned back around, flushing.

Christian called out to Hext and Inigo. "I'm going. Settle things here and follow with the other women."

He kicked his horse into a trot. Eleanora clutched at his arms. Her basket swung out to hit him in the ribs, and he ground his teeth together as something inside it yipped. Two fuzzy heads poked from beneath a cover. Puppies.

He was about to snarl at the two creatures when the wind swirled Eleanora's hair around his face again. He hauled on the reins until his horse stopped. Prying her hands from his arms, he slipped one arm around her waist. The little hands fastened on it, and he realized she was afraid he would drop her. He pried her grip loose, but offered the concession of holding her firmly against him.

"God deliver me from virginal sweetmeats," he muttered. He dragged strands of her hair from his shoulders and face, and his fingers burrowed through curls as soft as the fur on an ermine's belly. He jerked them free as if they had touched a white-hot brand.

Kicking his horse into motion, Christian snapped, "I do so hate black hair."

Chapter II

Nora Becket came awake with a small squeak. It was the call of the watch that had roused her. She unwound herself from the protective curve of Christian de Rivers's body and sat up straight on the horse. Two days of riding with him hadn't made her any more comfortable in his arms.

She had decided it had been divinely ordained that she would be the victim of a robbery, only to be rescued by a young man whose reputation was worse than that of a highwayman. He behaved as if she'd purposely thwarted his plan to skewer that villain with the silly name. For the past two days Lord Montfort had exhibited the fury of a spurned courtesan, and he vented that fury with verbal floggings that made her cringe. Her only comfort lay in the realization that he could reduce even the most false hearted thief or callous dock hand to blancmange. Why did her rescuer have to come in the form of this violet-eyed cobra with the terrible smile? What ill fortune.

Nora comforted herself with the thought that she'd soon be rid of Lord Montfort and back safe in the palace. She might not be an ornament to the court, but Queen Mary was kind to her. And best of all, Nora had found at last a purpose to fill the

weary emptiness of her life. Unfortunately, that purpose was likely to get her killed if it were ever discovered.

Her secret was well kept, however. Her current uneasiness rose from the violence of the man who now held her in his impersonal grip. He would have left her to the highwaymen; of this she was convinced. She knew a little of Christian de Rivers from court gossip. He and his father, the Earl of Vasterne, had been attacked by bandits when Christian was eight. The father had been left for dead and the boy taken. The Earl had recovered his son, but not until four years later, and then only by chance. Any young man who had spent that much time among the cutpurses, anglers, and bawds of England would have no qualms about feeding a girl to a pack of thieves. So in a sense, Nora supposed she'd been blessed by God's protection when Edward Hext had insisted she be escorted back to court.

Sitting straight and stiff in front of Lord Montfort, Nora took stock of their surroundings. The sun was dipping below church steeples, and the putrid odor that rose from the muddy road told her they were in London at last. Trying to hold her eyes open against weariness, she did not speak until she noticed that they weren't headed for Whitehall Palace.

"My lord, the palace . . ."

"Is locked tighter than a chastity belt," he said. "We're going to my house. And don't fret. My father is in residence, so your honor is safe. Not that it wouldn't be, considering the ride I had last night."

Nora pressed her lips closed. She'd learned quickly not to respond to the wasp stings of his temper. It only made him more vicious. So she let pass his reference to the big-breasted tavern maid who had battled off three of her sisters to get to him the evening before. It had been disgusting. They'd fought a mock duel for him.

Letting out an inaudible sigh, Nora contemplated once more the disastrous meeting with Jack Midnight and Lord Montfort, whom the highwayman had called Kit. When her party was attacked, she had been a coward. The fierce strength of the men, the violence and the blood had frozen her wits. She had never been able to stomach cruelty. And when that boy had taken his knives to her, she'd wilted like a rose in a kiln. How mortifying.

If only it hadn't been Lord Montfort who'd come upon them.

He was one of the ornaments of the Queen's court, declared so by Mary herself. And in fact, Lord Montfort held a court within the court, presiding over the raucous, quarrelsome, and dangerous aristocratic youths, who found little to attract them to a middle-aged, fanatically religious woman ruler. Christian de Rivers was unofficial crown prince of pleasure and earl marshal of as ruthless a band of noblemen as any who'd roamed England in the days of the old Plantagenet kings.

And the crown prince was bored with her. Nora knew what he thought of her. The mouse. That was her nickname, given to her by the dashing court ladies and taken up by the gentlemen. She could see him think "mouse" each time he looked at her. To her relief, he didn't look at her often.

They were riding along the Strand, that area of London beside the Thames that was beaded with the jeweled houses of dukes and bishops. Between the two men who rode with them was the boy called Blade, trussed to his horse as if he were a piglet ready for market. He'd tried to escape the first night of their journey. She didn't know what Lord Montfort had done to him when he caught the youth, but Blade had come back pale and trembling, and had not bolted into the night again. Of course, if she'd been hauled back, hands bound and dragged on a tether fastened to Lord Montfort's saddle, she would have been cowed, too.

They entered a stone courtyard through gates topped with rampant Montfort dragons. Before them wide white steps spread out in a graceful fan. Men in silver and crimson livery approached with torches. Lord Montfort snapped at one of them, and Blade was snatched from his horse and carried away.

Nora blinked at the flames of a torch, barely aware of the warm support at her back withdrawing. Looking down, she saw Lord Montfort standing beside the horse, reaching up to her. He said something, but she was too sleepy to make sense of it, and he laughed.

Abruptly she was sailing through the air to land in a cradle of satin and muscle. If he'd given her a chance, she would have told him she could walk. Instead, holding her tightly, he ran up the stairs and into the dimly lit entryway of his house. She glimpsed a black and white marble floor, gleaming oak walls, and another Christian de Rivers. Squinting, she studied the man who blocked their path. He was Lord Montfort's twin.

The arm that supported her legs dropped, and she scrambled to get her feet under her. Lord Montfort kept hold of her arm until she steadied, then left her to kneel at the feet of the other man. Nora's mouth almost fell open. In the last few days she'd seen men kneel to Lord Montfort, and almost every woman; she had yet to see him do more than incline his head in regal acceptance of homage. Now he submitted himself with grace, charm, and a cloak of childlike humility.

"My lord," he said.

Nora's eyes grew as big as pomander balls as she saw Lord Montfort kiss the man's hand.

"What have you done, Chris?"

"Feats of chivalry, my lord father. I have rescued a baby crow named Eleanora Becket from highwaymen."

The Earl of Vasterne, from whom Christian had obviously inherited his wide-set eyes and clarion voice, frowned. "You found Jack Midnight."

"Never fear," Christian said. He rose and jerked his dark head at Nora. "She foiled my murder. The only reason I didn't kill her for it was that I'd have to take care of two puppies in a basket and decapitate her men-at-arms."

At that point Nora wanted to melt into the cracks between the marble tiles, but a door burst open and three old men stumbled out. All wore the long robes and flat caps of which merchants and clerics were fond. Two were short and balding, but the third was tall, with a long, sparse beard, gray and wrinkled. His eyes burned at them with the virulence of a devil, then the three scurried into the dark recesses at the back of the house.

It was like watching rats race for cover, Nora thought. She looked back at Christian de Rivers, but he was staring at his father, excluding her completely from his attention. The older man moved his head in a gesture so slight, Nora wasn't sure she'd seen it. Christian whirled in one of those abrupt, facile movements that reminded her of the hurtling acrobatics of a hawk. He strolled to the nearby stairs, rested a hand on the banister, and glanced back over his shoulder.

"Sire, I beg you to put the lady-child in a closet. She's a rich sweetmeat, a sugared rose petal, pink-cheeked and ripe, but

in need of a bed. Alas, it must be a solitary one.'' With a smile
of lurid purity, he began to ascend the stairs.

Nora's cheeks burned. She was too full of Lord Montfort's
nastiness to remain silent. She said,

> *Whate'er the case, where'er he be,*
> *Or does, he smiles; with him it is a vice,*
> *And not, I think, a pretty one, nor nice.*

She bit her lip, aghast at her bravery. Lord Montfort had stopped
with his back to her. Now he twisted around, impaling her with
the violent eyes of an angel, and laughed.

"She quotes Catullus at me," he said. "Lord, the girl is a
cleric and feasts on my entrails while pretending to be a ewe-
lamb.''

Launching himself up the stairs, Lord Montfort left her with
her ears on fire and his laughter cascading down from on high.

Nora was left alone with the Earl of Vasterne. While a
chamber was being prepared for her, he led her to a parlor where
he plied her with wine and sweetbreads and inconvenient questions. Nora couldn't help feeling he already knew too much about
her, and the similarity between himself and his son made her
expect the same callous treatment from the Earl. She was wrong.
The Earl's concern wrapped her in a down coverlet of safety. He
worried over her health, her feelings, her possessions so much
that in a short time she realized this man was as gentle and
gracious as his son was violent and cavalier.

"Mistress Becket," he asked as she sipped her wine, "how
haps it that you were traveling from your father's house with
such a small escort?''

Nora studied the tips of her shoes where they peeped out
from beneath her riding gown. "The sweating sickness took hold
of many on our way, my lord, and we had to leave them behind.''

She knew he didn't believe her, but he nodded and asked
more questions. "And you left court suddenly. Is there aught
wrong with your father? May I offer assistance of some kind?''

"No, I thank you, my lord. My f-father sent for me to
announce his coming marriage.''

The Earl expressed the customary good wishes, but all the

time Nora suspected that he knew how she felt—that he knew how her spirits and her hopes had taken flight upon receiving her father's summons. Perhaps, at last, she had thought, she'd earned his regard. She should have known better. All she had received was a browbeating for not having caught the eye of a suitable nobleman.

Christian's father was looking at her. Nora glanced at him, but she couldn't keep her gaze from falling to the floor again.

"I want to thank you, mistress, for coming between my son and Jack Midnight."

At that, she lifted her eyes to the earl. He smiled at her, as if he sympathized with her plight at being the recipient of Christian's displeasure.

"You are much the little wren, are you not?" he said. "But there must be something of the she-wolf in you to have survived Christian's anger and not retreat into madness."

She shook her head, but could think of nothing to say that wouldn't insult the Earl's only son.

"He doesn't usually bait ladies quite so thoroughly as he has you," the earl said. "I wonder what it is about you that set him off like a hawk teasing a hare."

"I don't know."

"Neither do I, mistress, but I will give you some advice that has benefited me in my dealings with Christian. He is most vicious when he wants to hide something, or is afraid. When he fears, he attacks. Don't back down from him. He won't respect you."

"Thank you, my lord," Nora said. "But I doubt that I will be called upon to stand up to Lord Montfort at all after tonight. At least, I shall pray that I don't have to."

The next morning Nora returned to court happy to be out of Lord Montfort's way. Upon arriving at Whitehall Palace, she spent a few hours in her small closet. She shared the room with another of the Queen's gentlewomen, but the lady was on duty. Soon Nora would attend as well, and she must gird herself for the smirks and contemptuous looks that would come her way when the Queen wasn't paying attention.

Divining why she was the object of such looks had taken

her a few months. At first she'd thought it was because somehow
the secret of her bastardy had gotten about, but her father kept
the knowledge and the shame to himself. It was Queen Mary
herself who offered Nora the reason for the ladies' scorn—Nora's
dress. Not just her dress, but her manners as well.

"My dear Nora," the Queen had said, "your gable headdress is charming. It reminds me of the ones my mother used
to wear."

The comment had made Nora's heart thump. Mary's mother
had been Catherine of Aragon, persecuted first wife of King
Henry VIII. Catherine had been set aside to make way for Princess Elizabeth's mother, Anne Boleyn, the one the people had
called whore, the one for whom Henry had wrecked the Catholic
Church in England and denied the Pope.

But the Queen was pleased with Nora. Mary liked her mod-
esty, her quietness, her old-fashioned appearance that reminded
the Queen of the golden days of her youth, before her father
hounded her mother to death in order to marry his mistress.
From the Queen's comments and from looking around the glittering chambers filled with ladies in gowns with tight sleeves
and wearing veiled French hoods, Nora perceived that her wardrobe was fashioned in a style twenty years old. That was what
came of living most of her life in the backwater country estate
where her father had banished her.

Nora left off her more ornate gabled headdresses in favor of
the French hoods that only partially covered her hair, but she
hadn't the funds to redesign her whole wardrobe. Her father had
made it clear that she was at court to catch a husband. He expected results, for Sir William Becket was a rich man, and he
would pay a handsome dowry to get rid of her. Nora cracked a
sour smile. Her father hadn't counted on his daughter being
thought an unfashionable mouse.

Her page, Arthur, broke into Nora's reverie. The Queen
requested Nora's attendance in the presence chamber. The royal
musicians were about to play, and Her Majesty knew how much
Nora enjoyed music. Nora adjusted the bell sleeves of her overgown, which made her hands seem even smaller than they were.
She could do nothing about the high waistline of the overgown,
dated as it was. And she wasn't about to remove the yoke of
fabric that covered her neck and the tops of her breasts. Even if

she hadn't sported a cut over one breast, she had no desire to prance about, jiggling and bouncing with diamonds or emeralds nestling in her cleavage the way some of the Queen's women did.

Satisfied that she was decently if unfashionably covered, Nora marched behind her page through the connecting rooms of the palace until she reached the presence chamber. As she entered, she kept her head erect and her gaze on the small, soap-scrubbed, and plain face of the Queen. Before she reached her mistress, though, she sank to her knee three times, as required. Around her, muted voices splashed and dripped in a gentle, mannered rain. Chimes filled the air as goblets of silver and gold touched. Nora could smell cinnamon comfits and cloves, and roses. As she knelt for the last time before the Queen, Mary spoke to her in that deep, almost-man's voice that sat so oddly with her small frame.

"God has kept you safe, my good Nora. I hope you have thanked Him."

"Every day, Your Majesty."

The Queen's hand, weighted down with rings on each of her stubby fingers, gestured for Nora to rise. When she got up, Nora was near enough for the short sighted Queen to see her clearly. Noting the Queen's lucid gaze and steady hands, Nora was thankful that the poor woman was having one of her good days. On a bad one she wept ceaselessly, longed for her absent husband, cursed the French and all heretics, and looked under cupboards and beds for assassins. But this was a good day, and the Queen smiled. She gestured to someone behind Nora.

"Lord Montfort, come to us and tell the tale of your chivalry."

Nora bit her lip and studied one of the velvet cushions on the floor beside the Queen's chair. He was here, devil take him. Even if the Queen hadn't called him, she would have known he'd entered the presence chamber by the sudden turmoil among the ladies in waiting.

He strode up to the Queen, planting his swordlike body beside Nora. To hide her anxiety, she bent her head as she made her curtsy. Christian bowed to her at the same time, and as they sank together, he whispered low, so that only she could hear.

"If you gainsay my tale, I'll finish the work Blade started on your lovely breast."

She jerked her gaze to his face, then blinked. He was wearing a ruby in his ear. It nestled, crimson and flagrant, amid the dark topaz of his hair. As they both straightened, he bestowed upon her one of his seraph's smiles. With his threat rattling around in her head, she could do no more than make one-word replies to the Queen's questions and nod her agreement to the man's outrageous story. Lord Montfort soon had Mary guffawing at a tale in which he routed the thieves with a tree branch. And not once did he mention Jack Midnight.

"Such gallantry, even with a stick, deserves reward," the Queen said. "I will have Mistress Clarencieux write to Lady Nora's father."

Nora was struck with shame. Lord Montfort's help had been inadvertent and ungracious, but she was alive for all that. And she hadn't thanked him. Not that he seemed to want her thanks. Her gratitude was likely to be the only reward he received anyway. No such sentiment would come from her father, and no token of gratitude either. If an acknowledgment was to be made, she would have to make it. And that meant braving the gauntlet of this man's dislike at least once more.

Nervous anticipation of such an ordeal caused her to miss the Queen's request. Abruptly she found her hand in Lord Montfort's. He was leading her away from Mary.

"Wake up, my throstle," he murmured, "or you'll trip over your skirt."

"What are you doing?"

"We're to dance for the Queen."

He deposited her at the head of a line of women, took his place in the row of gentlemen opposite, and bowed to her. She held out her hand to him, as required by the dance. He grasped it, and they turned and began a slow, measured walk down the chamber to the accompaniment of flute, virginals, and drum. Stopping, they faced each other and stepped close. Lord Montfort lifted her hand so that their arms formed an arch for their heads. He leaned close to her, so close she could see the violet flecks in his eyes. The ruby winked at her.

"Why do you cover up that magnificent chest?"

She froze, but Lord Montfort shoved her away, bowed over

her hand, and knelt. His hand tugged at hers, and she began her circle around him. When she completed it and curtsied, he rose over her. Placing his palms against hers, he smiled at her.

"Your skin is like milk and strawberries. It's stupid to cover it up."

Now she was blushing in front of the whole court. Nora opened her mouth, but nothing would come out. To her relief, it was time for the ladies to skip away from the gentlemen. She skipped most enthusiastically. Lord Montfort laughed at her and joined the other men in marching toward the women. When he reached her, he caught both her hands and led her in a gliding movement between the other men and women.

" 'Maidens' acts belie their mock complaints,' " he whispered to her, " 'affecting aversion for what they most desire.' You like Catullus's poetry, don't you? What debauched tutor gave you his poems?"

"I—"

"The mouse isn't such a mouse as she pretends. Not with those juicy mounds and that quivering, inviting voice."

Wanting to weep in the middle of the stately dance counted as one of the most humiliating experiences of her life. Nora clamped her teeth down on the inner surface of her mouth to keep the tears in her eyes from spilling. They reached the end of the row of dancers, and it was time for her to curtsy to him. He bent over her, and she spoke.

"I don't know why you want to hurt me, but I wish you would stop."

Their hands locked. Arms raised, they faced each other and paced in a circle. Nora couldn't look at him, and she was thankful he was silent. She should have known he wouldn't remain so for long.

"My poor little nuthatch, you haven't a notion of how to play the game."

He inclined his head, and she felt the down-soft brush of a curl, so near was his face. She frowned at him. For once he was looking at her without irritation or derision.

"I should give you a flail," he said, "and bare my back so that you can chastise me. But alas, my guilt rarely lasts longer than an angel's gasp, so you will no doubt have to forgo your vengeance. Take heart, Nora Becket, our dance is at an end."

He trundled her back to the Queen and abandoned her for his pack of bejeweled and laced ruffians. Forgotten, Nora sank down on a cushion near the Queen and spent the rest of her time in attendance on Mary and in castigating herself for not having the courage to slap Lord Montfort's face in the Queen's presence chamber.

Out near the palace stables, in an open shed surrounded by a wicket, were Nora's friends. It was the morning after the disastrous dance with Lord Montfort, and Nora was scurrying along the path behind the stables. Her little page, Arthur, trotted behind, carrying a basket. Nora carried a larger one that was too big for him to hold.

Although it was late April, the mornings were chill, and Nora wore an open fur-lined overgown. It was old, which suited her purpose. As she neared the shed, whimpers and yips joined in the chorus set up by robins and sparrows in the trees overhead. Nora opened the gate and slipped inside the enclosure. Arthur nipped in behind her and closed it. Immediately they were surrounded by squirming, fat puppies. A hound with three legs yelped happily at her, while a black and white mongrel chased its tale in ecstasy.

She left Arthur to feed the crew of orphans while she took a bowl containing a meat pasty to the shed. In a pile of straw slept the two mastiff puppies she'd been carrying with her when Jack Midnight had attacked. Setting the bowl before them, she laughed as their noses twitched. Soon their faces were buried in the bowl. When they were finished, she scooped them up and deposited them in the large basket that had contained kitchen scraps for her brood. Arthur covered them with a piece of old velvet. Tummies full, the two curled up with grunts and sighs.

Nora looked down at the wriggling velvet. "Arthur, I'm not sure about this."

"Mastiffs are valuable, my lady. These two, when they're big, will rest their forepaws on a man's shoulders."

Smiling at the boy's enthusiasm, Nora gave one of his blond locks a tug. He was a sweet, lively boy, who'd been orphaned like her brood in the wicket. She'd met him one day two years ago, when she'd been home at the estate where her father had

exiled her. Her bailiff had hauled Arthur before her, bruised and
bleeding, and accused him of stealing bread from the kitchens
and, even worse, a book. It had taken her hours to pry the story
of his destitution from the boy. His parents were dead from the
sweat. At only seven years, he was too young to be of use to
anyone in the fields, so he survived in the scullery of her house,
scrubbing pots and living on scraps. His empty stomach pained
him so that he hadn't been able to resist the bread. The book he
was unable to read, but he longed to see what written words
looked like. That day Arthur became her page, and Nora had
someone besides herself to care for.

Leaving Arthur to tend the puppies, she went back to her
closet alone. There she settled on a cushion to finish an important task that had to be done before she could leave the palace
later that morning. From her sleeve she withdrew a scrap of
paper and folded it small enough to fit beneath a gold clothing
ornament. Taking up a perfumed glove of kid, she placed the
paper beneath the ornament and rested both in place within the
embroidered design on the cuff of the glove. She sewed the ornament to the leather, making sure the paper was invisible.

When the last stitch was tied off, she summoned her maid
and donned a black dress trimmed sparingly with silver lace
from a gown she'd outgrown several years before. Fastening her
best cloak about her shoulders, she set out alone for an abandoned privy garden in the palace grounds. Once there, she wandered aimlessly amid shrubs clipped into geometric shapes and
rare flowers about to bloom, while playing with her glove.

At this time of day few courtiers were about to witness her
passage, and not many servants. Nora strolled to a corner of the
garden and perched on a crumbling stone bench. Her hand fell
to her side, hidden by the thick billows of her skirt, and she
dropped the newly sewn glove behind the bench. After gazing
into the morning sky for a few moments, she rose and wandered
over to a fountain where a naked cherub poured water from a
shell. She listened to the gurgling waterfall for a while, then
walked slowly back to the door to the palace.

As she opened the door she looked over her shoulder to see
one of the gardeners kneel by the old bench and poke at a weed
growing beneath it. He picked up the glove and stuffed it in his
shirt. Nora nodded to herself in satisfaction and left the garden.

She hadn't been a spy for long. Only since that day a few months ago when she'd witnessed a burning. The Queen burned heretics, and at Smithfield a crowd had gathered to witness the latest spectacle. The heretic was a girl. She couldn't have been over fourteen, and Nora heard from someone in the crowd that she was an ignorant farm girl who hadn't been able to answer the bishops' questions about the meaning of the Mass.

Nora arrived in Smithfield as the flames were licking at the girl's face. The gunpowder meant to explode before she suffered too greatly hadn't ignited, and she was screaming through singed lips. The skin over her belly burst open, and her entrails spilled out. Nora, in a party of the nobility, fell to the ground in a faint with the sweet smell of burning flesh in her nostrils.

Until that day Nora had been a dutiful subject, loyal to the sovereign. Queen Mary was a Catholic and determined to bring England back to the old church. At least half the kingdom was still Catholic, but London and its environs were stuffed with Protestants. Mary was a good woman, but heresy was the ultimate sin to her. She punished it as did her husband, the King of Spain, by fire. All this Nora knew, but she hadn't understood the horror of burning. That night, half-drunk on wine and in bed but unable to sleep, Nora changed.

Her life had been filled with atonement for her own birth, and with duty and obedience. Something within her rebelled that night. Her conscience sought answers from God, and when the sun rose, she had them. Whatever the church said, Christ would never condone the obscene cruelty of burning. The Queen was wrong. The Catholic kings of Spain and France were wrong.

But the Queen was the Queen. Hope lay with her sister, the tolerant and brilliant Elizabeth. Princess Elizabeth was a suspected heretic, but Mary couldn't burn her for fear of inviting her own death. For years the fanatic Catholics at court had urged Mary to cut off her sister's head. Elizabeth needed help.

As one of the Queen's women, Nora often heard snips and bits of gossip, whispers of plots. Certain some of this news would be helpful to Elizabeth, she sought out the Princess's friend Sir William Cecil on one of his rare visits to court. Brilliant and devious as his mistress, Cecil at first rejected Nora's overtures. When she persisted in seeking him out clandestinely, he became convinced of her sincerity and told her he'd be glad for her help. So now, whenever she heard something, she put her information in a cipher, concealed it in her glove, and left it in the garden. Eventually the cipher got to Cecil, and the glove was returned.

Today her cipher contained news of a hunt for three heretics, writers of scurrilous ballads and pamphlets that lampooned the Queen, her foreign husband, and her burnings. One of them, Archibald Dymoke, had called the Queen Bloody Mary.

From the garden Nora returned to her room to collect Arthur, the puppies, and her maid. The three of them went down to the courtyard, where a coach awaited them. A groom handed Nora in, then boosted Arthur inside. Next came the basket and her maid. Nora pulled her cloak tight around her shoulders, then straightened her spine.

"I hope you're right about mastiffs," she said to Arthur. "I truly hope you're right."

Chapter
III

After their dance before the Queen, Christian helped Nora Becket settle on a cushion. He felt no remorse at having tormented her. It served her right for keeping him swollen with lust for days. Even when he'd been furious at her for thwarting his revenge on Jack Midnight, he'd wanted her. It was the way she covered herself from neck to toe. All that shrouding made him want to tear off her clothes to see what she was like beneath.

Some women wore their innocence like a halberd, he mused. Women like Nora. He preferred an honest bawd, one who served beer and meat in an open-necked gown with her breasts exposed in invitation. In the years since his father had found him again, he'd had his fill of noblewomen who eyed his codpiece from behind their fans and sent cloying notes to him, begging for an assignation.

No matter their station, women wanted him for his beauty, a beauty that had caused him more pain than pleasure. None could see the patchwork creature that capered in the disguise of an earl's son. He was both wool and satin, felt and velvet, knitted together with threads of gold and a good bit of frayed twine.

Rejoining his friends, Christian deliberately took part in a card game with Roger Mortimer so that he could sit with his back to the girl everyone called the mouse and who he knew was no mouse at all, but a phoenix. He was winning a fortune from the old Marquess of Winchester when Edmund Bonner was announced. A couple of men hissed behind their hands, another man muttered a curse, and some of the Queen's council looked as if they'd like to spit.

Bloody Bonner, the people called him. Bishop of London, burner of heretics. Roger Mortimer had told Christian that Bonner had just sentenced an aged cobbler for heresy. The old man was ignorant; he didn't know the Mass from a bushkin. Christian turned sideways in his chair to watch Bonner waddle up to the Queen. He was so fat, his skin looked like it was in danger of splitting. Sweat dripped from beneath his cap, down his bulging cheeks, and into the neck of his robe. Christian yawned, tossed a card on the table, and through half-lowered lashes stared at the papers Bonner carried.

After presenting the papers to the Queen, Bonner signaled to the servant who followed him. The man came forward with a lap desk and held it for the Queen. Mary glanced at the sheets of paper, then signed them while talking to the bishop.

A man who had entered with Bonner suddenly turned and caught Christian watching the group. Moonlight-silver hair curled over his ears. In spite of his lean build and prowling wolf eyes, Luiz de Ateca managed to convey imperial power and splendor in his dress and demeanor. De Ateca smiled a gloating smile at Christian and bowed. Christian turned back to his cards.

Bonner retrieved the signed papers from the Queen, and he and his party left the presence chamber. Luiz de Ateca followed, but stopped beside Christian.

"You weren't at Mass."

Christian threw down a card, but didn't look up at de Ateca. "I worship at home."

"If at all," de Ateca said. "It's unseemly for the Queen's great nobles to absent themselves from court Mass."

"Do you keep count of our absences and send word to His Majesty? How tedious, Spaniard. And how expected."

De Ateca's hand slipped to the hilt of his sword. He threw back the edge of his cloak and sneered at Christian.

"Do you think I like being exiled on this barbaric and backward island? I could be fighting in the Netherlands or in France."

Christian laid down his cards and clicked his tongue in sympathy. "And instead you're forced to roost here on this miserable little island and seduce boys." His hand snaked out to grasp de Ateca's arm before the man could draw his dagger. "Careful. If you challenge, the Queen will want to know the cause of our wrangle."

The Spaniard lifted his hand away from the weapon. His face was crimson with the effort to control his rage.

"Leave English youths alone for your own health," Christian said. "From now on choose older prey who can take care of themselves."

De Ateca smiled.

"I tried, but you wriggled out of my trap." With a lightness of step that belied the anger in his eyes, de Ateca left the presence chamber.

Unruffled by the exchange, Christian returned to his card play, but whatever was in Bishop Bonner's documents had put the Queen out of temper. She retreated to her privy chamber, and her women went with her. Christian looked up from his bow in time to glimpse the small, intriguing back of Nora Becket before it vanished. Roger Mortimer sidled up to him.

"Someday you'll touch de Ateca's honor too nearly," Roger said.

"Our comely Luiz helped bring the Inquisition to this kingdom. I want to duel with him."

Roger shrugged and changed the subject. "Bonner's on the trail of Archibald Dymoke."

Christian turned back to the table and swept his brightly painted cards into a pile. "Bonner is always hunting someone."

"But he knows Dymoke is in London, and he's determined to catch him. Someone should run a pike through Bonner's fat paunch."

Spreading his hand of cards before his face like a fan, Christian waved them as if to cool himself and studied his friend. Roger conformed to the Queen's Mass like everyone at court, but like Princess Elizabeth he was too much an intellect and a humanist to be a fanatic.

"Better to put him to a treadmill," Christian said. He folded his cards and tapped them on Roger's sleeve. "But then he'd sweat like a roasted pig and flood the Thames."

Roger gave a bark of laughter. Christian threw the cards on the table and turned away. Roger's hand touched his arm.

"Do you go to the bear baiting tomorrow?"

"Why not? If I can't watch a heretic roast, I might as well gaze upon a pack of starving dogs maul a blind bear."

Roger's hand tightened. "After the baiting we can go to a play."

"Are you still sniffing after that strumpet with the golden hair?" Christian asked. "Ah, the suburbs of pleasure. Southwark is my favorite district in London, dear Mortimer. Perhaps I'll help you track your girlish bawd."

"That's what I'm counting on. With you at my side, all I have to do is sit back and wait for the women to swarm. I'll act as your bodyguard while I wait for her to show herself."

Christian escaped with a promise to see Roger the next day. He was soon back at Vasterne House, where another, more reluctant disciple awaited him. Leaving off his cloak, doublet, and sword, Christian poured two goblets of wine and climbed the stairs to the third floor of the house. In a corner tower, he paused for a guard to let him into a locked chamber. He slipped inside and leaned against the door to close it. Crossing his ankles, he cocked his head and studied his prisoner.

Blade had been sitting in the window seat contemplating the sheer drop to the flagstones below. When Christian entered, Blade flung himself out of the seat and stood tall and defiant, with his back to the window. His chin lifted as Christian raked his gaze over him from curls to boots.

"You filthy spawn of a trugging house," Blade said, "let me go."

Christian shoved away from the door, walked toward the youth with a light, graceful tread, and held out a goblet. Blade swore, but he took the wine.

"You have the key to your emancipation," Christian said. He collapsed into the window seat and rested his arm on a bent knee. "Tell me where to find Jack Midnight and you may prance out of my house like a Morris dancer."

Noting how Blade stared at the door, he smiled. "It's not locked."

"I don't repeat my mistakes," Blade said.

"Then you're ready to tell me your real name."

"Go piss off one of your towers." He took a long drink of the wine.

"Dear boy," Christian said, "a vocabulary that consists mostly of profanity is a sign either of limited intelligence or lack of education. Desist from lewd language, I beg of you. It's boring."

Scowling at his captor, Blade absently tried to strangle his goblet.

Christian turned his head away from the youth and gazed out the window. "Can it be, my ill-tempered colt, that the reason you refuse to give your name is because you don't know it?"

With a twist of his body, he whirled around in time to catch the empty goblet Blade hurled at him. He tossed both vessels aside, heedless of his wine splattering on the floor. Blade let out a surprised curse as he was swiftly captured, and one of his arms was twisted behind his back. Christian shoved the youth across the room until Blade was smashed against the wall. He bent the boy's arm up and was rewarded with a gasp.

"I'm not a patient man. London has eighteen prisons to choose from, and I can put you in any one of them. I assure you, your accommodations won't be on the master's side, with a lovely bed and board. It will be the Hole for you, where you'll dine with rats and lie down with corpses."

"You don't frighten me," Blade said through whitening lips. "I've seen Newgate."

Christian again rammed his captive against the wall. "But have you been on holiday inside the Wood Street Counter? No food but what passersby throw through the window at street level, prisoners dying of festering sores, children crying over the bodies of their parents. You might get better treatment, though, if you bared yourself for the gaolers."

Blade laughed, then sucked in his breath at the onslaught of pain from his twisted arm. "You're trying to frighten me. Do you think, having been with Midnight, that such prospects hold any terror for me?"

Christian was quiet for a moment, then stepped back, easing the youth's arm out of its contorted position. He kept hold of it and began rubbing the abused joints at elbow and wrist. Blade suffered the treatment only because he couldn't get his arm back.

"Jack Midnight attacked me and my father when we were out hunting," Christian said in the amiable voice of a troubadour. "He skewered the earl and tossed me over his saddle. I thought my father was dead. I tried to escape for months and spent most of my time bleeding from his whip. Eventually I learned not to try to leave, and then my memories faded. I liked being a rogue."

Blade pulled his arm away. "I can't help you."

"I was right. You don't know your own name."

"You bleeding ass," the youth said.

"Is that how he kept you? Only he knows your identity, and unless you obey, he won't tell it. Rich. But consider that Jack Midnight is likely to keep you dangling from his belt strap until you die. Would you like to know why he'll do it?"

"Go to Hades," Blade said. "You made up a fairy tale and convinced yourself that it's the truth."

Christian walked back to the window seat and perched there. "But, my dear, your accent. When you're puffing like a bellows and all roused up, you sound like an Oxford cleric. If Midnight took you as my substitute, I want to know it. You see, Midnight hates noblemen with a festering, putrid virulence that makes Bloody Bonner look like St. Francis."

Blade shook his head. "You're lying."

Hopping to his feet, Christian stretched his arms lazily, then sauntered to the door. "It appears, my dear, that you must either suffer or be seduced. I shall ponder on which will be more edifying to your soul."

Late the next morning Christian wandered home in the company of Inigo Culpepper and a few ladies from the most luxurious brothel in Southwark. He returned armed with information and a smile that Inigo said made his stomach feel as if it were lined with knives. They all retired to his chambers, where Christian submerged himself in the hot water of a bath and soft female hands. Inigo lounged on his bed and sucked at a wine bottle. Christian was just tying his hose when a servant brought word that Nora Becket was below.

Shoving his feet into velvet shoes, Christian pushed away the woman who was playing with the open ends of his shirt. He hadn't suspected it of Nora. Some women were aroused by rough treatment; he'd been wrong to think she wasn't one of them. Here she was at his door when she should be eschewing his company like a nun confronted with a pimp. Christian laughed and twirled about. The full sleeves of his shirt fluttered like wings.

"I'm off to company, sweetings. Make merry with Inigo."

He raced downstairs, heedless of serving men and maids, and threw open the doors to the great hall. She was standing just inside the entrance, all tricked out in a gown better suited to a merchant's wife. He cast an irritated look at the black velvet yoke over her bosom. At least she'd removed her black silk mask, which she wore whenever she was about in the city.

"It's the mouse," he said, slamming the door shut. He stalked to her, caught the turned-back edge of her collar, and tugged at it.

"Oxen wear yokes, my dear. Leave them off next time or I'll have to resort to Blade's methods of exposing your lovely skin."

Her mouth popped open, and Christian had to kiss it. His lips fastened on the cherry-colored flesh, and he felt a puff of air as she gasped. Pulling back a bit he whispered, "Softly, easy and slow, like spring rain, like the melting of a candle." He kissed her again, sucking at her tongue, and felt her small body tremble. Her hands made fists in his shirt as she tried to shove him away.

He was about to tear the cursed yoke when something pulled at his shirt. He tried to ignore it, but the fabric was yanked sharply three more times. Lifting his head, he looked down. A cherub in Becket livery was scowling at him, a small fist twisted in the cambric of Christian's shirt. Sunbeams from a window cast light on curls as bright as polished gold.

"Unhand the lady, my lord."

Christian glanced at the blushing Nora. "An unlikely duenna. Is he supposed to swear to your innocence when you lose it?"

"No," Nora said. She tried to pull free of him, but Christian gathered her closer and nuzzled her neck.

"Get rid of him," he said.

The brat kicked him. Thrusting Nora from him, he swooped down and picked the boy up. The boy hollered and kicked, trying to bite Christian as he held him high in the air.

"Cherubs shouldn't act like pixies," Christian said. "Shall I hang you from a roof beam?" He ducked a kick. "The flat of my hand on your bum is what you need."

"No!" Nora cried out. She fastened both hands around his arm and pulled.

"It wasn't his fault," she said. "You misunderstood, my lord. I only came to bring you the puppies."

Christian lowered the boy to the floor, but kept hold of the back of his cloak. "The puppies?"

She nodded and cleared her throat. "Will you wait?"

After releasing the child, Christian spread his arms wide. She darted away and returned with a covered basket.

"I haven't the means to show my gratitude properly," she babbled as she shoved the container at him. "And I'm afraid my f-father is . . . difficult. But I wanted to do the honorable thing, to express my indebtedness. They are pure-bred, and great fighters, and they will protect . . ."

He realized she couldn't go on because he was staring at her. He lowered his gaze to the basket. The cover was moving, and he shoved it aside. Two fat, tawny mastiff puppies snuffled at his hand. One tried to bite his finger while the other gnawed on his signet ring. Christian touched the tip of a wet nose, then looked up into Nora Becket's earnest, glowing eyes.

"I know the gift must seem poor," she said. "But it comes with my heart's good wishes."

"God's toes, she's brought me puppies."

They stared at each other as Christian struggled with the unaccustomed experience of finding himself without words.

"I'll take them back," Nora said.

"You will not." He walked to the door, opened it, and handed the basket to a serving man. Turning back to Nora, he said, "Go away, Nora Becket. I beseech thee. Get thee from my sight and let me hear no more prattling of debts and gratitude. I want none of it, and none of you."

• • •

She'd given him puppies.

Christian leaned back on a cushioned bench in the bear garden on the South Bank of the Thames. Below, in the circular arena, the bearward and his men were staking out the bear. Scarred, slavering, and mad, the creature rocked from side to side and bared its fangs. In the stall with Christian sat Roger Mortimer and his current amour, Ned Howard, and several other young savages drunk on beer and anticipation of sport. Barbara White sat beside Christian. Her guffaws had ceased to make him wince, for he'd long since stopped listening to her.

Nora Becket had given him puppies to thank him for saving her life. Not jewels, not plate, not her body. Puppies.

It was clear she expected no gift of gratitude to come for him from her father. Christian supposed that a man who would send his daughter to court alone and without a proper wardrobe would hold her life cheap as well.

Their names were Homer and Virgil. That miniature bodyguard Arthur had told him so. He'd also said that Christian was lucky, for his mistress entrusted few with her orphans. Christian laughed at that memory, earning himself a speculative look from Roger. Those two puppies had already tried to gnaw his sword scabbard and had relieved themselves on the cushions on the floor of his bedchamber.

If only she hadn't given him puppies. Then he would have left her alone. He had cast out of his mind, but she'd come tripping back in with her great, luminous brown eyes, her humility and shy ways. It was too late to ignore her, and already he was plotting to have her with all the energy and obsession he brought to finding Jack Midnight.

The sun was bright and hot and sent waves of smelly heat rising up to the box where he sulked. Closely packed bodies, the odor of dog and bear, the smell of fresh pastries and beer all surrounded him. Idly he watched a nip and a foist work the crowd below with the help of a doxy who distracted potential victims. They were of Mag's pack from down at the Bald Pelican.

Mag. Christian smiled to himself at the memory of the woman. Almost six feet tall, she ran an alehouse that, like others of its kind, sheltered the activities of a band of thieves and swindlers, as enterprising a crew as any in London. Mag even ran a training school for pickpockets—nips—and cutpurses—foists. It was to Mag that he'd run when he'd escaped Jack Midnight when he was twelve.

Christian abruptly forgot about Mag when he heard Nora's name. Odd, he mused, how he could hear her name even above the catcalls, the hawking of vendors, and the rumble of the crowd.

"What did you say?" he asked Barbara.

"I said I couldn't believe Nora Becket deigned to come here." Barbara nodded to the benches on their right.

There she was. Nora Becket lifted her skirts and slid onto a bench. Her features partially concealed by a black silk mask, she was with several of the more adventuresome court ladies. She clasped her hands in her lap and kept her gaze trained straight ahead. She was pale. He couldn't see her eyes, but what he could see of her face was immobile, as if she dared not move for fear of breaking. Not once did she look down into the arena where the baiting was about to commence.

Roger whistled. "I didn't think she'd do it."

"What?" Christian asked.

"Come here. Last night at the palace Jane Dormer taunted her that she was a mouse and hadn't the stomach to join in true sport like bear baiting. She called Mistress Becket a mouse to her face, and so Nora wagered that she would come today."

Grasping the rail in front of him, Christian watched the girl. When the dogs were released, her hands jerked in her lap, then went still. She was still staring into the distance. One of the ladies whispered something to her, and Nora slowly lowered her gaze to the pit.

Five mastiffs were snapping at the bear. One charged and ripped into a leg. Blood spurted from torn flesh as the bear swatted the dog from its thigh. Two more dogs charged, and the bear caught one in its jaws. The mastiff screamed. Yellow fangs bit into the dog's back while the rest of the mongrels fell upon the bear.

Christian glanced from the spectacle to Nora. She grasped her silk mask and tore it from her head, then dropped it as she lurched to her feet. One hand clutched at her throat while the other groped for and found the scented pomander ball hanging from her girdle. She held it to her nose. Above her hand, her eyes were wide and fixed. Christian was up and running for the stairs before she fled.

He waited for her on the second landing. Hearing light, uneven footsteps, he moved closer to the stairs. She didn't see him. She dropped the pomander and almost fell down the last three steps in front of him. He caught her by the arms.

Eyes wide and unfocused, she stared at him.

"Lord Montfort."

Her face had lost all color and her skin was damp. When her throat convulsed and she tried to pull free, he swept her up in his arms.

"Try to hold it until I set you down," he said.

Running downstairs, he accosted an attendant and asked for a place of privacy. He was shown to an uninhabited office. Placing Nora on a bench, he slipped one arm around her waist and cupped the back of her neck with his other hand. He shoved her head between her knees while she muttered a protest.

The attendant brought a basin, damp cloths, and beer. After dismissing the man with the reward of a few coins, Christian placed the basin on the floor and applied a cloth to Nora's face and neck. She was still white, but her breathing was no longer so rapid. He wiped a bead of sweat from her cheek, but another followed. They were tears. Pulling away from him, she buried her face in her hands and sobbed.

Christian sat beside her, cloth suspended in the air, and waited. The sobs grew until he thought she would choke on them. Her body shook with the force of her grief, and she wrapped her arms around her stomach as though she were in pain. The violence of her grief stunned Christian. Then he remembered the puppies.

He pounced on her. Lifting her onto his lap, he shoved her face into his shoulder and squeezed his arms tight around her. He felt her tip-tilted nose burrow into his neck. The muscles in his chest contracted.

"You little fool," he said into her veil. "Goose. Idiot. Your heart is tied to your sleeve, and you can't go about letting others use it for a shuttlecock."

He felt her nod. Smiling, he buried his hand in her velvety black hair. His fingers found her neck. It was moist and hot; he kneaded the muscles. As he held her, a roar came from the bear. It was muffled, but Nora jumped and began to tremble again.

"Don't think about it," Christian said. He swore when she started to sob again. His hands bracketed her face, and he fastened his mouth on hers. Her sobs vibrated in his mouth for brief seconds before she drew back. He let her go, setting her beside him on the bench. Rising, he offered his hand.

"I'm taking you back across the river, sweet mouse. We'll go in my barge."

"I came with—"

"Let them wallow in blood," he snapped, then groaned silently when she flinched. He hadn't meant to sound so harsh.

He took her arm and conducted her out of the arena. His pleasure barge waited on the bank of the Thames. Pennanted and gilded, stuffed with cushions and covers, it was a gift from his father. Christian had Nora safely tucked into the cushions before she'd decided she shouldn't be going anywhere with him. She started to protest, but he hushed her.

"We're casting off," he said, "so there's nothing to do but wait."

A light, pattering sound drew his attention. Along the bank a small angel in Becket livery raced toward them. The page Arthur hurled his body across the increasing distance between the barge and the shore. Christian sighed and braced himself. As the boy arced toward him, he reached out and yanked at his flying cloak. Arthur landed on his bottom on the floor of the boat. Nora laughed at him and helped him up. Arthur plopped himself down on the floor again so that he was between Christian and Nora. The child lifted a rounded chin and scowled at his adversary.

"I accompany my lady at all times." Arthur pounded his fist on the deck to emphasize this announcement.

"Not if I drown you in the river," Christian said.

Arthur folded his arms over his chest and kept scowling. Nora admonished the boy, and Christian smiled at him nastily. His men oared quickly, and Christian distracted Nora from the silent and resentful Arthur by telling her a story about a black witch who turned a goldsmith's apprentice into an eel.

"Witches," Nora said. "Fie."

"Fie!" Christian put his fists on his hips and frowned. Suddenly he pointed into the water. "See. There it is now. The very one."

Nora leaned over the side of the barge. Christian dipped his hand into the river and flicked a spray of water at her face. She squealed, then jumped back and gawked at him. He leaned against his cushions and chuckled. His mirth ended abruptly when a pillow hit him square in the face. He caught it and held it up as a shield, but Nora's barrage was over. She was eyeing him warily, as if she regretted her rash familiarity and expected him to hit her. He lowered the pillow and grinned at her.

She gave him a tiny smile in return. "Thank you, my lord, for rescuing me again."

"I shall apply to the Queen for a license and monopoly. Snatching you from disaster is beginning to take a lot of my time."

"I regret it, my lord."

"Christian."

She shook her head.

"I'm going to call you Nora, so you might as well call me Christian."

She didn't answer. Turning her head, she gazed out at the houses along the river. Around them sculls and barges swarmed over the water. The sound of waves hitting the barge mixed with hailing calls from oarsmen. Arthur was still frowning at him, watching him as if he expected Christian to leap upon his mistress at any moment.

Christian let Nora be, however. He was content to study her profile. She had the blush of a Dutch tulip in her lips and cheeks. Her forehead was a gentle curve that sank into the bridge of her nose. Wispy black curls at her temples danced in the breeze. He avoided looking below her neck.

He should take her back to the palace, but he wasn't going to. Where could he take this gentle yet lush young woman, though? He let his hand trail in the water while he thought of the stews, taverns, and gardens that were his favorite haunts.

"We'll pass the rest of the afternoon in pleasance, my lady," he said, smiling lazily. He ignored her shake of the head and started singing an old French song.

> *Down the broad way do I go*
> *Young and unregretting,*
> *Wrap me in my vices up,*
> *Virtue all forgetting.*
> *Greedier for all delight*
> *Than heaven to enter in*
> *Since the soul in me is dead,*
> *Better save the skin.*

The boat hit the northern bank as he finished. He pulled Nora up and helped her onto the dock. Giving her no opportunity to protest, he clasped her by the arm and hustled her into the streets of London.

"Come along, my night-black mouse, and I'll wrap you up in my vices."

Chapter
IV

Christian sat on a bench in the back courtyard of the Golden Unicorn, leaning his weight on one hand and smiling at the chortles coming from Nora's little shrike of a guardian. It hadn't taken Christian long to conjure up a troop of players to distract his guests, and Bogo Littlefoot made an absurd spectacle as the sheriff of Nottingham. Using a pot for a helmet, a serving tray for a shield, and a roasting spit for a sword, Bogo waddled about the makeshift stage like a metal-clad lump of pudding with feet.

Judging that Nora had forgotten the bear baiting and was cheered by the combination of merrymaking, food, and the sight of Arthur's pleasure, Christian took her hand and gestured for her to follow him. Arthur and two of Christians's men-at-arms were cheering Robin Hood. Nora glanced over her shoulder at them, but Christian pulled her into the inn. Crossing through the kitchen, parlors, and the main hall, he got as far as the entryway before Nora dug in her heels.

"Where are you taking me, my lord?"

"Christian. I remembered just now that my lord father asked me to pick up something for him. He's had a cup made to present to the Queen when she attends our banquet."

Nora shook her head. "I can't go alone with you."

"Do you think I'd trip about London with a gold cup and a maid by myself? We'll have escort."

"But Arthur . . ."

Holding up a finger, Christian silenced her. Over the talk of the inn's patrons they could still hear laughter from the courtyard. "Arthur is well settled. You wouldn't want to deny him his pleasure, would you?" To forestall more objections, he caught her hand and whisked her into the stabling yard. "It's not far, anyway. We can walk."

Followed by several men-at-arms, he walked quickly so that she had to trot to keep up with him and had no chance to make excuses. She was too busy dodging loose cobblestones and ruts. He pulled her down a crowded street, around a corner, and across an intersection in front of a lumbering coach. The vehicle creaked and groaned as it sank into a mud hole, and Christian lifted Nora by the waist to swing her over the muck. When he reached for her hand again, she slapped his away.

"Ouch! Marry, lady, you are too cruel."

"Take me back."

"But we've arrived." He nodded toward a timber and plaster structure at her back.

Nora turned and stood in silence. She took a step, hesitated, then glided to the windows to study the treasures set out in them. Christian followed, a gratified smile playing about his lips. He inclined his head at two apprentices standing guard at the shop door, and they smirked at him knowingly.

The shop of Hugo Unthank was unique, for Hugo was a collector of rarities. Having spent his youth traveling in Europe and the Middle East, he had settled in London during old King Harry's days to purvey foreign goods. No one knew how he obtained the fabulous and exotic pieces that graced his shop, for Unthank discouraged questions. Joining Nora at the window, Christian glanced at a gold cross set with rubies, then at her.

She wasn't looking at the window display. He followed her line of sight and found the object of her perusal. In a gilded cage suspended from a stand sat a parrot—a giant green and crimson parrot. Scowling, Christian muttered a curse. She was supposed to be looking at the jewels, the watches made to be suspended from a lady's girdle, the illuminated book of hours, the ivory and lace fans. While he was scowling, Nora brushed past him and slipped into the shop. When he caught up with her she was stroking with one finger a tail feather that stuck out between the bars of the cage.

"Unthank!"

Nora jumped at Christian's shout. So did the apprentice who was walking toward them.

"Anon, my lord. No need to bellow." Hugo Unthank emerged from behind an arras at the back of the shop. "Indeed, indeed." He paused to brush a speck of dust from his velvet coat, adjusted his cap with the gold feather, then approached to give his bow.

"There are laws about commoners wearing velvets and the like, Unthank," Christian said.

The merchant smiled and flicked the feather in his cap. "Indeed, my lord, indeed. How may I serve you?"

Christian remembered his purpose. While Nora was making friends with the parrot, he took Unthank aside. "I've come for the cup my lord father ordered. But also find something to beguile the lady. Do it quickly, sirrah, and none of your cheap trinkets. I want wonders, marvels, anything to get her attention off that cursed bird."

The parrot squawked, making Christian wince, and Nora laughed and clapped her hands. Unthank disappeared behind the arras again and returned some minutes later trailed by three assistants bearing coffers. These were set on a table covered with damask. Christian walked over to the gilded cage.

"Nora." His quest was whispering endearments to the parrot. Christian raised his voice. "Nora, aren't you interested in the Queen's cup?"

Nora ceased her blandishments, but her gaze never left the bird. "Of course, my lord."

Christian sighed, snatched her hand, and led her to a chair set before the display table. Gesturing for Unthank to begin, he watched Nora. Unthank set a tall cabinet of ebony before her, took a key from his purse, and unlocked the door. Inside, nestled in velvet, rested a covered pedestal cup wrought in silver gilt and translucent violet enamel. Scenes of the Queen's coronation decorated the bowl, and the lid was crowned with a cluster of Spanish pomegranates and Tudor roses.

"Think you the Queen will like it?" Christian asked.

"Oh, yes."

He bent down to look directly into Nora's eyes. "Is that all you have to say after my poor sire spent a fat merchant's fortune on the thing?"

"It's very nice."

"God's teeth!" Christian threw up his hands and turned to Unthank. "Did you hear the lady? Nice. There. Look you, Nora, you've insulted Unthank. His feather's all aquiver and he's got the countenance of a grieving widow. Show her something else, man."

The cabinet was put aside, and a cherrywood coffer took its place. With the air of a wizard about to reveal the secrets of magic, Unthank tipped back the lid of the coffer, exposing a pile of jewels that would have made Princess Elizabeth's eyes gleam with acquisitiveness. Unthank's nimble fingers descended into the mass of glitter to pluck out a pendant. It was a phoenix cast in gold, encircled by rubies.

Nora nodded politely, but to Christian's disgust her head swiveled in the direction of the cage and its noisy occupant. Unthank cleared his throat, and she turned back to murmur her approval of a gold and enamel ring with an onyx cameo of the Queen.

Christian whirled away from Nora to yank on Unthank's cloak. "Do something, you befeathered grub. I want to know what she likes."

The merchant scurried into the recesses of his shop again and returned with another box, a small one this time.

"She won't be able to resist this, my lord," he whispered to Christian. "None of the ladies of the court has anything so fine."

Christian grabbed the box and dropped to one knee beside Nora. She was gazing at the parrot once more, but remembered herself enough to turn her attention back to him when he approached.

"Look, sweeting, a surprise."

He removed the lid of the box to reveal a small egg-shaped case made entirely of intricately engraved gold. He opened it. Inside the egg rested a watch so small, it would fit in Nora's palm. All of crystal and gold, it was made to be worn on a chain about the neck. Christian spilled the watch into his hand and raised his eyes to Nora's.

All he saw was the swirl of her skirts as she dashed to the shop window. A group of roughly clad men rushed past in the street outside. One of them held a bag, and something inside it wiggled and cried.

Nora was out the door and gone before Christian could stand. He threw the case and watch at Unthank, shouted for his men to remain behind, and took off after her. Insulted, his pride bruised if not cut, he vowed to catch this black-haired sprite and show her where her attention should be pinned. All thought of chiding her vanished, however, when he saw her hurtle after the three men into an alley. Clamping his hand on his sword, he dashed into the alley after her.

He was seconds behind her, but he was too late. As he ran toward her, he saw Nora reach out and poke the tallest, burliest man on the shoulder. The man turned around, and Christian recognized Pigsey Watt, a horse thief known to every ruffler, whipjack, and cutpurse in London for his unerring nose for swaybacked and diseased horseflesh. Poor Pigsey was a dullard, and his awareness of his shortcomings had made him mean. Christian groaned when he heard Nora. She would choose this moment to abandon mousehood.

"You've got kittens in that sack," she said to Pigsey. "They're frightened. Let them out."

Pigsey gaped at her. His two friends dug elbows into each other's ribs and sniggered.

"Them's my animals, mistress," Pigsey said. "We're going to use them in football, we are."

"You are not." Nora pulled herself up to her full height and pointed a finger at Pigsey. "Give those kittens to me, sirrah."

"Them's mine."

Pigsey was nothing if not consistent. Thus far, his presence had gone unnoticed by the three men. He was still a few yards from the group, and in the shadows of the buildings on one side of the alley.

"I'm not going to let you hurt them," Nora said. "Give them to me."

"Won't."

"You will."

Pigsey's face took on what Christian assumed was his clever look, which meant he appeared to be suffering from gas pains. Apparently Pigsey decided to solve the problem of this interfering lady by attempting to barrel past her. As his bulk loomed near, Nora shrank back. But Pigsey overreached himself. He boxed the sack he was holding.

A kitten yelped, and Nora sprang. Shoving her foot in front of Pigsey, she hooked this thick calf and pulled. Pigsey barked in surprise and tumbled to the ground. His two friends knew better than to loiter while Pigsey wrestled with a gentlewoman. They ran past Christian as he headed for Nora. He was drawing his sword, but Pigsey had caught Nora's ankle. He clawed at her skirt with his other hand. Christian knew the strength of those hands. If Pigsey got hold of her neck, he could kill Nora.

His sword cleared its scabbard as he closed the distance between himself and Nora. He shouted at Pigsey, all the while cursing himself for waiting too long. Pigsey's hand reached for Nora's neck, and she kicked him. Instantly, the man bucked and shrieked. Christian skidded to a standstill in front of the horse thief in time to see Nora withdraw her foot from the man's groin. Shivering at the sight of Pigsey doubled over on the ground and moaning, Christian sheathed his sword and took Nora's arm.

"By God, woman, you're as lackwitted as a guinea fowl. Pigsey could have killed you."

She pulled her arm free and leapt for the sack that Pigsey had dropped. Christian stalked over to her.

"I'm speaking to you, lady. I said you could have gotten yourself killed."

"Give me your dagger."

Christian ground his teeth together. "The saints preserve my temperance." Nora held out her hand without speaking. He growled and handed her the weapon.

While Nora was freeing the kittens, Christian fussed. "I don't understand it. I truly don't. You can't defend yourself from silly maids at court. You wilt like a babe in need of physick at the least harsh word, and tremble at the attack of thieves, and yet you furbish up your courage in an instant to attack three knaves over a sack of kittens."

She freed the last kitten and set it on the ground. "And you'd let them torture the poor creatures, I trow."

Christian felt his mouth drop open. "I would not!"

"You didn't even notice them." She picked up a kitten and thrust it at him, forcing him to grab it. "You were too busy looking at—at trinkets."

Christian cursed. The kitten sank its tiny claws into the back of his hand, and he cursed again. Nora picked up the remaining kittens and marched back to the shop of Hugo Unthank. Christian stayed in the alley, peeling the kitten from his flesh. By the time he reached the shop, he was in a fine temper. He could feel the blood rushing to his face, and when he saw Nora handing the kittens to Unthank with a smile of gratitude, the urge to swat the girl on the rump was almost unbearable.

"Master Unthank is going to find the kittens a home," Nora said to him.

"So," Christian said as he handed over his charge to an apprentice. "So."

Nora glanced at him. "So, my lord?"

"So, you fawn over a common merchant, all fat and foggy with praise because he takes in your pets. If I hadn't been at the bear baiting, you'd have puked on the stairs."

"What has the one to do with the other?" she asked.

Christian squeezed his eyes shut and recited the Greek alphabet. When he opened them, Nora was studying him in confusion.

"Don't look at me like that," he said. "It's your fault for behaving like a mouse and then attacking like the god Mars. Don't you know what it does to a man to see a woman burst into fire and passion like that?"

"I was furious," she said in protest. "When we first met, you chastised me for lacking courage."

He groaned and rubbed his forehead. "God's teeth, she's furious. Don't you understand that you should defend yourself as well as you did those kittens?"

"It's not the same."

"You're right, my sweeting. You're more important than the kittens."

She lifted her skirts and stepped into the street. "Oh, no,

I'm not. Animals are creatures of God, too, and someone has to care for them."

"You need to take care of yourself first, Nora Becket."

She shook her head and laughed. Seeing her eyes brighten, for once at him, Christian felt his humor return. Setting himself to be pleasant until he could return her to the palace, he kept his objections to himself. She didn't seem to think her behavior inconsistent—which made him wonder who had taught her that she counted for naught, for less than the stray cats and dogs that roamed the streets of London Town.

Nora stood in the privy chamber behind the older ladies-in-waiting and listened to the Queen's sobs. The royal bedchamber was dark, although it was not yet midday, for all the hangings were drawn across the windows. It was May, and the court hadn't quitted London due to the Queen's condition. Glancing over her shoulder at the closed door that led to the outside world, Nora couldn't decide whether it was better to endure the Queen's growing derangement or Lord Montfort's stalking. Mary's raised voice distracted her.

"Why doesn't he come?" the Queen cried. "He knows I'm with child again, and I need his comfort. And the war with France. I need counsel."

Mary leaned on the arm of her favorite waiting woman and ranted at Luiz de Ateca. Shrouded in black, her belly swollen, and her eyes red with weeping, she cast her gaze to ыιe ceiling. "Why does God punish me? Is it because my kingdom is full of heretics? I search for them constantly."

Nora couldn't hear de Ateca's reply, but she could guess that the man was indulging in his usual tactics of reassuring Mary of King Philip's fidelity while urging her to burn more heretics. It had been three weeks since she'd made the mistake of going to the bear baiting. In that time the Queen's state had worsened. She'd taken to wearing armor again and grieving inconsolably over the absence of her husband.

Mary saw the estrangement between Philip and herself as the work of the devil and his minions, the Protestant heretics. The more distraught and gloomy Mary became, the more tense and oppressive grew her court. Rumors swarmed, flylike, in this atmosphere, and Nora stayed busy keeping William Cecil abreast of the latest gossip.

The newest rumor had it that the Queen would name her Catholic cousin Mary, Queen of Scots, her heir in place of Princess Elizabeth. Nora didn't have to tell Cecil that such an act would mean civil war.

The Queen waved de Ateca away and hobbled to her great bed of state, sobbing once more. Nora and the other ladies hovered nearby, helpless. Nora clasped her hands together to stop them from trembling. Poor Mary. To be cast aside by her father, then be called a bastard and made to humble herself before her father's mistress, Elizabeth's mother. It was no wonder the Queen was unhappy.

For years she'd lived in fear that her father would cut off her head to keep her from the throne. And now she'd succeeded to the crown, only to find herself hated by the people whose souls she was trying to save.

One of the Queen's friends shooed the ladies out of the chamber, and Nora tried not to run from the room. In the last few days the Queen had refused to leave the palace, and that had sparked more rumors. Some said Princess Elizabeth had been taken to the Tower; she had been murdered by order of the Queen. Once it was bruited that the Queen had been murdered. Next people were sure that the Queen had called for troops from her Spanish husband in order to arrest and try scores of heretics. The next day everyone said the Queen had sent the crown of England to Mary, Queen of Scots and her French husband.

The last out of the privy chamber, Nora scurried along behind the other ladies-in-waiting and darted glances around the palace chambers. Lord Montfort wasn't about, and she relaxed. Perhaps he was busy with arrangements for that night's feast. The Queen insisted that the event take place in spite of her illness, and she was sending her ladies in her place.

Nora's heels tapped on the palace floor as she followed a fat countess. Tonight's banquet didn't signify. She'd been successful—for the most part—in avoiding Lord Montfort since the quarrel over those kittens; she could survive a feast at his house among a hundred guests.

Gaining her own chamber, she went to the window seat and took up her embroidery. Arthur joined her with his new lute, and she listened to him practice chords. Yes, she had outwitted Christian de Rivers, who seemed determined to pounce on her anywhere, from the presence chamber to the yew maze in the royal garden.

"I think Lord Montfort has given up," she said to Arthur.

"Good, my lady." Arthur didn't approve of Lord Montfort, in spite of the lord's attempts to bribe him with comfits and a new bow.

"It's not that I'm not grateful to him for saving my life," she added.

"Yes, my lady."

Nora smiled. She and Arthur often sat like this, with her talking more to herself than to him, and the page making polite noises of interest. Regardless of his youth, she trusted him where she did not trust the girls at court her own age.

"It's just that," she went on, "no matter his blandishments and attentions, I'm sure he hasn't changed his opinion of me. He thinks I'm a—a mouse."

"The snark." Arthur plucked a minor chord and sniffed.

Nora blinked at her page's choice of words. "And anyway, he's not comfortable."

"My lady?"

"When he looks at me, I feel, well, uncomfortable. I don't know." She studied the French knot she was making with gold thread. "You've seen duels, Arthur. You know that look that comes upon a fencer just before the duel begins, when he knows he must concentrate on his opponent and nothing else or die. That's the way Lord Montfort looks at me. It isn't comfortable."

Arthur put his lute aside and looked around as if in search of eavesdroppers. Seeing that they were alone, he whispered, "Mayhap he's a cunning man, a sorcerer, my lady. The other pages say he consorts with roughs and knaves, that he's never given up the evil he was raised to."

Frowning, Nora considered the possibility that Christian de Rivers was a sorcerer. The Queen's priests said that the Devil sent his servants among the unsuspecting in many disguisings. If the Evil One had sent Lord Montfort, the disguise was most pleasing—and therefore most dangerous. Nora congratulated herself for having escaped him. Indeed, he was not a comfortable or virtuous man.

There was a knock at her chamber door. Arthur answered it and returned bearing a letter. Nora almost snatched it from his hand, for she recognized her father's handwriting. Breaking the seal, she read the note quickly, only to let the paper fall to her lap. She stared unseeing at her embroidery hoop.

He was coming. He was coming to London, and would see her. He was coming, and he was angry. It was her fault, for she'd failed to catch the notice of a family with a rich heir. She should have been married years ago, but how could she have married then, when she'd spent most of her time in the country? Her companions had been her nurse, her tutors, and now Arthur.

She had tried to make herself worthy. From the fading memories of her mother before she died of the sweat, Nora recalled a quiet voice praising her for her clever wits. Hearing of the great scholarship, brilliance, and daring of Princess Elizabeth, she had set the royal lady up as Nora's standard. Elizabeth could speak French, Latin, Greek, and Italian. Elizabeth stood up to privy councillors and flayed them with her tongue. She had survived plots to have her beheaded and emerged from the Tower to the cheers of the people when Queen Mary let her go for lack of proof of treason.

Elizabeth was brave and beautiful, sophisticated and daring. Nora was none of those things. Her father said so, often, and now he was coming to court. He would arrive that night.

As she did when her father paid one of his rare visits to her country home, Nora spent the next few hours alternately fussing over her appearance and trying to think of excuses for the faults he was sure to point out. Since the list of her faults was endless, the hour of her father's arrival came quickly. Still feeling unprepared to face him, Nora hid behind an ornamental screen in a gallery through which her father would pass on his way to the closet where they would meet.

She had paid the sergeant at arms to come this way so that she could observe her father unseen. It was an old habit, this spying. It arose from the time when her father had first conceived of the idea that she was a bastard.

She could remember the day clearly, for he had come to her while she was at her spelling lesson, dismissed her governess, and told her of his suspicion. From that day on, though he kept his suspicion a secret from all but her and her mother, Nora

never saw the blessing of his smile. Her mother spent much of
her time pleading with him and crying, but always when she
thought Nora couldn't hear her. A few months later, Mother fell
ill of the sweat. Exhausted by her grief, she had little strength
to fight for life, and soon left off trying.

To be ten years old and cast out of a father's heart and then
lose one's mother was to be lost and bewildered, a battered and
storm-tossed little dingy on an ocean of hostility. Soon Nora
began to suspect that she was to blame for the unhappiness of
her parents. It seemed only logical that if Mother hadn't been
unhappy because of her, she wouldn't have died.

Afraid and burdened with guilt, Nora shrank in upon herself. Inside, she curled up as a fox curls up against the chill of
a winter's night. She was alone.

As the months passed, she grew used to missing her mother,
but not her father. Mother was gone, but Father was not. She
saw him every day, and yet he eschewed her company. To re-
capture a small amount of sunshine in her life, she decided to
spy on her father. She would creep into corners and behind tapestries so that she could see the smile he never gave her, hear
the laughter reserved for his friends and his mistresses. When
he finally sent her away, it was a blessing. In the old country
estate of her mother's mother, she learned to put grief behind
her and fill her life with sunshine of her own.

Now she waited again for the swift thud of boots as she had
when she was little. Her father's tread was distinctive. Always
quick and always loud with the bulk of his thick frame, it reminded her of the tread of an enthusiastic bull who had spotted
an intruder in his pasture and was happily running him down.
Nora giggled at the image of her father galloping across a pasture, then clamped a hand over her mouth. The rapid tap of
leather on polished wood signaled Father's arrival.

In a sweep of brown velvet and gold chains, William Becket
charged into view. Gold of hair and massive of frame, he neither
glanced about the court nor took notice of the curious stares that
always greeted the arrival of a newcomer. He preserved about
his person the reserve and isolation of an abbot. This reserve
dropped away when he was at leisure, or when he was angry.
The tepid waters of his temper could boil in the flicker of a
candle flame, as they had when William decided that a black-

haired mite such as Nora couldn't have been sired by a golden giant like himself.

William was past her in moments, and Nora raced to gain the closet before he arrived. She burst through the door, trotted to a side table decked with food and wine, and passed a shaking hand over the silver flagon and goblets that waited there. The door opened and closed before she could catch her breath. She licked her lips briefly, lifted her eyes, then lowered her gaze to the floor as she curtsied.

A grunt served as her acknowledgment. Nora murmured her own greeting, but William brushed past her to grab the wine flagon. He filled a goblet and drank it down before addressing her.

"Get up from that ridiculous half curtsy," he said. "I'm tired and I want to go to bed. A fine thing it is to be full of joy and good tidings and yet find a goose-witted fool one's only audience."

He slammed the goblet onto the side table and crashed down into the only chair in the room. Nora opened her mouth to apologize—she wasn't sure why—but William ignored her.

"God has answered my prayers," he said. "My wife is pregnant, and I've come to town to purchase gifts for her. I'm going to have a child of my own. You know what this means?"

Nora gaped at her father. She'd known his reason for marrying again had been to get an heir he didn't suspect of being another man's child. What could she say?

"It means my honor is restored," he said when she remained silent.

Wrinkling her brow, Nora shifted her weight from one foot to the other and tried to follow this line of reasoning.

"And I want you disposed of before my son or daughter arrives. I should have known better than to send you to court. I thought you might grow pretty under the tutelage of the finest noblewomen in the kingdom, but I was foolish to expect it of you."

Heat spread up her neck and face, and she ducked her head. "I tried, but the clothes . . ." Her voice faded as her courage withered under William's regard.

"I should have known no one would want you. You're plain and stupid, and no man wants a plain and stupid wife. So I've taken care of the matter myself. You're going to marry Percivale Flegge, son of Sir Badulf. And you're going to do it in three months' time, before my heir is born."

"Percivale Flegge," Nora whispered. She wet her lips and forced herself to speak up. "But Percivale Flegge . . . everyone knows he's got the—the pox. That's why he can't get a wife. The pox is eating his face and his wits as well."

"That's all gossip." William rose from his chair with the air of a man who had accomplished an unpleasant task. "Forsooth, I'm weary. It's off to the town house for me. A good joint of meat and cool beer is what I need."

He eyed the used goblet on the sideboard. While Nora stood in a daze, he whisked it away, hiding it under the chair behind one of the legs. Irrelevant thoughts swarmed in Nora's head. Her father never could stand the sight of soiled plate or clothing, or a dirty floor. At mealtimes he insisted that each dish be taken out of his sight as it was used and replaced with a clean one. He had to keep three extra sculleries for the purpose.

She woke from her standing dream when her father headed for the door. "Not Percivale Flegge," she said.

William's head whipped around, and she jumped at the sudden boom of his voice. "Not Percivale Flegge? By God's wounds! A woman needs but three virtues, chastity, silence, and obedience. They are all your sex is capable of, and I expect them from you, mistress. God strike me if I haven't behaved toward you with Christian charity." He strode up to her and bent over her, thrusting his face in front of hers. "When I knew you were not my spawn, I didn't cast you out. I've fed you and clothed you for years for the love I bore your mother, but I'll be damned if I'll do it any longer. You're an old maid, and it's time you married. I'll not have my new seed despoiled by contact with the Devil's offspring."

Nora shrank back from the rage that hit her like the heat from a kiln. "But, Father—"

"Silence! I'm signing the betrothal contract next month. Willing or no, you're going to marry, and I don't care how or to whom. If I have to truss you up like a stoat being taken to market, you're going to marry."

He grasped her shoulder and shoved her away. Without looking at her again, he stalked from the room.

Massaging her bruised shoulder, Nora stood gaping at the door. Percivale Flegge. Everyone said Percivale Flegge had festered lips and suffered from fits of violence, all from diseases arising from his debauchery. They said he'd been away from court because his family was trying to hide him. They needed an heir from Percivale desperately, but the young man's plight was too well known among the nobility.

Nora crossed herself and sank to her knees. Words of supplication tumbled from her lips. Surely God would help her. Even she, plain and stupid as she was, didn't deserve Percivale Flegge. Did she? The words of her prayer faltered as she wavered. Was this God's punishment? Was she all the things that her father accused her of being? Nora squeezed her eyes shut and resumed her prayers. God protected even the worst sinners. If she prayed hard enough, he might protect her.

Chapter V

Christian raced across the hall, dodging serving men carrying plate and sculleries wrestling with benches. Bursting through the doors on the far side, he hurtled toward the back stairs that would take him to the tower room where Blade was kept. A call from his father arrested his flight.

Sebastian de Rivers sat at a table in his library with his back to a sunlit window. A book lay before him, its pages bright with new print and shining in the blaze of a candelabra. Christian went to his father and knelt.

Keeping his gaze trained on the book, Sebastian reached out and stroked Christian's tangle of dark curls. "Are you going to torture that boy again?"

Christian glanced up at his father, but the earl was reading as calmly as a priest sings at vespers.

"I've played the mouse hunt too often these past few days and neglected poor Blade."

"I like to see you hunt women more than I like to see you hunt Jack Midnight." Sebastian shoved his chair away from the table and leaned back to study his son. "However, you've chosen a virtuous mouse this time."

"Marry, sire, you've touched the matter nearly. Each time I set out ahunting, I come back with my points still laced and my codpiece fair to bursting." Christian thrust his jaw out as his father's laughter rained down on him.

"A fitting penance for all your mischief, my headstrong. Perhaps you'll have better luck tonight at the banquet."

Christian smiled but said nothing. He rose to go, but Sebastian lifted a hand to stay him.

"You haven't distracted me from my purpose." Sebastian pointed to the window seat. "Sit."

"My charge will be hungry, and I was to bring him his meal."

"Sit down, young baggage. You sow discord like barley, and I like it not. And don't stick your jaw out at me. You're going to listen."

Christian subsided onto the window seat, hooking an arm around one knee, and glared at his father. Unlike Inigo and Three-Tooth Poll, Sebastian didn't shrink or start. He ignored the signs of impending fireworks and leaned against the wall beside Christian.

"Do you know why I hide Protestants?" he asked.

Frowning, Christian shook his head. "What has that to do with Blade?"

"Hush." Sebastian tilted his head back and studied the plastered and gilded ceiling. "When Midnight took you from me and I couldn't find you for so long, I took refuge in the new learning."

"Sire, that was long ago."

Sebastian waved a silencing hand. "After about three fortnights of flying around the countryside, I realized that I couldn't search the whole of England by myself, so I came here and began to direct my men in the search. I'd promised my physicians that I would rest, but I couldn't sleep without dreaming of you, so I read. I discovered so much in Aristotle, Socrates, Plato, Ovid—much more than when I was schooled. I would read through the night to avoid torturing myself with thoughts of you."

"I used to imagine you looking for me."

"I never stopped. And as the months went by and I still couldn't find you, I read instead of eating. And as I read, I marveled at the wisdom of these people who lived before Our Lord's Son. But one day it occurred to me that the church would condemn every Greek and Roman scholar as a heretic. Their souls were doomed. According to the church, that is.''

"That's why you hide Protestants?" Christian asked.

"Yes."

"Because the priests would condemn Aristotle's soul?"

"Are you confused?"

Christian nodded.

"Excellent," Sebastian said. "Then you won't be so likely to argue with me when I ask you once again to give up seeking revenge upon Jack Midnight.''

Christian stirred as if to rise, but a look from his father stilled him.

"Remember the day I found you?" Sebastian asked.

"Found me? I cut your purse. If I'd seen your face, I wouldn't have chosen you for a coney, but all I saw was your cap and a pouch fat with coin.''

Christian smiled at his father. Christian had been in London only a few months, pricked up with admiration for himself for escaping Jack Midnight after four years of slavery. Having apprenticed himself to the best school for cutpurses in town, he'd been practicing his skills near St. Paul's Cathedral and had tried to cut his own father's purse.

'Will you tell me now,'' Sebastian asked, "why you didn't come to me when you got away from Midnight?''

Christian leaped from the window seat, and strode to the table, bracing himself against it with his hands flat on the top. "You know I don't talk about that.''

"I've let you imprison that boy in my house, Chris. It's wrong and could get you in trouble. I want to know why I should risk losing you again.''

Fingering the edge of the book that lay before him, Christian remained silent. Behind him, his father waited, never moving. Christian could feel those gentle eyes study him.

"It was long ago," Sebastian said. "You can tell me, for I love you.''

Christian sighed and closed his eyes. "He said that after the things I'd done, that he'd done to me, you wouldn't want me. He even told me he'd tried to ransom me, only you'd refused the sum he demanded.''

"By God's wounds!''

Whirling about, Christian held out a supplicating hand. "I'm sorry. I was too young, and he beat me. I didn't want to do those things. Not at first.''

"I will hear no apologies from you." Sebastian shoved him into the chair and grasped his shoulders. "Haven't I told you to leave the past behind? You did what you had to do to live, and I thank God that He watched over you until I could reclaim you.''

Christian hunched his shoulders and whispered, "But that isn't the only reason I didn't come back." Lifting his chin, he faced his father. "I didn't come back because—because by then, I liked it. I liked thievery, the life of a highwayman. I belong with cutpurses, trulls, and knaves. If I were virtuous and godly, I wouldn't have liked the excitement. I wouldn't have found fellowship and pleasure in a thieves' camp or in a trugging house before I was twelve.''

Sinking down to one knee, Sebastian shook his head. "You're so much my son, Chris. Our minds work alike, don't you think? But you're much more practical than I. You took on the outer trappings of thievery to survive. The sin lies on Jack Midnight's soul, not yours.''

"So you've told me, and I intend to see that he expiates his sins.''

"But as to liking thievery, what boy does not? What lad wouldn't run wild, gad about the countryside living off stolen pies and poached meat if given the chance? Especially if the choice is between being a knave and doing one's duty as heir to responsibility and care." Sebastian eyed his son's down-curved mouth. "This is well-traveled country for you and me, and I've not convinced you yet.''

"No, sire.''

"Stubborn lackwit. It's no wonder I call you my headstrong. Be off with you then.''

Christian got up, plucked a book from one of the shelves, and sighed again. "I still say you'd be married by now if it weren't for my sins.''

"And I still tell you I favor a dagger-witted merchant's

daughter whom the Queen would never allow me to marry. It's not your doing that her family had to take refuge from Mary in Scotland. Content you, for I'll be traveling north before winter to see her.''

Studying his father's face, Christian nodded. ''We shouldn't speak of such things on a fine spring feast day. My wits are addled from chasing that pretty mite all over the palace.''

''Well then, stop chasing her.''

''I can't. Nora Becket needs tending. She doesn't stand up for herself. She shrinks and cowers and lets those women of the Queen's drive her like a calf without a mother.''

''So you would be her champion and reap a champion's reward.''

Christian widened his eyes in innocence. ''I but seek to improve her character.''

''If your mother hadn't died when you were a babe, you wouldn't be so rapacious toward women. I'm convinced of it. Don't turn that angel's stare on me, young wretch.''

Resuming his seat at the table, the Earl put his fingertips together so that they formed a steeple and gazed over them at Christian. Christian swerved away from that quiet contemplation and began tapping the spines of books on a shelf and singing under his breath.

There was a loud snap as his father closed the book he'd taken up. Christian pursed his lips and traced the gilded spine of a translation of the *Iliad*.

''I've been thinking about Nora Becket,'' Sebastian said. ''The word is all about the town that her father has betrothed her to Percivale Flegge. You'll have to give up the hunt.''

Christian's finger paused in its journey down the spine of the book, then resumed its movement. ''Flegge is a pox-ravaged leach.''

''Becket doesn't care. His new wife is with child, and he wants rid of Nora. I suppose the girl will object. Perhaps she'll put up a fight. Then you can play the mouse hunt again.''

''Nora Becket fights for nothing that doesn't have four legs and fur.'' Christian spun around, avoiding his father's eyes, and sauntered to the door. ''What woe, what woe. At last I find a girl of wit and good cheer, and she's betrothed. I shall put her from my thoughts until she's been wed a few weeks. That much time in the company of Flegge should make the fruit ripe indeed. I shall put her from my thoughts.''

Sebastian's snort followed Christian out of the library. "Lying is a sin, Chris, even if you're only lying to yourself.''

Cursing his father's perceptiveness, Christian made his way to the kitchens, where a meal was being prepared for Blade. The place was as raucous as a bear pit with the preparations for the night's banquet. Subsiding at a table in a corner where a serving man had placed the tray containing Blade's meal, Christian took up a knife and jabbed at the roast capon on the tray.

Percivale Flegge, he thought. By God's teeth, how could a father give his only daughter to that? And Nora wouldn't have the courage to refuse. He was sure of her cowardice, for she'd been running from him for weeks faster than a mouse from a ferret. Why, only a few days ago he'd tried to speak to her at a fencing match in one of the palace courtyards, but she had hidden behind the skirts of those old duennas the Queen kept as ladies-in-waiting. The clanging of pots and the growls of cooks faded as Christian remembered Nora's quick dash behind a wall of brocade and velvet.

Instead of pursuing the girl, he'd faded away into the crowd around the fencers and watched her. He could tell she had lost sight of him. Nora stood on her toes and peeked around the bulging girth of a Spanish noblewoman, her eyes searching the crowd for him. At last she appeared to cast aside her wariness and observe the fencers once more. When he was sure she no longer looked for him, Christian began to edge his way around the crowd toward her. As he did so, he saw her slip away.

Trailing her into the palace, he lurked in the shadows of entryways and around corners until she disappeared through a doorway. It led to a small garden used infrequently because of its proximity to the stench of a leaking sewer pipe. Christian sidled up to the doorway and peered through it to see Nora pick up a basket. Using a pair of scissors from the basket, she stooped and cut a rose. He watched her progress, cutting more blossoms, until she reached a honeysuckle.

She stopped in front of the bush with her back to him. Fumbling with basket and scissors, she appeared to be having difficulty removing her gloves. She got them off at last, placed them in the basket beneath the roses, and shoved the basket under a bench beside the honeysuckle. Christian grinned when she glanced around, as if in search of intruders. As she bent to sniff the honeysuckle, he slithered into the garden and up behind her.

" 'There is a garden in her face, Where roses and white lilies grow.' "

With a squeal, Nora lurched upright and twirled around. He snatched her hand before she could flee, but she jerked free. Instead off running as he expected, she scuttled sideways, knocking her basket over, and sank onto the bench. After gawking at him for a moment, she glanced down at her basket, then cried out and swooped down upon it.

Christian knelt beside her, picked up one of her gloves, and laughed. "You cavort like a jester, beautiful Nora."

"Give me my glove!"

"How now, mistress, you berate me for my chivalry." He extended the glove, only to have it ripped from his hand and stuffed in the basket. "How haps it that you steal away from the fencing match to do servants' work?"

She dumped the roses back on top of her gloves and stood, clutching the basket to her chest. Christian rose with her and closed the distance between them. She backed up until her leg hit the bench and she toppled onto it.

"Go away," she said.

He slid onto the bench. Bracing himself on one arm, he leaned close to her. She turned toward him, with the basket held between them like a shield.

He glanced down at her bulwark, then lifted an eyebrow. "Never have I known such a puling coward. You should thank God He made you a woman. I do."

He expected her to shriek and run. Once again she surprised him. Instead of cowering, she looked at the basket lodged against her chest, sucked in her breath, and went white. Abruptly she thrust the basket under the bench, giving it a shove so it disappeared beneath her skirt.

In an instant Christian snaked an arm behind her back and pulled her close. As the heat of her squirming body reached his skin, he wrapped his arms tighter around her. Instinct guided him to mutter reassurances with what little sense he had left. A river of blood roared inside his head and churned

to his legs and groin. His hearing vanished, its place taken by
the feel of her soft cheek against his lips.

He wasn't sure just when Nora stopped squirming. He only
knew that small fingers reached up to touch his face, lightly, like
leaves blown by a breeze. That uncertain touch woke him from
his hot, dreamlike state long enough to look at her. She was
staring up at him, lips trembling. She tried to speak.

"Shhh," he whispered.

Brushing his lips across her cheek, he felt her shiver. Of
their own accord, his arms tightened even more, and he continued to skim the surface of her flesh with his lips. He traced her
jawline, the skin below her ear, the length of her neck to where
the pulse beat in her throat. She was breathing almost as quickly
as he was now.

He pressed her backward so that her only support was his
arm, then slowly lowered her until she was lying on the bench.
She tried to slip her arms between their bodies, but he quickly
pressed his chest to hers and covered her mouth. Sliding a hand
up her rib cage, he sought and found the soft hill of her breast.
She started at the touch. He was sucking at her mouth when
something tugged sharply at his hair. His head snapped back.

"Ouch!" He blinked and tried to rouse himself from the
warm heaviness that had invaded his body.

She released his hair and clasped his face in both hands.
"You don't like me."

"What?"

"You think me a coward, my lord."

Bracing himself on his elbows, he captured her hands. "This
is no time to acquire courage and fight me, sweeting. Be a coward." Holding on to her wrists, he again fastened his mouth on
hers while pressing his body against hers.

He was shifting so his thigh could force its way between
her legs when he heard a sob. Arousal vanished. Lifting his
head, he beheld her tightly shut eyes and the single tear that slid
down her temple. He released her at once, lifting his body from
hers and drawing her upright.

Nora hugged herself and bit her lower lip. Christian winced,
then brushed a lock of hair back from his brow and cursed.
Often it suited his purposes to frighten, but never before had he
felt the monster he did now upon seeing Nora tremble in fear of

him. He'd spent days of frustration, a wolf cheated of its prey, only to find that his taste for blood had vanished at the moment of the kill. He touched her cheek, and she cringed. Slipping to the ground in front of her, he knelt on both knees and extended his hand to her.

"G-go away." She wiped tears from her face with the palms of her hands.

"I beg you to forgive me, sweeting. I thought even you would have been touched by at least one man before now."

Fidgeting on the bench, she sniffled and straightened her skirts. "Go away."

"No."

He thought she would run. She didn't, and he frowned at her. She scooted away from him, and her dress caught on the basket. She scooted back, lifted her skirt to cover the basket again, and faced him, her teeth tearing at her lower lip.

He put his fingertips against the abused flesh. "Don't. You're hurting yourself, and I can't bear that any more than I could hurt you myself. What have you done?"

"I haven't done anything. Please, go away."

"You must have done something, or I wouldn't have stopped." He rubbed his chin and muttered to himself in awe. "I stopped." He shook his head. "I must need a physick. Perhaps ill humors have built up in my body."

"It is I," Nora whispered. "I am ill. I tingle and—and I'm not comfortable."

He caught his breath, then laughed so hard that Nora jumped again. She recovered and stared at him while he sank down on his haunches and guffawed. When he could speak, he looked up at her again.

"My innocent, my sweet lackwit."

"I told you that you didn't like me."

He shook his head, smiling. "You don't like what you feel when I touch you?"

"No. It's not comfortable."

"What you feel isn't discomfort. It is pleasure."

"Fah."

"It is. Look." He slowly reached out and placed his hand on her shoulder. "What do you feel?"

"Warm."

"Where?" he asked.

"Where you touch me."

"And?"

She flushed and shut her mouth tightly.

"Here?" He put his other hand on her thigh, and she began to squirm again. Before she could move, he slid his hand up to her pelvis. His fingers pressed into the flesh of her stomach near the join of her thighs. His voice was rough as he said, "Here as well, I wager."

She slapped his hand.

"God's teeth, woman!" Christian sucked the back of his fingers to take away the sting. A pity nothing would ease the pain between his legs.

"You choose the most inconvenient times to put aside your timidity."

Nora leaped to her feet. Crossing her arms over her chest, she scowled at him. "I am expected in the presence chamber anon, my lord."

"Witch."

"Go away."

"I've not finished with you." He stood and took a step toward her, but halted at the sound of the garden door swinging open.

Glancing over his shoulder, Christian saw a gardener enter carrying buckets of compost. Turning back to Nora, he spoke low enough so that only she could hear.

"Be warned, sweeting. I'm not used to playing the supplicant. I grew up thieving, and I know how to steal what I want. Hide from me all you wish. It will do no good."

Returning to the present with a grunt of disgust, Christian again jabbed the knife into the capon. The blade sliced through meat and hit the metal tray with a *clink*.

"I do believe the maid's never been kissed," he said to himself. "Well past a marriageable fourteen and she feels 'uncomfortable.' "

"My lord?"

He glanced up at a serving man who carried a loaf of bread. The man placed the bread on the tray and gawked at the impaled capon. Scowling at the confused servant, Christian grabbed the tray, then stomped from the kitchens.

A guard let him into the tower room. Blade was lying on his bed, one leg propped on a knee, staring up at the canopy. A pile of unopened books took up most of the surface of the table near the bed. Christian shoved some of them aside to make room for the tray.

"Where is the Latin I gave you last night?" he asked.

"You know I can't read it," Blade said.

Christian picked up a book, rifled through its pages, and read, " *'Disce bonas artes, moneo, Romana inventus, Non tantum trepidos ut tueare reos; Quan populus iudexque gravis lectusque senatus, Tam dabit elequoiu victa puella manus.'* Translate."

"Stow you!"

"You'd rather tend pigs?"

Blade thrust his slim body. Crouching on all fours, he snarled at his captor. "I can't read Latin. I never could. Never."

"Your accent gives you the lie." Christian glanced down at the passage and translated it himself. " 'Learn noble arts, I counsel you, young men of Rome, not only that you may defend trembling clients; a woman, no less than populace, grave judge or chosen senate, will surrender, defeated, to eloquence.' *The Art of Love*, Ovid."

"You're trying to make me into a gentry cove. I'm a cozener, a lockpick, a cutpurse and dagger, not some lost nobleman's spawn."

Christian picked up the knife from the tray, stabbed a chunk of the half-butchered capon, and held it out to Blade. The boy eyed the offering and Christian with distrust, then snatched the meat.

"Why do you think I bundled you from tradesman to artisan for over a fortnight?" Christian asked.

Blade swallowed the meat and shrugged. "To drive me mad."

"When I set you to work for my father's steward, he said you couldn't carve a peacock, you know nothing of polishing plate, and that you can't even fold linen."

"The steward is a fat ass."

"I arranged to have you serve a tanner, a smithy, and a pigkeeper. None of these trades could you master."

"I told you, I'm a dagger."

"You're a fool."

Christian opened the chamber door and snapped out an order to the guard. The man produced two swords, and Christian faced Blade. Hurling one of the swords at his captive, he saluted with his own weapon.

"Listen closely or you'll be worms' meat. *Pasado*." After saying the word, Christian brought his sword down and thrust forward, aiming at Blade's chest. Even as he moved, Blade's steel flew up into position to parry.

"*Punto reverso,*" Blade said. Leaping back, he executed a backhanded stroke that hit Christian's sword, and the two weapons slid together until they locked at the hilt.

The two faced each other over the cross formed by their swords.

Christian smiled. "You move like a student of a first fencing house, my cutpurse. And answer to the *pasado* in the Italian manner."

A furrow appeared in Blade's brow. Gazing at the crossed swords, he muttered, "Midnight said he taught me."

"Midnight speaks no foreign tongue. He's a franklin, Blade, tossed off his land by some greedy noble who enclosed his estates for profit. Why do you think he hates the highborn? His wife and two sons died of exposure when their lord cast them out. Midnight speaks no foreign tongue."

"But I—"

"Answer to Italian while fencing, as one taught by a master." Christian stepped back, withdrawing his sword.

Letting his own weapon fall, Blade stared at Christian, his thoughts obviously distant.

Christian raised his voice to break into the boy's reverie. "*Honi soit qui mal y pense.*"

"Shamed be he who thinks evil of it," Blade replied without hestitation. "Oh."

His sword swinging in his left hand, Christian sauntered over to him and whispered in his prisoner's ear. "Yes, think upon it, my surprised one. How is it that you can translate the motto of the Order of the Garter?" He watched the color ebb from Blade's smooth cheeks and quickly slipped a hand under his arm. "Sit you down before you fall. And let this be your lesson—*fronti nulla fides.*"

Blade sank down onto the bed. "No reliance can be placed on appearance." He put his hands over his ears and shut his eyes. "Stop, please."

"You can't ignore Jack Midnight's duplicity."

"Christian."

It was the earl. Christian straightened from his looming stance over Blade and turned to face his father.

"What have you done?" Sebastian asked. He stepped between his son and Blade. "The lad's pale as a whitefish and shakes as if he has an ague."

Christian bent and picked up the sword he'd cast aside. "He's quaking because he's found out Jack Midnight isn't a bloody saint."

Sebastian eased Blade into a reclining position. "Fear not, boy. Christian has a banquet to host and Nora Becket to seduce. He won't have time to put you to the rack further today."

"Oh, there's time aplenty," Christian said.

The earl sighed and left the room, shoving Christian before him. Christian stumbled out onto the landing that led to the tower stairs, then caught himself and whirled around. His arms crossed over his chest.

"You will leave that boy alone tonight. It is my wish."

"He needs—"

"Peace. The lad needs peace. I ought to know. I've reformed young knaves before."

Christian ground his teeth together. "Yes, sire."

"And speaking of knaves," Sebastian said as he walked his son down the stairs, "our three guests haven't made their departure."

Halting on a stone step, Christian gaped at his father. "What happened?"

"Bloody Bonner is watching the port. The ship's captain took fright and sailed without them, and I must arrange passage all over again."

"God's arse. We're entertaining Bloody Bonner and his minions tonight, and those three heretical weasels are still under our roof."

"I'll put them in the cellar," Sebastian said.

"And I'll find a lock even Blade couldn't pick."

"There are new guests." Sebastian stepped down so that he shared a stair with Christian. "I saw Becket at Unthank's and invited him. And Flegge."

"Sire, what jocund wit you have. I do believe you seek to discomfort me."

"Not at all, my son. If the truth be sought, I think Nora Becket an unsound choice for a wife for any man. Too quiet, too plain, and she fidgets and dithers when faced with travail of any kind. If I thought you entertained yearnings for her other than physical ones, I would forbid you to seek her out."

Christian nodded, his wits unraveling like the threads of an old tapestry. "Too quiet and plain. Fidgets, yes, she fidgets."

"And dithers."

"Dithers, yes. An unsound choice." Christian took another step down. "Mark you, sire, I wasn't thinking of Nora Becket for a wife."

"Then we agree."

"Of course," Christian said in a faint voice. He shook his head and managed a chuckle. "Besides, what man wants a woman who prattles that he makes her uncomfortable?"

Chapter
VI

Nora took the empty posset cup from the Queen and adjusted the blanket around Mary's shoulders. Her hands brushed the cold metal of the armor the Queen had donned that morning after seeing the latest pamphlet calling upon all godly subjects to overthrow her. Shortly after her father left, Nora had been called to attend Mary, but was having difficulty thrusting aside her own unhappiness in favor of courtly decorum.

"It's that daughter of sin who puts them up to such indecencies," Mary said. She hurled a pamphlet to the floor. Resting her hands on her swollen stomach, she cursed and hunched down in her chair. "What ails you, girl? Your nose is red and your eyes are swollen. I can't have sick people around me, you know. I must think of the babe."

"I'm not sick, Your Majesty."

"What then? Have you been weeping? Why? Out with it, Nora. I have enough sorrow to contend with without my ladies adding to it."

Nora studied the posset cup in her hands. "It's naught, Your Grace."

"Nonsense. You're unhappy, and I want to know why. Tell me at once."

"Oh, Your Majesty, I'm to marry Percivale Flegge," Nora said. Once she started, she couldn't hold the words back. "I know a daughter's duty to her father, but—but Percivale Flegge."

"And what's wrong with Flegge? I saw him a few days ago. He's a well-looking man."

"But Your Majesty, everyone says he is diseased."

"God's blood, this court is a wasps' nest of rumor. Flegge himself assured me that the report was a lie spread by the Howards because he is a son of the true church. And I saw for myself that the man has a nose, and all his other parts, too. Be comforted, Nora."

Placing the posset cup on a sideboard, Nora expelled a long breath. Only some of her fear was dispelled. What if Percivale Flegge saw her and didn't want her? Plain, possessed of no great wit or charm, how could she hope to inspire admiration and love?

"Another long face," the Queen said. "By the rood, Nora, I'm glad you're going to the de Rivers banquet tonight, for it will cheer you."

"I don't think so, Your Majesty."

"And why not? Quit biting your lip and speak up, girl."

"I'm not worthy, Your Majesty. I'm such a mouse."

The Queen made a grumbling noise. "Look you, Nora. It's true that women are inherently the Devil's instrument and not God's, but as long as a girl is chaste, obedient, and intelligent, there's no reason she can't also be pretty. God delights in beauty devoted to His works."

"Think you so, Your Grace?"

"My father used to say so all the time. And he was, after all, the great King Harry."

Nora contemplated this new idea. If England's powerful and fearsome Henry VIII approved, it wasn't for her to question. Tentatively, she said, "I have thought about altering my gown for the banquet. There's to be a masque, and the Duchess of Suffolk says my dress is more suited to a funeral than merrymaking."

"Begone with you, silly baggage. My good Frances knows what benefits a woman. If she says your dress is lacking, you may be sure it is. I'll send my seamstress to you."

Hours later Nora stood in front of the Queen's full-length

mirror and surveyed the results of her newfound audacity. She
wore a gown remade from one of her mother's. The white silk
overgown fit tightly to her arms and torso, then swept over her
hips to her feet. Split in the front, the overgown revealed a petticoat of black silk beaded with pearls that matched those covering the outer dress. A matching French hood with a white silk
fall set off the black curls that tumbled from beneath the veil.

As she gazed at her reflection, she suffered misgivings about
her chemise. Of fine black lawn, it had been designed to hug
her neck and chest, concealing what the low, square-cut neck of
the gown revealed. She'd had the seamstress adjust the chemise,
and it hid beneath the neckline of the gown. The chilly draft on
her bosom told her she was fashionably dressed. The black
sleeves of the chemise peeked out from beneath the full over-
sleeves of her gown but were no comfort. She would have been
far more comfortable if she could have reversed the adjustments
and pulled the neck of the chemise to her chin and bared her
arms instead.

A waiting woman interrupted Nora's worries. Bearing a casket engraved with Queen Mary's initials, she proffered it to Nora.
Nora opened it and gasped at the string of pearls that lay within.
Cascades of them rippled from a central pendant containing a
cabochon ruby. It was a piece Mary rarely wore, for it had been
taken from her mother by King Henry and given to Elizabeth's
mother.

"The Queen says," the waiting woman said, "to tell you
the pearls should be worn by a lady of both beauty and virtue."

With the servant's help, Nora donned the necklace. It wound
around her neck so that the ruby pendant rested just above the
cleft between her breasts, and strands of pearls draped down her
shoulders to disappear beneath the neck of her gown.

Nora gaped at her reflection. "Why, I'm pretty."

The waiting woman looked at her as if she were addled.
"Of course, my lady."

Blushing, Nora clasped her hands together and chastised
herself for her foolishness. Hadn't her father always said females
were inherently sinful? She had just proved him right by boast-
ing.

The waiting woman touched Nora's sleeve. "Pardon, my
lady, but don't you go letting those other ladies chide you. You're

as pretty as any of them. All the servants think you're the
sweetest lady of the court.''

Nora murmured her thanks, and the woman left her alone.
Wrestling with the experience of unfamiliar praise, Nora tried
not to feel undeserving. The woman didn't know that Nora secretly hoped to attract the interest of someone other than Percivale Flegge that night. Even if all those rumors of Flegge's
disease weren't true, she didn't want to marry a man who spent
so much time at trugging houses that his friends accused him of
owning them.

Gathering her skirts, Nora slipped out of the robing chamber. This evening would be a night of trials. Not only had she
to face Percivale Flegge, but also somehow she must survive
another encounter with Lord Montfort. As she walked through
the palace in search of Arthur, she cringed inwardly at the
thought. That last time in the garden, Christian had interrupted
her when she'd been about to conceal Cecil's message. And the
things he'd done to her.

He'd given her a contagion. That was the only explanation.
Otherwise she wouldn't have fevered dreams at night and search
for his violet eyes in the countenance of every man at court.
Once, when she was seven, she had allowed an older boy to
touch her leg. Her mother had whipped her with a willow switch.
The experience hadn't been worth the punishment, but now she
thought she'd endure any number of whippings if they brought
her the feel of Christian's hips against hers and the warmth of
his lips.

"Stop!" she told herself. "Don't think such things."

"My lady?"

She looked up to see Arthur hurrying toward her across the
gallery where she'd stopped.

"It's naught," she said. "Please fetch my cloak."

Merciful Savior, she couldn't go to the banquet thinking
ribald thoughts about the infamous Lord Montfort. She'd seen
at least five different court beauties, their breasts heaving and
lips slack, offer themselves to him in the past month.

She had other worries. God knew she had troubles enough
without succumbing to a man who had merely to walk into a
room to seduce a woman. Mayhap they wanted him because of
his lurid reputation. Christian de Rivers carried about him the

allure of the forbidden. The Duchess of Suffolk speculated openly about his career as a highwayman and cutpurse, while the light in her bean-sized, piggy eyes revealed an unspoken curiosity about the compelling sensuality of the man.

Nora was no match for him, as he'd told her plainly, so she wouldn't pit herself against him. She would seek the admiration of a good man who would protect her and take her away from court. If she escaped the court, she would escape Lord Montfort, and then perhaps she wouldn't dream about him anymore.

Wedged between her father and Percivale Flegge, Nora started at the trumpet call that announced the next course of the Earl of Vasterne's banquet. Her hands shook as she raised a silver goblet to her lips. While her face was partially concealed by the vessel, she glanced at Flegge. He had a nose. It was a small, straight nose as free of disfigurement as the rest of his body. Indeed, he was almost as desirable as Lord Montfort. He was long of leg, and his hose covered knots of muscle built in hours of fencing and riding. As she watched Flegge, her father said something to him over her head, and the man laughed.

"Ah-ha hic ah-ha hic ah-ha hic, ah-ha hic."

Nora closed her eyes and prayed. Heads turned nonetheless.

Nora opened her eyes and ducked her head. On the dais, Frances, Duchess of Suffolk, sniggered. Draping a fat hand on Christian de Rivers's sleeve, she whispered to him. Christian speared a piece of roast boar and offered it to the woman. He murmured something to her, but did not turn his attention to the noise at the table so near his own.

She couldn't marry that laugh, Nora thought. Especially when Flegge's idea of amusement was a story about the antics of dying animals at a bear baiting. But what could she do?

A stuffed peacock sailed by her on its way to the dais. Beak gilded, feathers shining, it stared out at the revelers in frozen dignity. At that moment, Nora felt like the peacock—all garnished and gilded on the outside, and minced on the inside. It mattered not that Roger Mortimer had complimented her, or that her appearance in the hall had caused Christian to stutter and forget his address to the Duchess of Suffolk. Nora loathed Flegge.

Only a few times in her life had she taken an immediate

dislike to someone. There had been the false beggar who'd accosted her in the village near her home. There was the distaste she'd suffered upon meeting Bishop Bonner, the churchman engorged with sweat and sadism. And now there was Flegge. In spite of his pleasing appearance, he disgusted her. His mind dwelled in the gutter, where his body lay so frequently. And, of course, there was that laugh.

More courses passed through the hall—swan, partridges in wine, artichokes, salads, veal, and kid. Nora was still toying with an artichoke when four men bore in a confection of marchpane formed into a castle surrounded by dragons.

Soon after the appearance of the marchpane castle, but not soon enough for Nora, she was able to leave the table. The earl invited everyone to follow him, and the whole party adjourned in order of precedence. Flanked by her father and Percivale Flegge, she trudged into the Montforts' disguising house, where a masque was to be held.

Built a short distance from the earl's palace, the disguising house was a small theater much like the one Henry VIII had built. Rows of cushioned benches ringed a central stage, and behind the stage were storage closets and changing rooms for actors. The whole building was alight this evening in preparation for the masque. Nora took her place in the tiers of seats reserved for the ladies, relieved of Flegge's company for the moment.

From behind a curtain erupted a howl and a roar. The women seated near it shrieked. The curtain jerked aside, and a man in golden armor burst into the theater pursued by a dragon. The ladies stopped shrieking and began to cheer the hero. The gentlemen took wagers on whether the dragon or the man would win.

Two women in front of Nora ignored the dragon. They were more intent on talking about Christian.

"It's no use," one said. "He won't see me. This morning his father sent me away. Last night Roger Mortimer and that awful Inigo Culpepper slept in his room. The man has more defenders to protect the sanctity of his body than a virgin princess."

"His friends have always guarded his privacy, Jayne," the other replied.

"He wanted me not a fortnight past. What has changed

him? Do you know what he said to me? He said the only way I could have him again would be to make him a present of Jack Midnight's head. Then he'd whore for me as long as I wanted. Think you a man should treat a lady so?''

"You knew he had a viper's tongue when you sought him out. Take heart, my dear. He cast a spell over Lady Sybil and then kicked her out of his bed one night, naked into the streets. And all because he said she stank of lilac and horse sweat.''

A roar from the dragon drowned out Jayne's reply. By the time Nora was able to eavesdrop again, the two women were discussing their husbands. Sitting motionless except for her hands twisting in her lap, Nora discovered something about herself. She could boil with fury.

The lecher. He knew nothing but swilling, gulling, and carousing. He shouldn't touch her if he was going to touch someone else. By God's mercy, she wanted to reach down and yank Jayne's hair from her scalp. Balling her hands into fists, Nora eyed the top of Jayne's head. She wasn't so pretty. Christian's appetites had led him astray if he would have this skinny, buzzard-faced harlot in his bed.

The satyr. Cuckolding innocent husbands. He was fast transforming the court into his own bawdyhouse. Nora's fury overcame her. Growling, she rammed her fist into her thigh and kicked the bench in front of her, earning herself a glare from Jayne. Nora scowled back at the woman, and Jayne blinked in surprise. Then the woman's eyes narrowed, and she tried to shove Nora off her bench. Nora caught herself, cursed, and drew back her fist.

As Nora took aim at Jayne's nose, a blast from a hunting horn sounded, and a gang of men dressed in the rough wool and leather of highwaymen invaded the hall. Sliding down ropes hanging from rafters and burrowing out from under seats and tables, the brigands attacked the maskers dancing before the company, as well as the men in the audience.

One man in a leather jerkin and kid boots dropped from the air, to land at Nora's feet. Masked in black, his hair covered by a red scarf, the knave sprang up and drew his sword.

"I have the ladies!'' he yelled.

Jayne and her friend squealed, popping up from their seats to scurry away from the man. The highwayman leaped onto the bench the women had vacated and shouted for silence. Nora got on her hands and knees on the bench and eased backward to stand up. As she got to her feet, the man in front of her twisted snakelike and pointed his sword at her throat.

"Stay you, lady. I'm not weary of the sight of you yet."

The highwayman turned back to his audience. Each of his men had captured a lady and were fighting off rescuers while they backed toward their leader. As they drew nearer, Nora caught sight of Roger Mortimer charging a brigand, whooping and grinning all the while.

"Christian, you foul bawd," Roger called out, "release the ladies!" He slipped around his opponent and jumped on top of the railing that protected the first tier of seats.

In a single motion Christian swept Nora up in one arm and whirled to face Roger. "I told you I could steal them." Christian waved the tip of his sword at Roger's nose. "I have six ladies, and you lose the wager."

Nora squirmed in Christian's grip. Everyone knew it was he and his knavish friends. The wretch hadn't bothered to disguise his acrobat's body, and she would know that taunting, love-spell voice anywhere. The Duchess of Suffolk was laughing as Nora and the other women kicked and struggled to get free.

Roger groaned. "Nora Becket, you've cost me my new Barbary stallion."

"Release me," Nora said as she tried to pry herself from Christian's embrace.

He chuckled and whispered to her, "Not yet, sweeting. It's all part of the masque, you know. You must play your part. Do shriek and struggle all you want. Call out to your laughing weasel of a betrothed and beg him to rescue you from me."

She clamped her mouth shut. Christian looked down at her, grinning nastily.

"No wails and cries? Ah, well, I'll have to carry on without your help then."

Shifting his grip, he sheathed his sword and grasped the rope he'd used to leap upon the seats. Nora caught her breath and squeezed her eyes shut as he swung them out, past Roger and over the floor below. As they swung, Christian released the rope and they dropped. His feet hit the floor before her, and he caught her as she followed him down. His men followed with their captives.

As soon as she landed, Nora tried to run, but Christian grabbed her wrist and pulled her after him. He raced across the floor with his characteristic gazelle's run, heading for a giant gilt mountain that had been constructed at one end of the disguising house. She had to lift her skirts and use his momentum to keep up.

Stopping at the foot of the mountain, Christian gathered his men around him. He kept Nora beside him as he stepped forth to address the crowd of noblemen shouting amiable insults at his band of knaves.

"Good gentles," he called, "mark you that I, Kit the high-wayman, and my men have invaded your domain and captured the fairest maidens we could find. We now challenge you to contest with sword and dagger our possession of the maids. The winner shall keep the company of his maid for the rest of the masque. My good fellow, Robin Cutpurse, will take any challenger for his maid first."

Nora twisted her wrist in an effort to break free from Christian, but he held on and guided her to the rear of his band of highwaymen.

"Let go, my lord." She tried to pry his fingers loose, but to no avail.

Christian ignored her, sidling closer to the base of the gilt mountain, then slipping inside it through a leather cover painted to look like the rest of the mountain. He hauled her after him into a dark cavern.

"Papier-mâché and wood framework," he said near her ear. "All to conceal my pleasure."

In the darkness she felt his lips brush across her cheek. She gasped and turned toward him, making it easier for his mouth to search out hers. In a moment his lips teased hers and parted them. As his tongue slipped inside her mouth, she tried to grab a handful of his hair to pull him back, but her fingers found his scarf instead.

The scarf came free, and her fingers laced through soft curls. She tried to speak, but his mouth prevented it, so all that came out was a groan.

"That's it, sweeting, moan for me."

"I'm not moaning, and you must stop."

"No."

She saw the black shadow of his head duck toward her, and she turned her face so his lips grazed her cheek.

"God's teeth," he muttered.

Her feet slipped out from under her as he picked her up again. She was whirled around and then found herself on the floor before she understood what was happening. As she gathered breath for a scream, his body came down on hers.

"I'm tired of the mouse," he said against her lips. "Show me the little dragon that near devoured my mouth in the Queen's garden."

He kissed her again, and she felt him sucking at her tongue, rhythmically, in time with the slow flexing of his hips. At first she was startled by his weight and the invasion of her person, but as he continued to move with that strange, enticing cadence, her blood heated and her fears vanished. It seemed natural to kiss him back, to allow him to slip one leg, and then the other, between hers. All the while his hips thrust against her, pressing hard, raising, pressing hard again, and his tongue did the same in her mouth.

Tingling heat built in her veins, searing her breasts and invading her loins. As sensation after sensation rushed upon her, Nora breathed a sigh. She had been fighting the urge to explore Christian's body, but the tingling in her breasts and loins overpowered her shyness, and she groped for his hips. She allowed her hands to ride those pumping muscles before she lost all control and grasped his firm buttocks. As her fingers dug into his flesh through his hose, he muttered encouragement.

"Yes, feel me, touch me, sweeting. All of me." He ran his tongue down her neck to her breasts and nipped at her bare flesh. "Say you'll come to my bed, sweeting. I can't take you here."

Her eyes popped open. "Oh, dear."

"I want you."

"Oh." Nora's desire vanished. "Oh. No."

"Yes." He slipped his fingers beneath the neck of her gown and down the cleft between her breasts. "Give me your promise."

"You don't like me," she said. She wriggled and shoved at

his chest. "Lord Montfort, you don't like me. Please don't do this."

He lifted his head. "Who told you I dislike you?"

"No one. You're cruel to mock me, saying I'm a pretty maid when I'm so plain, and making a spectacle of me in front of everyone."

"S'blood! Why do you think you're plain?"

"Father says—"

"Falseness. Do you think I devote myself to seducing ugly women?"

"But—"

"Come to my bed and I'll show you how beautiful you are. Come." He thrust his hips against hers again as he spoke. "Come, come, come to me."

"Don't." The word was a drawn-out wail. "You're unfair, my lord, to tease me so when I must betroth myself."

"Flegge is worms' meat on legs. Cast him aside, for I'll couple with you if I have to kill him to do it."

Startled, Nora began to struggle again. "No, sweeting," Christian whispered. "I'm sorry I frightened you, but you're driving me to madness, and we don't have much time. And by the by, I don't couple with anyone I don't like."

"But you're cruel," she repeated.

"I'm not cruel in bed."

She groaned and pounded a fist against his chest. "Don't you listen? Percivale Flegge."

"Cast him aside."

"I can't. Father has chosen him for me. And it's terrible, because I hate his—"

"Laugh. The fool laughs like a demented peacock. And his soul is three parts cesspool and one part jade. Deny him."

"I can't." She swallowed a sob. To be aroused by a man who seemed to want to spend the whole evening resting atop her body while half the court jeered and whooped a few yards away was agony.

"You can," Christian said. "I've seen you deny a ruffian for less reason. Look you, I'll arrange for you to meet both your father and Flegge during the dancing. I'll conceal myself nearby and lend aid. You can do this, sweeting. You must learn to defend yourself."

"But Father—"

"He will admire your hearty stomach."

She shook her head. "I don't think so."

"He will. You'll see, and you can thank me later tonight."

"Oh, no."

"Come," he said, lifting his body off hers. "We must leave our cavern or we'll be missed. It's almost time for me to fight to possess you, and I need something to take my thoughts from the ache beneath my codpiece."

He gently pushed her out of the mountain. She stumbled forth, blinking in the light of dozens of torches. John St. Vincent was hacking away at Robin Cutpurse for the hand of his betrothed. No one noticed her as she crept forward, followed by Christian. He took her hand and escorted her to the front of the crowd that surrounded the pair of fencers. As the match ended, Nora pressed her hands to her burning cheeks in an attempt to cool them. So flustered was she, she missed Christian's challenge until she heard her name on his lips. He had challenged Percivale Flegge, since Flegge had shown no desire to challenge him.

Nora watched Flegge step from the crowd to face Christian. Catcalls and taunts rained down upon the two men, but Flegge smiled and raised his voice.

"Alas, good gentles, I must decline, for I am recovering from a terrible ague that has kept me from court these long months and have yet to regain my strength."

A host's smile upon his lips, Christian bowed to Flegge, but Nora heard the words Christian spoke low enough for only the three of them to hear.

"Dear Flegge, God grant you succor in your weakness. I am befuddled, though. How is it that you can marry and yield your fleshly sword but can't ply the one in your scabbard?"

Flegge's complexion turned to blotches of red and white, and his hand moved in the direction of his sword. Christian remained still, appearing unconcerned at the threat. His catlike gaze caressed Flegge's mottled features, and he smiled a smile of open good humor. Christian's composure was nearly Flegge's undoing. He touched the hilt of his sword. Christian began to shove Nora away from him when Roger jumped between the two men with a challenge of his own. They were quickly surrounded by Christian's knaves and herded to opposite ends of the circle formed by the guests. Percivale Flegge disappeared.

The duel was swift and difficult to follow, for the two moved with the quickness of adders. It seemed to Nora that she glanced away for only a second, and when she looked back, Christian was standing over Roger, his swordtip pressing into the velvet of his friend's doublet. Roger moaned and bewailed the loss of a pretty maid on top of his best stallion, and loudly cried out for some kind lady to comfort him. Plump Mistress Mary Wentworth scurried to his side and crushed him to her breast, to the enthusiastic cheers of highwaymen and nobles alike.

Christian put up his sword and took possession of Nora's hand again. He addressed the guests. "Good gentles, now that our quarrel is settled, it is time to seek refreshment and dance."

Nora looked about. She saw her father standing at the edge of the crowd, scowling at her. Flegge lurked at his side, evidently considering himself safe in her father's company. Guilt crept over Nora, but the warmth of Christian's hand surrounding hers lent her courage. God wouldn't want her to marry a fool and a coward. Perhaps He had sent Lord Montfort to teach her the virtue of courage. She would be brave and refuse Percivale Flegge. With Christian there to guide her, she could convince her father that marriage with Flegge was wrong. However, Christian was mistaken if he thought she was fool enough to believe his aid worth her virginity.

Nora smiled to herself. She might be a mouse, but she was by no means a stupid mouse. It was time Christian de Rivers learned that lesson.

Chapter VII

Christian bowed to Lady Jayne, who curtsied according to the moves of the pavane they were dancing. Having returned to the great hall with his guests, he'd been captured by the woman and forced to partner her or appear rude. Jayne tried to burn him with her eyes, but he was distracted by the sight of Nora pacing by with her father. He had had to give her up to Becket. One couldn't refuse a maid's own father, but if he weren't careful Flegge would try to steal her again.

"The disguising house."

He glanced down at Jayne. "What?"

"Meet me at the disguising house."

"Do you have Jack Midnight's head in a bag beneath your skirt?"

"Of course not."

"Then tender me no invitations."

Jayne dug her fingernail into the skin of his palm. "Foul urchin, you're bored with me already, are you not?"

"Cease gouging my flesh at once, or I'll step on the hem of your own gown and your breasts will pop out of their mooring."

Releasing Christian's hand, Jayne did a stately prance in a circle, then returned to him. They began to pace forward once more.

"Such lewd suggestions, my lord. It must be all those years you spent with Midnight that turned you into a ruthless bawd."

He scowled at her. "God's teeth, you're aroused."

"That's what you wanted, wasn't it?"

Bowing as the music ended, Christian shook his head. "Go away." Giving Jayne no time to protest, he slipped past her to catch up with the retreating Nora and her father.

As he reached the pair, Flegge appeared and snatched Nora's hand. Pressing it to his lips, he begged for a dance. Flegge was about to kiss her hand again, but Christian shoved his own hand beneath the descending mouth and grasped Nora's. Flegge jerked his head back, glaring at Christian.

"I told you, Sir Percivale," Christian said, "Nora Becket's company is forfeit to me and me alone, saving her father." He bowed to William.

Before Flegge or William could reply, Christian hustled Nora away to take up a position among the dancers for another pavane.

"Look what you've done," Nora said as she swayed along beside him. "Father is furious."

"Don't quiver so. He's only a little irked. If you nearly faint at the thought of annoying him, how are you going to tell him you're not marrying the fatuous Flegge?"

"I can't tell him that."

"Yes, you can."

"No, I can't. That's why I'm dressed this way." Abruptly, she frowned and pursed her lips.

"What mean you? You're turning red." Christian stared at the delightful flush, then chuckled. "So that's what convinced you to take my advice and uncover yourself. Fear of Flegge has made you bold."

"Please, my lord. It isn't charitable of you to tease me when I'm so desperate."

"Gather up your courage and tell your father you won't marry Flegge."

"I can't. Father would cast me out. He said so."

"Idle threats. All you need do is stand firm. Once he sees

that you won't change your mind, your father will admire your spirit. Men like women of stomach and valor.''

''But—''

''Bow, Nora.''

She bowed and gave Christian her hand as the dance came to a close.

''My lord.''

''I'm going to help you.''

''But I can't.''

''Yes, you can, if I'm there to give you solace. I'll send your father to the library in a few minutes. When I nod at you, you must leave and meet us there. I'll stand behind the arras in front of the northern door. You stay near it, and I can talk to you without being perceived.''

''What will I say?''

''Tell him you won't marry Flegge, lackwit.'' He escorted Nora to a place near the Duchess of Suffolk's chair. As he turned to leave her, she grabbed his arm.

''I'll never be able to do it,'' she whispered.

''Do you know where the library is?''

''Yes, but I don't think this is a good idea.''

''I'll warn the guards to expect you so that you aren't stopped.''

Ignoring Nora's anxious look, Christian set about finding Becket and directing him to the library on the excuse that the earl wanted a private word with him. To Christian's annoyance, Flegge attached himself to Becket's side and accompanied the older man out of the hall.

God's teeth, Christian thought. Nora could hardly face her father. Having Flegge there, too, would send her into a fit. He glanced around the hall in search of Nora. She was still planted beside the Duchess, but she looked too calm to have seen Flegge leave with her father. Christian nodded to her. She pursed her lips, swallowed, and excused herself to the Duchess.

Leaving his father to play host alone, Christian took a circuitous path through the scullery and kitchens to reach the chamber next to the library. There was a connecting door between the room and the library, and an arras hung in the small entryway that joined them. Christian slipped through the entryway and peered into the library by the gap between the arras and the door frame.

Flegge and Becket stood next to a table in the middle of the room, inspecting the shelves of books. Christian ground his teeth together upon sighting Flegge. The man looked like a fox anticipating making a meal of some unsuspecting chicken.

"And so we agree on the settlement?" Flegge asked.

"I'll have my clerk draw up the documents tomorrow."

"You're sure your daughter won't mind forfeiting her dower house or the income from her lands in Norfolk?"

"You've met Nora. Biddable, that's what she is. Why, I can't remember a time when she disobeyed me. Give her a few pets and some books, and she's happy."

"I'll give her babes, my lord. My family wants issue from this union quickly."

Becket shifted from one foot to the other. "Where is the earl? It's not like him to keep a friend waiting."

Christian backed away from the arras and looked down at his hand in surprise, for it was wrapped tightly around the hilt of his dagger. He didn't remember drawing the weapon.

"S'blood," he whispered.

Fading away, he stalked from chamber to chamber in search of Nora. If she didn't hurry, Becket would have her married that night, so eager was the man to rid himself of his daughter.

His search took him down a gallery and out onto a back landing. Only one candle had been lit there, and he searched the darkness for a glimpse of Nora's white gown.

"Oh, dear."

The words floated up to him from the bottom of the stairs.

"Nora?"

"My lord? I'm lost."

"Marry, lady, I know that. You're almost in the cellar." Christian cursed under his breath as he realized what he'd said. "Hold! Nora, stay where you are. Don't go any farther."

Snatching the candle from its sconce on the wall, Christian charged down the stairs to the first sharp turn. There Nora stood, skirts gathered in both hands, blinking at him.

"Your father is waiting," he said.

"Ahhh!"

Nora jumped and dashed behind Christian, then peered down the stairs into darkness.

"What was that?" she asked.

"Nothing. Probably servants at my ale kegs again." Christian turned and began shoving her up the stairs in front of him.

"Eeeeh."

"God's sacred body," Christian said as old Tom Birch whizzed up the stairs beside him. "Get you gone, crackbrain."

Christian lifted a foot to kick the lackwitted heretic, but Tom shrank against a wall and shook his head so vigorously, his beard seemed to take flight.

"Rats, my lord. Rats as big as dogs be living down there."

Moving to stand in front of the curious Nora, Christian grabbed the neck of Tom's gown and lifted the smaller man off his feet. Controlling his rage, Christian spoke quietly, yet Tom cringed.

"Get your puling carcass below or I'll mince your flesh for a pasty." Christian dropped his victim, and Tom scuttled backward, his mouth working noiselessly. He stumbled back down the stairs.

Nora poked her head around Christian's shoulder. "Who was that?"

"A lazy old minion of my father's."

"He didn't look like a servant."

"Father spoils old Tom with gifts of clothing and an allowance because Tom had charge of him when he was a child. Hurry. Your father may be gone by now."

He urged her up the stairs again, giving her no chance to ponder old Tom. Christian was going to get rid of those thrice-cursed heretics upon the morrow. He was lucky it was only Nora who'd seen Tom.

They reached the library door. Christian left Nora there and crept into position behind the arras. By the time he got there, Nora was in the room. She stood huddled against the door as if she were a deer cornered by wolves. Since Becket and Flegge had their backs to him, Christian parted the arras and beckoned to Nora. In her panic she'd forgotten to stand near him.

Her eyes widened when she saw him peer out from behind the tapestry, and she stuttered in her greeting of Flegge. Christian slipped back behind the cloth and watched her walk around her father and come toward him, wringing her hands.

"Sir Percivale has consented to the betrothal," Becket was saying. "We will sign the contracts tomorrow."

Flegge began a courtly address to Nora that sent Christian's hand groping for his dagger again. And Nora stood silent. Christian scowled at her back through the slim gap of the two halves of the arras, then jabbed her ribs with his finger. She squeaked, but only he heard her. Still she said nothing, and Flegge progressed to the crimsom beauty of her cheeks. From the smirk on his face, Christian knew he wasn't talking about Nora's face. He poked her again. Nora stuttered, but Flegge ignored her and continued his address.

Christian put his lips close to the arras and hissed at her, "Speak up."

Silence.

"Tell him."

Nothing.

Neither Flegge nor Becket were looking at Nora. In desperation, Christian reached and pinched her bottom.

"Oh!" She jumped and thrust her hands behind her back.

Flegge paused in his discourse. Becket looked up from the book he was studying, and both men stared at Nora.

Christian cupped a hand to his mouth and whispered, "I do not wish for this betrothal."

"I do not wish for this betrothal," Nora said.

Flegge's mouth went slack, and he turned to Becket.

Roaring his daughter's name, Becket pounded his fist on the table. "You must be possessed. You would deny my word? By God, I'll teach you obedience."

Nora gasped and took a step back from her father as he stalked around the table to stand beside Flegge.

Again Christian whispered, "I won't marry Percivale Flegge."

"I w-won't—"

This time Becket's roar made even Flegge cringe. It sent Nora farther back into the arras, and Christian had to steady her with a hand against her back. He couldn't see anything with her so close, but he could hear her stuttering protest and Becket's curses.

"You'll obey me or suffer for it," Becket said. "I'll give you this night to contemplate your sin before I beat some virtue into your dimwitted skull."

To Christian's alarm, Becket grasped Nora by the arm and thrust her out of the room. He apologized to Flegge, muttered something about finding out what had happened to the earl, and left. Christian was about to leave as well to find Nora, when he heard Flegge growl.

"A pox on it," the man said to himself. "What a man must endure for the sake of gold and an heir."

Christian lifted the arras and stepped into the library. "Methinks you'd avoid any mention of the pox."

Flegge whirled around to face Christian.

"What do you here, Montfort?"

"This is my house," Christian replied. "I can't take a moment's respite from a host's duties without coming upon disputations and discord."

Puffing up his chest, Flegge began to circle around Christian like a fencer looking for an opponent's weakness. "You were spying."

"What makes you think you can father an heir? You've never begotten so much as one whelp on any of your whores."

"You presume to concern yourself with my affairs?"

Christian took no notice of the circling Flegge. He rested his hips on a table and leaned back, contemplating a bookstand.

"You make bold with an innocent like Nora Becket," he said, "when you'd do better to mate with a woman whose appetites match your own." He finally stabbed Flegge with his glance, and the man paused. " 'Forgo your dream, poor fool of love.' "

Flegge planted himself in front of Christian. Crossing his arms over his chest, he jeered at the younger man. "I'll marry where I list."

Thrusting his body upright, Christian curled one hand around the neck of Flegge's brocaded doublet while placing his other hand on the hilt of his dagger.

"Marry Nora Becket and I'll send you to hell much sooner than you'd wish."

Flegge tugged at Christian's fist and snarled. "Get your foul hands from me, Montfort. I know your game. You want her for yourself, and haven't been able to seduce her yet. Becket's offer is ill-timed for your schemes. You want her for yourself.''

Flegge succeeded in freeing his doublet because Christian suddenly dropped it. He turned away to stroll idly over to the bookstand. He flipped through a few pages of the Greek text resting there as he spoke.

"Say rather that I don't want you to have her."

"You'd have me believe you've turned virtue's champion after years of teaching the most jaded lords in the kingdom new sins?" Flegge snorted. "There is naught so vile as a jade masquerading as a saint. If you're going to cultivate a virtue, Montfort, try honesty. Admit that your cock is leading your brain and you can't endure the thought of anyone else having what you want."

Closing the book, Christian spread his hands out flat on the leather backing. He could hear Flegge's breathing, labored from his prancing around the room. It was the only sound in the library. Without turning around to face Flegge, Christian jerked his head in the direction of the door.

"Get out."

"I want your word that you'll leave Nora be."

"Begone, you simpleminded grub, before I decide to cut out your tongue and make you eat it."

Christian waited until he heard the door close before lifting his hands from the book. They were shaking with the fury that threatened to consume him. What ailed everyone? His father, Flegge, even Inigo Culpepper accused him of being besotted. He held up his right hand and watched it tremble. Balling it into a fist, he struggled to deny the urge to fly after Percivale Flegge and beat the man until his bones turned to sand.

Christian was honest with himself. He'd never denied wanting Nora, so why was everyone treating him as if he'd lost his wits? God's teeth, he'd seduced women before. True, none was like Nora. No one was like Nora—timid yet possessed of a secret strength; all milk skin and blush-rose cheeks, yet humble and unaware of her charm. Groaning, Christian leaned on the bookstand and rested his forehead on his arm. He was dwelling on a maid's charms like a randy and infatuated schoolboy. And he'd never been infatuated in his whole twenty-six years.

"Beshrew her," he muttered. "All I want is a little dalliance."

He let himself out of the library, intending to check on his father's pet heretics before rejoining the festivities. At the head of the stairs leading to the cellar, he encountered the earl. Sebastian had one foot on the first step when Christian reached him.

"I came to tell you the guards just stopped Luiz de Ateca from leaving the hall," Sebastian said. "He claimed he was going in search of Nora Becket for the Duchess, but he was headed for the kitchens." Sebastian waited for Christian's reply. "Chris? Christian!"

"Yes, sire."

"Did you hear what I said about de Ateca?"

"Yes, sire, but he can't get belowstairs. Culpepper stands guard with a few goodly men."

Sebastian threw up his hands. "Culpepper. You might as well set Morris dancers to guard as him and his band. Oh, leave that for now. We must return to the hall. But I wanted to tell you that Cecil has sent a warning that rumors concerning his activities are reaching the Queen through Bonner. We are to be cautious and wait a while longer to move Tom and the others."

Linking arms with his father, Christian headed back toward the hall with him. Worry about Nora receded as his thoughts pursued secret avenues and navigated the Byzantine intrigues of court and kingdom.

Christian needed to find out what Bonner knew, yet none of the old priests and nobles who were continually in the man's company would trust him. There was de Ateca, but the Spaniard knew of Christian's antipathy toward him. Were Christian suddenly to become friendly, he would invite suspicion, and unwanted advances as well. Who could approach de Ateca?

"My headstrong, you're not listening to me."

"Forgive me, sire. I was thinking about de Ateca."

"I said you haven't been as clever as you thought in your games with Nora Becket. What did you do to Percivale Flegge? He's fled. Skittered out of the house as though running from the watch."

Christian clenched his jaw and met his father's gaze. "I told him not to marry her. He's not good enough."

"That may be true, but her father has chosen him for the girl, and it is her duty to accept him." Sebastian forestalled his son's protest with a raised hand. "You're no more suited for Nora than Flegge. She needs a gentle, kind man, and—as I love you, my headstrong—you are neither gentle nor kind."

"Mayhap you're right, but all I'm trying to do is strengthen her backbone. She needs a little meanness stuffed into that sweet body." Christian stopped walking and turned to his father. "If there is one thing Jack Midnight taught me, it's that weakness invites cruelty and strength commands respect. The day I struck back was the day he stopped beating me."

"You can't make Nora Becket into something she is not. No, we won't speak of it further. I forbid you to interfere in this betrothal. And don't scowl at me, young baggage. I have to attend the Duchess, and I want to do so knowing I have your promise to leave off."

"I can't give it."

"We'll see about that," Sebastian said.

"Yes, sire."

Christian frowned as his father walked away from him. He watched Sebastian enter the hall through a service door, then cursed his bad luck when Lady Jayne winnowed her way through it and shut it behind her.

"Trapped," Christian said to himself.

Jayne had that look of a determined mule that he'd grown to dread. Then she surprised him with a smile.

"There you are," she said. "I've been sent on a quest by the Duchess. She wants to see that basilisk costume from the last performance. And she wants to hire your costumemaker. I told her you always refuse to reveal his identity, but she thinks she can persuade you."

"I haven't time to parade costumes," Christian said.

"Very well. I'll hunt for it myself."

"No." He blocked her path. "They're probably all still in the disguising house. This way."

As he led Jayne back through the hall on their way to the disguising house, he searched for Nora Becket among the dancers and merrymakers. He found her in a corner, staring down at Roger Mortimer as the nobleman bent low over her hand. She was casting wet-eyed glances of unhappiness at her father until

Roger kissed her hand. Eyes round with astonishment, she burst into laughter as Roger clutched his breast in imitation of heart-sick ardor. Her laughter jolted through Christian's body, and he stopped so suddenly, Jayne bumped into him. Nora never laughed like that for him.

"I am not besotted."

"What?" Jayne asked.

Christian deliberately turned his back on the laughing couple and bowed toward Jayne. When he straightened, a slow, indolent smile spread across his lips.

Jayne caught her breath. "Indeed, my lord, you are capricious with your favor."

"You don't want my favors?"

"Oh, I want them."

Saying nothing more, Christian threaded his way through the crowd in the hall and out into the courtyard that separated the house from the disguising hall. Jayne stuck fast to his side, clinging to his arm. She waited only until a unicorn fountain was between them and the house to dig in her heels and tug him so that he fell against her. She wrapped her arms around his neck and pulled his head down for a kiss. Her lips pressed against his, then she nipped at them with her teeth between whispers.

"You're not teasing me, are you?"

Christian shivered as she nibbled on his neck and sucked at the skin at the base of his throat. "No."

"I won't have to pay you with some ruffian's head?" Her fingers skittered to the fastenings of his doublet.

He tore his lips from hers. "Damn you, don't speak of Midnight." He sucked in a deep breath, for Jayne's wandering fingers had discovered his codpiece. Grabbing her hand, he held it away from his groin. "Harlot, wait until we're inside."

Jayne complied, refraining from touching him again until he shut the door to the tiring room that held boxes and trunks of costumes. The fantastic raiment of that night's masque lay discarded in heaps about the place. The head of a hobby horse rested atop the silver and green dragon's body.

Turning from closing the door, Christian found that Jayne had snatched up the costume of a fairy princess. It was a gossamer thing of white shot with gold. Of a sudden, the glittering piece turned to silk with black trimmings, and the image of Nora's rose and cream body filled the garment. He was back on a garden bench, pressing a trembling body beneath him, seeking entrance. . . .

"Put it down," he said in a quiet voice.

Jayne froze, and the costume dropped to the floor. Christian watched it pool like sunlit water before he turned away.

"You've changed again," Jayne said. "It's not fair. I had you before that simple goose Nora Becket caught your eye. My claim is the better. And besides, everyone knows she's going to marry Percivale Flegge."

Bending over a pile of regalia, Christian lifted a mask to his face. It was of a falcon. Gilded feathers swept back to reveal slits for his eyes. The beak jutted out, gold and hard over his own nose.

He fastened the band at the back of his head and moved his neck in imitation of the sharp, swift movement of the bird. The mask ended below his nose, leaving uncovered his mouth and chin. He raised his arms like wings and hissed like an angered falcon. He swooped at Jayne, toppling her onto a pile of dresses.

She giggled, but left off when Christian didn't speak to her. Breasts heaving, she studied him as if trying to discover his mood. Christian kept his weight on top of her and held her gaze with his while he yanked at the laces of her gown.

"The mask," she said. "I can't see your eyes."

He jerked hard at the bodice of her gown, and it ripped, parting to reveal her breasts. They were heaving with her agitated breathing. Still staring into her eyes, Christian covered one of them with his hand. He did nothing else.

Jayne squirmed, but he pressed his hips down over hers and held her still. Propped up on one arm, he could see her growing arousal, and smiled.

"Take off your clothes," she said.

Heedless of her words, he pulled at the already loosened laces at his groin. When Jayne saw what he was about, she cursed and bucked, but his weight was too great.

"No," she said. "I want you naked."

His smile grew malicious as he jerked skirts and stiffened petticoats up to Jayne's waist, then lowered himself between her legs. He was hard put not to groan when his swollen flesh nudged her loins. His smile faded, and he trapped Jayne's arms with his own. She had abandoned her protests and was gazing into his eyes.

"Take off the mask," she whispered. "Do you hear me? Say something."

He stared down at her, trying to force himself to go on, while a nasty little voice droned in his head, *It's not Nora. Not the one you want. Not Nora, not Nora, not Nora, not Nora.* Nearly crying out in angry frustration, he flung himself away from Jayne. Rolling onto his back, he tore the mask off and threw his arm over his eyes.

"God's mercy," he said.

Jayne had scrambled to her feet and was struggling to right her clothes while viciously cursing him.

"You dare treat me like this?" she said in a dangerously low voice.

He moved his arm and looked up at her. He was still too stunned by his own actions to care much about her. "I treat you as you allow yourself to be treated," he said.

Her eyes narrowed, and he tensed, thinking for a moment she might hurl herself at him. But she only whirled away and stomped from the room, leaving him alone with his unquenched lust and his disquieting thoughts of Nora.

Chapter
VIII

Christian de Rivers kept heretics in his cellar.

Nora rested her chin on her fist and pretended to watch the Queen's gentlemen pensioners play at bowls. While all the ladies cooed over the players, Nora tried to make sense of the previous night's tempest. Too many things had happened at once, and she was confused.

The discovery that shocked her the most was that the man she had thought a selfish and cruel dissolute was trying to save old men's lives. The rat man was Tom Birch. She knew because Bishop Bonner had posted his likeness throughout the kingdom, along with that of Archibald Dymoke and John Pecksmith. The three were heretics wanted for composing and distributing treasonous billets calling for the people to depose Mary and put Elizabeth on the throne to save England from popery. If Bonner caught them, all three would be hanged, drawn, and quartered. She would have to write a cipher telling Cecil this news.

Dear God, if Christian was captured with those men, he would be tortured to death, too. She swallowed the bile that rose in her throat as she pictured Christian stripped, hanged, then cut down alive and his bowels sliced out while he still lived. Dear

God. Nora pressed her fingertips to her mouth. She couldn't think about it anymore. She would warn Cecil. Cecil would take care of Christian.

It was too late to stop her revulsion, though. She had thought of the punishment for treason, and images of the gory acts forced themselves upon her. She squeezed her eyes shut. The brightness of the afternoon sun made her see red shadows that reminded her of blood. God's mercy, what would she do if Christian de Rivers were arrested? If he died, she would never be able to . . .

What was she thinking? Her eyes popped open, but she didn't see the bowling green. She saw Christian's violet eyes, their corners crinkling with mirth. They changed and took on that rabid-wolf look she'd learned meant he wanted to touch her. By God's mercy, she loved him.

But he didn't love her. He thought her a lackwitted coward. No stomach, he said. He only tried to seduce her to be perverse. Mayhap he wanted to shock the court by turning her from a sparrow into a swan.

Something tugged at her skirt. It was Arthur. Everyone was standing and applauding the gentlemen pensioners. Nora scrambled to her feet and clapped a few times, then trailed after the Queen's ladies with Arthur at her side. On the pretense of going to her chamber, she took Arthur and slipped away to hide in a grove of yew trees on the palace grounds. She wanted to compose a cipher about the three heretics, and needed secrecy.

Arthur trotted along beside her carrying a basket of embroidery threads and writing materials. They settled beneath the trees, and she set Arthur to separating threads into colors while she wrote on a small piece of paper. Her latest cipher from Cecil had contained instructions to insert the paper inside a large, hollow silver bead.

"Mistress," Arthur said, "are you going to marry Sir Percivale Flegge?"

She glanced at Arthur, her spirits dropping even farther at the mention of Flegge. "My father has decided that I will. What's wrong, chuck? You look unhappy."

Arthur screwed up his mouth, and his small hands twisted a skein of thread into knots. "Sir Percivale, he doesn't like me."

"What did you do, Arthur?"

"Nothing, mistress. An accident it was. When he arrived

at the banquet, you know I was helping with the cloaks." Arthur began kicking at a dead tree branch. "His was too long, and he threw it at me, and it landed on my head. I couldn't see and I tried to get out of it. It wasn't my fault," Arthur cried. "I couldn't see, and I had to get the cloak off my head, so I shoved it and it came off. Only it landed on Sir Percivale's legs as he was walking away."

Arthur jabbed at the branch with his heel and grunted. Nora could see unshed tears in his eyes, but she hesitated to offer comfort. Arthur hated it if he thought she was cosseting him.

"He fell on his face," Arthur said. "And when he got up, he tried to hit me, but Lord Montfort came between us and said something to Sir Percivale in Latin that made him turn red and make noises like a bubbling stew. Lord Montfort sent me to the kitchens to eat marchpane and told me to stay there until it was time to go."

"That mean, petty, bullying"—Nora searched her mind for a disgusting epithet—"cankerworm."

Arthur gawked at her as she thrust the completed cipher in the pocket of her gown and set pen and ink aside. The thought of Flegge hurting Arthur ignited her temper as no injustice to herself could. She jumped to her feet and paced about the grove.

"Disgusting," she said. "Disgusting habits, disgusting laugh, mean spirit. I don't care if his family is ancient and his appearance pleasing." She stopped in front of Arthur, but she wasn't paying attention to the startled boy. "I don't want him. I want . . ." She stumbled over the basket of embroidery threads and kicked it. "Oh, merciful Father in Heaven." She pressed her palms to her temples and groaned. "It's impossible, but I want . . ."

"Want what, mistress?"

She recovered and shook her head. "Nothing. Help me pick up all these threads."

Kneeling amid the bright strands, Nora tried to hide her agitation from Arthur. The exhilaration of love's discovery sent shivers through her body. Longing grew until she ached with it. What was she going to do? He'd never love her. He was too beautiful, too blessed with wit and grace, and possessed of more charm than a siren. As changeable as light, as mysterious as the motions of the stars, he was as dangerous to try to capture as a wolf. One might succeed, but was certain to get hurt in the catching.

"Arthur," Nora said. She studied the boy kneeling amid the crimson, gold, and silver threads. "Arthur, do you like Lord Montfort?"

The page dumped a handful of threads and leaves into the basket. "I didn't at first, mistress, but after he saved me from Sir Percivale, I changed my mind. And after all, he is part thief, and he promised to show me how to cut a purse from a fat merchant."

"He did, did he? Well, don't think I'm going to allow such knavery. I'll speak to Lord Montfort and make sure he doesn't show you at all."

"Mistress!"

"I will allow him to take you to a fencing school, though."

Arthur's face transformed into a sunburst. So excited that his body wriggled in several directions at once, he danced circles around Nora all the way back to her room. While Arthur enjoyed the prospect of seeing a fencing master, Nora grew more and more apprehensive.

How was she going to avoid marrying Percivale Flegge? She was so ashamed of her failure to defy her father. After all Christian's efforts to help her, when Father had yelled, she'd crumbled. And Christian had been there to see her fail. Another humiliation in front of him. It seemed that whenever they met, she made a fool of herself.

She so longed for him to admire her. Now that she knew he hated cruelty as she did, hated fanatics who committed atrocities in the name of religion as she did, she yearned to share more with him. They could fight for Princess Elizabeth together. Mayhap if he knew she was brave enough to send ciphers to William Cecil, he would realize that she wasn't a mouse. But she couldn't tell him.

Still in her whirlwind of confusion, Nora took the basket from Arthur, dismissed him, and headed for the privy garden where she always left her messages. It was almost the hour after midday, one of the appointed times for her to leave messages. She avoided the Queen's private chambers, slipping quietly through the throngs of courtiers and petitioners who clustered about the palace. Thinking herself unobserved, she had her hand on the latch of a door that led to the wing of the palace nearest the garden, when someone called her name. Luiz de Ateca.

"Have I frightened you, Mistress Becket?" he asked, gliding up to her.

She curtsied to de Ateca and shook her head.

"That is good," he said, "because I would like to speak to you."

He offered his arm, and Nora had no choice but to shift her basket to one hand and place the other on the damask sleeve of the Spanish nobleman. He escorted her to a window seat in a chamber set aside for card playing. Groups of courtiers were gaming there, but none took notice of the newcomers. De Ateca waited for Nora to sit, then leaned over her, bracing his shoulder on the wall beside her. Cut off from the rest of the room by his body, Nora could only wait for him to say what he wished. She prayed he spoke quickly, for she didn't have much time left.

"The earl's banquet was magnificent, was it not?" de Ateca said. "Except for the typical English lack of decorum, that is."

Nora hesitated before answering, for de Ateca's English was heavily accented. Once she had translated "bonket" and "mog-neefeeceent," she hastened to agree with him. She'd agree to anything to avoid irking one of King Philip's chief henchmen. De Ateca smiled at her, and she couldn't help comparing the man to a well-dressed lizard. His face was shaped like the wedge of an orange, his body thin and supple. Blond hair as straight as his legs, light blue eyes, and pale skin all lent an air of asceticism to the man, but this effect was offset by the ruby and gold opulence of his dress.

Her body growing cold, Nora regarded de Ateca warily. He'd never spoken to her much before, and now he was bestowing upon her an executioner's smile, one that said he would be happy to wield the ax that chopped through her neck.

"By the rood, mistress," he continued after a long pause, "the whole court buzzes with the suspicion that the fabulous Kit has conceived a passion for you."

"My lord, it cannot be. These are foolish tales."

"I think not. For if they were foolish, you wouldn't blush and cast down your eyes with maiden shamefacedness." De Ateca's gaze sliced up and down Nora's figure. "It hasn't been Lord Montfort's wont, this yearning after maidens."

"He doesn't yearn after me, my lord."

"Yet he calls you fairest of maids before the court and fights for your company."

"All of that was but pretense, a jest and wager made between Lord Montfort and Roger Mortimer."

"I think not."

Nora gave de Ateca a blank look. She could think of nothing to say.

De Ateca rubbed his fingertips over the rubies that studded the gold chain across his shoulders. "Great misfortune could befall a woman who attaches herself to a man as wild as Lord Montfort. Not a thought will he give to your virtue or your future. Take heed, mistress."

"I've done nothing," Nora said, but de Ateca wasn't listening to her.

He was looking across the room. Nora watched his eyes widen, then narrow. His hand twisted in the gold links of his chain before he made an obvious effort to control his reaction. He freed his hand and put it behind him. It was then that Nora searched the room for the object of the man's fascination.

Christian de Rivers was strolling around the chamber with another young man. Introducing his companion as he went, he paused by a group of card players, bending and kissing the hand of the lady who had the most gold coins before her. When he straightened, the lady shrieked, for her coins were gone. Christian held his arms away from his body and chuckled.

"I protest my innocence, Lady Marjorie," he said. "Marry, you may search for your coins upon my person if it will satisfy you."

Another lady said, "Faith, Marjorie, if you won't, I will. Come, hellion, and let me search. I promise to be most thorough."

Lady Marjorie needed no help, however. She leaped up from her cushions and began to run her hands over Christian's torso. His companion stood by with a bored expression on his face, yet wasn't quite able to conceal his shock when Lady Marjorie's hands wandered to the insides of Christian's thighs. The room grew silent as everyone waited to see who would falter, Lady Marjorie or her victim.

In the end it was neither, for Luiz de Ateca walked over to

Christian, grasped his arm, and shook it. Gold coins rained from his sleeve, hitting the floor and scattering in all directions. Christian had gone still when de Ateca approached, his eyes engaging in a duel with the Spaniard. He twisted out of de Ateca's grip while the card players hooted at Lady Marjorie.

"Be of good cheer, Marjorie," one gentleman said between chuckles. "I'll purloin your money if you promise to hunt for it in a like manner."

Nora remained on the window seat, watching the merry-makers. She had been about to hurl her basket at Lady Marjorie's head when de Ateca moved. Unaccustomed to the rage that had boiled inside her when the woman touched Christian, she sat in silence, furious with everyone who made light of such wantonness, furious most of all with Christian de Rivers. All worry over missing her appointed time for leaving messages vanished. He ought not to tempt women with his body. Who could blame them if they succumbed? She knew how hard it was to refrain from touching him.

For once her anger burgeoned so great that she forgot herself. Nora hopped to her feet, squeezing her hands tightly on the handle of her basket, and marched toward Christian. They met halfway across the room, for Christian had swerved away from Luiz de Ateca like a sparrow hawk dodging an eagle, and was headed in her direction.

He bowed, then stepped closer for his kiss of greeting. "Well met, my sweet marchpane."

"Lewdness deserves no kiss of greeting, my lord."

Inclining his head to one side, Christian pursed his lips and whistled low. "She does notice. I thought I might have to ride through the palace naked on a black stallion to find out."

"Allowing that woman to paw you."

"Have you met my cousin from the North country?"

"In front of the court."

"Where did he go?" Christian craned his neck to search the groups of courtiers behind them.

"She would have put her hands on your—your . . ."

Christian waved at his companion and turned back to Nora. "Body, sweeting. The word you want is body. It will suffice, because I know you won't say cock."

She tilted her chin up and piously quoted the Bible to him.

" 'They that are after the flesh do mind the things of the flesh; but they that are after the Spirit the things of the Spirit. For to be carnally minded is death.' "

Throwing back his head, Christian laughed. It was a sound Nora usually enjoyed, but she only scowled at him this time. If Luiz de Ateca hadn't joined them, she would have given Christian more of her opinions.

"Mistress Becket and I were conversing when you burst upon us, my lord," de Ateca said.

He made a slight bow in Christian's direction. As he did so, Christian's cousin appeared. Nora studied the brown-haired stranger, taking in his long legs and young-old eyes. Absently she acknowledged Christian's introduction.

"This is my cousin, Lord Richard Fitzwalter."

The young man lifted his brows at the sound of his name and bowed to Nora and de Ateca. As he bent, his cloak, which he wore slung over one shoulder, swung out to reveal an ornate silver dagger at his side. It glinted in a beam of sunlight, hurting Nora's eyes, and she gasped.

"Blade," she said.

"God's teeth, you remembered," Christian said. He snatched her basket from her, took both of her hands, and planted a kiss on her cheek. While his face was close to hers, he whispered, "Please, sweeting, quiet."

Only interested in distancing herself from Blade, Nora skittered around to Christian's other side while de Ateca moved between her and the young highwayman. Christian grasped her arm and squeezed. Nora clamped her lips together.

Christian was eyeing de Ateca. "We call my cousin Blade for a good reason," he told the Spaniard. "Come, my friends, and we'll have Blade show us how he earned the name."

Holding Nora's hand, Christian led the group out of the palace to an old oak tree on the grounds. Selecting a golden thread from Nora's basket and a red rosebud from a nearby bush, he secured the bloom to the oak tree. He, Nora, and de Ateca stood to one side, and Blade walked back toward the palace, going so far that Nora thought he was leaving them. Finally he stopped and turned around, dagger in hand.

"Would you make a wager?" Christian asked de Ateca.

De Ateca shrugged. "He'll never hit the rosebud at that

distance. I wouldn't shrink from taking advantage of you, my lord, but not in this manner.''

"My lady?" Christian asked. "A wager. If Blade hits the rose, I claim a kiss.''

Nora had been a victim of Blade's skill. Christian knew this, and she could see that knowledge in his eyes. He watched her, hawklike, awaiting her reply.

"I'll accept the wager," she said in a faint voice. Aghast at her own temerity, Nora could no longer look at Christian.

"Come now, de Ateca," he said. "Are you of a weaker stomach than the lady?''

Nora watched de Ateca's body tense. A message passed between the two men, one she didn't understand. All she knew was that there was an undercurrent of fierce tension in the air. Both men were aware of it, and every word they spoke in superficial jocularity covered a menace that unnerved Nora.

Christian and de Ateca were caught in a battle with their eyes. Nora lifted her hand to touch Christian's arm, but the tension was broken when Blade called out to them. Christian turned from de Ateca and waved at the boy. Blade trotted back to them.

"Fair cousin," Christian said, "the *conde* disbelieves your skill so much that he won't wager.''

Blade pulled his soft toque from his head, revealing straight, dark hair that gleamed in the sunlight. Tossing the cap to the ground, Blade drew his dagger and trailed the blade across his open palm, back and forth, while he studied de Ateca. For the first time the Spaniard turned his full attention to the youth, watching the path of the silver blade as it slid over the boy's flesh. Then de Ateca lifted his gaze to Blade's face, and a catlike smile crept across the Spaniard's lips.

"If you hit the rose, fair Blade, I'll give you an evening in the best taverns of the city. I imagine you haven't seen their like if you've spent most of your time in the North country.''

"No," Christian said.

De Ateca's gaze never left Blade's face. "I didn't know you English had male duennas.''

"I haven't had a nurse since I was four," Blade said. He touched his lips with the tip of his dagger and glanced at Christian. "I'll take the wager, cousin.''

"Vexatious young cockerel, I weary of protecting your virtue," Christian said. "Guard yourself if you can."

"I need no help," Blade said, his voice rising.

"Please," Nora said. The men turned to her. "Please, my lords, This is a friendly contest, is it not?"

Christian had been glaring at Blade, but when Nora spoke, his mood lightened. "Carry on, cousin. Mistress Becket will forgive us our lapse if you entertain her. And I have a kiss at stake."

Blade turned to go.

"Wait," Christian said. "To win, you must hit the stem, not the bud."

"Unfair," de Ateca said.

"Fear not, my lord. It's an easy task." Blade smiled lazily at de Ateca.

The Spaniard looked from Christian's taut face to Blade's, and inclined his head in submission. "Perhaps God has blessed you with both skill and beauty, my lord, as He has your cousin."

Blade left them to resume his stance near the palace. Looking at the distance between him and his target, Nora doubted even Blade's ability to hit the stem of the rosebud. She saw the youth's arm draw back and flick forward. There was a whizzing sound just before the dagger buried itself in the bark of the tree.

Nora scurried along after Christian and de Ateca as they rushed to the oak. They beheld the silver dagger, its blade implanted in the stem of the rosebud about an inch below the petals. Christian folded his arms and faced de Ateca. Blade strolled over to join them, seemingly unconcerned by the animosity between his cousin and the Spaniard.

That animosity wore on Nora, though, combining with her agitation over the need to pass on her cipher. When the two older men began their gamecock hissing and spitting again, she excused herself.

As she'd expected, Christian was too busy vivisecting de Ateca with his poetic gifts to heed her disappearance. She slipped away, taking a little-traveled path that would lead to her cipher garden. Once there, she went about her usual occupations, pretending to be absorbed in gathering blooms.

The apple tree near the ancient bench was in bloom, and between the apple tree were two wooden bowls. A gar-

dener had been gathering figs and strawberries in these contain-
ers, but he was nowhere to be seen.

Sitting on the bench, Nora pulled the cipher from her
pocket, along with the hollow, cylindrical bead. Rolling the paper to its smallest size, she inserted it in the bead. Laughter
floated over the wall that separated the garden from the palace
grounds, and Nora cringed. Always it took every scrap of hard-
won courage for her to sneak into the garden and leave her message. Any noise made her cower. Even a violent breeze could
send her skittering for cover.

Fingers shaking, stomach doing the lavolta dance, she
scooped up a fig from one of the bowls and pressed an end of
the bead into the skin of the fruit, pushing until the cylinder
disappeared inside the fig. She'd chosen one of the less ripe
fruits so that the job wasn't too messy.

"I knew you'd be here."

Nora jumped, and the fig dropped like a lead pellet, rolling
over and over until it collided with the velvet tip of Christian de
Rivers's shoe. Her tongue wetting dry lips, Nora stared at the
fig, then lifted her gaze to Christian's ankle—small for so tall a
man—and up the swell of his calf muscle and the long line of
his thighs. From there her gaze skipped to his face.

He was smiling at her, but his eyes held that burning fury
she'd only recently learned wasn't fury at all, but something
much more dangerous for her. Merciful Lord, not again. She
would go mad if he tortured her with his hands while she suffered the fear of discovery. She held her breath, as he swept up
the fallen fig, then released it as he dropped beside her on the
bench and held it out to her.

"Not quite ripe," he said, "unlike yourself."

She snatched the fig from him and placed it in the bowl
with the others. "I would like to take a walk." She tried to get
up, but he put an arm across her chest.

"I wouldn't."

Leaning so close that she could smell the forest scent of the
soap he used, Christian blew at the feathery curls near her ear
that had escaped her French hood. His gaze caressed her cheek
and lips, then paused at her temple. Frowning, he pulled the cap
and veil from her head. She snatched them back from him, but
was distracted by his voice.

He breathed a word, low and vibrant, and it sent sparks of pleasure shooting through her body. "Eleanora."

Nora shivered. She tried to face him, but he turned her profile to him with a finger beneath her chin. The finger left as he blew at the curls near her temple again. His tongue darted out and touched her earlobe, fleetingly, leaving the skin there cold. The coldness immediately receded as heat suffused her, and the heat built into a fire as Christian brushed his lips over her ear. The caress was so light, it raised goose bumps all over her body. He hadn't touched her anywhere else, and yet he had her ready to curl her hands in his shirt and rip it off him.

Her body roused to the point where sensation became pain, Nora found herself absorbed in the ruby glittering in Christian's ear. She wanted to touch her lips to the soft skin concealed by that jewel, but she couldn't. She couldn't let him remain in the cipher garden. If she did, she would end up on the ground in front of the bench with him on top of her, and beside them would be the bowl of figs. When Christian began to run the tip of his tongue along her jawline, she blurted out the first thing she could think of.

"Blade."

Christian returned his lips to her ear. "You don't want Blade," he whispered. "He's too young, and the *conde* has staked a claim."

Latching onto this mystery to save herself, Nora pulled away from Christian's devastating mouth and faced her tormentor.

"What machinations are you about? Why is that ruffian at your side, and why are you thrusting him at Luiz de Ateca?"

"I promised to break the little beast to my will, and I have," Christian said. He attempted to slide his hand around her waist, but she batted it away. "Blade isn't your concern."

"He is. He tried to kill me.'

"If he had tried, he would have succeeded."

Her cap and veil in one hand, Nora put her fists on her hips. "You're flaunting him in order to attract that Jack Midnight."

"God's blood!"

Sucking in her breath, she backed away from the raw and menacing rage that came over Christian. His head thrown back, he snarled at her.

"Speak not of Jack Midnight. It unbalances the humors of my body and makes me want to kill."

Terror gave Nora wings. Dropping her French hood, she sprang to her feet and was out of the garden before Christian could move. She ran from his fury as if it could take form and pursue her without him. She heard him call to her, heard his footsteps behind her.

Blindly, with no other thought than to escape the rage that had turned a voluptuous seducer into a demon, she hurtled into the palace. She rounded a corner, skirts held high, and stumbled to a halt before Queen Mary. Behind the Queen stood several ladies-in-waiting, and at her side, Bishop Bonner, berobed and adorned with sweat. Nora sank to her knees. As she did so, Christian flew around the same corner. She heard him stop, and glanced to the side to see him drop gracefully to his knees.

The Queen had paused, hands folded in front of her swollen stomach, while her two subjects knelt. She stepped forward now. Stopping in front of Christian, she placed her fingers beneath his chin and lifted his face to inspect it.

"What signifies this unseemly haste, my lord? Nay, we have more weighty matters to discuss. We have been hearing tales of treason, Lord Montfort. Tales of spying and betrayal. You are one of our chiefest jewels, and we have decided to speak to you instead of handing you over to our lord bishop for questioning."

Nora's heart jerked inside her chest as she listened to the Queen. Treason. Dear God in heaven, treason. She knew. The Queen knew about the heretics.

Christian hadn't moved. Arms at his side, he gazed into the half-mad eyes of his Queen. Nora wanted to scream at him to run. Tightening her hands into fists, she watched as Bloody Bonner waddled forward to loom over Christian like a pale and bloated spider.

Where she got the courage to speak, Nora could not have said. She simply licked her lips, and of a sudden, the words tumbled out.

"I beg Your Majesty's leave to speak."

"Nora," the Queen said, turning to her, "we had forgotten you were here, child. Run away. We have business."

"Please, Your Majesty."

Mary scowled at her, but nodded.

"Faith, Your Majesty," Nora said, "I can't understand how Lord Montfort could think of treason when he spends most of his time trying to—to . . ."

"Out with it, girl."

Nora gritted her teeth and attempted to ignore her own blush. "He—he spends most of his time trying to seduce me, Your Majesty."

Frowning, the Queen cast an inquiring look at Christian.

Bishop Bonner rubbed his double chin with a damp palm. "Debauchery and treason go hand in hand, Your Majesty."

Mary came closer to Nora and peered into the younger woman's eyes, then looked back at Christian's still, tense body.

"God has given Mistress Becket innocence, honesty, and virtue," the Queen said. "When innocence speaks in defense of the accused, we must listen. We will all retire to the state chamber."

Two royal guards flanked Christian and took hold of his arms. Aghast at the role she had cast for herself, Nora could do nothing but follow the Queen and the bishop. She dared not look back at Christian. She was afraid of what she might see in his eyes, afraid she would see that he hated her for taking his life in her hands. For that was what she had done. One misspoken word, only one, and she would send this firebird, this saber-tongued giver of pleasure, to a death of such horror that its equal could not be found in Hell itself.

Chapter
IX

Christian let stillness surround him. He'd learned to do so after months of suffering under the hand of Jack Midnight. It must serve him now, for he could smell the bloodlust exuding from Bonner. It wafted toward him with the man's peculiar odor as he was escorted after the Queen and her attendants into the state chamber. Christ's wounds, why had Nora spoken for him? He could take care of himself, but fear for her was disturbing the calm he needed to survive.

The Queen lowered herself into her canopied chair of state. Her ladies were dismissed, and Bonner positioned himself beside her. Christian breathed in the fresh scent of Nora as he dropped to his knees beside the girl. She took a step closer to him and, using her skirt as a shield, caught his arm, giving it a squeeze. Beshrew her, he thought. She couldn't stand up to her father, so what was she doing defying the Queen? "Get you gone," he whispered harshly. "Now."

She ignored him. Christian's fists doubled in frustration, and the guards, who stood behind him, clamped their hands on his shoulders and touched their sword hilts in warning. Lowering his eyes, he concealed his anger behind his lashes and stared at the carpet.

The Queen began speaking, droning on about her desire to restore England to the Catholic faith. Her eyes burned with a fire brighter than the ones that seared heretics. Christian knew he had little time to gather his wits. He was suspected, as he'd often imagined he would be. Only he'd never considered he might also endanger an innocent whose very presence scoured every emotion but lust from his soul.

Drawing in a long breath, he stuffed his worry about Nora into a corner of his mind, summoned all the skills of deception he possessed, and raised wide-open eyes to the pair who judged him. The Queen was still engaged in her tirade, but Bonner was staring at him. Across the ten paces that separated them, Christian could feel the man's desire for blood. It rushed at him in ravening waves. Bonner rubbed his chin and his upper lip. His bulk seemed to strain toward Christian as their eyes met, but the Queen finished speaking.

"Because of the love we bear you and your father," she said to Christian, "we do you the honor of informing you of the accusations against you." She nodded to Bonner.

The bishop folded his hands together over his protruding stomach. "Christian Richard Villard de Rivers, Lord Montfort, you are charged with heresy."

As he wrinkled his brow, Christian heard Nora's small "No!" and he cast a glance of angelic bewilderment at the Queen.

"Please, Your Majesty, I don't understand. Was I not shown the true faith years ago by your own priests?"

Mary bent toward him. "Our own sister was schooled in a like manner, but we are not fooled by her cozening and mouthing of blandishments and false piety. Are we, Bonner?"

"Nay, Your Majesty. If it please Your Grace, give Lord Montfort into my keeping, and I will persuade him to confess his heresy." Bonner could contain himself no longer. While the Queen appeared to consider his request, he waddled over to Christian. Bending with difficulty over the bulge between his neck and his feet, he stuck his face in Christian's. "Bethink you to fool the Queen's majesty with your wiles? Think you your pretty face will save you from God's judgment? I tell you it will not be. Only a full confession and repentance can save you now."

Christian drew back from the man's foul breath and shook

his head. It was all he could do to maintain his facade of innocence and bemusement, for he wanted to sink his fingers into the flab around Bonner's neck and choke him until his weasel's eyes popped. He didn't, though. Instead, he continued to shake his head from side to side and lifted his hands in a gesture of helplessness.

"I don't understand," he said.

"You're famed for your brilliance, de Rivers," Bonner said. "Belabor us not with lies." The bishop straightened and put a hand on Christian's shoulder. "Mayhap you need reminding of the punishment for heresy. I'm sure Her Majesty would see to it that you witnessed a burning. Sometimes the wood is green and doesn't burn all at once, or the gunpowder doesn't explode as it's meant to in order to spare the heretic pain." Bonner's hand kneaded Christian's shoulder. "And when that happens, the torso is burned away while the sinner is still conscious."

Christian could feel the blood drain from his face. At his side, he saw Nora's body begin to tremble. He couldn't comfort her. It took all his strength of will not to throw that fat hand off his body and pounce on Bonner. Grinding his teeth together, he girded himself to endure Bonner's pawing.

"I saw one man," Bonner went on, "still moving his lips even though his throat had been burned away. At the last, he had no mouth, and all he could do was wave the stumps that were left of his arms until the skin on them charred and burst."

As Bonner grinned at him, Christian shrank away from the leering face and prying fingers. He spoke so that only Bonner heard him. "You're mad."

"Enough," the Queen said. "You've made Nora cry, Bishop."

Bonner lifted his hand from Christian's shoulder and bowed to the Queen. "Forgive me, Your Majesty. I but seek to convince this corrupt boy of the foulness of his sins by showing him the severity of the punishment he faces. Give me a week with him, Your Majesty, and I will return him to you obedient and free of heresy, or begging to die."

"Bonner!" Mary's voice whipped through the room, causing everyone to start. "Control your tongue."

The bishop again begged the Queen's pardon.

While Bonner's attention was elsewhere, Christian glanced at Nora. She was biting her lip, trying not to sob. She looked at him, and he winked at her. Startled, she quit weeping. All the while, Christian was slowly moving his hand to the neck of his doublet. Unlooping a jeweled button, he lifted his other hand and tugged at the lacing of his shirt. His fingers slipped beneath the white silk and caught on a gold chain. Drawing it forth, he wrapped his hand around the object suspended from it.

Suffusing his voice with unhappy confusion, he begged the Queen for permission to speak. Mary scowled at him, but at a pleading look from Nora, granted his request.

"Please, Your Majesty, I don't understand. How have I committed this terrible sin?" Christian searched Mary's face as if seeking salvation from it, all the while exuding wounded innocence. Once Mary was looking into his eyes, he held them for a long moment before glancing down as if in shame. He spoke quietly. "Your Majesty knows that I was cast into sin as a boy."

"And you've corrupted others now that you've grown," Bonner said.

Christian kept his eyes downcast. His shoulders drooped in submission. He almost smirked when the Queen lashed out at Bonner for interrupting. Mary ordered Christian to continue.

"I've never spoken of this to anyone, Your Majesty, because of my shame. I—I fought my father when he tried to reclaim me. For over two years, until the day Father brought me to court to be presented to the great King Harry."

Mary nodded. "Father often told the story of you being dragged into his presence as furious as a cornered alley cat."

"My father threw me at the King's feet. It wasn't until I beheld the King's face that I realized I was in the presence of majesty, and I was afraid."

Mary bobbed her head. "Everyone felt it. My father was chosen by God for greatness."

"Yes, Your Majesty. I was afraid, but the King laughed that giant's laugh of his and tapped me on the head with his walking stick." Christian paused, for everyone was looking at him, waiting. "And then . . ." Queen Mary scooted forward in her chair to hear him better. "And then . . ." Bonner's eyes bore into

Christian's. "And then the King ordered me to play the lute and sing for him, and said if I wasn't obedient, he'd throw me in the Tower and hang me. So I sang."

"What did you sing?" Nora asked, then covered her mouth with her hand.

"Yes," the Queen said. "What did you sing?"

Christian's mouth twitched, then he began to sing.

> *My little fool*
> *Is gone to play,*
> *She will tarry no longer with me.*
> *Hey ho, frisk-a jolly,*
> *Under the greenwood tree!*
> *Hey ho, frisk-a jolly,*
> *Under the greenwood tree!*
> *Hey ho, frisk-a jolly.*

He'd done it, Christian thought as he finished the song. He'd nudged the Queen's mood from suspicion into reverie. Like breeze-tossed ribbons on a maypole, her moods flapped, sailed, and jerked according to some hidden derangement Christian could not understand but had learned to influence.

The Queen's deep bark of laughter brought smiles to Christian's and Nora's faces.

An imitation of a smile distorted Bonner's lips. "Your wit is blazoned throughout the kingdom, Lord Montfort, but not all your fabled intellect can reason out of this. You consort daily with heretics."

It took the schooling of a runagate to keep Christian's smile in place. The Queen's merriment vanished, and he beheld the fires of Smithfield in her gaze. Bonner knew, Christian was certain, about Dymoke and the cellar.

Raising a sausage of a finger, the bishop pointed at Christian. "You consort with heretics."

"I do not," Christian said.

"I have one in gaol to prove that you do."

"One?"

"A foul doxy called Three-Tooth Poll. Why, the woman can't even tell what a Mass is, or whether or not the sacramental wine turns to Christ's blood."

Christian tightened his hand over the object it held. "You have Poll?" Of all the possibilities for disaster, he'd not thought once of this one.

"And a scrawny cutpurse who refuses to acknowledge the Pope."

"Inigo Culpepper." Christian could barely hear his own voice, so faint was it.

"Heretics."

"Oh, Your Majesty, no," Nora said. She had been so quiet, they all looked at her as if one of the tapestries had spoken.

Christian tried to glare her into silence, but she wasn't looking at him.

"Forgive my boldness, Your Majesty." Nora rushed to the Queen and threw herself at Mary's feet. "The good bishop is mistaken."

"I know heresy when I hear it!" Bonner roared.

"Of course, my lord." Nora's voice quavered, yet she persisted. "But Lord Montfort consorts with these knaves and thieves apurpose, Your Majesty."

"Nora, what could excuse habiting with the Devil's minions?" Mary asked.

"Why, to save them from the heresy he is accused of adopting, Your Majesty."

Christian raised his eyes to the ceiling. They were never going to believe that piece of fabrication. Not unless he helped Nora with her lies. Why did she have to screw up her courage and risk her life now, when she'd be better off playing the mouse? Confident in her newfound mendacity, she busily dressed up her tale.

"For months he has been leading them toward the true religion, Your Majesty. How often have I heard you lament that our well-born lead their baser charges astray from the true religion? Lord Montfort has taken your lamentations to heart. He seeks to spread the truth among those who need it most."

"Nonsense," Bonner said. "This fair report is nothing but a veil he spreads in front of virtuous eyes. He spends his time swilling and carousing. He wallows and cavorts with sinners because he, too, is a sinner. Look upon the face of his sin, Your Majesty."

Bonner signaled to a guard at the door, and the door was

thrown open. A man was hurled into the chamber to land on his stomach beside Christian. Whirling toward the man, Christian turned him over. It was Inigo. Eyes swollen shut and bloodied, lips distorted and cut, he coughed blood. Christian held his friend while the battered body spasmed. When Inigo was quiet, Christian raised his eyes to Bonner's and silently promised the bishop death.

Bonner smiled.

"Oh, Your Majesty," Nora said, "this is one of the creatures Lord Montfort was teaching." She was still kneeling beside the Queen, and her face was white. "Inigo Culpepper."

"How do you know this?" the Queen asked.

"Lord Montfort asked me to recommend a priest who could help him, Your Majesty, and—and he asked me to help him pick out rosary beads to give to Inigo."

"Falseness again," Bonner said. "A thief teaching a thief. The boy hasn't the virtue to instruct."

Christian removed his cloak and covered Inigo with it. Standing, he confronted Bonner. "You're right, my lord bishop, but I don't rely on my soiled virtue. I rely upon this."

Catching hold of the gold chain at his neck, Christian pulled it over his head. A heavy gold cross set with diamonds hung from the chain. He turned the cross over, laid it flat on his palm, and held it out to the Queen. Etched on its surface was an inscription. *To Christian. Henry R.*

Mary rose, slowly, her gaze fixed to the cross. She reached out to touch the inscription, and a single tear leaked from one eye.

"He gave it to me a few months after I sang for him," Christian said. "To show me that God rewarded his servants better than the devil, he said. Now I am trying to save my thieves' souls by teaching them of the true church. They're a hard lot, Your Majesty, and I couldn't convince them until one day I showed them King Harry's gift. I'll admit at first they were lured by the gold and diamonds, but at least they're listening to me."

He held his breath while the Queen studied the cross. She muttered something about her father and God; then, covering his hand with hers, she closed his fingers around the cross.

"I believe you," she said.

Inclining his head to one side, Christian smiled at the Queen.

"Such an angel's smile, my lord," she said, "when we know for ourselves that your nature leans more toward that of an imp." She took the chain from Christian and replaced it around his neck, then rested her hand on the top of his head. "God has spoken to you through our father and through Mistress Becket, we trow. Hie you hence, and take our Nora and your ruffian with you. We have had enough of misunderstandings for one day." Mary held up a finger. "But mark you, we like not this cavorting with a betrothed maid. Decorum, my lord, practice decorum."

With this last warning, Mary retired to her bedchamber. Christian lifted Inigo onto his shoulder, and Nora led him to the royal antechamber. The bishop followed them spewing apologies for the misunderstanding until the door to the Queen's chamber shut. He let Nora pass out of the antechamber but lifted his arm to bar Christian's way.

"De Ateca said you were as supple of mind as you are of body," the bishop said.

"What has the *conde* to do with me?"

"Naught, Christian de Rivers. But mark you. You're tainted with corruption and heresy, lie you ever so well to our good Queen. If I were you, I would study to become a martyr, for if ever there was a soul that needed purging by fire, it is yours."

"A pox on you, Bonner. And God protect me from men who dare set themselves in His place as judges."

Christian strode into the antechamber, and not until he heard Nora call for a stretcher and serving men did he allow himself to believe he wasn't going to one of Bloody Bonner's cells. He blinked rapidly and stared at Nora's back as she spoke to a royal guard. She had saved him. Not that he couldn't have saved himself. But she had risked her own life for his. The idea brought on odd feelings—anger, incredulity, and a desire to assuage his fears and rage with her body.

"I'm going mad," he said.

Turning his thoughts from the vexing Nora, he looked down at the senseless Inigo. Someone had constructed this monstrous trap and handed it to Bonner. He didn't think the man clever enough to have thought of it alone. And his little mouse turned dragon had sprung the trap before it gobbled him up.

How curious, he mused. She was jealous, and she defended him at her own peril. And he wanted her. Still. Ever. Marry, it was a curious thing, this lust that would not ebb, his fascination with this mouse-dragon. He left Inigo to join Nora. The guard saluted and vanished as Christian leaned down to murmur in her ear.

" 'Who is she that looketh forth as the morning, fair as the moon, clear as the sun, and terrible as an army with banners?' "

The Bald Pelican nestled in the odorous stews of South London, disreputable, hospitable, and notorious. This night, patrons of the ordinary abandoned their ale, cards, and dice to duck beneath tables and behind chairs at the sound of a lion's roar coming from the landing above. Bawd, cutpurse, angler, and vagabond gambler all cowered, for Kit was back, and in one of his rages.

A pottery beaker sailed out of one of the three upstairs doorways and smashed against the edge of a gaming table. A leather case followed it, hitting the floor. Knives and scalpels burst from the case, and two gamblers pounced on them, beginning a fight of their own over who was going to purloin the leach's instruments. A frightened cry set the two scurrying for cover, though. An angry Mars in a cambric shirt, hose, and boots appeared on the landing, holding what looked to be a ferret in a tradesman's gown and cap.

"Puling worms' meat!" the tall figure shouted. He grasped the neck of the ferret's gown in both hands and shoved the wriggling and shrieking creature over the banister, dangling him above the floor of the ordinary.

The leach's arms and legs flailed, and the patrons were treated to the sight of hairy white flesh, most of it blotched with dirt.

"Pandering excrement!"

The man holding the leach braced his legs far apart, banged his victim's head against the banister, and dropped him. The leach fell on a hapless pot boy. The boy yelped as the man hit his shoulders, then dodged out from beneath the missile. The leach landed bottom first and fell prone, groaning and whimpering. At a nearby table, Edward Hext sank his teeth into a meat pie and ignored the sufferer.

Marvelous Mag, proprietress of the Bald Pelican and tutor to many an aspiring London thief, sauntered out from the kitchen, hands on her hips. Blowing a blond sweat-drenched curl from her face, she shouted up at the man still standing on the landing.

"You asked for a leach, my beauty, and now you've broken him."

The man in white cambric scowled down at Mag. "You gave me a mountebank. He prodded Inigo's cuts with dirty fingers and tried to bleed him."

"As I said, Kit, he's a proper leach."

"I don't care. I've seen men die from unclean wounds and loss of blood. May God rot his testicles." Kit fingered the hilt of his dagger.

"Now, now, beauty," Mag said as she mounted the stairs. "I'll get rid of the leach for you. No need to kill him just because you're mad at someone else."

She reached Kit and touched his arm. He darted away from her and propped himself on the banister.

"They should be here by now," he said.

"Patience. It takes time to get someone out of gaol. Don't you worry. Poll's spent many a night there."

Kit whipped away from Mag, stalking back into the room where Inigo lay. "I'm not worried about Poll. I'm afraid I'll be stuck raising that grimy whelp of hers. Get me fresh water and more cloths, and send up a joint of mutton and wine for me. Soup for Inigo."

Mag cursed and stomped after Kit. He was standing at a table in the bedchamber, and she planted herself opposite him. He took a cloth from the table and held it in both hands, testing the strength of the weave.

"You've had my house in a tempest for hours now," Mag said.

He smiled nastily at her over the cloth.

Undaunted, Mag inspected his body from head to foot. "You need a good toss in the bed to drain all that choler."

The smile remained as Kit jerked at the cloth, ripping it in half. "I'm not in the mood."

"You left my school too soon to learn everything, beauty."

"You taught me enough." He ripped another cloth in half, and another.

From the open doorway came a giggle. Two of Mag's girls, Annie and Gertrude, scurried in bearing trays of food.

"Food, Kit," said Annie.

"Wine, Kit," said Gertrude.

Kit paid them no heed. He gathered his cloths and carried them to the bed where Inigo lay sleeping. With fresh water and the cloths, he finished cleaning his friend's wounds and bound those that needed it. As he was tying the last bandage, a woman's hand pulled his fingers from the cloth and finished it for him. Other hands drew him from the bed.

"He's sleeping," Gertrude said.

"You can't do anything else," Annie said.

Mag left Inigo's side to approach Kit, who was trying to avoid Gertrude and Annie. He retreated toward a side door. They followed.

"I'm not hungry anymore," he said.

Mag closed in on him from the front while Gertrude and Annie came at him from the sides.

"I know you, beauty," Mag said. "You're in a rage, and no one will be safe until you've rid yourself of it."

"Bring the leach back in here," he said. "I'll skewer him to improve my humor."

Mag shook her head and stopped close to Kit. "You need exercise."

"Killing is great exercise. Don't touch me."

Running her nails up his thighs, Mag chuckled. "Too late."

Annie slipped her hands inside Kit's shirt. "Too late."

"Much too late," said Gertrude as she planted her mouth on his.

Kit jerked his head away. "I don't think so," he said, and shoved backward, pushing open the door behind him.

Mag gave a joyous whoop, lunging after him. Kit stumbled under her weight and found himself propelled back into the chamber. His legs hit something, and he fell. He landed on a bed big enough to hold five, which was fortunate, because at that moment it acquired four occupants.

Kit disappeared beneath skirts and bosoms.

He pawed at masses of brown and blond hair as fingers plucked at the lacings of his hose and codpiece. Both came loose, and his flesh sprang free. Mag grasped him in both hands and stroked him once with practiced ease. Kit swore again and tried to pull his hips away, but Mag stroked him again, rapidly. He sank back under Gertrude's weight as she sat on his chest. Annie caught his arms and held them over his head while she kissed him.

Between his legs, Mag bent her head. "You're surrounded, my beauty." She kissed him. "Give." Kit arched his back, trying to buck all three of them off, but Mag kissed him again. "Give, beauty."

Kit cursed at her, and Mag chuckled as his thighs relaxed and his hips began to thrust.

"That's it, beauty. Show us just how killing mad you are."

This time it was Gertrude and Annie who came sailing out onto the landing to the enjoyment of the patrons of the Bald Pelican. Mag was climbing the stairs with a pot of ale in her hands when Annie screamed and burst through the bedchamber door. Gertrude squawked as she bounced out of the chamber under the encouragement of a booted foot.

Kit lunged after her, his torn shirt revealing sweat-drenched and tense biceps and a heaving chest. "No more, you jades. I told you to keep your hands out of my codpiece."

Annie stuck out her tongue at him. Gertrude did, too, while the crowd below hooted and whistled. Mag grinned at Kit, who turned away from her to reenter the chamber. She smacked him on the buttocks. Rounding on her, Kit stalked her with an eye on the ale jar. Mag held up one hand, giggling all the while.

"Now beauty, don't spoil your good temper after all the work we did on it. Be a sweet boy."

" 'S blood, was I not sweet enough? This will teach me to venture forth without a goodly escort." Stomping back into Inigo's chamber, he snapped at Mag, "I'm locking the door."

The portal crashed shut to lend emphasis to his words, and

the ruffians below groaned in disappointment that their entertainment was over. They were wrong, for as Kit closed the bedchamber door, the one leading to the street burst open, and a
whirlwind in a green velvet cloak launched itself into the tavern.
Those playing at dice and cards scrambled to protect their money
from the flying cloak.

Two men clambered in after the youth, who darted between
a serving woman and a pot boy. Shoving those two at his pursuers, he leaped to the bar and ran lightly down its length, hurling epithets at the two men as he went.

"Trugging house spawn. May your cocks rot. I'll use your
balls for chair cushions." A silver dagger appeared in the youth's
hand, then vanished.

One of the pursuers wasn't quick enough, and he yelped.
Looking down, he found the dagger pinning his doublet to the
wall at a point uncomfortably near his groin. Everyone had been
laughing at the sight of two grown men chasing after a youth.
Now the room went still, except for the impaled man, who was
wriggling in an attempt to free himself, and then, to the last pot
boy, everyone ducked underneath the nearest piece of furniture.
All but Hext, who had planted himself in front of the fireplace
in a high-backed chair and had been napping.

He opened one eye. "Everyone get up. He's just a cub."

"A cub," the impaled man wailed. "He's near took my leg
off."

The youth laughed, stooped from his perch on the bar, and
filched a dagger from the belt of a patron. "Next time it will be
your cock, Simon Spry." The boy dodged the grasping hands
of the dagger's owner and ran down the bar toward the back of
the ordinary.

As he neared the end of the bar, he stopped abruptly, for a
man had vaulted over the landing above the bar and landed in
front of him. He glared at the man, holding his dagger at ready.

"You sent them after me like two bewhiskered wet nurses,"
Blade said.

Kit gave him a cool glance. "Come and meet our hostess,
my fruit sucket."

Blade tossed the dagger from one hand to the other while
slowly shaking his head. In the middle of a toss, Kit dropped to
his haunches. One leg shot out and swept Blade's feet out from

under him. Blade crashed to the bar, furious and red-faced, as Kit easily caught the falling dagger and stood back up without ever losing his balance.

"God rot your soul," Blade said to him.

"I love you as well." Kit held out his hand. When Blade refused to take it, he chuckled and sat down beside his ward on the bar. Casually, he got rid of the dagger by burying its tip in a slice of bread on a table on the other side of the room. Blade's face froze. He stared at the dagger, then jerked his attention back to Kit when the older man began to sing into his ear.

> *She breweth nappy ale,*
> *And maketh thereof fast sale,*
> *To travelers, to tinkers,*
> *To sweaters, to swinkers*
> *And all good ale-drinkers.*

"Mag will have my head if we disturb her house any more tonight," Kit added. "Shall we retire?"

Hopping off the bar, he once more offered his hand. Blade jumped off on his own power, and Kit sighed as if wounded.

"By my troth, comfit," he said, "I begin to think I have spoiled some escape plan of yours by sending old Spry to look after you."

Blade threw his cloak over one shoulder. "I gave my word, damn you. You said going among the nobility might prod my memory. Well, it hasn't."

Kit swiped a cup from a passing pot boy and thrust it at Blade. "De Ateca's company has spoiled your disposition. Come."

In the sickchamber, Kit pointed to a stool and waited for Blade to sit. Standing over the youth, he folded his arms over his chest.

"What have you learned?"

"That de Ateca isn't a fool," Blade said. "He spent the whole time complimenting me, entertaining me, and encouraging my anger toward you. And I preened and pranced as you instructed, but he doesn't trust me." Blade snatched off his cap and tossed it on a sideboard. "It would help if I knew what you want."

Kit left Blade to straighten the sheets that covered Inigo. "I don't trust you yet either, so you'll have to labor in ignorance. He asked you to attend the hunt tomorrow, didn't he?"

"Yes, and my stomach roils at the idea of spending a whole day in the company of Spaniards. This treatment isn't going to work. I haven't remembered anything, no matter how many bows I make or pretty speeches I hear." Blade got up and sent Kit a disgusted look. Turning his back, Blade headed for the door.

"My lord," Kit said softly.

"Yes?" Blade stopped as he said the word, then pivoted slowly to face Kit. His jaw worked, and he lifted his fingers to his temple. "Did you hear?"

"I took a chance and was rewarded. Don't look so frightened. Father is writing to all the families he knows who don't like court. Don't you see? If your people had been seekers of power, or greedy, or close to the royal family, we would have heard of a missing boy."

Blade took a few hesitant steps back into the room. "You don't fool me. You're after Jack Midnight, and you think I'll help you if you winnow your way into my affections by giving me back my memory."

"Clever Blade. Spiteful, vexatious, and bloodthirsty, but clever. Leave off your hostility for the night and join me in a drink." Kit gestured around the room. "After all, we're in our accustomed burrow, you and I. So cry truce, and we'll do some drinking and wenching. It won't improve our tempers, but it will pass the time. For tomorrow I must to court again."

"To see Nora Becket."

"Aye, to see Nora Becket, and mayhap to kill a certain jackanapes with a mad laugh and the humors of a fiend."

Chapter
X

By the next day Nora had resorted to hiding. She peeped through the barely open door in her cipher garden, looking for her father and Percivale Flegge. Arthur shoved aside her skirts and stuck his face to the crack as well.

"They're gone, mistress," he said.

Nora shut the door. "Help me pull the bench over here. It should hold if someone tries to open the door."

Heaving and grunting, the two managed to haul the bench to the door. They collapsed on it and gulped in air.

"I vow that awful Flegge must have set spies upon me," Nora said, "for he accused me of deceiving him with Lord Montfort. Lord Montfort indeed."

"But mistress, you said Lord Montfort was the bravest, most handsome man in the kingdom."

She shook a finger in Arthur's face. "You're never to repeat that. May your tongue rot if you do."

Arthur stuck out his tongue and tried to look at it until his eyes crossed.

Sinking back against the door, Nora struggled not to wallow in despair. The day before she had saved Christian de Rivers's life, and after Bonner had left them, she'd hoped Christian would finally look at her with admiration and love. Instead, he'd pulled her into an alcove while Inigo Culpepper was being lifted onto a litter and kissed her, delving his tongue into her mouth and rubbing his hands all over her body.

Then the Queen had sent Mistress Clarencieaux. The old woman had marched up while Nora and Christian were thus engaged and whacked Christian on the head with her fan. As he jumped and rubbed his head, Mistress Clarencieaux had snatched Nora from him. Spouting threats against his manhood, she had dragged Nora away, and Nora hadn't seen him since.

This morning her father had arrived early to inform her that the ceremony of betrothal and the signing of the contracts would take place at once. She was to dress richly and come to the Queen's chapel. Nora had dressed and gone to the chapel, but upon seeing Percivale Flegge, her antipathy had risen to choke her. She'd fled, and now here she was, hiding.

"What am I going to do?"

"Hide until he goes away," Arthur said. He had given up trying to see his tongue and was drawing a picture of a bow in the dirt with a stick.

"But there are too many people in the palace looking for me."

Arthur dropped his stick and looked at her with eager relish. "We should steal out of the palace and hide at that inn where we saw the Robin Hood play." Holding his cap in place, Arthur jumped up to stand on the bench. "We can do it, mistress."

"But for how long? No, I must stop hiding now, before my father finds me for himself."

They both cringed as someone bellowed her name. It was Flegge, and he was on the opposite side of the northern garden wall. The bellowing stopped abruptly, and Nora and Arthur exchanged curious glances. Arthur got up and trotted over to the fig tree near the wall. Nora followed, watching him climb up into the branches and disappear behind a curtain of leaves.

She waited, but the boy didn't return. He was silent and still for so long, she finally tucked her skirts into her girdle and climbed up after him. Arthur was lying along a branch with his head sticking out over the garden wall, his gaze transfixed on something below. She clambored to a perch beside him and looked down.

Flegge was standing on a shrub-lined path, slowly turning in place and looking in all directions. He shouted Nora's name again, and both she and Arthur winced. Flegge would have the Queen's guard on him if he didn't stop making so much noise, Nora thought. His voice rose an octave to become the screech of a dying chicken, then was cut off. Nora's eyes widened as she watched the man hold his breath until his face was swollen and raw-meat red. At last he let out a long howl of frustration that rivaled the roar of a baited bear. As he howled he pounded his thighs over and over again with his fists.

Nora and Arthur put their arms around each other, too surprised to move. The spectacle continued as the man flounced to his knees and smote the dirt as if it were a mortal enemy. Face dripping sweat, mouth wet with spittle, he collapsed on his back in exhaustion, only to beat the defenseless earth with his heels and his fists.

Nora inched back on the branch, pulling Arthur with her. Together they climbed down while listening to the subsiding tantrum of Percivale Flegge. By the time they reached the ground, the man had resorted to obscenities periodically emphasized with more pounding. Nora and Arthur fled to the bench, covering their ears with their hands. After a while, they uncovered their ears. Hearing Flegge tramp off in another direction, they settled on the lawn beneath the fig tree.

"I don't like that man," Arthur said.

"I don't either."

Nora twisted a lock of her hair in her fingers, winding and unwinding the curl in an effort to keep from screaming. She didn't want to frighten Arthur, but if he hadn't been frightened by that scene at the wall, he was braver than she.

"Arthur, it seems as if we're going to have to keep hiding."

"Good."

"I can't marry that animal."

"No, we don't like him, and he might beat us instead of the ground."

"He might." She shivered. "He must be possessed by the Devil, but Father will make me marry him."

"And then we couldn't marry Lord Montfort."

"What?"

Nora looked at Arthur, but the boy was intent on his own thoughts, solemnly tearing hunks of grass from the lawn.

"But if we hide and find Lord Montfort," the boy went on, "he'll marry us and protect us from Sir Percivale."

Nora couldn't help smiling. " 'We' ?"

Arthur nodded. "We have to marry Lord Montfort. He likes us, so we should marry him instead."

"Yes, I suppose we should."

Christian de Rivers's plans to kill Percivale Flegge had been thwarted by his heretical guests. Their ship had arrived, and he was put to the trouble of escorting them to it. All that day he busied himself with preparations, summoning his disreputable band for escort and conceiving of a plan to get the old men out of his father's house and to the docks.

To Christian's annoyance, it began to rain as he and his father entered their private chapel that night. They were holding a special service in thanksgiving for Christian being found innocent of heresy by the Queen. Several clergymen had already entered the chapel, and the Mass began as soon as Christian and his father were seated.

At the end of the service, the household departed, leaving the two noblemen behind. The Earl's chaplain—a successful thief Dominby day—retired, and Christian left his pew to join four Franciscan brothers who hovered in a shadowed corner of the chapel.

"It's time," Christian said. "Follow me."

Three of the brothers followed him, while the fourth, Edward Hext, stood guard.

The Earl was already standing behind the altar. As Christian and the others joined him, he threw back the Turkish carpet to expose gray flagstones. With his dagger he pried one of the stones loose, revealing an iron ring. He pulled the ring and a door lifted, giving access to a set of stairs. Christian herded the three brothers down the staircase, and the Earl and Hext followed. The chaplain reappeared with a taper, which he handed to the Earl before closing the trapdoor again.

"Damp and cold down here," one of the brothers said.

"And dark," another said. "I'm tired of the dark. We should go back."

"God's toes," Christian said. "How you can be so brave on paper and such puking cowards about a short walk to the docks is a mystery."

Sebastian's lips twitched in amusement. "I do hope the rain dampens your temper, Chris. Take this habit, and here are the beads and the cross."

Christian fought his way into the dark grey-brown wool. His head popped through the neck of the gown, and his father dragged the skirt down until it covered Christian's riding boots.

"Cecil would hie off to France at this moment," Christian muttered. "My knaves say the house isn't being watched, but Cecil would know who at court set Bonner upon me. It could have been de Ateca, or Hampton, or that angelic idiot Pole."

"It matters not," Sebastian said as he donned his own habit. "The Queen thinks you the savior of London's runagates. Now, do I look like a friar?"

"As much as I look like a bishop."

"That doesn't bode well for our disguise, my headstrong."

Christian bent and rummaged through the basket from which they'd taken the robes. "That's why I brought padding." He thrust a pillow and twine at his father. "Tie this around me, and I'll look as fat and useless as any brother in Christendom."

Their disguising complete, Christian led his party through the tunnel to its exit just outside the wall that surrounded the earl's residence. Simon Spry awaited them there, rain-drenched, with a donkey and cart. It was just after ten, and though they had only a short walk to the river and then downstream to the docks, they would follow the Thames upstream. Once far enough out of the city, which would take them a good two hours, they would take a boat to the docks as though they had just arrived from the country.

With his father's help, Christian bundled the three heretics into the cart. Sebastian sat with them, his head towering above the other three. Christian wiped raindrops from his chin and motioned for Spry and Hext to follow him down the muddy lane that paralleled the river.

His close brush with death the day before must have affected him more than he'd thought, for he imagined that every snort of the donkey, every snap of a twig heralded an attack. His boots slithered on the packed earth made slick by the rainfall. The moon wasn't out, and a cloying mist surrounded them, making his chest tighten. In the darkness, the creaking of the cart and the grunts of the donkey seemed loud enough to hurt his ears.

In spite of his agitation, the trip was made safely and quickly. They transferred from donkey cart to small launch, then alighted from the launch at the docks when it was still dark. Christian helped the gouty Archibald Dymoke onto land. The earl and the other two men followed. Spry and Hext remained with the boat, for only a short distance remained to be traveled.

This was the segment of the trip Christian hated the most. He was almost rid of them, these fanatic bumblers, and he itched to thrust them in the direction of their Dutch ship and be away with his father. Instead, he set his jaw and preceded the other four down an alley that would lead to their destination.

Hand on his concealed sword, Christian slipped ahead to inspect the intersection of another alley. He clung to the rotten wood of a shed at the corner. All was clear, but the cross-alley dead-ended to the left, and that made him wary. Looking back over his shoulder, he found himself alone.

His father and the heretics were several yards back. The Earl was yanking on the habit of one of the old men, but the heretic was well planted. Christian sped back toward them, stopping halfway when he heard Dymoke whine.

"I can't bear it anymore, to be enshrouded in the trappings of heresy. I must rid myself of the raiment of evil."

Christian almost picked up a rock and threw it at Dymoke's head. "You slug-witted fools," he whispered fiercely at the men, "cease this braying and follow me now, for by God's wrath I won't stay to be made gallows meat."

Without waiting to see if the heretics followed, Christian flew back down the alley to the shed. Sliding his body along the wet planks that made up one side of the shed, he put one hand around the corner to feel his way. It skimmed over mold growing on the wood, and he could smell rot and dead fish. The heretics had shut their mouths, and he strained to catch any sound. He heard nothing but the fall of rain.

Glancing back, he saw his father shooing the heretics into

motion. Christian's gaze darted about the intersection, touching rain-slick cobbles, shadows, and roof line. He stepped out into the open, shot looks in all directions, then whipped across the empty space to cling to the building on the opposite corner. Behind him he saw his father help one of the heretics, who had slipped in a puddle of water.

Christian pushed away from his hiding place, intending to go back and help. As he moved, he heard the sound of a blade sliding out of a sheath. He turned in the direction of the sound, ripping open his habit and drawing his own weapon. Hampered by the pillow at his stomach, he barely got the sword drawn before they were upon him.

He had no time to do more than shout a warning to his father. Three armed men who wore no livery or badge came at Christian at once, and he knew he had to kill one quickly or they would surround him.

It seemed as if a spell had been cast to slow the world down, for he was able to block a sword, jam his foot into the paunch of the second attacker, and duck the slicing blow of the third. Jumping backward, he heard sounds of battle behind him and knew that his father was under attack as well.

Christian swung his sword like a battle-ax, cutting an arc around his body, and his assailants scattered long enough for him to glimpse his father parrying the blows of two swordsmen. Dymoke and his fellows offered no help. In his hands and knees, Dymoke was crawling away from the Earl. Another heretic sat in a puddle and howled while the third cowered with his back to a wall.

"Dymoke, you worm, fight!" Christian shouted.

He ducked a sword that came at his neck, then rolled on his back and onto his feet again. As he rolled, the pillow at his waist pulled free. He threw it at one of his attackers and headed for his father, but another was there to block his way.

Bending and twisting, stabbing and slashing, he felt his strength begin to ebb as precious moments slipped by. To his horror, he caught sight of another man heading for his father. The distraction was enough. The tip of a blade jabbed his thigh, and Christian sank to one knee. He drew his dagger from his belt, but before he could throw it, he was forced to parry a storm of blows from all three men.

Blood trickled from the cut on his leg and down into his boot. He slipped as he was forced away from Sebastian under the onslaught of the three men, and as he slipped, a knife darted out to slice at his chest. It came away with his blood on it, but the knife-wielder paid for his daring with his life. Christian feinted to the left, threw his body to the right, and hurled his dagger at the man as the enemy prepared to knife him again.

The price of that victory was high, for an attacker slipped under Christian's dagger arm. Christian felt the sting of sliced flesh at his side and hurled himself backward. No longer able to move quickly, he stumbled, his sword wobbling. The two remaining attackers closed in, their own swords raised. Christian fastened both hands on the hilt of his weapon, not daring to look for his father again.

The slowness spell took him once more, though, and he couldn't seem to lift his blade quickly enough. He watched two sword points fly at his chest, slicing the air as they would slice his gut. Instinctively, he dropped to his knees. In the same moment, a whistle cut through the sounds of battle, a whistle that had haunted Christian's dreams since he was eight.

The sword points still came at him. Christian lifted his blade. It struck one weapon. The other was free, and it continued on its path. Christian watched it aim for his heart, only to be chopped aside by another, larger blade.

"Kit, love, you must save your fights for me," Jack Midnight said with a laugh.

Christian shot to his feet, sword held in front of his body with two hands, and waited for Midnight to attack. He couldn't believe his senses when Midnight whistled again, and two ruffians pounced on Christian's assailants. Gathering his wits, Christian shoved Midnight aside. He spotted his father still fending off his two attackers and launched into a wobbly run.

As he ran, his wounded leg threatened to buckle under him, slowing him at the moment he most needed his speed. He fought to keep his bad leg beneath his body. His chest heaved with the effort to stay exhaustion and shock. And all the while he watched the Earl turn to counter a blow, leaving his back exposed to a man he'd battered to the ground. Christian screamed.

"Father, behind you!"

Sebastian twisted as he parried, but his foot caught on the

heretic who still groveled in the mud puddle. The assailant on the ground lurched up and jabbed, sinking a knife into Sebastian's back.

"No!" Christian hurled himself the last few feet that separated him from his father.

He landed on all fours between his fallen father and the two murderers. Raising his sword, he lashed at the men while covering Sebastian's body with his own. The assailants ran at him, sensing Christian's weakness, but before they could reach their prey, there was a whizzing sound and two muffled thuds. The murderers' bodies jerked and halted. Christian watched them fall on their faces, arrows protruding from their backs.

He had no time to reason out Jack Midnight's actions. He lifted himself off his father. The Earl lay on his stomach, a knife sticking out of his left shoulder. When Christian saw the position of the knife, he stopped breathing. Midnight joined him, but Christian paid no heed to him and drew the blade from Sebastian's body.

"I need cloth," he said.

Jack Midnight ripped a habit from one of the cowering heretics and handed it to Christian. With shaking hands, Christian bound the wound. As he did so, Hext barreled into the alley, sword drawn. He lowered it as he approached Christian.

"Outnumbered," he said.

Not glancing up from his father, Christian shook his head. "Nay, Midnight has played the rescuer this time. I have to get him home at once, but he can't be jostled."

Midnight helped Christian turn the Earl over on his back.

"God's ass," Midnight said. "This is your father. I help no murdering blue bloods."

Midnight stood. "Come with me, Kit."

Christian pulled Sebastian's cloak around his body. "You'll have to kill me."

"And me," Hext said.

"The watch will be here soon," Midnight said to Christian. "And you're too weak to fight me."

"There's no time for this idiocy. I must get him home."

The highwayman glanced at the Earl. "He's going to die, Kit."

Midnight hit the ground under the full force of Christian's

body. Christian straddled his tormentor, fists tangled in Midnight's cloak.

"He's not going to die, and if you don't help me I'll kill Blade."

"Now, Kit, I followed you all this way because I thought you were moving Blade out of my reach."

"I swear it. I'll break his pretty neck with my own hands and I'll . . ." Christian's head felt heavy of a sudden, and he blinked at Midnight.

Midnight shoved his hands aside and caught him before he sank to the ground.

"I'll kill Blade," Christian said, his words as blurry as his vision.

"I believe you, Kit." Midnight helped him to his feet and signaled to his men.

"Don't touch me," Christian said.

"If I don't hold you up, how will you get to the river, love?"

"Promise," Christian said. He clutched at the neck of Midnight's shirt. "Promise you'll get him home safely. You can do what you want with me."

"Ah, love, I've waited years to hear you say that, and now you're too diced for me to do anything but patch you up."

Christian wasn't listening, for Hext and Midnight's men were lifting his father gently and heading for the riverbank. He took a step to follow, but his wounded leg buckled under him. He heard Midnight chuckle, and he was lifted. Midnight dragged one of his arms around his shoulder, and Christian was forced to allow his enemy to half-carry him in the wake of his father's bearers.

"I'll remember your promise," Midnight said. "And if your father lives, you'll owe me a double debt. It's a fine night, my treasure. A fine night for killing . . . and for promises."

Nora waited all day for the uproar over her disappearance to subside, but the royal guards and servants didn't stop searching the palace until well after dark. She and Arthur hid in the fig tree. While the royal household was at the evening meal, they slipped out of the palace in stolen servants' cloaks.

Never having been in the streets of London unescorted, Nora was fearful and agitated as they crept their way to Arthur's Robin Hood inn. They took a room and tried to rest, but with the first appearance of light, Nora was up. After much worry, she sent a note to one of the palace cooks who helped her with her or-phaned animals, giving them over into his care. She and Arthur downed a quick meal, then hurried to the river, where they took a boat to the Earl of Vasterne's landing. She marched past the guards at the gate, so intent on gaining sanctuary that she had no time to allow them to question her. The steward who an-swered her knock nearly soiled his beautiful Montfort livery, so great was his shock at seeing her. Addled herself, Nora scurried in while the man gaped at her.

Something was wrong. She knew it the moment she got inside. Serving men and women were rushing up and down the main staircase with linens and jugs of water. Guards were po-sitioned about the house, and Nora saw almost twenty of the Earl's men-at-arms gathered in the hall. The whole household was up and dressed.

The steward recovered enough to send one of the Earl's lieutenants to her as she stood at the foot of the staircase, Ar-thur's hand clasped in her own.

"My lady, is something wrong?" the young man asked, but he didn't wait for her to answer. "You must allow me to escort you back to the palace, for the Earl can't see you. He is ill."

"What's wrong?"

"He was attacked by thieves last night, my lady. Lord Montfort as well. My lady!"

Nora was already racing up the stairs with Arthur in tow. That nuisance of a lieutenant plucked at her cloak, but she slapped his hand away and ran. It wasn't difficult to decide which was the Earl's chamber. It had to be the one with the gaggle of physicians hovering outside. She pushed two of them aside and thrust through a half-open doorway.

She collided with the solid Edward Hext.

"My lady," Hext said as he grasped her arm.

"Let me past. Let go."

She was in an antechamber. Beyond was the door to the Earl's bedchamber, but Hext wouldn't release her. Arthur and the lieutenant scrambled into the room, halting when they saw her and Hext.

"My lady," Hext said, "the Earl is grievously wounded, and you must leave."

She shook her head. "Lord Montfort."

"There isn't time, my lady. I'm trying to convince Lord Montfort to see a physician. He's been with the Earl since they returned home after the attack, and he won't leave his father's side. I fear for his life as well if his wounds aren't seen to."

"I can help," Nora said. She saw the disbelief on Hext's face. "I can."

"I don't see how."

"I saved him from the Queen, didn't I?"

Hext chewed his lip but finally stepped aside. While the lieutenant protested, Nora walked into the Earl's bedchamber. The windows were still shrouded against the night's cold. She smelled beeswax candles, the sweet scent of rosewood furniture, and spices. Across the expanse of the room she saw a bed hung with the Earl's colors and standard. On it lay the Earl covered in white linens, and sitting on the bed beside his father was Christian.

Christian's back was to her. Neither man moved, and Nora thought they resembled a tableau on one of the marble sepulchers in her family's burial vault at home. The Earl was almost as white as one of the vaults. And though Christian's hand covered his father's, she detected no movement in it.

As if approaching an altar, her dread growing with each step, she crossed the room to them. She crept to the side of the bed on which Christian perched, and when she was an arm's length away she noticed the wide bandage fastened around his upper thigh. Dark with old blood, it was moist, and new trails of bright red trickled down his leg. He rested on his right hip, keeping the injured leg stretched out and braced on the floor. His left arm hugged his body unnaturally, and Nora was sure it was damaged also.

She moved into the light shed by the candles on a table beside the bed, but Christian showed no sign that he knew she was there. His gaze remained fixed on the Earl. Nora took another step, gaining a better view of the desecration of Christian's body. His doublet had been sliced diagonally from right shoulder to left hip and hung in two bloody halves. His shirt had slipped off one shoulder to reveal a neat cut that began at the join of arm and torso.

His face was untouched, yet ravaged. And it was his face that most frightened Nora. Drained of emotion, it was like the face of one of those figures clockmakers mounted on their more costly creations. The Queen had one on which a knight, fashioned in silver, knelt before his sword as if it were a cross. Silver, cold, and unreal.

He was so unmoving she was afraid to speak. She hesitated, wishing her own breathing weren't so loud, wishing she had the courage to say something. Then she remembered the first time she'd seen Christian with his father. At the sight of the Earl he had transformed from a viper into a submissive angel. This man who tormented and toyed with murderers called Sebastian "sire," as a nobleman addresses his king.

Nora held her breath and put out a hand. She touched the bleeding arm with one finger.

"Get out," Christian said, "before I kill you."

Chapter
XI

Once she would have bolted at his threat. Mayhap she'd heard too many threats from men these past few days and had grown used to them. Mayhap she was too frightened by the death-vault stillness of Christian and his father to take heed. Or mayhap she'd lost what few wits she had after a day of running and hiding.

Whatever the reason, she didn't run now. She waited for Christian to say something more or to move. He did neither, so she reached out again to touch his arm. The touch was light, but he sucked in his breath and jerked away, his hand coming up to ward off another liberty.

"Don't make me throw you out into the streets," he said. "They're littered enough as it is."

At least he was talking. "What happened?"

"We were out whoring and were attacked. Would you like to know what we bought and how we used it?"

"I—I'm not going, my lord." She covered her ears with her hands.

Christian didn't smile, but she could see a glimmer of half-hearted amusement in his eyes. His shout caught her off guard.

"Hext!"

The man appeared, his face alight with hope. "Get some of my men to cart this parcel back to the palace," Christian said.

He was going to throw her out. Nora lifted her skirts and sprang away from Christian, running around to the other side of the bed as he shoved himself to his feet. Limping, he nevertheless caught her before she could dodge him. He snagged her arm, dragged her to Hext and thrust her at the man.

"At once, Hext. And see to it that she understands just how unwelcome she is." He turned away, back to his father.

Hext started pulling Nora out of the chamber, and she panicked.

"No, please. I can't go back."

Arthur burst in, drawn by her cries. "Take your hands from my lady!" He kicked Hext's shin, and the man yelped.

"You let her go!" Arthur proceeded to shout and kick at Hext while pounding him with both fists.

Christian's roar made the boy squeak and hide behind his victim and Nora. "Silence! By God, I've had a surfeit of whining and whimpering."

Reaching behind Hext, Christian fished Arthur out by the neck of his shirt and held him off the ground, wriggling like a river eel. He dropped the boy in front of Hext, who grabbed Arthur's hair with one hand while he kept hold of Nora with the other. He began to drag them away.

"God rot your soul," Arthur said. "We aren't going back and marry that devil's minion."

Christian had resumed his vigil at the Earl's side. At Arthur's words, though, he lifted a hand, and Hext immediately stopped.

"What did you say?" Christian asked Arthur.

Nora made shushing noises, but Arthur stuck out his chin and glared at the man across the room.

"They tried to make us sign those marrying papers, but we hid. And we aren't going to marry that man. He has fits."

Christian glanced at his father, then rose and walked with an uneven gait back to the three of them. "Hext, take this golden-headed shrike to the kitchens and feed him."

"We aren't going back," Arthur repeated.

"Don't try my patience, you infant Mars, or I'll put my good hand to your arse."

Arthur stomped out followed by Hext, and Christian returned to his father. Left by herself, Nora had no idea if she was meant to go with the others or stay. Christian wasn't going to throw her out, at least not at the moment. Perhaps she should leave. She could speak to him when he'd rested. Only he wasn't going to rest. She could see that he intended to keep vigil at his father's bedside until he bled to death. Tiptoeing as quietly as she could, she crept back to the two men on the bed.

Christian didn't acknowledge her, but he didn't try to chase her away either. His inattention allowed her to gather her courage to speak.

"What do the physicians say?"

"What they always say. He is in God's hands."

She winced at his laugh. A tortured, lost-soul's laugh it was, and it turned her insides to boiled cabbage.

"He was in God's hands last night," Christian said, "but I was there to see that he fell out of them and into the path of a dagger."

Speaking before she lost the resolve, Nora asked, "Mean you that those brigands were yours?"

"Don't be any more of an ass than you can help."

"Mean you that you knew there would be trouble this night?"

"Of course not. Beshrew you. I can't take much more of your foolishness."

"But, my lord, you can't mean that you are responsible for the evil of men who try to attack honest subjects in the dark any more than you could help being taken by that terrible outlaw Jack Midnight."

From the table beside the bed, Christian grabbed a cloth and gently touched it to his father's brow. The Earl hadn't moved in spite of all the commotion around him.

"Go away," Christian said. "My steward will give you chambers."

"I'll stay."

"This is no time for you to become a little donkey. And I've no patience left."

He stood, and Nora knew he was going to toss her out. She skipped backward when he reached for her.

"Please," she said.

"No, I don't please."

He limped toward her, and it was the limp that gave her the idea. She stopped skipping away from him. Allowing him to catch her, she let her body go boneless. Christian caught her and stooped to lift her in his arms. His leg gave way. Dropping to his knees, he cursed as his arms lost their strength.

Nora scrambled out of his grip in time to slip her shoulder beneath his arm as he swayed. His free hand came up to grasp her other shoulder, and she felt the slick, wet smear of blood. Knowing she would draw his fury if she called for help, she pried him upright. It took all her strength, but she succeeded in dragging him to the bed. When they reached it, he fell on his side, gasping and clutching at his thigh.

"My lord," she began.

"I'll call my guards."

Clasping her hands in front of her, she mimicked Arthur by sticking out her chin. "If you do, I—I'll wait until you fall down from loss of blood and come back."

"God's blood."

"It's yours that is sprinkled about this chamber, my lord."

He bit the inside of his mouth. "Why don't you run from me like you do from your father?"

"If you don't let me tend your wounds, you won't be able to watch over your father at all."

She waited, but there was no blast of obscenities, no threat to hurl her into a dung heap. Silence was as much acquiescence as Christian de Rivers would give her, and Nora took it. Moving slowly so as not to invite rejection, she placed one hand on Christian's chest and braced his back with her arm. Exerting only slight pressure, she lowered him to rest beside his father.

Nora didn't give him a chance to change his mind, but set about immediately removing the stained bandages and clothing. She'd tended many an injured pup and stray cat, but never a man. It was unnerving, too, the way this one ignored her. He lay quietly, allowing her to touch him but not looking at her. Either he turned his head to watch his father or he stared up at the velvet canopy that topped the bed.

She was beginning to know him, Nora thought as she realized his blank stare concealed a maelstrom. She longed to ask what troubled him, yet at the same time she feared to know. He traveled paths of darkness, did Christian de Rivers, black alleys peopled with phantoms and beasts in human form, such as Jack Midnight. She wavered between the desire to call him from his world of darkness and the urge to flee.

She left him to request supplies from one of the serving men who waited outside the Earl's chamber. When she returned with a basket, Christian was lying as she had left him. She produced scissors and began to cut away his doublet and shirt. Once the garments were in shreds, she peeled them away from his chest, then stopped with her hands poised over him.

She was an evil person. She was devouring the sight of him as though he were a cup of sack and she a thirsty pilgrim. She couldn't prevent her eyes from stealing glances at the way his flesh stretched tight over his ribs, then sank as it topped his lowest rib and descended to his waist. Perspiration formed on her brow, and she patted it with her sleeve before removing the remnants of his shirt.

Next she pulled off his boots. As she tossed them to the floor, her hand came to rest on his ankle. His flesh was cold, and she flushed, contrite at the way she hesitated to remove his hose when he so obviously needed her help. Biting her lower lip, she plucked at the laces at the side of his hip. The material tugged, drawing tight over his codpiece, and she finally gained his attention.

His hand grabbed her wrist, and she met his bleak stare.

"Sweeting," he said, "if I weren't in Hell, I would be glad to let you continue. Turn away."

When he called her back, she found him lying beneath the sheet, his body clearly outlined by its white folds. She lifted the sheet a fraction of an inch, sure that he would make some terrible jest. He surprised her by pulling the cover back to expose his thigh while casting a worried glance at his father. Chiding herself once more for her lack of fortitude, Nora set about cleaning the gash in his thigh. As she wiped away dried blood, she realized the wound would have to be stitched, as well as the one on his arm.

She busied herself gathering needle, thread, and cloths. Noticing a bottle lying in the basket, she remembered the serving man's comment that there was sleeping potion among the other supplies. The dosage was written on the outside of the bottle. She poured a dash of the liquid in a cup of water and held the cup out to Christian.

"What is it?" he asked.

"I have to stitch your wounds."

"That's not what I asked."

"A sleeping draft."

"No."

"I will hurt you."

"Which will hurt worse, do you think—a little embroidery, or waking up and finding him dead?"

She set the cup aside and took up her needle. Unlike her injured puppies and cats, he gave no sign of his pain beyond a tightening of his mouth as she closed the wounds. The whole business was accomplished in silence. By the time she finished binding the thigh and arm, Nora could almost believe he hadn't noticed what she was doing at all.

"He doesn't stir," he said as she straightened.

"When a creature is wounded, its body sleeps in order to husband strength for healing."

"Or to die."

She couldn't think of a believable lie, so she remained quiet. Christian stirred; he raised himself on his elbows and took hold of the sheet that covered him.

"What are you doing?" she asked.

"I need clothing, and I have inquiries afoot that need seeing to. God's blood, woman, do you think this attack is a chance happening? It comes on the heels of Bonner's attempt to take me and break all the bones in my body one at a time."

She didn't answer. She simply put her hands on his bare chest and shoved.

He fought her. "Get your hands off me or I'll—"

"You're weaker than a newborn pup."

"And that's the only reason you'd dare defy me, you sniveling mouse."

She pressed him down in the bed and straightened the sheet that had fallen to his groin. He reached for the cover again, but she grabbed his wrists and forced them down to either side of his head. His strength gave way suddenly, and she plopped down on his chest. Her nose bumped his shoulder hard enough to sting. She lifted her head to find him furious at being subdued so easily. Her nose throbbed and itched, or she might have shrunk from him. Instead, she was reduced to holding him down with both hands while wriggling her nose in an effort to prevent a sneeze. Christian stopped fighting her and stared, his mouth falling open at the dance her nose was performing. Nora made a little squeak, turned her head, and sneezed.

Mortified, she buried her head in the crook of her shoulder. Her face was hot with embarrassment, but she lifted it because she couldn't remain perched on Christian's naked chest forever.

He was lying beneath her without protest now, his wrists no longer flexing and twisting to get free. His gaze, still flat and shadowed, traveled over her features, and the barest of smiles formed on his lips.

" 'Untimely grinning is the silliest sin,' " he said. His smile vanished, and he closed his eyes. "You've cost me what strength I had left, damn you."

Nora pressed her advantage. "I will keep vigil for you, my lord. I give you my word, before God, I'll wake you at the slightest change."

She caught a glimpse of dark violet as he tried to open his eyes.

"I command lords and cutpurses, ladies and bawds," he said. "Why is it that I find myself surrendering to a mouse?"

She released him, relief flooding her to the bone. "Mayhap it is as you said, and I am but a dragon in the guise of a mouse."

"Promise. No bleeding, no physicians."

"I promise."

As she gave her word, Christian's body seemed to release its tension. He turned his head toward his father. His lashes fluttered, then lay still.

Nora heard his breathing deepen and knew that he was asleep. Drawing a chair to the bed, she settled herself to watch both men. Hours passed during which she tended them and struggled to find an answer to her own predicament. Sometime during the day Hext returned with the Earl's steward, and she accepted their gratitude for convincing Christian to rest.

Their gratitude vanished when she objected to the entry of

the Earl's three learned doctors. Sensing a battle, Hext retreated along with the steward. Harpylike, the physicians descended on the sickbed, their thin fingers twitching with eagerness.

One, a spider with a beard that reached to his knees, whispered to the other two. "At least the fires are high. They might keep out the evil vapors." The spider lifted his brows at Nora and bowed. "Hobart Dogdyke, physician, Mistress Becket. The steward made us aware of your kind offer to nurse the Earl and his heir."

The physician's voice rose in a question, and Nora could see the dubious and scandalized expression he tried to hide. Suddenly aware of the consequences of her mad flight, she twisted her hands together and inclined her head in silent acknowledgment of his words.

"This is Thimbleby, my colleague," Dogdyke went on, "who studied with me in Padua. And that is Clopton the apothecary. If you will pardon us, mistress, we will bleed the Earl now."

Dogdyke bustled past Nora, followed by Thimbleby, who carried a bag. The apothecary left and returned with several metal basins, while Nora looked on with growing horror. Dogdyke possessed an air of authority that confused her, but she couldn't break her promise to Lord Montfort. She would rather die.

Dogdyke fished in the bag and withdrew a lancet. "I told Lord Montfort," he said to her, "that most people have too much blood in them. Reducing it relieves the body, and when I examine the blood as it flows, I can better perceive the patient's malady."

"I—I forbid it," Nora said.

Wiping his sharpened blade on a cloth, Dogdyke watched the apothecary bare the Earl's chest. "Fear not, mistress. The Earl's health is under the influence of the planet Saturn, and I have a new tincture of bitter apple, mercury, turpentine—"

"I said no!" She swept up to the physician and thrust her arm between Dogdyke and the Earl. "No."

"The Earl was left in my charge," Dogdyke said. He edged closer to the Earl, his lancet at the ready. "I can't let you interfere and cost me the life of my most important patient."

Nora stumbled as Dogdyke shouldered her out of the way.

He bent over the Earl while Thimbleby and the apothecary moved to stand between Nora and the bed. She heard the Earl moan.

"He's waking," she exclaimed. "Stop."

No one paid attention, but Christian stirred at the sound. He rose on one arm to find the doctors looming over his father.

"Bloody carrion," he said, his words slurred. "Get you gone from here."

He heaved himself up on his knees and grabbed Dogdyke by the throat. The movement must have torn his wounded thigh, because he gasped and lurched to the side. He caught himself before he collapsed on top of his father, and Thimbleby jumped into the fray by clutching Christian's wounded arm. The apothecary let out a terrified whimper and fled.

Nora stared at what her dithering had caused. Christian fought the two men, cursing and bleeding all the while. If he lost, Dogdyke would bleed his father and Christian would be next. She looked around for something to use as a weapon, and found Christian's sword in its scabbard tilted against a chest in the corner. Rushing to it, she unsheathed the weapon, then hurled herself at the doctors.

Nora gripped the sword hilt with both hands and hit Thimbleby on his rear with the flat of the blade. The doctor yowled and brought his hands around to protect his buttocks. She lifted the sword and bashed him on the head. Thimbleby plummeted to his knees and fell on his face. She clambored over his back, hefted the sword again, and brought it crashing down on the head of Dogdyke.

The blow made no impression on the fervent doctor, who was busy peeling Christian's hands from his throat. Dogdyke fastened his own hand over Christian's wounded arm and squeezed. Crying out, Christian froze, enabling Dogdyke to tear the choking hands from his neck.

"You are under the influence of evil humors, my lord." Dogdyke shoved Christian, and Christian fell on his injured leg with a moan.

Fury suffused Nora with strength. She swung the sword, whirling it over her head and dashing in against the physician's thick skull. Dogdyke teetered, and his scrawny body tilted toward the Earl. Christian's arm shot out, and he sank his fist into the man's gut. Dogdyke backpedaled, and Nora finished him off by tripping him with the sword. The doctor crashed to the floor and lay shaking his head.

Nora stood over him, sword poised. "Out."

Dogdyke opened his mouth. She slapped his arm with the sword, and the physician screamed. Flailing his arms and legs, he managed to get them moving in unison and burst out of the chamber on all fours.

Nora followed him, slammed the door shut, and bolted it. Dropping the sword, she returned to the bed to hover over the Earl. Christian lay with his arm draped protectively over his father. Pale, his skin damp with sweat and his mouth tight with pain, he nevertheless managed a weak chuckle before sinking onto his back.

"God's cock, what a fighter," he said.

Satisfying herself that the Earl was holding his own, Nora rounded the bed to check Christian. As she did so, she realized what her fury hadn't allowed her to notice in the scuffle. He was naked and bleeding all over the sheets.

She shut her eyes while her face heated like a baked tart. When no ribald comments were hurled at her head, she opened her eyes. Christian lay on his back, one leg bent and the wounded one out straight. He clutched the wounded leg with his good arm, while he kept his face turned away from her. Contrite, Nora realized he was in too much pain and far too weak to do anything.

"Drowsy syrup," she said, her embarrassment forgotten.

She snatched the bottle of sleeping draft from a table and poured another dose into a cup of water. Giving Christian no opportunity to refuse, she crept up on him while his eyes were shut in pain and forced the cup to his mouth. His eyes flew open, and so did his mouth. She tipped the contents down his throat. He coughed and sputtered, but he was no match for her, and she won. Most of the liquid went down his throat before he could stop her.

"I'll flay your arse," he swore, "you sneaking, sniveling little witch."

She skittered away from him and waited for the potion to take effect. He tried to rise from the bed, but his arms folded.

"Damn your soul, Nora Becket. Promise. Promise."

"I already promised, and I didn't betray you. Please, my lord, rest, and trust me."

"Trust a mouse."

He pointed a finger at her, and she watched it weave back and forth.

"Trust is for children and fools," he said. "Are you going to make me a fool?"

She touched his finger. When he didn't attack her, she wrapped her hand around his and lowered it gently to his chest, where she held it between her own two hands.

"I promised before God. And . . . I could never betray you. I—I love you."

"Jack Midnight was there. He saved my life." Christian stared up at the canopy. "The mouse rescues me. I feel like a sick snail, and she confounds my will at every turn. At every turn."

His dark lashes fell, and his voice faded. Nora let out the breath she'd been holding.

With Christian asleep, she was able to tend to both men in peace. In spite of the furor around him, the Earl hadn't awakened. She checked his wound, smoothed the covers over his body, and devoted her attention to Christian.

Although he had wrenched his wounds, none of his stitches had torn. Nora refastened his bandages, but once this was accomplished, she could no longer ignore the rest of him. God's mercy, who could? He was all long, straight lines of flesh broken by tight curves of muscle. His intimidating strength was concealed by deceptively smooth skin.

His legs were tangled in the sheets, and she began to untwist them. Grasping material near his groin, she paused and flushed, her brows furrowing. Looking over her shoulder, she reassured herself that she was alone and resumed her inspection.

She was no stranger to the male anatomy. She'd handled too many animals. But stay now, something wasn't right. He was too small, and if she touched him, he would be soft. Yet his codpiece . . .

Men were such cozeners, liars, cheats. Perhaps Lord Montfort did not deign to wear outsized protection, but there were many at court who did. The liars. What would happen if she touched him?

"Nora Becket," she murmured to herself, "you're fast becoming the bawd he'd like you to be." She pulled the covers free and spread them over his body. Much better, she decided. It wasn't proper for her to ogle him like a common trull.

From behind the door, she heard Arthur calling her name. She let him in and held her finger to her lips.

"Mistress," he whispered. "Hext and I have been out. To the palace."

"That busybody."

"No, mistress, it's good that we went. I'm learning better how to sneak."

"A godly pastime," Nora said.

"We heard about you. The whole palace was bustling, and when your father saw that the Queen was disturbed, he put it about that you'd vanished because of a sudden attack of a bad tooth." Arthur bobbed his head up and down when Nora gave him an astonished look. "Hext says it was to save his honor and prevent the Queen from interfering. Everyone thinks you're at the town house suffering, and meanwhile, your father searches for you by stealth."

"Then we have a respite. But we won't if you prance about the streets of London and catch my father's eye."

"I'll take care, mistress."

"I know, you've learned to sneak and lurk. Holy Mary forgive me for casting the child among knaves."

Arthur grinned at her, and she dismissed him. Returning to her vigil, she had time to think of the Earl's state. His wound was near the heart, though a clean one. No wonder the physicians hadn't dared to probe it. There was no way to tell how deep the puncture was and thus how grave the damage. The only thing to do was to keep the wound clean and the man still—and pray.

Christian's wounds were much less grave, yet she'd seen animals die of like injuries. Putrefaction could set in for no reason that she could perceive. If it did, this beautiful man would die a long and agonizing death. From her experience, keeping his wounds clean would increase his chances of healing. Why, she wasn't sure, but mayhap it was because God loved cleanliness.

Settling in the chair she'd put near Christian, she tried to rest while keeping alert for movement from either man. She couldn't resist reaching her hand out and resting it on Christian's bare arm. He hadn't heard her confession of love, but it was for the best. He was too ill and too distraught to bother about her.

Or had he instead ignored her because he didn't love her and didn't want her to love him? Nonsense. He didn't want her to marry the awful Flegge. But mayhap he felt sorry for her, or wanted to bed her first, or both. She didn't understand him, and she longed to ask him about his true feelings. Yet in all likelihood, if she did ask, he wouldn't tell. The possibility of getting Christian de Rivers to tell her his real feelings was as likely as getting the Pope to recognize the Princess Elizabeth as legitimate.

Nora brushed a dark lock of hair from his forehead. It was softer than her own hair, and its color was jewel-like in its intensity. She left off stroking it, for each stroke increased her longing for him and her urge to protect him. And his father, who loved Christian with a fierce, protective love that rivaled her own. What would she do if she lost both men when she'd only just discovered the miracle of their existence?

Sinking to her knees by the bed, Nora rested her forehead on the mattress and prayed. God wouldn't let them die. He was kind, and He knew that she needed Christian. Christian opened her up, freed her from a prison of uncertainty and fear, teased and plagued her into believing in herself. No, God wouldn't let him die. And when he got well, she would gather her courage until she was strong enough to ask him for his hand. Yes, that was what she would do.

Lifting her head, she whispered to Christian, " 'With you I should love to live, with you be ready to die.' "

Chapter
XII

Idleness was the root of all vices, according to some. For the next three days, Nora was safe from vice, for she had no time to do more than nap for an hour at a stretch. She changed bandages, sponged sweating and fevered bodies, changed bed linens, stoked fires, and tried to convince Lord Montfort to eat.

As his father succumbed to an ague brought on by his wound, Christian rested less and less. By the fourth day, with the Earl either delirious or unconscious the entire time, Nora feared that God would take the Earl for His own. That afternoon, though, he was lucid for a few minutes, and he came near to breaking her heart with his lack of concern for his own condition. His first thought upon awakening was for his son.

Nora was tucking a sheet under the mattress near the Earl's head when he stirred. She looked up to find a pair of dark blue eyes squinting at her. They grew round as recognition set in, but the effort to reason was too much, and he closed his eyes again before he spoke.

"My son."

"He is well, my lord. He lies beside you. He wouldn't budge, though I tried to wrest him from your side. Can I get you water?"

The Earl's hand fished blindly across the covers until it met his son's arm. "He sleeps?"

"Yes, my lord. I'll wake him. I promised I would if you woke."

"No." The Earl's hand dropped and he tried to lift his head. "No time. Tell him my wish . . . my wish . . . He should rid himself of hate. God will punish as he cannot."

Nora patted the Earl's hand, alarmed at the way his voice thinned like smoke in a gale. She had to put her head close to his to make out his words.

"Tell him I love him, and he is to—keep himself safe."

At first she thought he was dead, but then she felt the shallow movement of his chest as he breathed. The Earl's face blurred as she looked at him through her tears. He knew. He knew he had little chance of surviving, and even in dying he cared only to protect his son.

A strangled sound caused her to look up. She'd been so absorbed in the Earl, she hadn't seen Christian wake at the sound of his father's voice. He was propped up on his forearms, one hand fisted in the coverlet near the Earl's shoulder, his face buried in the crook of his other arm.

Nora sensed more than heard one lone sob muffled by the force of an indomitable will. Heedless of her own tears, she touched Christian's bare shoulder.

"By God's mercy, leave me," he choked out.

She didn't abandon sick strays; she wasn't about to abandon this man. She walked around the bed to him, knowing what she had to do. Coming up behind him, she grasped his upper body and hauled him into her arms in a sudden, rough attack that had him cradled to her body before he knew what she intended.

His head dropped to rest naturally on her breast, and for an almost imperceptible moment he clung to her. Then he began to fight, thrusting away from her with both hands. She merely wrapped one arm around his shoulders and the other around his neck and head. Squeezing, she pressed him to her, nestling his face against her neck.

He stiffened as his lips touched her skin. He sucked in his breath, shuddered, then burrowed his face into her neck. Sensing her victory, she hugged him with all her strength, and he let out a cry of pain stopped only by her flesh. She held him, rocking gently back and forth, while he trembled with unspoken grief.

The privilege of holding him and comforting him lasted only a short time. Too soon he lifted his head, pulled back from her, and peered at her tear-stained face. She felt his hand tangle in the hair at the back of her head.

Slowly, while he held her gaze with his own pained-filled one, he drew her down to his lips. It was a mystery to her that a kiss could hold off grief and seek solace, yet tell her through some unspoken language that he had become pain. His lips trembled, and she could feel the same quivering in his body. She delved into his mouth, kissing him roughly in an attempt to give him the ease he needed so badly.

At last she felt the trembling cease. It was her warning. He drew back, leaving her with a craving that wouldn't soon go away. As she suspected, he withdrew his body from her and lay back with his face turned to the side. He studied his father in silence while Nora scooted off the bed. She stood with her hands buried up the cuffs of her full-over sleeves, and as the silence lengthened, her fear grew.

"Give o'er, lady," he said at last.

"My lord?"

"Give o'er, for I will not need you. You may have my wanting, but I'll never surrender to need. Think you I want to feel this agony more than once in my life?" He turned his violet eyes on her. "I've been schooled in subtleties, beguilings, and fell corruption. It is my protection, and I need no other. Now leave me."

She opened her mouth to protest, but he shut his eyes and turned his face away again. She could feel the ice with which he infused his nature and knew that if she stayed, she risked an attack of words that would make burning at the stake seem a country lark. Weary and troubled, she left, closing the door to the bedchamber behind her.

He was afraid! He wouldn't be afraid if he didn't need her. And he wouldn't need her if he didn't like her. In a trice, her shattered spirits soared. A priceless discovery, his fear.

Marveling at her unlooked-for success, Nora set off in search of ingredients for a tincture she fed her strays when they suffered from ague. That evening the crisis in the Earl's sickness reached its zenith. She and Christian attended the injured man throughout the night as he battled the fever that threatened his life. Twice more she fended off attempts by the Earl's retainers to send in physicians. The battles passed unnoticed by Christian, who in spite of his own fever tried to keep his father's body cool by bathing it constantly, with Nora's help.

Refusing food, and taking water only because Nora said he would collapse if he didn't, Christian held his father while Nora periodically administered her concoction. She thought about giving it to Christian as well, but decided the perverse creature would balk. So they bathed, dosed, stoked fires, and changed sweat-soaked linen hour after hour until, as light began to filter through the diamond panes of the windows, Christian bent over his father with a damp cloth and fainted.

"God's mercy." Nora grasped Christian's shoulder and pulled. He was too heavy for her to move far, so she pushed a chair close and maneuvered him so that he fell into it. "My lord?" Brushing strands of hair from his face, she felt Christian's brow. His skin was flushed, damp with perspiration, and it burned almost as hot as the Earl's. Her dread burgeoned into real fear.

She tried to loosen the ties at the neck of his shirt, and as she did so, he moved. In disbelief, she saw his eyelids flutter, then watched him drag himself back from desperately needed rest. Slowly his eyes opened. The pupils were enormous, and his gaze lacked direction, but she could see the stirring of that unbeatable will. It roused, dragging the remnants of his senses with it.

"Father," he said softly.

She knew it was a request, and she moved aside so he could see the Earl. Christian lurched forward in the chair, his hand groping for the bed.

"He doesn't move," he said.

She turned, stooping to examine the older man, and felt the skin of his cheek. "God is merciful."

"*No!*"

Realizing that Christian had misunderstood, she quickly grasped his hand where it dug into the mattress. "No, my lord. His fever is broken, and I think he will live. God is merciful."

She had to help Christian from the chair and support him so he could touch the cool skin for himself, before he was convinced his father would live. Once Christian was settled in his chair again, she left the two so she could give the good news to the household. Seeking out Hext, she imparted her tidings, and soon the whole great house echoed with the sounds of cheers and whistles.

The next several days passed more easily for Nora's charges, and gradually she was able to get some rest herself. On the fourth morning after the Earl's recovery began, she was starting upstairs with a new batch of her herbal concoction when she happened to see Arthur's golden curls disappear through the front doors of the house. The heavy oak boomed shut, sealing off her cry. The little fool was off to practice his lurking and sneaking again, she thought. Her mind free of worry for the Earl, she could afford to devote herself to the proper behavior of her page. Lifting her skirts, she marched out of the house after Arthur.

He was already across the long court and through the gates, waving at the guards as he went. Muttering to herself, Nora dashed after him, slipping through the iron wings of the gates just before the guards slammed them shut.

She hadn't expected the street outside to be crowded, and she blundered into the path of a pair of Thoroughbreds. One was ridden by Blade, who hauled back on his reins. His big roan danced sideways, shouldering Luiz de Ateca's black stallion.

Nora spared the youth a glance and a peremptory smile. He'd visited the sickroom twice. Both times Christian had treated him to a round of orders and threats that would have propelled Nora in search of dark corners in which to hide. Blade had lashed back at first with gutter curses and threats of his own, then showed more restraint once he perceived the gravity of the Earl's condition.

At the moment all of Blade's considerable talents were put to use subduing his mount. Nora called out an apology and danced out of his way. She hurried down the street a few steps, shouting Arthur's name. When she came to the corner of the brick wall that surrounded the Earl's residence, a gloved hand shot out and grabbed her arm. She stumbled, put her hands up against a velvet-covered chest, and shoved.

"Got you at last," a man crowed.

She looked up. "Percivale." She stopped shoving simply from the shock of seeing the man. She'd forgotten him.

"You cursed woman. I'll teach you to humiliate me." Flegge began to drag her down the street. He whistled, and a groom appeared with his horse. "I've skulked about for days trying to find you. Finally spotted that whelp of yours, God curse his hide."

Nora dug in her heels, bringing Flegge up short. Blade called her name, and panic gave her own voice power.

"Blade, help!"

Twisting in Flegge's grip, she was able to face Blade and de Ateca. Blade was staring at her in confusion. She kicked backward at Flegge's legs and shouted again. She was rewarded by the sudden comprehension that flooded Blade's face. The youth's hand snaked to the dagger at his side, and he rose in his stirrups as Flegge threw Nora across his saddle.

Nora landed on hard leather. Instantly she braced her arms against the horse's withers and thrust her head up as the animal danced beneath her, unnerved by its master's sudden violence. She glimpsed Blade, his arm raised to throw the dagger. As the youth aimed, de Ateca lunged and caught his arm. Blade cursed, trying to free himself, but de Ateca wrenched the arm, pulling the boy off balance.

Blade slipped, and de Ateca used the momentum to haul him from his roan and slam him down across his own saddle. At that moment, the Earl's guards rushed in, and the *conde* and Blade were pushed from the black. The horse reared, and the guards scrambled for safety.

Nora felt Flegge mount behind her while he kept his hand on her back to hold her down. She called to Blade, but the youth was on the ground, pinned beneath the *conde*. Nora's last sight was of de Ateca straddling Blade, smiling as he gently tapped the youth's chin with his fist. Nora shouted for Blade, useless as it was, but Flegge had gained control of his horse, and she was jounced and bumped so hard, her vision blurred.

When she could lift her head again, the Earl's house was nowhere in sight. Flegge slowed his horse to a walk long enough to haul her upright to sit sideways.

He smirked at her and hugged her body to his. "You're going to pay, mistress. God's arse, you're going to pay."

In the chapel of her father's town house Nora sat, alone except for two guards, and prayed. She prayed for God to strike Percivale Flegge down before he could enter the chapel and make her his wife. She prayed that her father would change his mind, that she could sprout wings and fly away, anything that would prevent this marriage.

Flegge had spotted and followed Arthur two days earlier, and had thereby discovered her hiding place. He'd waited with much-tried patience for her to show her face outside the walls of the de Rivers gates. After snatching her, he had brought her directly to her father's house. With a curse and a backhanded slap to her face, William had announced that the marriage ceremony would take place at once.

That was half an hour ago. The priest would be there soon, and her father had promised to break all her fingers if she made a scene again. Exhaustion and anxiety had blurred her perception, and her lack of sleep had transformed the events and people around her into a slow dream.

Mayhap it was because she didn't want to believe that what was happening was real. Whatever the reason, she couldn't seem to grasp what was said to her as quickly as she should. As weariness dragged at her body, Nora mumbled prayers and pleadings until she heard the chapel doors being thrust open. Squeezing her eyes more tightly shut, she held her breath while she listened to the approach of her father and betrothed.

She was snatched to her feet, and William dragged her around to face Percivale Flegge. Nora blinked slowly at the man, then went on to study the household retainers gathered to witness the ceremony. Her father was ranting, but she couldn't seem to hear him. She examined the faces of her father's steward, an equerry, a clerk. Once, long ago, they'd been familiar to her, for she, too, had been part of William's household.

Her father shook her arm. "Stand up straight, girl." He shoved her hand into Flegge's and signaled to the priest.

Nora stared at her hand. It had disappeared. Her father had thrust it into Flegge's as though it were a torn glove for which he had no use. By God's mercy, she was tired of being shoved and pushed about at the whim of others. Resentment swelled into anger, and she clamped her jaw shut, grinding her teeth together, as she stared at the priest. They'd skipped the Mass, and the priest was prancing through the marriage ceremony at royal-post speed. Flegge muttered his responses, and Nora scowled at his complacent, gloating face.

The priest said something to Nora. She transferred her scowl to him and pursed her lips. In the quiet brought on by her refusal to speak, she could hear someone shuffle his feet. The clerk coughed.

Silence.

The priest repeated his question. Nora jerked her hand from Flegge's and folded her arms across her chest. William strode up behind her and yanked her to him by her hair, and she screamed.

A long whistle drowned out her cry. The chapel doors burst open, and a river of bodies flooded through them in waves, streaming over pews, down aisles, and toppling guards and retainers in its wake. William released Nora's hair to put his hand to his sword hilt. It was halfway drawn when a giant in home-spun planted his foot gently in William's stomach.

"Outnumbered, coney," the giant said.

William huffed and retreated from the bulk in front of him, his hand falling away from his weapon.

Peering about her in confusion, Nora witnessed several scuffles. An acrobat in scarlet, yellow, and green backflipped into a guard who was trying to strangle a minstrel. A young man who wore the riding outfit of a nobleman threatened to slice off the nose of the steward, while a beggar with false sores jumped on the back of the clerk and pounded his head.

Down the central aisle, the wave of intruders parted as the scuffling subsided. Quiet slowly prevailed, and Nora saw that the odd jumble of strangers had the upper hand. The giant beside her father whistled again, and the band turned to look at the doors. A tall figure appeared and strode toward the group in front of the priest.

Flegge growled. "Montfort."

Christian de Rivers strolled down the aisle slapping his riding gloves against his thigh, his pace rapid and businesslike. He stopped two paces from Flegge and surveyed the man, with his brows lifted.

"I warned you, Flegge." Christian ignored Flegge's cursing and nodded to William. "My lord, well met."

"Montfort, what madness is this?"

"I beg leave to introduce my friends," Christian said with a sweep of his arm and an easy disregard for William's irritation. "My father's men you know, and Roger Mortimer."

Nora's mouth nearly dropped open when she spied Roger grinning at her. Several young noblemen positioned around the chapel bowed to the group at the altar.

"But you've yet to meet my jewels, my treasures, my prized coursers," Christian added. He waved a hand at the jester, the beggar, and other ruffians. "Conjurers, priggers, whipjacks, prison-breakers. Victims of enclosures and evictions, rent raisings or lewd birth. As fine a band of spreaders of discontent to spoil, rob, and raven as were ever whipped at the cart's tail— my bosom family."

Nora slid between the giant and her father to stand beside Christian. He looked down at her, his eyes bright, his face flushed and damp. She almost touched her fingertips to his cheek, but he was in that mood. That fearsome, raw, and high-strung nastiness gleamed from his eyes, and she knew better than to touch him. His gaze flicked over the bruise on her cheek.

"As I said, Flegge, I warned you." Christian spoke lightly as he stroked his soft leather gloves across the palm of one hand. He clucked his tongue against the roof of his mouth. "You've irritated me, taking the lady from beneath my very roof when I was at my father's sickbed."

William burst in, confronting Flegge. "You said she was at an inn."

The two launched into an argument. Their voices rose, and Nora saw Christian's mouth twitch. It was the merest spasm, hardly noticeable, but she had seen it before.

"You shouldn't have left the bedchamber," she said, shaking her head in exasperation. "You were resting when I left."

The simpleton grinned at her.

"Bedchamber?" William's voice rose to a screech. "Bedchamber?"

Belatedly Nora covered her mouth with both hands. Christian's grin widened as she turned crimson.

Flegge backed away from the furious William. "It doesn't matter. I said I'd marry her and I will."

"Oh, no, you won't," Christian said.

"I will. The ceremony is almost complete. All it needs is for the girl to say 'I will' and we'll be married. Say it, Nora."

"Say it," William said.

Catching her father's glare, Nora cringed. He would hate her if she refused, she saw that now. Still the words wouldn't come out of her mouth. She tried to move her lips, but they stayed closed. Her eyes ached from holding back tears that came from wishing for what she couldn't have. Lord Montfort had come to help her out of pity, and perhaps gratitude. And she was making a spectacle of herself. Her tongue forced its way out to moisten her lips. She opened her mouth. As she did, Christian trampled over her newborn words.

"God's blood, of course she'll say 'I will,' but not to you, Flegge. To me."

"She's betrothed to me!" Flegge exclaimed. "It was I who was made to look the fool when she ran. I deserve her."

"You don't deserve the hand of Medusa in marriage," Christian said.

"My daughter is betrothed." William eyed Christian speculatively. "She's in the middle of marrying Flegge."

"Beshrew me, sir, for contradicting you, but Nora was in the middle of sharing a bed with me when Flegge interrupted."

William's roar made Nora cringe. Her face drained of color, and she felt her legs wobble. An arm wrapped around her shoulders, and she was dragged into the shelter of Christian's body.

"I'll still marry her," Flegge said.

Sighing, Christian addressed the giant. "Anthony Now-Now, my good fellow, toss this ferret into the Thames at once."

Flegge was snatched up by the collar, his arms and legs flailing, and carried from the chapel to the jeers of Lord Montfort's ruffians. Nora almost smiled, so great was her satisfaction at witnessing Flegge's humiliation. She looked up at Christian, but he was returning the calculating gaze of her father.

"You've dishonored my daughter."

"It's a fault, I know."

"I'll complain to the Queen."

"She hears complaints about me daily."

"Your title won't protect you."

"I know. Nothing seems to protect me from your daughter, so I've decided to rid myself of the necessity of protection by marrying her."

"Good."

"What?" Nora twisted beneath Christian's arm to gawk at him.

He was rubbing his damp brow. "My wits are addled from this fever."

"Get you home to rest when we finish here," William said. "We must petition the Queen for permission."

"Unbalanced humors, that's what it is." Christian gave his head a slight shake.

Nora chewed her lip as she assessed Christian's flushed skin and bleary eyes. "Father, Lord Montfort suffers from an ague. He doesn't know what he's doing."

"Of course I know." Christian whirled away from her, spreading his arms wide. "Come, kittens, our business here is finished, and if I stay, she'll dose me with her foul stew of roots and branches."

"Montfort, we haven't finished discussing terms," William said.

Christian vanished in the midst of knights, beggars, and thieves.

"Montfort, you're not running away from this. Montfort!"

"It's no use," Nora said. "He never listens to anything he doesn't want to hear."

"He'll listen to me," William said. "Son of an earl or no, he's not going to ruin my family's honor. The banns have been waived, all we have to do is change the name on the contracts. It shouldn't take more than a week to arrange."

"But the Earl is dangerously ill, and Lord Montfort suffers, too."

"It matters not," William said. "By next week, the Earl will either be dead or recovering, and either way, Christian de Rivers will have himself a bride if I have to bring the priest to his father's bier."

Nora shook her head and whispered, "He would kill you."

''Nonsense. In any case, you have no say in the matter. Get you to your chambers and refresh yourself. You look like you've spent the night in a rabbit's burrow.''

William strode away, intent on his plans to corner Lord Montfort. Hugging her waist, Nora sank down on a pew and tried to make sense of what had happened. Had Christian meant to offer for her hand when he invaded the chapel? He'd been so fevered, she wasn't sure he hadn't merely intended to ruin the ceremony. After all, he was distraught over his father and ill himself. To hold him to promises made while in such pain would be dishonest.

And he'd told everyone he'd seduced her! Though she herself had implied such attempts to the Queen, she hadn't gone so far as to claim carnal relations. But Lord Montfort's scruples were as rare as scales on a bear.

Sinking back, Nora rested her head on the hard wood of the pew. Ah, well, she'd wanted him, so what right did she have to complain about the way she got him? For she did indeed have him. Her father and the Queen would see to that. But in guarding her honor, they would also see to it that she would never know if he wanted her for herself—or out of charity.

Chapter XIII

Christian hopped down from the cart laden with baskets of freshly baked pastries. Simon Spry and Anthony Now-Now followed and began to unload pies, bread, and buns. Dressed in a white smock, his head enveloped in a baker's shapeless cap, Christian made a show of directing the delivery to his father's kitchens.

Grabbing a double-handled basket himself, he ducked into the house. Heat suffused the main kitchen, and he was engulfed in the bustle and scurry of preparations for the morning meal. No one paid attention to the baker and his apprentices, and Christian slipped out of the main kitchen with his basket and up the back stairs. At the doors to the Earl's chambers, the men on watch only lifted their brows at the sight of the heir sporting a dirty silver wig and a thick coating of flour on most of his exposed skin.

"How is he?" Christian asked of them.

"Fair, my lord," one said. "But he tried to sit up and took bad."

Christian shut his eyes for a moment, cursing his need to leave his father. Then he sighed and went in. Walking lightly, he approached the bed and stood, clutching the basket in front of him, and watched his father. Sebastian was sleeping. Pale, he seemed to have shrunk like a withering plant in a flowerbed.

"You smell like peach tart," Sebastian said with his eyes closed. He opened them and surveyed his son from cap to shoes. "And you look like you belong in an oven along with your pastries."

Christian set the basket on the floor and took out one of the small pies. He waved it before Sebastian. "Does it tempt you? Tarts are my specialty."

"What have you been doing, my headstrong?"

"Toiling in the kitchens of Bloody Bonner."

The Earl sat up too quickly and groaned. "God's wounds, I'm never going to get well if you keep scaring me like this."

Christian tossed the pie into the basket and pressed his father back down against the pillows.

"Forgive me, sire."

"You have plenty of clowns and disguisers among your minions. Why must you risk yourself?"

"Because I'm better at it than most, and I'm in a hurry. Think you I want to marry with the headsman's ax waiting outside the bridal chamber?"

Christian tugged the cap and wig from his head and ran his flour-covered fingers through his hair. He stopped when his father shook his head and chuckled at him, as he used to when Christian was seven. Sebastian's smiled faded, though, and he patted the mattress beside him. Christian lowered his weight to the bed gently so as not to jostle the sick man.

"What have you discovered?" Sebastian asked.

"Nothing," Christian said. "His clerks are clams, and his priests stuff their mouths with so much capon and mince pie that all I could hear was the smacking of lips and burping. But fear not, there are other ways. Mag will snare at least one or two of his priests in her house, for they're mighty fond of riding something other than donkeys of an evening."

"And the Queen?"

"Scolded like a godmother." Christian pounded his thigh, and a puff of flour rose from his smock. "She boxed my ears and threatened to fine me into poverty if I didn't marry Nora. God curse Her Bloody-Minded-Majesty."

"But she doesn't question your faith, you careless baggage."

"Nay, only my honor."

Sebastian breathed deeply, then let out a sigh. "Good. I was worried that she was privy to the attack."

"She's dying. Everyone knows it but the Queen herself. The whole city lets loose its bowels every time she takes to her bed. Blade has it from de Ateca that the Spaniards fear the country will go to Mary of Scotland and her French husband. I do believe they'd rather have our young Bess. Philip could marry her and keep England."

"She'll never consent to that."

"To sharing power? The Lady Elizabeth's grace? Not until cabbages sprout legs and walk." Christian stood, brushing flakes of dried dough from his apron. "I must bathe before I turn into a loaf and start to rise."

The Earl stayed him with a lift of his hand. "Before you go, you'll tell me why you must risk your life on the day of your wedding."

"There won't be time for disguisings after. I've sent word to Cecil that I must curtail my intelligencing for a few months. Someone has made Bonner suspicious of me, and I can't risk involving you or Nora, or my friends."

"You've already involved Nora. You're marrying her tonight."

"I've tried to explain, sire." Christian stooped to retrieve his discarded wig and cap and began brushing white dust from both. "It's not my fault she exposed herself to dishonor. The widgeon blurted out her presence in my bedchamber, and even a rook such as I couldn't stand by while she married that pestilence of a Flegge."

Shifting uneasily under his father's gaze, Christian began to hum the melody to a bawdy song.

"You were forced to it," Sebastian said.

"My wits sizzled by an ague."

"But bound to it by honor."

"Body racked with seizures, mind plagued and deviled."

The Earl snorted. "You know my feelings upon the matter."

"She's not so delicate or so timid as either of us thought."

Christian suddenly chuckled and spun around in a circle, his arms flung wide. "God's sweet patience, sire, you should have seen her prick those doctors with my sword. She had to lift it with both hands, but she never balked once. Whipped and kicked their tails out of the room with all the enthusiasm of a gaoler from the clink. I think my lessons and nagging have borne fruit."

"I've never seen you like this," Sebastian said.

Christian left off smiling to himself and flushed. With difficulty he met his father's gaze. "She saved your life, and I tried to get rid of her in spite of it. And then Flegge took her, and I nearly went mad. When they told me she'd been taken, I almost convinced myself it was for the best. But then Blade said something I'll never forget. He said I should think about what my life would be like without her in it." Christian grimaced. "He knows, you see, what it's like to have no one. So he railed at me that I deserved to lose her. Strange how fond of her he's grown since she doesn't approve of him any more than she does of me."

"And what would your life be like without the timid Mistress Becket?"

"I don't know," Christian said with a fierce laugh. "And do you know why? Because I'm afraid to imagine such a thing. Maggots must have taken up nesting in my brain."

Sebastian let out a deep sigh and settled back on his pillows. "Good."

"Your concern for me touches my heart."

"I feared you only lusted after the girl, but it is love, and I am content."

"Shhhh!" Christian raced to the door to make certain it was closed, then returned. "You don't have to let anyone else know my foolishness."

"It was good of the Queen to consent to hold the ceremony here. It would have grieved me to miss your wedding, my head-strong."

"You won't say anything about it, will you?"

"What?" The Earl grinned at his son.

Christian twisted the cap and wig. "Love."

"That is for you to do, and soon, for I'm sure you've tormented the poor girl into thinking you're marrying her out of perverse and reluctant duty, or to protect her. And since this isn't an arranged match, I can hardly speak for you. Get you gone, whelp. I tire, and you're dancing about the chamber like a destrier before a battle.''

Christian took the ring of three hoops with him and went in search of his betrothed. Flour-free, clothed in green and gold damask, and as nervous as a rabbit in a kennel, he gained entrance to the palace two hours after being dismissed by his father.

The ring he'd gotten from Unthank. It was of a deep reddish gold, filigreed, and made of interlocking rings. One was the betrothal ring. The other two they would exchange that night. And afterward, he would have Nora to himself. At last. The thought was enough to make him swell so much, it was difficult to walk comfortably.

As usual, he couldn't find Nora in any of the places she was supposed to be. Even her pen of strays was deserted except for the page Arthur. Christian showered the boy with comfits and promises of lessons at the bow, and resumed his search. Recollecting at last where he'd found her before, he realized he should have thought of that noisome garden sooner. She was bound to be there collecting fruit or herbs and hiding from the censurious eyes of Mistress Clarencieaux.

Wanting to surprise her, Christian cracked the door open and pressed his face to the gap. The sun had yet to reach its high point, and its rays still touched off silver fire in the remaining dew on leaf and petal. He could smell freshly turned earth.

Nora was gathering herbs, her gown a pink blossom amid the darker greens around her. A spade stuck in the ground near a rose bush warned him that a gardener might return soon, yet he stayed a moment to enjoy the sight of Nora. She wasn't a beauty like many at court, nor did she possess the wanton, pleasure-loving bawdiness of his dear Mag. Still, she had his heart tied to the chain suspended from her girdle, right alongside her enameled perfume case.

He saw she'd gathered some angelica root and was tying it in a bundle. Next she began cutting heartsease, her small fingers holding the plant while she cut the stem with her scissors.

Heartsease. It was used to invoke love. He'd tried to embarrass her once by pointing out this function, but she'd gazed at him somberly, assuring him it was more used to cure the pox. Christian remembered her air of gravity and concern, the way she'd completely missed his attempt to lure her into titillating conversation. He felt again the shock he'd experienced at discovering purity, kindness, and a gentle heart set down before him in the package of a rose and milk-skinned gosling.

What was she doing? He eased the door open a bit wider to get a better look, for Nora had collected a bunch of heartsease and seemed to be hunched over it. Abruptly, she jerked erect and darted glances around the deserted garden. Her movements were quick, and she'd paled. She looked his way, and he backed from the door. She'd seen nothing, however, for she sighed and crossed to the bench near the fig tree.

Intrigued, Christian watched her tie the heartsease into a bundle to be put in her herb basket along with the angelica. Once the bouquet was secure, she peered around the garden again, her head turning slowly, her eyes seeking out each corner and shadow. Her inspection complete, she fumbled at the neck of her gown.

She lifted the white lace over her breast, exposed a good bit of flesh, then searched beneath it with her fingers. When she withdrew them, she held something, but it was too small for Christian to see. Slipping the object into the bundle of heartsease, she tied another piece of string around the bouquet and placed it beside the angelica. Her hand hovered over the herbs, touched a petal, withdrew. Again she gave the empty garden a piercing examination.

Christian rubbed his upper lip with a forefinger, wondering what mischief she'd gotten into now. He was sure she'd just concealed a message of some kind. Mayhap she was plotting to rescue more abused creatures or adopt another abusive urchin such as Arthur. Whatever it was, he would have to interfere. She couldn't act on her own anymore; she must ask his permission and be guided by his word.

He stepped into the garden, locking the door behind him. As the bolt shot, Nora jumped up from the bench and yelped. Christian grinned at her astounded look, but stopped when she twisted her hands together and almost sobbed. As he approached, her eyes grew wider and wider, until he at last stopped before her.

She was afraid, he realized, and it was his fault for staying away when he should have sought her out immediately upon signing those contracts with her father. Only his father had been so weak, and he'd been so furious with himself for a yearning for her that he couldn't shirk.

"Don't quake so, chuck," he said. "I've come to throw myself at your feet in abasement."

Instead of bursting into a smile of gratitude, she gave a little whimper and dashed past him. Startled, Christian didn't catch her until she was at the door. Sweeping her up in his arms, he carried her back to the bench and sat down with her in his lap.

"God's breath," he said. "I admit I frighten whipjacks and gamers, but I thought we'd gotten 'round this skittishness. Be still, sweeting. I'm not going to eat you, not yet."

Nora subsided, her hands pressing against the gold embroidery of his doublet. He smiled at her, and for once tried to hold in check both lust and the urge to tease. His restraint was rewarded, for her eyes lost that trapped-animal intensity and her body relaxed.

"Are you listening to me now?" he asked.

"Yes, my lord."

"Are you ready to marry me?"

Her features twisted, and she looked down. "I . . ."

Christian hardly breathed, sensing that she was trying to say something of great import.

"I . . ."

"Yes, chuck?"

At last she spat the words out like a drowning victim spits water. "I love you, but you don't have to marry me, I won't hold you to it, I know you were just trying to help me get rid of Flegge, and I'm grateful, but really you only find me amusing and like to touch me, but you never wanted to do more than bed me, so it's quite all right. I understand, and I'm sure we can think of something, but you really can't keep trying to seduce me after this, because, you see, I do love you so much I think I'll die of it."

Christian stared at her, his mind working over that last bit of chirping desperation. "God has honored me with his blessing," he said at last.

She glanced up at him, but then cast her eyes down once more. "Yes. Yes. Well then, we agree."

"Marry, lady, we do not."

"We don't?"

"Nay. We haven't agreed upon anything, and we won't until you quit chattering like a peacock being chased by a cook. Keep still and close your mouth." He captured both of her hands. "I didn't say I'd marry you for charity's sake. I did it for my own sake. It seems I must have you. I know it doesn't make sense, but there it is. It doesn't matter whether I'm beset with an ague or well, furious with you or pleased, inspired to quote poetry or spew curses at you. No matter what happens—and many odd things happen when you're near, my sweeting—I can't rid myself of this desire."

"But—"

He shook her, causing her French hood to slide askew. "I love you, you cursed mite." Annoyed at having to say it, he thrust her from him and snapped like an angry turtle. "God's blood. Silly gentry mort. Teasing little badger."

Something tickled his cheek, and his blustering ground to a halt as Nora's lips brushed his jaw. He turned his head.

"Don't cry, chuck. I'm sorry." He pulled her back into his arms. "God help me, I've never been in love, and it's damned . . . uncomfortable." He heard Nora chuckle. "I feel beset by enchantment, set upon and befuddled."

"And it gives you a harpy's tongue," she said.

His gaze drifted to her lips. "Come dull the edge of my tongue then."

He slipped his tongue into her mouth and pulled it out again. She started and gaped at him, but he nipped at her lower lip, at her chin and jaw. Running his tongue down her neck, he licked his way to the lace of her gown. He rested his cheek on her soft flesh and cupped his hand over her breast.

He stayed there, holding her, testing his control and tormenting himself at the same time. His groin ached and his thigh muscles tensed as he sought to remain motionless. He broke quickly. Turning his face to her chest, he buried his nose in her softness and squeezed her breast.

"Christ, Nora." He tore his hands from her and again thrust her away. "Run."

"My lord?"

"Run." His voice rose to cruelty. "Run now, or I won't stop until I have you beneath me with my phallus buried between your legs. Run!"

He didn't hear her go. Hands braced on the bench, he fought the throbbing, the roaring lust, the pain. At last he was able to lower his body to the bench, lying half on the ground and half on its surface, his burning cheek pressed against the cool stone. In time he opened his eyes, and they lighted on the herb basket. He touched a finger to a blossom of the heartsease, and a glint of metal winked at him. Smiling, he remembered Nora's secretive manner. She'd hidden something in the flowers.

Fishing inside the bouquet, he retrieved a small metal bead. From it protruded the edge of a piece of paper. Christian teased it forth. Unrolling it, he studied the senseless markings while ice poured into his veins. A cipher. Matters of import were put into cipher, not the contrivings of innocent maids. What had Nora gotten herself into?

He rolled the cipher back into a cylinder and inserted it in his cuff. His clerk would translate the cipher, then he would go to Nora with it and demand an accounting. Whatever she was doing would have to stop. Foolish mouse. He wouldn't permit her to engage in any court intrigues, no matter how her soft heart ached to champion some lost soul. Her safety was more important. It was the most important thing in his life—next to killing Jack Midnight.

He returned to find his house in the condition of a wrecked ship. From his sickbed the Earl had given commands that the mansion be prepared for the wedding of his heir. Christian had forgotten to do so himself. The steward rushed continually from the great hall to the kitchens to the stables and back to the hall, bellowing orders and working his staff into a frenzy.

The clatter of furniture being moved and the quarreling of servants drove Christian abovestairs. He'd given Nora's cipher to his clerk with orders to break the code. Expecting the cipher to be translated easily, he forgot about it and retreated to the reading room he'd had built off his bedchamber.

They were waiting for him. Christian stepped inside the chamber and met four pairs of accusing eyes. Inigo Culpepper bowed, but remained out of arm's reach as Christian glared at him for allowing this intrusion. His castigation was forestalled when Mag rushed at him. Throwing herself into his arms, she chuckled and planted a hard kiss on his mouth. Three of her girls surrounded him, and his body was invaded by small hands.

"Kit, my succulent," Mag said, "if you're to cleave to a wife from now on, we want a last taste."

"Mrrw—mmmmhhh." Christian tore his lips free of Holly Cushion's. "No you don't. Inigo, you sod, get them out."

"Now, Kit," Inigo said, throwing up his hands. "You know Mag does what pleases her."

"And you do please me, Kit." Mag walked around Christian, hands on hips, and eyed him from head to toe. "God's cock, you've pleased me since the day I taught you how. You were such a wild thing when I first had you, so young but full of need. And never had I a better pupil in my thieves' school."

Christian twisted in Holly's arms and ducked out of the circle of female flesh. He dashed around Inigo, putting the cutpurse between him and the women.

"And I'm grateful, Mag, but I need no more lessons, and I'll be damned if I want you draining me dry before my wedding night. Begone or I'll feed you to my men."

"Ah, you're breaking my heart."

"What heart?"

Mag laughed and beckoned to her friends. "Come, gossips, our charger resists being mounted, and we've plenty of those who don't resist and who do pay."

The girls left, and Mag held out her hand to Christian. He came out from behind Inigo and took it. She put her palm to his cheek and looked into his eyes.

"I came to see if you were happy, my madcap." She studied him for a moment before kissing him. When his lips remained still under hers, she freed them. "You could have come to say farewell."

"I'm not going anywhere."

She stroked his cheek. "No, you're not, but I think we're

family, you and I and Inigo and the rest. And we're losing you to a gentry mort more surely than if they'd clapped you in the Tower.''

"Nothing will change."

"Then you'll come to me of an evening and carouse with Inigo and Spry and Now-Now?"

"Sometimes."

"And I still have leave to do this?" She kissed him once more while her hands slithered down his body to cup him. When he shoved her hand away, she stepped back, shaking her head. "Do I?"

"No."

"Why not, Kit, if nothing's changed?"

Christian hurled himself away from her. "God's curse on you! I don't know why. Must I account to you and Inigo and every other runagate and trull . . ." He stopped, sucking in air between clenched teeth. "Leave me be, Mag. I'm not fit for company, and I'll broil you on the spit of my ill temper. Give me peace on this day, and I'll come to you with gifts and songs on another."

"Ahhhh."

"Don't look down your nose at me. Inigo, show her the door."

"He's been choleric and maggoty-headed since he met that Becket gentry mort," Inigo said.

"I have not, you son of a bawdy basket. Get out, both of you."

Mag slipped her arm through Inigo's and nodded. "He's worse the longer he has to wait to get between her legs."

"I'll garrote the pair of you," Christian said. "No. Where's my whip?"

A guffaw from the cutpurse made Christian cast about for something to hurl at his head, but Mag hauled Inigo out of the chamber and slammed the door. Her chuckles intertwined with Inigo's laughs, and Christian vaulted over the table to follow them. His steps faltered before he reached the door.

He had no wish to make himself a spectacle, and the pair of them had joined forces to bait him. Christian knew when to bide his time. Subsiding into a chair, he dragged a heavy tome onto his lap. He turned the pages of the book, forcing himself to translate the Latin. After a while, his hand stole to the pouch at his belt and withdrew the three filigree rings. He was linking them and unlinking them when his body servant came to fetch him to the Earl's chamber.

Anxious, he questioned the man on the way, and was relieved that nothing had happened to his father. He arrived to find the Earl lying in the midst of clothes of violet and silver satin.

Propped up on a mass of pillows, Sebastian was stroking a silver feather in a cap of violet. "There you are," he said to his son. "Hext, get him undressed and into that tub at once."

"What means this?" Christian asked as his man took his arm and led him to a wooden tub.

"It's late, you foolish baggage," Sebastian said, "and we've been searching for you for an hour."

Christian glanced out the window. "It's night."

"You were always a bright child."

"I hadn't noticed."

"I've taken care of everything."

Christian was shoved gently into the tub, and he sank down into the warm water. He'd been musing in that reading room for hours. He was indeed maggoty-brained.

"I ordered this outfit made up yesterday," his father added. "Hurry, Chris."

Feeling that events were getting beyond him, Christian set himself to regaining his composure while body servants readied him. By the time his wits reassembled themselves, he was dressed. He held up his arm. It was encased in violet satin slit with silver. He frowned.

"It's the color of your eyes," the Earl said. "My heir must marry in finery that befits his station, and I wanted you to enchant your delicate lady."

"You're not well," Christian said. "You shouldn't tax your strength with unimportant matters."

"I'm fine. And someone has to take charge. You're not yourself, my headstrong." Sebastian lay back on his pillows. "But I shall rest until time for the Queen to arrive. I have a few minutes."

The servants were tidying the Earl's bedchamber in anticipation of the Queen's presence. A chair of state and canopy were

already in place. Christian chewed his lip while he looked at his
father, worried that his negligence had cost the Earl badly needed
rest. As more candles were lit about the chamber, he heard the
voice of his clerk.

"My lord," the man whispered, "the cipher."

The clerk was standing at Christian's elbow, strangling his
cap with his hands. His complexion was white splotched with
two blotches of red on his cheeks, and his body strained toward
his master.

Christian turned away. "Not now."

"My lord, the cipher." The clerk's vice vibrated with sup-
pressed urgency.

Christian sighed. "Follow me."

In his own chamber, Christian held out his hand. The clerk
produced a parchment from beneath his robe and handed it to
Christian. He shuffled back toward the door, under his master's
perplexed eye. Then Christian read what was written on the
parchment.

*I know not what became of heretics who were in Montfort's
house, and they must be found. The Earl still lives.*

Christian looked up at the clerk without seeing him. "You're
sure of the words?"

"Yes, my lord."

"You may go."

Alone, Christian read the two sentences again and again
until the words jumbled together. His brain refused to work. He
stood in the middle of his chamber reading each word like a boy
at his lesson. He repeated them in a whisper until they drummed
a tattoo in his head: *The Earl still lives, the Earl still lives, the
Earl still lives.* But for how long?

She was a spy. For the Queen, or for Bonner. Who better
to capture a jaded knave like himself than an innocent mouse of
an intelligencer? And her pryings and plottings had almost killed
his father.

"God's entrails."

Christian squeezed his eyes shut to blot out the smell of his
father's blood, the gut-searing helplessness he'd felt as he
watched Sebastian waste away before his eyes. She'd been part
of it. He wasn't sure how, but she'd known about the heretics,

and from the note, it was clear she'd been telling someone else about them.

No wonder she'd planted herself in his house as a nurse. She'd been looking for the heretics and needed an excuse. She had been spying for someone, and that someone had laid a trap that had nearly killed the one person to whom Christian gave his love. His father might still lose his life. Often those severely wounded appeared to recover, only to die suddenly of a fever.

His hands shaking, Christian went to a sideboard and poured a goblet of wine. He wrapped both hands around the bowl of the vessel and stared at a tapestry without seeing it. She'd nearly killed his father, the sniveling bitch. Lying, whining, mewling virgin harpy.

And he was trapped. He couldn't refuse to marry her without inviting the Queen's wrath and suspicion. The maggots in his brain were back, and they chased each other back and forth inside his head, buzzing and stinging until he exploded with rage. A great bellow erupted from his chest and throat, and he flung the goblet across the room. It hit the wall and bounced, clattering its way to rest against the foot of his bed.

Christian stood motionless, legs planted wide apart, fists clenched, chest heaving. Fury at his own stupidity and impotence burned through his awareness, purging him of all schooling, all civility, all restraint. As he cursed his way through every obscenity learned in the stews and alleys of London, he vaguely realized that he had to regain his sanity. And quickly.

The Queen was coming. And with her, Nora. He clung to his bedpost, body hunched, while he fought to master his rage. Eventually he was able to stand erect and release the post. After long moments, a layer of ice flowed over the cauldron of his hatred, wrapping him in a veneer of stability.

He wiped his brow with the back of a trembling hand. Remorse at the pain he'd unwittingly caused his father nearly cost him hard-won control. He shoved the dangerous thought away.

There was no choice. He would have to marry the bitch. Marry the woman who'd nearly killed his father, and might still do so if he wasn't careful. But she wouldn't get the chance, because she would be too busy worrying about whether her husband was going to kill her. And he would kill her.

Imagining his hands wrapped around Nora's throat, he saw himself squeeze and squeeze, saw her face turn purple. No!

"Damn your soul, Nora Becket."

Very well. He couldn't kill her. After all, she had failed. But he would have revenge, and in having it, tear her out of his heart.

Slowly, muscles trembling, breathing ragging, Christian lowered himself to sit on the bed. He fell on his back and covered his eyes with his arm. Words from Catullus spun through his brain.

> *I hate, I love—the cause thereof*
> *Belike you ask of me:*
> *I do not know, but feel 'tis so,*
> *And am in agony.*

Chapter XIV

God had answered her prayers, but Nora hadn't expected Him to work His will in so fantastic a manner. Yet she was a little ashamed. If she'd been one of King Arthur's knights, she wouldn't have searched for the Holy Grail. Instead she would have sought a living, virile treasure with the temper of a basilisk and the eyes of a summer night. But the treasure didn't know how unworthy she was to capture him. Her birth and thus her self might be tainted, and in any case, she possessed neither beauty, nor great wealth, nor clever wits. It was a perplexity. Why did he want her?

Nora was ensconced in the Queen's barge, packed into a gown more costly than any she'd ever worn. A gift from her troubled mistress, it was of stiff yellow damask that chafed her skin. Already she had scraped her palm on the setting of five diamonds that marched down the front of the bodice. Her hand toyed with another of the gems, which perched above her waist.

Still puzzling over Lord Montfort's attachment to her, she paled at the memory of his last visit. He'd done it again—burst upon her when she thought herself concealed, and almost discovered her secret. She would have to ask Cecil for a new way to pass ciphers when he returned from France. Her heart thumped painfully as she remembered how frightened she'd been when Christian surprised her, and how frantic had been her desire to lure him from the garden. He hadn't noticed, though. He'd been too concerned with declaring his love. And the declaration had caught her unaware.

Had he not kissed her, she could have persuaded him to come away from the garden. The ways of the Lord were unfathomable, for she was sure it was His plan that Christian de Rivers corner her in her secret place and torment her. He'd done it too often.

So she'd found herself teetering on a pinnacle above a sheer drop, swaying between fear of discovery and lust. After he'd sent her away, she'd had no opportunity to sneak back to the garden and assure herself that her cipher was still hidden, for Mistress Clarencieaux had swept her up in preparations for the wedding.

Flustered, that's what Nora was. She'd been caught up in her shock, it had been time to go to the Montforts' house before she knew it. Her daze hardly lifted until she found herself climbing the stairs to the Earl's chambers. On either side of the staircase stood the Montfort retainers. She tried to lift her chin and greet them with a smile, but the feat was beyond her.

What was she doing? She didn't know this man. Not at all. And she was about to submit herself to his care for the rest of her life. She couldn't. But if she didn't she would lose him, and he was as necessary to her as food and drink.

She reached the landing and forced her legs to move as the Queen, her ladies-in-waiting, and Nora's father approached the Earl's chamber. Arthur walked in front of her with another page, holding the bride's laces. The yellow ribbons hung from her sleeves, and Arthur had nearly tripped on one coming upstairs. Another royal page walked before Arthur, carrying a silver cup filled with spiced wine and decorated with a spring of gilded rosemary. Nearby, musicians played lutes, viols, and flutes.

Trying not to stumble, Nora at last gained the Earl's chamber. Sebastian was bowing to the Queen as best he could while sitting up in bed, and Nora heard them conversing. Suddenly the Earl looked at Nora, giving her a smile of reassurance that evoked a grateful smile from her own lips. The Queen took her chair of state, and a door opened near it.

Fear crawled and wriggled through Nora's body as Christian stepped into the room. At first all she saw was his face. Warm, almost dusky skin, set jaw, and too-calm eyes. He made his obeisance to the Queen, then turned to her. Smiling a smile that would have beguiled a mad Turk, he approached and took her hand.

It was the touch of his hand that calmed her, for his beauty sent her into fits of agony. How could she ever hope to be worthy of someone so rare and so charmed? Glancing around, she noted his friends and those of the Earl, her father, and the Queen's attendants. Roger Mortimer stood close by, and she spotted Inigo Culpepper half concealed by bed hangings.

What was wrong with her? she wondered. She was so addled, she missed the Mass. She'd participated in the wedding ceremony and exchange of rings in a state of agitation brought about by a war between her own uncertainty and her inability to believe she'd gotten what she craved so desperately.

A whoop from Roger Mortimer woke her from her daze. Hot lips covered hers, transporting her into unaccustomed happiness. She tasted sweet wine flavored with spices and opened her mouth for Christian. He lifted his head and stared into her eyes as though he'd lost something there. His fingers dug into the flesh of her upper arms, and she winced.

"Forgive me, dear wife," he said. "My desire overcomes me."

"My lord," she said with a smile of indulgence. "Perhaps it is the wine."

"I think not, for I've only had two bottles."

"Two." She noted the steadiness of his body, the directness of his gaze. "Are you sure you had two whole bottles?"

"And part of another. It's not an ordinary day. Now open your mouth again."

Another shout of joy from Roger, and then they were surrounded by laughing, jibing young men. Scrambling over one another, they snatched at the bride's laces, eager for trophies. Christian laughed and called for wine.

"Bring the contracting cup."

The silver cup was brought forth, and Christian held it for Nora. She drank, and then he, and after him the entire company. As the cup passed from one to another, Christian led Nora to the Queen for her blessing. When this obligation was over, Mary retired, taking her aura of gloom with her. Nora watched her new husband stare after the woman, his thoughts concealed behind a courtier's respect. When the Queen was gone, he escorted her to his father.

"Sire, I present my wife to you for your blessing."

Nora flushed and curtsied to the Earl, who held out his hand. She knelt, and Sebastian placed his hand on her head.

"I bestow upon you my blessing, Nora de Rivers, though I'm sure in the months to come there will be times when you'll swear you're cursed. The boy is all gale, squall, and tempest."

"But my lord," she said, "such a beautiful storm."

The Earl laughed, and Christian knelt beside her. "I beg of you, sire, don't frighten my bride before I've taken her to me. I'm not so terrifying." He cocked his head and met Nora's gaze. "And I wouldn't want her to feel cursed. After all, I married her for love, not punishment. So let there be no talk of chastisement for my sweet chuck, no yammering about chains or flagellation, as bachelors are wont to do."

"What do you mean?" Nora asked, frowning.

"I but try to tell you that I'm not one of those howling bucks who rail at their fate upon taking a wife, my innocent."

The Earl laughed again, and Nora cast her eyes down. Unused to flattery, she had no answer. She needed none, though, for Christian swept her away to accept the congratulations of their guests. Immediately after, they were carried below to a feast of celebration. Lamb, kid, pig, and venison paraded before them. Christian plied her with swan and peacock, but kept her cup filled with cider instead of wine. His own goblet was filled and refilled with a heavy charneco. He let her taste the wine—a port—and she grimaced.

"Serves you right," he said. "Drink your cider, chuck. I don't want a mizzled bride in my bed tonight."

Nora turned red, until she feared her skin would burn and char. The devil leaned back in his chair and laughed so hard, the retainers below the salt craned their necks to look at them. Christian lifted his goblet and drained the whole of it. Although certain he'd finished off another bottle, Nora had yet to discern any mark of drunkenness in him. His eyes had grown heavy-lidded and he moved with the lazy grace of a well-fed wolf, but then, he'd often fooled her with his ability to feign a torpor foreign to his nature.

The feast progressed, and Nora found herself growing excited and a bit fearful. Tonight there would be no holding back, no fear of discovery. Tonight she could touch him, hold him, revel in the pleasure of his body. If she had the courage. His fingers touched her neck, and she jumped.

He was looking at her through half-closed eyes, his dark lashes concealing his thoughts. "It's time. I can endure no longer." He rose, taking her with him, and brushed his lips over her hand. "Go to my bed now."

She stood still, gaping at him, until he signaled to a waiting woman. He turned Nora around by her shoulders and gave her a push. Immediately she was surrounded by women and, to the accompaniment of bawdy songs and jests, was escorted upstairs to Lord Montfort's chambers.

She was surprised when the procession turned away from the apartments occupied by the Earl and his son and took a path to a separate wing of the house. Mistress Clarencieaux squeezed her hand reassuringly when Nora asked about their destination.

"You're blessed, my dear, to have married so dashing and courtly a nobleman. The Earl told me that his son conceived of this idea only minutes before you arrived for the ceremony. A hidey-hole for the two of you. No one uses this wing, and Lord Montfort has had chambers prepared at the farthest end of it, so that none will disturb you. It's not every bride whose husband wishes to devote all of his attention to her alone."

"But the Earl is still sick," Nora said.

"And improving. He would tell you to set your mind to pleasing your husband."

The new suite Christian had chosen was indeed isolated. They paraded through unoccupied rooms, one after the other, until they reached open double doors sentried by Nora's own smiling maid and an assistant given to her by the Earl. Inside, beyond an antechamber, Nora found a sitting room and two bedchambers.One was flooded with light from dozens of candelabras, its velvet-draped bed the center of the yellow glow. Roses and honeysuckle decorated the room and filled it with their scent.

In spite of the beauty of the room, Nora grew more apprehensive as she allowed the women to prepare her for the night. She was afraid again. As long as he was with her, she felt more love than fear, but when they parted, her old feelings of unworthiness haunted her. She knew what to expect of him this night. She didn't know what to expect of herself, however, or what he would ask of her.

Worried and skittish, she climbed into the bed, feeling small and insignificant in its confines. The minutes passed while her companions tidied the room until at last they all stood about casting glances of confusion at one another. Where were the men?

Mistress Clarencieaux left to inquire. She returned in fits of laughter.

"They're chasing Lord Montfort." She collapsed against the bedpost and chuckled. "Lord Montfort vowed they weren't going to strip him like a new babe and frighten his lady with their bawdy jests and ribaldry, so Roger Mortimer jumped on him. Now they're all clambering after Lord Montfort, who has led them a chase to the stable roof. He's on top of it with a bottle of wine jeering at the others. They're all too drunk to make the climb to him, so they're trying to snare him with nets and ropes."

"He could be hurt!" Nora exclaimed. She threw back the covers and began to climb out of bed, to the protests of the ladies.

"Nay," said Mistress Clarencieaux. "They've snared themselves instead. Mortimer is tangled in a net with that young cousin of Lord Montfort's and two of the Howards. The rest are trying to free them, but they only make the tangle worse."

Nora covered her mouth, but a giggle escaped anyway, and soon every lady in the room was laughing.

"A tangle indeed."

The low male tones doused the sparks of laughter. Nora, who was sitting on her heels in the middle of the bed, leaned around Mistress Clarencieaux to find her ladies backing away from Lord Montfort. He stood with his back to the closed door of the chamber, his legs crossed at the ankles, and surveyed the women through deceptively drowsy eyes. A bottle dangled from the fingers of one hand, while the other hand was splayed against the dark oak behind him.

He ignored the women who smiled at him in favor of studying Nora. Her mouth went dry under his stare, and she ducked back behind Mistress Clarencieaux. Ashamed of her cowardice, she ran her hand over her nightgown, fiddling with lace and ribbons. Christian remained where he was as the women's whispering and giggles died. When the room was quiet, he inclined his head at Mistress Clarencieaux, flung the door wide, and bowed.

"My thanks, good ladies, for your care of my bride. I bid you all good even."

He bolted the door shut after the last woman, then turned back to Nora.

"You were on the stable roof," she said.

He grinned and saluted her with the wine bottle. "Am I not clever, sweeting? I knew you'd die a thousand mouse deaths if Mortimer and his gang threw me into your bed naked."

It was mortifying, but she put her head under the sheet while he laughed.

"Come out of there, widgeon."

She pulled the sheet down, and her hair fell about her face. Parting it so that she could see, she found Christian had resumed his pose against the door. He was watching her, all trace of humor gone.

"I deserve to be called mouse," she said in disgust.

"Perhaps." He drank from his bottle without moving his gaze from her face. "But a dragon lurks within that too-sweet body. You and I both know that."

She wet her lips and saw his gaze fasten on her mouth. "A dragon?"

He didn't seem to hear her.

"Do you like Tom Wyatt's poetry?" he asked. He drank from the bottle again, then quoted a bit of the nobleman's verse.

> Driven by desire, I did this deed,
> To danger myself without cause why,
> To trust the untrue, not like to speed,
> To speak and promise faithfully.
> But now the proof doth verify
> That whoso trusteth ere he know
> Both hurt himself and please his foe.

Nora's forehead puckered, and she stopped trying to strangle the lace of her gown. "I don't understand."

"God's blood, why do you have to be so—lush?"

"Have I done something wrong, my lord?"

Christian didn't answer. Shaking his head, he thrust away from the door and glided over to the bed. Nora longed to reach out and touch this silver and violet fulfillment of her dreams, but he was in a rare, contemplative mood, and she hesitated.

The spring shower of his laughter caught her off guard. He threw his arms wide and collapsed on the bed, legs hanging off the side. His arms flew out, and she snatched the wine bottle before it fell from his hand.

"I'm befuddled, chuck, and you must forgive me. I think of myself as a dangler after bawds, not a husband, and finding myself charged with the care of a faery sprite turns my wits to porridge." Lifting only his head, he leered up at her. "Shall I woo you in the courtly style?"

His head dropped back on the covers. Screwing up his mouth more in concentration, he clasped his hands together and recited again. " 'What would ye more of me, your slave, require than for to ask and have that ye desire?' "

"You, my slave?" Nora giggled. "I think not, my lord." She felt the tight knot of apprehension in her chest dissolve as he grinned up at her.

"Very well. If you won't believe me enslaved, believe me enchanted."

He came upright suddenly, giving her a start as he captured her in his arms and brought his lips close to hers. She tried to steady her breathing, for he was sure to notice she was panting.

"Don't be afraid, chuck. This act, this mating, I decree that there be nothing but pleasure in it for you. I want you to remember the pleasure." He paused, closing his eyes and pressing his lips together, then said three words: "Remember it well."

Confused, Nora tried to turn her head aside, but he followed her, touching her lips with his. She relaxed at the feel of their warmth and pliancy. Sprinkling her face with raindrop kisses, he slid his hands up and down her arms, lightly, barely touching, teasing. He ran the tip of his tongue down her neck, stopping just above her breast.

His hand gently cupped her, then he backed away to leave her crouching on the bed with her eyes closed. When she opened them, he'd already begun to divest himself of his clothing. She caught a glimpse of a frown, but it vanished, burned away by a grin that held all the bawdiness and lechery of the finest of London stews.

He winked at her. " 'To teach thee, I am naked first; why then, what needst thou have more covering than a man.' "

As he spoke those last words, his hose flew across the room, and Nora watched him stalk toward her. She had little time to view him, but it was enough. An expanse of chest with a shallow valley down the middle separated by hillocks of tight muscles covering his ribs; straining thighs, at the apex of which burst forth an engorged phallus.

Curiosity and horror warred within her as Christian put one knee on the bed. The moment he angled his body toward her, she scrambled away.

"You aren't like my animals," she said.

He paused, noting the direction of her gaze. "No, but God fashioned men and women to take pleasure of each other, and we're a man and a woman." He touched her hand. "Don't be afraid."

"I don't think I like this." She was telling the truth. He'd changed. There was a tension about him, and he stared at her body's most private parts.

"I've given you too much time to think."

Taking her by the shoulders, he lifted her to him. He wrapped her in his arms and kissed her gently, then increased the pressure of his lips with each new kiss. The arm that supported her back flexed, the muscle bunching and then loosening. Its ceaseless movements told Nora of the force he held in check. The arm tensed again, and he leaned into her body until she was prone on the bed.

Her gown spread out on the bed, and Christian covered it and her with his nude body. At the feel of his weight, she instinctively pushed at his chest, but he whispered into her ear, his breath tickling her skin.

"The hunt is over."

The rest of his words made no sense to her, for his breath

heated her flesh and made her fingers and toes tingle. That tingling caused her to dig her fingers into the bunched muscles on his upper arms, and she discovered how pleasing it was to caress them.

While she let him explore her mouth, she began to explore the vast lengths of his exposed flesh. She rubbed her palms over hot skin, learning the planes of his back, the feel of his ribs, the dip at his waist. Her arm stretched to its fullest length and her hand touched springy, taut flesh. She dug her fingers into the muscles of his buttock.

At her touch, Christian arched his back and cursed, driving his hips into hers with the nightgown still between them. She could feel the pressure of his sex, its heaviness, churning into her loins, rousing them. Without instruction from him, she clutched his buttocks in both hands and forced his groin to the place where she needed it to be.

Her actions elicited another curse from Christian. He lifted his body and tore her gown away, then settled himself between her thighs. Frightened by his sudden violence, Nora cringed, but when his warm body lay on hers and he nudged her with his engorged flesh, fear vanished.

She was growing moist, swelling and aching. As he rubbed his sex against her loins, directing his movements to a single point that throbbed with each stroke, her thighs spread wide. Digging her nails into his flesh, she pushed his hips down and her own up. Bucking, she almost lifted him off the bed, and when she did, he slammed her back down, hard, and bit her neck.

He slipped his hand between their bodies. She caught her breath, then nearly screamed when he touched the place he'd aroused with his sex. His fingers stroked and teased and pinched, and she lost all sense of herself, of him, of the room. Pleasure coiled tighter and tighter through her body as he stimulated her, driving her to madness. She pressed herself against his fingers and cried out at the spasms his touch released at last. He whispered to her, urgent, erotic words that sucked her into climax.

While Nora shuddered, Christian shifted, lifting his hips. She groaned, still in that delightful agony, as she felt his penis butt against her swollen flesh. Her eyes flew open. His were filled with a violet rage, but then he shut them and ground his teeth together. He slipped his phallus into her body, pushing gently. Still in the throes of her own pleasure, she writhed against him.

"No! Don't," he said. His arms quivered as he held himself above her. "No."

Ignoring him, Nora squirmed again, trying to draw the source of her arousal deeper, to massage the ache within her. Christian resisted for a moment longer, then cried out helplessly and rammed his flesh into her body. Stings of pain jolted Nora from her passion. Sinking her teeth into the flesh above his nipple, she gasped with each thrust of his body. Lost beneath him, she could hear his ragged, uncontrolled gasps. Then he shouted, jamming his phallus deep into her, and she felt the tip of it touch her womb. He kept it there, holding himself stiff while his flesh throbbed and burst.

Impaled, Nora felt her own pain recede. After a while, Christian seemed to regain the sanity he'd lost and released her, slowly lowering himself from his arched, strained position. He collapsed on her, arms and legs spread wide, and turned his face away. He said nothing, but kissed her shoulder. Nora lay quietly, her hands skimming over his back. She could feel his penis still throbbing inside her. The sensation made her smile and bury her face in his neck.

After a moment, she sensed a change in him. The muscles in his arms flexed again, over and over, but he remained silent. His weight was making it hard for her to breathe. She pushed up on his chest, and he rose to support himself on his forearms. His face was flushed. Beads of moisture dotted his forehead and upper lip. She brushed a lock of his hair from his cheek.

His gaze raked her face, then danced over her chest and down to the point where their bodies joined. Surprised at his continued silence and the sudden tension in his body, Nora lifted her brows.

"My lord, is something wrong?"

He put a hand to her cheek. His thumb traced over her lips, then he slipped the hand down to her neck. He looked into her eyes.

"Have I brought you pleasure?"

She ducked her head and nodded. Placing his hands on

either side of her face, he drew her up to meet his gaze. Puzzled, she watched his eyes brighten.

He smiled at her. It was a sweet, yearning smile that reached to his voice as well. "Do you love me?"

Nora was sure God had granted her heaven when he smiled and asked so shyly of her love.

"Oh, yes. I—I've loved you for the longest time."

"Pleasure and love, I thought so."

Without warning he pulled free of her body. He was gone so quickly that Nora lay where she was for a moment. Then she sat up, gawking at him while he walked to a chest and withdrew a robe of red silk. Donning it, he came back to her, eyeing her as he tied the belt.

"I, too, am pleased, for it's not every day a man marries a spy who has tried to kill him."

"What—"

"I found your cipher, you little bitch." He folded his arms and stood over her, bare feet braced apart. "You've been spying on me all this time, and you betrayed me to someone. You betrayed me and almost caused my father's death."

She clutched the sheet to her breasts. "No."

"And if you don't tell me who the cipher was for, I'll make you wish I had the stomach to kill you."

Nora looked into his eyes and saw the detached gaze of the executioner. In that moment she realized he'd cut himself off from her and was picturing her death.

"You nearly killed my father," he said softly.

Feeling the strength drain from her body with each quiet word, she shook her head. "I didn't. I would never do that. It was meant for—" She bit her lip. How quickly he'd frightened her into almost blurting out the truth.

"For whom was it meant? Save yourself, Nora. Try again." When she refused to look at him, he leaned over her, catching her wrist and squeezing it. "God, I want to kill you. Why can't I kill you?"

She gasped at the pain, trying to free herself but to no avail. "I tell you the cipher was harmless."

"I'll have the truth from you. To whom did you send your messages?"

"I can't tell you." The fingers around her wrist tightened, bringing tears to her eyes.

"You can publish my doings like a purveyor of broadsheets, so you can damn well tell me who benefited from your sneaking and prying."

She cried out as he began to shake her, jerking her about until she feared her neck would snap in two. Then she felt her body leap as she was thrown across the bed. Landing on her back, she blinked to steady her vision. When she could see, Christian appeared above her.

"Tell me what I want to know, Nora."

She'd heard that tone before. He'd used it on de Ateca and Jack Midnight. Void of anger, flat and distant, it heralded the retreat of compassion, of pity, of honor, of conscience. Disbelieving, Nora could only shake her head. As she did, Christian drew away from her. Before her eyes, he changed, transforming into Kit. Loose-limbed, relaxed, a touch of mirth in his eyes, he burst into light chuckles.

"Very well, I'll find out for myself. It won't take long." The laughter stopped, and his eyes narrowed. "And now I'll give you the truth, though you've withheld yours from me."

Leaning against the bedpost, he caressed the velvet hangings while he watched her, his eyes mere slits. Nora drew her knees up to her chest, still unable to take in all that was happening.

"The truth, dear fool, is that I lied."

"About what?" she asked fearfully.

"About loving you, of course. Do you really think I could love a plain mouse of a thing whose prattle of kittens and puppies evokes the sleep of the dead?" His hand kept stroking the velvet. "Ah, no. It was a plot, you see. At first I only wanted to see what it was like to delve between the legs of a country virgin. Later I needed to keep you out of mischief and in thrall while I poked about to see what your evil had wrought."

Like a child's stick puppet, Nora kept shaking her head. Her body hunched as if she could protect her soul from his cruelty by curling into a ball.

"Y-you don't love me?"

A trill of laughter stabbed at her. Once she would have exulted in its beauty.

"Love you?" He shook his head as if marveling at her

gullibility. "Mayhap I should make it clear to you for your own good that your father is quite right. No man would want you. Does a man love clumsiness, pasty-faced, cooking-pot plainness? Can you believe that I really hanker to bind myself to a small crow with the stomach of a worm, who snivels and whines all day and grubs about in the dirt after weeds?"

Some kinds of pain were too great to take in all at once. As she listened to the man she loved reveal his disgust and hatred of her, Nora died in small bits, her happiness pouring from her in streams of tears. It was true, what people said about hearts breaking. Spasms of agony ripped through her own, making her clutch her chest and moan. He was still talking, hurling gibes at her, but she was already drowning in pain and couldn't hear all of them.

"By God's holy foot, you should whimper," he said. "I want you to whimper and cower and whine. That way I don't feel so guilty for not killing you."

He stepped closer to her, studying her as a butcher studies a carcass he has dismembered. "You see, I wanted so badly to kill you. But even I, lost to decency as I am, can't kill a woman. So I'll comfort myself with your suffering. If I can't kill your body, I'll kill your happiness, your pleasure, your blessings of life, and any small enjoyments I detect that give you respite from my revenge."

"Please," Nora said between sobs that nearly choked her. She couldn't look at him and kept her face buried in the crook of her arm. "Please, I d-did n-nothing."

Christian grabbed her hair and snatched her to him. She gasped, trying to tear his hands away, but he stuck his face in front of hers.

"I hate you. Almost as much, no, more than I hate Jack Midnight. You're my wife now, in my control, and you'll stay that way for the rest of your life—unloved, unwelcome, surrounded by people who know what you are and hate you for it."

He cast her from him, then disappeared into the adjoining chamber, slamming the door behind him. Nora lay where he'd thrown her and gaped at the place where he'd last stood. His words, the ugliness of his true feelings for her, beat at her like spiked maces, drawing her soul's blood.

Plain, unloved, stupid. Plain. Stupid. Plain, stupid, plain, plain, plain. I hate you.

Shrill and piercing, Nora's cry shattered the silence of the deserted wing of Vasterne House. And close on her cry came the sound of Christian de Rivers's laughter.

Chapter
XV

The bridal chamber smelled of candle wax, roses, and honeysuckle. The last flame guttered and vanished, throwing the room into complete darkness. Garments lay strewn about, over stool and chest and vacant bed. In the corner farthest from the canopied scene of her destruction, Nora crouched. Her wild hair drawn up in a knot, her body wrapped in a sheet, she pressed herself against the paneling of the wall.

The agony had ebbed with her strength, and now it only lapped at the edges of her perception while the rest of her mind fell into blessed vacancy. When she began to hear noises, the ordinary creaks and moans that beset a house at night, she cringed, thinking he had returned. Once roused, her thoughts stirred, and she plunged into despair.

She was afraid. More afraid than when Jack Midnight and his band had attacked. More afraid than when her father had tried to make her marry Percivale Flegge. Lord Montfort hated her. What lunacy had possessed her to make her think he might want her?

He had confirmed all her doubts, all her secret fears that she didn't deserve what she most craved. And when she faced her own unworthiness, saw it reflected in his eyes, she gave up hope.

Relief was to be found in death, and Nora dearly wanted that relief. Sometime during the night, after her tears stopped, she had gone so far as to search the chamber for the means to kill herself. She found a dagger in one of the chests and pointed it at her heart, but the act was beyond her. Of all the causes of her pain, this was perhaps the most costly, for she found she was too much of a coward to kill herself.

Nora shifted her weight, for her hip was going numb. Her back ached, and her eyes and mouth were dry. Wondrous strange it was, that small discomforts seemed so important when she faced the death of love.

She gave in to the discomfort and uncurled her body from the corner. She felt as stiff as a farthingale as she propped herself upright. Holding the sheet around her with one hand and lifting its trailing end from the floor with the other, she took slow, hesitant steps, unsure of her direction. As she hovered in the middle of the room, she heard sounds from the next chamber. Lord Montfort's body servant was greeting his master. The night was over—for everyone except her.

What was she going to do? He hated her, but his hatred was based on misunderstanding. If only she could convince him that she hadn't betrayed him. He might not love her, or even like her, but at least he wouldn't try to kill her with humiliation and ridicule. But she couldn't betray Cecil and, thereby, Princess Elizabeth. She must try to convince Lord Montfort of her innocence, yet in order to do that, she had to face him. She didn't think she could do that.

During her deliberations, Nora washed and dressed in a gown she found laid out in the dressing room next to her chamber. Hurt and blood-smeared, she feared being caught naked by the man who called himself her husband. She tugged at her heavy overgown until it draped smoothly over her petticoat. The brocade opened in a V below the waist in front to reveal the silk and lace of the undergarment. She was fastening a girdle and pomander at her waist when three whispering maids burst into the chamber, carrying water and towels. The girls stopped and gaped at her.

"My lady," one blurted out, "you're clothed."

Nora had no opportunity to answer, for her father appeared, barging past the maids. Casting a brief glance at her, William stalked into the bedchamber and stared at the wrecked bed.

"Gave you a rough tumble, did he?"

Nausea snaked through her vitals at his comment, and she pressed her fingers to her lips. William dug among the clothing and sheets, ripping them aside to reveal bloodstains.

"Good." Snatching the soiled sheet, he dragged it off the bed. "Now I can go home."

Nora watched her father leave without glancing her way a second time. The maids whispered among themselves, but Nora paid them no heed. His aims accomplished, her father was leaving—in the manner of a merchant abandoning the scene of an auction.

A well of emptiness opened deep inside Nora. The room vanished, and she felt herself sinking into a pool of nothingness. Into that murky void someone shouted her name. She started, waking to see the maids retreat.

"Nora."

It was Lord Montfort. She lifted her skirts, preparing to run, but he was in the room before she could move. Shadowed, violet eyes impaled her, and she backed away as her husband advanced. The ravaging Kit was gone, and in his place stood the imperious and furious Lord Montfort.

"Get downstairs," he ordered.

Nora kept backing up until she came up against a wall. Terror robbed her of speech. Lord Montfort stopped less than a hand's width from her, and she could feel the heat of his body and his wrath. That wrath seemed to feed on the sight of her. When she failed to move or answer, his hands fell to the lacings of his codpiece. Staring into her eyes, he smiled.

"I told you to get downstairs." Strong fingers jerked at the silk lacings.

Nora's gorge rose as she perceived his intentions, and she bolted. Running through the connecting chambers, she didn't see Inigo until she stepped on his feet.

"Christ, you witch. Have a care for my toes." Inigo steadied her with a hand on her arm, but she shied away from the anger that suffused his tone. This man hated her, too.

"What is it?" Lord Montfort asked.

Nora jumped and whirled to face him. He was walking toward them, his hands busy with his lacings.

Inigo jerked his head at her. "The master is asking to see both of you. Wants to visit with his son's beloved."

"No."

"Kit, he knows you're up and about. You know how he is—won't rest proper, too busy seeing to everyone's contentment. The steward is coming to fetch you and the little traitor."

"God's blood." The words were squeezed out between clenched teeth and stiff lips. Montfort turned on Nora, grabbing her arm.

She cried out at the pain of his grip, but he hauled her close and ground out his commands.

"You will dissemble in front of my father. We're in love. Joyous, silly with it, beset with fair madness. And you, my wondrous bitch, you are my willing, doting slave. Give my father cause to fret, and I'll make you wish it was Flegge who took you to wife."

Dazed, Nora could only nod. The gesture was sufficient, and she found herself dragged by the wrist out of the deserted wing and through the house to the Earl's chambers. Halting in the antechamber, Montfort pulled her to stand beside him. He snaked an arm around her waist and bent over her suddenly. Fastening his mouth over her own, he sucked at her lips until they stung.

Nora wriggled and made strangling noises as she fought him and her own fear. Just when she thought she would collapse with terror, he released her. She could hear his labored breathing, but her vision refused to clear. She could only stay where he held her, fighting for her own breath.

"Now you look like a maid newly initiated instead of a frightened duck," she heard him say.

The arm at her waist tightened, drawing her close, and Montfort guided her into his father's presence. Confusion reigned over Nora's thoughts, and she missed the Earl's greeting. She came to herself when Lord Montfort left her to kneel at his father's bedside. From a distance she watched him kiss his father's hand and bestow upon the older man a smile of jewel-like brilliance. Before she could gather enough of her wits to be surprised at Montfort's sudden change, he was back and leading her forward.

"Nora," Lord Montfort said, "Father is speaking to you."

"Don't chide, my headstrong," Sebastian said. "I can see for myself she's bewildered. Give me your hand, Nora."

Nora stuck out her hand, and the Earl took it.

"Are you well?" he asked.

Her lips ached and stung, and she cast her eyes down. "Yes, my lord."

The Earl patted her hand. "The blushes and discomfort will pass, my dear. But mind you, don't let Christian pleasure you into submission. He wants taming."

"Sire . . ." his son began.

"No protests," said the Earl. "I've spent too many years battling that will myself not to know what's best for you. Now sit. I've ordered our meal brought up, and then you both must retire to that bridal nest of yours. I've sent everyone away on the excuse of my health so that you'll have no interference."

Lord Montfort gently shoved Nora into a chair and stood behind it while he conversed with his father. Nora tried to follow their speech, but all her wits scattered when Montfort's hand dropped over the back of the chair and came to rest on her bare neck. She cringed, half-thinking to rise, but his hand was there to stop her. It stroked up and down her flesh, and she knew it would appear the gesture of an obsessed lover. Judging by Sebastian's smile, even his own father was convinced. Only she knew that her husband wanted to strangle rather than caress.

A meal was set before them, and Nora tried to eat. The idea of food was repellent, but the savagery in Montfort's gaze when she played with her knife spurred her to stuff bits of bread into her mouth. It seemed hours before the Earl told them to be gone, but she gained the outer chamber at last. Montfort's hand left her waist to fasten around her upper arm, and he dragged her back through the house to the bridal wing again.

Once in her bedchamber, he thrust her from him. She stumbled and rounded a chair, placing its bulk between them, but he wasn't paying attention. He strode up and down the length of the room, muttering to himself.

"He knows me too well. Soon or late, he'll begin to suspect.'' Montfort stopped, his fingers tapping the hilt of his dagger. ''He's stronger and has more color of late.''

Nora watched her husband warily, but he appeared to have forgotten her. Easing from behind the chair, she began to creep away.

''Come back here.''

Nora's feet sped faster.

''I said come back here. If I have to chase you, it will be with a whip.''

Sliding to a standstill, she clasped her shaking hands, then turned, taking a step in Montfort's direction. He was eyeing her with that special loathing he reserved for her, and it took all her meager courage to walk to him and stand before him. To her relief, he didn't touch her.

''We're leaving,'' he said. ''Pack at once, but don't bring a maid.''

''But—''

''Obedience,'' he snapped. ''I'll have your obedience, or would you rather I had you stuffed in a chest and trundled out of London in a wagon?''

''B-but—''

''Answer me. Do I have your obedience?''

''Yes.'' At his lifted brow, she corrected herself. ''Yes, my lord.''

He stalked away.

''But what of Arthur, my lord?'' she called after him. Please God he wouldn't make her entirely alone.

''The whelp will stay here and serve my father.''

''Oh, please—''

''Or I could throw him out on the streets.''

''No!'' She stretched out her hand in supplication.

''Then we understand each other. You submit to my will, and I allow the boy to remain in my father's household.''

He was waiting for her answer. Nora fought the urge to run, to hide. Hugging her waist with both arms, she said, ''Yes, my lord, we understand each other too well.''

Christian trudged down the path, dragging his pack behind him in the dust and trying not to think about the past two days. He'd believed himself well settled in his hate, enough to do things he hadn't done in years. Not so.

The pack thumped along behind him, bumping at his heels, somewhat like his anger at Nora, which nagged at him, following him, nipping at his sanity. Like the peddler's pack, his wife contained desirables, false treasures. It was his torment that he craved those treasures even when he most wanted to toss them in the nearest chamber pot.

And touching her had been Hell. He'd lost himself in her sweet nature, forgetting her duplicity as he touched Heaven. In loving her body, he'd found unlooked-for solace, a harbor that sheltered and delighted, teased and pleasured. By all God's mercy, he had yet to succeed in wiping from his mind and senses the taste and feel of Nora Becket—all roses and honeysuckle, pink lips and white-rose skin. His only cure lay in remembering his father's near death. This memory, this spur and goad, haunted him. It gnawed at his entrails even as his groin swelled at the mere thought of her body.

Christian stopped. The pack thumped his leg, and he kicked it.

"Christ!" He pressed his fists against his forehead as the twin serpents of his dilemma writhed and battled within him. His hands opened and slipped down to cover his mouth. Blindly he stared down the forest path.

I hate, I love . . . I'm in agony.

The trees before him blurred, and Christian closed his eyes. He opened himself to the feel of the wind on his skin, the creak of tree branch rubbing against tree branch, sounds that reminded him of years spent sleeping in the forest, hiding, fighting for survival and freedom from slavery. When he opened his eyes again, they were free of moisture.

He rounded a bend in the path and stopped once more. He could see the gate in the wall. It led to the kitchen yard at the house of Elizabeth's jailer-host.

Hauling his pack over one shoulder, he adjusted the hood of his patched and torn cloak and ambled toward the sentries who stood at the gate. One of them yawned while the other swatted flies away from his face. At his appearance, the two perked up.

Christian grinned. Country life was country life, from village to village all over England. If there wasn't a festival or fair, the days took on an unrelieved sameness that put the wits to sleep. A visit from a peddler toting city trinkets and the latest ballads and gossip set even the greatest household atwitter. He lifted a hand in greeting and began his cheap-jack's cant.

"What is't ye lack? What is't ye lack, my lads? I've come from the city with fine wrought shirts and smocks, sweet gloves and silk garters, fine combs and glasses to charm the lasses."

Both sentries grinned, and one threw open the gate for Christian. He ducked inside, calling to serving men, turnspits, maids, and cooks. At once he was surrounded by chattering, laughing folk. Christian swept his pack to the ground with a flourish and a bow.

"What will ye have, fair maids? Come buy, come buy, else I'll take my wares and fly."

The kitchen yard continued to fill with excited servants. Christian paraded masks for wearing abroad, perfume, pins and threads, lace, stomachers, and gold bracelets. He was dangling a scarlet ribbon in front of a milkmaid when one of the windows three floors above the yard was thrown back with a crash. A vase hurtled at him, and Christian jumped aside as it shattered on the cobblestones at his feet. A woman's deep voice shouted at the group below.

"By Great Harry's beard, what discord and noise is this?"

A pale face framed by red-gold hair poked out of the window, and Christian's customers scampered away, all except the sentries. Those two tried to hide behind their pikes.

"Peddler," the woman called, "begone with you."

Christian swept an arm out and bowed low. "Fine lace and gold pomanders for my lady," he said in his wheedling voice. "Rainbow ribbons and mysterious spices I have."

"Guard, beat this man for his impertinence and cast him out." The red-gold head retreated.

"Sweetmeats!"

The head reappeared.

"Delicacies from the East, my lady. Figs dipped in honey and Persian wine, sweet marchpane, cherries preserved in spices obtained from Greece and Turkey, tart of almonds."

"Bring the fellow up at once."

Christian was bundled into the manor house, his arms still

laden with trinkets. Several older men in velvet gowns clustered at the entrance to the lady's suite, and one of them lifted a hand, halting the sentries.

"Search him."

Rough hands pawed at his body, and Christian set up a yowling protest until one of the guards cuffed him. His wares were inspected and tossed back into his pack. A guard shoved him into an antechamber and slammed the door, shutting Christian inside. A maid beckoned to him, her manner that of a harried cat.

"Quickly, man. The Lady Elizabeth's grace has been discomfited by your noise. She threw a book at my head."

Christian hurried after the woman and into the princess's closet. As he stepped into the chamber, Elizabeth turned from the window. He bowed to her and set his pack down. The princess said nothing. Walking around him in a circle, she inspected his dusty jerkin and the worn hose that clung to his thighs.

"A ragamuffin peddler. A cheap-jack with the tongue of Judas and the wiles of a doxy, I trow. Your sweetmeats must needs be finer than your sweet self, my man, or I'll have you clapped in the stocks."

Christian pulled an ivory box from his pack.

"Alas, my lady, the poor comfits in this box can never rival your sweetness."

"A pox on you. Give them to me."

Christian held out the box with both hands. The princess took it and settled into a panel-back chair. Lifting the lid, she smiled and plucked a comfit from its nest. It disappeared into her mouth, and she chewed while surveying him. Between chews she demanded to see his wares, but when her lady-in-waiting squealed at the sight of a gold pomander, the princess hurled a chair cushion at her.

"Out with you, silly woman. Your shrieking will stop my heart or make me puke."

The maid squeaked and trotted from the chamber. A silence fell as the Princess stuffed a fig in her mouth and fingered a bottle of scent. With her mouth full, she addressed Christian.

"One of the jewels in my shoe is loose. Have you silk thread the color of a bluebird's wing?"

"Aye, gracious lady."

Elizabeth rose, jerked her skirts up, and rammed a velvet-clad foot down on a stool. "Amend it at once."

Kneeling at the Princess's feet, Christian grasped the shoe lightly. Elizabeth pulled her foot out of the slipper and stepped on his hand. Holding him trapped, she whispered while glancing around the room.

"The hose fit you better than the habit, my Lord of Misrule."

Christian spread his fingers out on the stool beneath Elizabeth's foot and kept his eyes down. "Your acquaintance remains in France and none has heard from him."

"Have you taken to wearing jester's paint, or are you trying to match the color of your eyes with those smudges under them?"

"King Philip takes the Queen to task for refusing to settle the succession. The council rant at her night and day to name your heir, though there are some who have sent missives to the Queen of Scots."

"She calls me bastard, does my cousin Mary of Scotland." Elizabeth removed her foot and sat back down in her chair. "She'd bring war to England and put the people to the French yoke."

Christian sank back on his haunches and took up needle and thread.

"I have counted your supporters, Your Grace. That is, I have stopped counting them, for they are too many."

Elizabeth pounded the chair arm with her fist. "They do me no good if my sister kills me before she dies."

"But that is what I've come to tell you, Your Grace. I've word that the Spanish have decided they hate you less than they hate the French, and that a weak young woman on England's throne is preferable to a young woman on England's throne who also has a French King for a husband."

"Who told you this?"

Jabbing his needle into the velvet shoe, Christian said, "De Ateca."

"And how did you persuade the *conde* to bare anything but his body to you?"

"I threw younger bait at him, and he tried to devour it. While he was stalking it, his tongue came loose from his brain."

There was a pause while Elizabeth drummed her fingers on

the arm of her chair. Christian plied his needle and kept his senses alert for the faintest sound that might herald an intrusion.

"The more ill she becomes," Elizabeth said at last, "the more nobles skulk away from court to throw themselves at my feet. If she hears of it, she might lose what is left of her mind and kill me."

"But Philip won't allow it."

"Mayhap."

"And your jailers seem more afraid of you than you of them."

Elizabeth grinned, then threw back her head and laughed. "God's arse, Christian, I thought to have you swearing to protect me and mouthing all sorts of comfort."

"Your Grace had a lion for a sire, as I well know. You'll devour this nest of rabbits they've set about you."

Biting off the knotted thread in Elizabeth's shoe, Christian moved to kneel before her. He slipped the shoe on her foot, then kissed her hand. As he made to rise, she put a hand on his shoulder, holding him in place. She searched his features.

"You look to play the ghost, my Lord of Misrule? I see pain in those violet eyes where once I saw mischief and wickedness."

"A trifling matter, Your Grace. Unworthy of your notice."

She lifted his chin with her fingers and forced him to look at her. "What few men I can trust, I can't afford to squander. You're in trouble."

"Bonner tried to get his hands on me."

"But he hasn't, and Bonner wouldn't rob you of your appetite. God's blood, you can't afford to waste that spare flesh of yours. What's wrong? Tell me quick, for my maid will return soon."

Christian sighed, and his shoulders sagged. "I've taken a wife, Your Grace."

"Beshrew you, what possessed you to do that?"

"She spies for someone, an enemy. And she nearly killed my father."

"Who is she?"

"Nora Becket."

Elizabeth shook her head. "You lie. You and little Nora the

mouse? Nora and Kit? Impossible. And she couldn't hurt anyone. You're addled, my boy."

Shoving his sleeve up to his elbow, Christian bared a long scar and held it up for the princess to inspect. "This is a token of her love for me. I have several, but she marked my father as well—a dagger in the back that just missed his heart."

Long fingers traced the scar, and Christian shivered.

"There is no suffering at another's betrayal where there is no love," Elizabeth said. "I've spent a lifetime on the edge of a chasm, balancing, spinning, teetering. I've learned to judge people. Nora brims with innocence and kindness, two qualities I've learned to prize since I don't possess them myself."

"I hate her."

"I know." Elizabeth paused to listen to the sound of women's voices in the next room. "They're coming back. Listen to me, my wild one. Take no action before you consult our acquaintance. He'll know the truth of it."

"As Your Grace wishes."

Christian kissed Elizabeth's hands, then turned to his pack. He was stuffing baubles in it when the Princess's ladies entered with the guards behind them. He was shoved out of the house and into the kitchen yard, where he was surrounded by household servants again. It was several hours before he could leave the manor and pretend to saunter along to the nearby village.

Anthony Now-Now waited for him in the forest with horses and fresh clothing. Christian threw his pack at the giant and stripped off the patched cloak.

"We got her to Falaise," Anthony said before Christian could ask, "but she weren't happy about it."

"And my guests?"

"Aye, Kit. Simon Spry, Inigo and his band, and Mag and her doxies. Most of them's there already."

Christian settled a black cloak on his shoulders and fastened its silver clasp. He cinched his belt tight and adjusted the scabbard that held his sword.

"And my father?"

"Walked about his chamber today. Sends his love."

Taking the reins of his horse from Anthony, Christian mounted. He removed a sealed letter from the pouch in his belt and handed it to his servant.

"Take this to the Earl and return to me at Falaise. And remember, not a word about our sweet traitor. And quit shying away from me, you dolt. It's not you I'm going to punish."

"We all jump and shrink in your presence these days, every whip-jack and bawd."

"Marry, sirrah, you've not the courage of a nursing babe."

"Nay, Kit. Every one of us owes you a life. Glad to pay back a little of your care, we are. It's just that we all seen you take vengeance before and feel sorry for the lady."

Anthony barely dodged a blow from Christian's whip.

"Sorry?" Christian hissed. "Sorry, is it? By God's mercy, it's my father you should feel sorry for. She put him in Hell, and me, too. I tell you I watched his life drain from him, slowly, knowing he suffered because of me." Christian's horse danced sideways at the sound of the whip and his raised voice. Christian subdued the animal without taking his eyes from Anthony. "Know you this, I'll hear no more mewling about my bitch of a wife and her misfortune. The next man to give her so much as a comforting look will find his eyes carved from his head."

Hauling his horse about, Christian kicked him into motion, leaving Anthony Now-Now to choke on dust and his master's fury.

No one was going to stop him, Christian told himself. He would listen to no persuasions from weak fools. His soul craved vengeance, and he would have it in spite of the voice in his head that whined and howled in protest. He wouldn't listen, for to listen was to weaken, and he'd promised himself long ago never to be weak again.

Chapter XVI

It was almost sunset the next day before Christian emerged from the forest to view the grass-covered plain that heralded the approach to Falaise, and Nora. A moated country house, Falaise rested on a hill that dominated the rolling meadows around it. It was old—his ancestors had built the manor even before the Tudors killed off the last of the Plantagenet kings nearly eighty years before—but Christian preferred the place to his family's seat, Castle Montfort. The castle was a great stone pile, dank, cold, and forbidding.

Perhaps the castle would have been a more appropriate prison for his wife, but Falaise was a day's ride from London, and he wanted to be close to his father. In addition, he'd sent men to search for the laborers who worked in the cipher garden and had to be near to receive any news from his intelligencers. And he felt better about taking Nora to his own house for punishment, for when he found out, his father was sure to cavil with him for what he'd done.

Kicking his horse into a trot, Christian rode across the meadows. As he neared Falaise, he could see reflections in the water of the moat—the bright green of the ivy clinging to the house, the creamy stone of its walls, the Persian-silk blue of the sky. Red brick chimneys jutted from the roof, concealing the corner room at the back of the house where he'd ordered Nora taken.

He slowed his mount as he rode over the drawbridge, acknowledging the ducking heads of several villagers on their way home from making deliveries at the lord's house. At the stairs in front of the main door, he pulled up. A groom took the horses's bridle, and Christian swung down. He was halfway up the stairs, cloak swinging with each stride, when a whizzing sound made him halt. A sliver of thin metal pierced the front door a moment before Simon Spry opened it. The thief blinked at the dagger that impaled the oak beside his nose, then stepped back inside the house and slammed the door.

Christian slapped his riding gloves against his palm and spoke to the dagger. "Good eventide, my comfit."

"Whoreson vicemonger," Blade said from somewhere at Christian's back.

"Odd how you manage to utter the vilest coney catcher's obscenities with the accent of an Oxford student. Have you remembered your past yet?"

Blade stamped across the courtyard and up the stairs, passing Christian and then whirling to face his captor, standing one step above him. "No, I haven't, but that's not what has me ready to piss melted lead. What have you done to Nora?"

"Attend to your own affairs, my sweet, or I'll teach you how."

Christian stepped around Blade, but the youth ran up the stairs to plant himself in front of the door.

"She's corpse pale and shivers in the sun's heat, and she won't talk to me. You've set your pack of wolves about her and let them take nips at her flesh. God's cock, I knew you were vicious, but I thought you fancied Nora. What's she done?"

Tucking his gloves in his belt, Christian slowly closed in on Blade, who set his feet wide apart and glared his defiance.

"Angel's morsel, get out of my way."

"What did she do to you?" Blade asked with a smirk. "Wasn't she a virgin?"

Christian's hands flashed out. Blade's arm was twisted behind his back while an arm choked his throat. Christian lifted his victim and proceeded to ram Blade's head into the door in rhythm with his couplet.

> You are, will be or have been
> Unchaste in fact or will.

After tossing the now limp Blade down the stairs, Christian stepped into the shadows of the entryway. "Unhappy consequences befall you when I hear the subject of my wife's chastity tripping off your tongue. I'll send someone to wipe your nose and carry you to bed, my comfit."

Inside, Simon Spry waited to take Christian's cloak. The older man jutted a whiskered chin at the door. "Hotter than Mag's petticoats, he's been. Furious at being made to wear the saddle after being ridden bareback all these weeks."

"Trust not the innocence of youth, Simon. Remember what I was like at his age."

"You're not much older than Blade now, and I trust you."

"Then you're crackbrained, you old prigger."

Christian handed Simon his gloves and walked into the hall, where the fireplace already burned logs in preparation for evening. Followed by Simon, his boots tapping against the black and white marble tiles of the floor, Christian kicked a stool aside and halted before the fire. He placed his forearms on the mantel and bathed his face in heat.

"You put her in the maid's chamber?" he asked.

"Aye, Kit, but are you sure that's the right one?"

"Fed her, did you?"

"She won't come to the dining chamber," Simon said. "When we got here, she didn't fuss at where she was put, just plopped down on the window seat and folded her hands. Makes me jittery, she does. All still and quiet. She's plotting something, sure as the stews stink."

"And no word from my clerk?"

"Not yet. Inigo has gone to the city to listen to your magpies sing, but he says that many of the Queen's household scattered when she left for Hampton Court three days ago. Sent to other palaces, they were." Simon paused, glancing at Christian's face. "Here, Kit, you look like you haven't slept since Yuletide."

Christian took the tankard of ale Simon handed him and drained it. All it seemed to do was fog his thoughts even more and aggravate his weariness. He refused another drink, for he still had Nora to face. Ordering that the evening meal be served in an hour, he set off for the room at the east corner of the house on the topmost floor.

The chamber was reached by the servants' stair, six steep flights that led to three rooms. Christian paused before one door and noted that Inigo had installed the massive silver-plated lock that usually went on Christian's own chamber at whichever of the family houses he stayed. Withdrawing a key from the pouch at his belt, he stood glaring at it.

It was happening again. Just knowing she was on the other side of the door was enough. Cursing under his breath, he braced both hands against the door. He called up images of heretics burning alive, victims of the rack, but the only real picture in his head was of Nora—naked, large-eyed, trusting Nora. If he didn't find relief, he was going to open the door and fall upon her like a beast, his lust and his hate rampant, and neither of them would survive the inferno unmaimed. So he thought of his father, of how Sebastian had put his hand on Nora's head and blessed her.

When the pain in his groin had ebbed slightly, he began to recite passages of the *Iliad* in Greek. After a long while, he was able to stand erect and enter Nora's chamber. His first impressions were of shadows pierced by fading light from a recessed window, and of dust floating in the air, blanketing a chest, bed hangings, a sideboard. He'd known the room wouldn't be ready for use. What furniture was there made the room look the size of a comfit box.

Nora was perched on the window seat, barely touched by the fast-dimming light. She had removed her French hood, and her hair tumbled around her shoulders and snarled in the faded embroidery of her riding habit. Crouching, her hands pressed against the whitewashed walls, she watched him silently.

"Do you approve of your new home?" Christian asked, watching her as closely as she watched him.

She started at the sound of his voice, then wrinkled her brow. She looked around the room as if giving it her attention for the first time. What she saw appeared not to interest her, for she quickly returned her gaze to him without making a reply.

"I asked how you found your chamber, wife."

"It's fine."

Irritated that she hadn't noticed her bare and incommodious surroundings, Christian tried again.

"And your servants, you approve of them as well?"

"Who?"

"The special retainers I've assigned to you—Simon Spry, horse thief and swindler, Odo Twitch, false beggar and pimp. And, of course, my dear Mag and her girls, but you won't have had time to meet them."

"They're fine," Nora said. "My lord, please, if you would but hear me."

"The only words I will listen to are the names of those you serve. To whom did you send the cipher?"

"I can't tell you."

"If I have to find out for myself, your punishment will be that much worse. Tell me now and I'll send you to Castle Mont-fort in peace. You'll be in gaol, but I'll forgo my other . . . plans."

Nora reached out a hand to him, but pulled it back abruptly. She laced her fingers together, twisting them while he watched her eyes fill with unshed tears.

"My lord, I beg you to listen."

Expelling a long-held breath, Christian turned to leave.

"Wait!"

With deliberate care, he returned to stand before his small wife, arms crossed and eyes blank. Saying nothing, he lifted a brow and waited. Nora's gaze wavered and sank to the floor.

"I know you suspect me of serving Bishop Bonner, but it's not true. We've misunderstood each other from the beginning, it seems. I thought . . . but I was wrong, and I don't fault you for not wanting me."

"So gracious of you not to blame me for not wanting a traitor for a wife. No, say nothing more. I told you I want noth-ing from you but the name of your master. Is it de Ateca?"

"No."

Christian narrowed his eyes. "I don't believe you, and my

patience is at an end. Dinner is in one hour. I'll come back to let you out of your cage then."

"I'll eat here."

"If you want to eat, you'll do it where I command and when I command." He backed away as she rose for the first time, bringing her near enough for him to catch the scent of honeysuckle that rose from her hair. "One hour," he repeated, and fled her presence.

Running away did no good, for he was back in her chamber when the hour was up, torn once again between desire and damnation. He bowed mockingly to her and held out his arm. She stared at it until he grabbed her hand and forced it to lace under his arm and rest in its crook. Then he marched her downstairs and into the main hall. Raucous laughter, belching, and cursing could be heard long before they entered, and the volume of noise rose as they walked the length of the hall to the dais reserved for the lord.

Christian studied Nora as they passed between two long trestle tables occupied by pockmarked, sweaty, and ripe-smelling retainers. He'd gotten her attention at last. The strangeness of his household was penetrating her wits. She wrinkled her nose, pulled her skirt close to her body, and slowed her steps. He tugged her along, noting that his people were falling silent as they perceived of their arrival.

As they neared the dais, Christian felt Nora halt. He looked down at her, then noted the direction of her stare. She'd seen Mag and the others sitting at the lord's table.

"My special friends, wife," he said. "They've come to meet you."

He grabbed Nora's arm and yanked her up the dais after him. Pausing before Mag, he took the woman's hand and kissed it. As he ran his tongue over Mag's knuckles, he heard Nora catch her breath. Slowly a smile spread over his face, and Mag's eyes lit with anticipation.

"Oh, Kit," she murmured, "you shouldn't make such promises in public."

"But I intend to keep them," he said. "And you may chastise me if I don't."

Mag laughed and rushed at Christian, pressing her body to his and forcing his lips open for a kiss. Whistles rose from those below, and a few stamped their feet. Christian lifted his head. Still holding Mag, he turned to them and raised his voice.

"My good people, I give you my wife, Nora." Beside him, Nora jerked her gaze away from Mag to look at him. He grinned at her. "A fair maid who's a maid no longer. Sweet, obedient, docile, and silent, everything a man could want in a wife."

Cheers rose from the ale-drunk crowd, and Christian bid them resume their meal. He led a red-faced Nora to the chair beside his, and Mag took a stool on his right.

"Wife, I present my dear and honorable friends." He stopped while Simon and Holly smirked. "Simon you know. And this plump morsel of sin is Holly, and the wench with her mouth full of goose is Annie. Annie, don't stuff your mouth so."

Annie swallowed and leered at him. "My mouth's been a lot fuller with you in it, Kit my delicious."

Nora's goblet toppled, splashing wine on the tablecloth. Christian righted the vessel while surveying Nora's pallid features.

"Does our banter disturb you?"

Nora wet her lips and shook her head.

"Good. Have some goose." He threw a drumstick on her trencher. "And some capon and an artichoke or two."

"And what about you, Kit?" Mag scooted close to Christian so that her breasts pressed against his arm. "Have some meat. You're going to need your strength."

Christian opened his mouth and allowed Mag to feed him. He licked the woman's fingers clean of juice before taking a drink of wine. When he glanced at Nora, he saw she was regarding him as if he were a devil's imp. Her hands were shaking as she sipped her wine.

"You aren't eating," he said. "Does the play disturb you?" He gestured at Simon Spry, who was toying with Annie's breast.

"I'm not hungry."

"I won't have my wife yammering and squalling about the honest pleasures of my friends. By God's cock, why is it that plain women are so prudish and spiteful?"

It should have given him great satisfaction to watch Nora turn the color of faded parchment and shiver as if she'd caught an ague. It didn't, and that made him furious with himself and wildly angry at her. He couldn't let her see him weaken, but he was going to have to suspend the torture for the moment, or he'd never carry out his next plan.

"Can you imagine," he asked in a light voice, "how pleasant it will be to spend the whole summer and fall in the company of these dear friends, wife?"

Nora turned to face him. The dazed expression he'd seen in her chamber had returned, and she didn't answer. He couldn't stand watching her eyes lose focus and her head and shoulders droop. How dare she look so pitiful when it was she who'd caused them to be trapped together in this Hell?

"You look tired," he said. "Go to bed."

When she failed to respond, he snarled at her. "Get out of my sight."

He watched her flee, hating the way her curls swayed with each light step as she ran, hating the bounce of her breasts and the hunted look in her eyes. He was so busy hating that he didn't feel Mag's hand rubbing his thigh until she cupped him and squeezed. He gasped and threw his body back in his chair.

"You were right, Kit," Mag said. "She's an evil hag. Let me help you forget her."

He captured Mag's invading hands. "Not yet, curse you. It's not time. Later," he added almost to himself, "upstairs, when I know she'll hear . . ."

Mag laughed at him, "Why not now, too, my sweeting?"

He shoved her away. "You're too greedy, woman. It's a fault you'd do well to curb. A man enjoys being pursued, but it's in his nature to also enjoy playing the hunter. Why do you think we prey on maidens?" Christian realized what he was saying and stopped. "Damnation."

Mag dipped her finger in his wine goblet and ran it over his lips. "Yes, Kit? What about maidens?"

"Nothing. I care naught for maidens or mice, or dragons either."

"Have you been swilling bad ale?"

"God's blood, woman, give me peace. Can't you see I'm eating?"

Nora had placed a pillow on a stool and lay her rosary on it soshe could look at the cross. It had been her mother's. It was

made of silver with intricately embossed beads, and a single
pearl dangled from it. Nora folded her hands and bent her head
in prayer, but she couldn't seem to talk to God. Mayhap it was
because she was afraid. Afraid that the horror of these last days
was of His designing.

Squeezing her hands tightly together, she tried to remember
a psalm. No words came to her. What she did remember was
that terrible walk down the hall between rows of belching and
contemptuous outlaws. As if it were a tableau from a stained-
glass window, she could see the figures on the dais.

That woman . . . Mag . . . she'd touched Lord Montfort as
if she owned him. She was much older than he, but her skin was
taut, her figure lithe. Blond and beautiful and possessing a body
that moved with confident sensuality, Mag possessed qualities
for which Nora longed. Mag, and Holly, and Annie, they had
all laughed at her, and Lord Montfort had said before them that
she was plain. Not that it was a thing to be missed by any with
eyes.

What was she doing? Self-pity was a sin, and she'd indulged
herself with it for the better part of the evening. Nora wasn't
sure how much time had passed since she'd left the hall. Ever
since her wedding night, time slipped by while she remained
still. She rose on stiff legs and began to undress by the light of
the single candle Simon Spry had given her.

What was he doing now? Foolishness, that speculation.
He caroused with those people, those purveyors of sin and
deception. He was with Mag. She wished he had beaten her
instead of flaying her alive with his rejection and hate. Each
day he slipped farther from her reach, and each night fed his
wrath.

Standing in the middle of the chamber, Nora glanced
about, her gown, petticoats, and farthingale in her arms. They'd
given her a small chest stuffed with a few of her things. She
draped her clothing on the window seat and searched the chest
for a smock. Yards of lawn appeared at the bottom, and she
tugged the nightgown free.

Once immersed in the soft garment, she doused the candle
and clambered onto the bed. Only after she'd seated herself on
top of the covers did she notice she was shivering. She drew the

spread around her shoulders but didn't lie down. From experience she knew it would be useless. The only way she'd be able to sleep was if she sat up or paced the chamber for a few hours.

So she sat. Blinking slowly at the darkness, she wondered if she could ask her father for help. A mad thought. The Queen? Not unless she wanted Lord Montfort clapped in the Tower, and much as she feared him and much as he'd hurt her, she couldn't bear to see him hurt in return.

After all, this misunderstanding wasn't his fault. She should have asked for a different hiding place for her ciphers the first time he invaded the garden. Lord Montfort was right. She wasn't at all clever, not at all.

She must have dozed, for she opened her eyes to find her nose buried in the spread. She was curled in the middle of the bed. Her eyes burned from weariness, and her legs ached from spending hours on her knees. Stretching them, she burrowed under the cover, anxious to sink into merciful blankness before her brain started working again and she remembered the unhappiness.

As she nuzzled into the bed, she heard someone groan. Bed ropes creaked against wood, but they weren't her bed ropes. She lifted her head. Eyes now accustomed to the darkness, she could make out the half-open door to her chamber. She'd closed it when she came back from the hall. Hadn't she? And Lord Montfort had said he would lock her in. Could he have forgotten?

She could see light through the open doorway, and the groan had come from beyond the door, in the direction of the light. There it was again. This time it was longer, softer. Someone was in pain, and it sounded like a woman.

Dragging the spread around her body, Nora scooted off the bed. She tiptoed across the chamber, the cover trailing behind. Bed ropes whined as she emerged from her chamber, and she turned to peer at the door of the chamber beside her. It was ajar, like her own.

She pursed her lips while she listened to a woman's moan. It had to be one of those bawds. What if she were sick from too much ale or had a cramp in her gut? Sometimes cramps could be dangerous. She would ask if she could help. Nora crept to the door and peeked into the chamber.

A lewd masque greeted her. A dark room. A bed surrounded by candles. Tousled sheets. A woman on her back, legs spread wide. A man lying over her, suckling on her breast. A man with honey-colored skin and soft hawk's-feather hair. Nora crinkled her brow as confusion settled over her. She stared at the man, his skin bathed in candle glow; watched his muscles flex as he lifted his head and rubbed his chest against the woman's breasts. Lifted his head and turned to the door.

Nora stumbled back, closing her eyes against the sight of Lord Montfort's face. Her shoulder hit the door frame, and she turned to run, her gorge rising.

"Perhaps my wife would like to join us."

Nora froze.

"Turn around," Lord Montfort said.

She shook her head. She held on to the door frame, afraid she would fall. A hand grabbed her arm, and she was yanked into the room. Her husband stood before her, naked, his phallus turgid. She shrank from him, and he released her. She huddled in her cover and kept her gaze on the floor.

"Look at me." He waited. "Look at me, or I'll lock you in this room and resume the ride you interrupted."

She could look at him, she decided, because her sight was blurred anyway. He put his fingers under her chin and stared at her with eyes as cold as his body was hot. "If you tell me the name of your master, I'll come back to your bed."

She blinked at him. Her lips moved, but nothing came out of her mouth. Without warning he caught her to him, thrusting aside the spread to press his heated flesh to her body. His leg forced its way between hers, and she felt his thigh nudge her groin. He squeezed her buttocks and murmured into her ear.

"Tell me." He began to move, thrusting against her to the beat of an unheard drum. "Tell me, tell me. Yield, Nora."

She cried out and hurled herself away from those erotic hips and demanding body. Every inch of her own body quivered, and all warmth drained from it as she scrambled for the safety of her chamber, nausea roiling in her stomach. She stumbled over the spread and let it fall as she ran. Gaining her room, she slammed the door shut, but Lord Montfort thrust it open and sauntered in to the accompaniment of Mag's giggles. He stopped when Nora fled to the far corner and put her back to it. Indulging

in a stretch, he spread his arms and legs wide, displaying himself
to her. She covered her mouth and swallowed bile.

"From your response," he said, "I take it you refuse my
offer."

Nora was too busy trying to keep from vomiting to answer.

"Very well. I'll have the news soon anyway, and I'll be
spared a tedious chore, for which I thank you. And since you
don't require my service, I'll go back to Mag."

He left, and Nora sank to the floor. It was possible to die
and still breathe, she realized, for she accomplished the feat
herself, there in that dusty room, on the night her husband lay
between the thighs of a whore while she watched. And since she
was dead inside, she couldn't be hurt again. So at last, she was
free.

As a child he had lived with terror. Jack Midnight used to play
with him, forcing him to steal or beg, then beating him if he
refused or failed. Day after day his captor thrust him into the
streets full of cutthroats and whores, and day after day he risked
his life so he could return for his reward: pain.

Once Jack hung him from a tree limb and whipped him with
a willow switch until he screamed for coming back empty-
handed. The next day he chose an old man as his coney. He
played the lost child, producing tears that came easily if he allowed himself to feel the pain of his wounds. The man took him
up, held him gently, comforted him. Kit pointed the way to his
fictitious house in an alley while fingering the man's purse. The
man set him down in the alley, and Kit launched his thin body
away from the coney.

He'd gone only a few yards when he heard the old man cry
out. Looking back, he saw Midnight carve an arc through the
man's throat. Silver metal traced a path across flesh, leaving a
trail of blood. Transfixed by exposed, quivering muscle and
spurting blood, Kit watched the flapping skin, listened to the
gurgling, muted scream, met the old man's frightened eyes.

Christian huddled on the floor outside Nora's chamber, naked and drowning in the gore of that memory. The old man's
eyes—why did he have to remember them now? Because Nora's
eyes held that same look of wounded terror.

"God's mercy, what have I done?"

Shivering, he rested his arms on his knees and pressed his forehead to them. He heard his own dry sob, and bit his lip to stop it. He'd become that tortured child-animal again, ever since he'd learned of Nora's betrayal. Just now, when he had touched her and offered to return to her bed, he'd expected to evoke the passion he'd discovered on their wedding night. He'd brought forth agony instead.

If he lived into the next century, he would never escape the vision of her eyes, those soft eyes that could brim with love and compassion for the weak and unwanted but now reflected the tortures of the rack, the stake, and the brand. And he—Christian de Rivers—he turned the rack, lit the faggots at the stake, wielded the brand. He couldn't do it anymore. He'd hoped to shame and hurt her this night with Mag, but it was himself he was torturing. He was killing his own soul.

"Kit?" Mag bent over him and touched his bare shoulder. "Kit, you've been out here forever. Come back to bed."

She leaned closer and brushed his hair back. Her voice grew louder. "Kit, what's wrong?"

"Go away," he said.

"What did she do to you?" Mag sank to her knees and held his face in her hands. "Dear God, what did she do to you?"

Pulling his head free, Christian stood up and propped an arm against the wall. "I did this to myself, dear Mag. I tried to put her in Hell, and put myself there, too."

"Come back to bed. I'll make you forget."

"No," he said as he moved to the stairs. "It's not a thing you can do for me."

"I can. I've done it before."

"I was a child then, Mag. No, don't fight me in this." His lips twisted into something like a smile. "I am become 'a monster fearful and hideous, vast and eyeless.' "

"That's pig's swill. She did you a bad turn, you said. Betrayed you. We all hate her for it, you know." Mag rushed to him and slipped her arms around his waist. She kissed his chest, but Christian didn't respond. He withdrew his body from her grasp and took a step down the stairs.

"Take the key I gave you and lock her in. Give the key to

Simon. And Mag, you have my thanks and my heart's fondness."

"I want more," she said. "You belong to me, Kit, and to those thieving runagates below."

"I'm cold. I'll see you in the morning."

"And ever after."

His hand strangled the banister as he regarded Mag. "I thought you learned long ago that I belong to myself."

"Do you, Kit?" Mag pointed at Nora's door. "Or do you belong to her, fight how you will to be rid of the chains she's wrapped about that touchable body of yours?"

"I'm cold and I'm going to bed. Rest you well, Mag." Christian descended the stairs, praying that Mag would let him go in peace. He should have known better.

"Send her away," she called down to him. "She's destroying you and you can't see it. Get rid of the bitch before she hurts you again, or the next time you may not survive."

Chapter
XVII

The birds of Falaise fell quiet in the afternoon heat. Dragonflies floated above the moat in lazy somnolence, and the porter at the gate nodded as the cutpurse Inigo Culpepper walked his horse under the portcullis. The courtyard was deserted except for a stable boy who swatted at gnats from his perch in the shade beneath the eaves. Inigo roused the boy with a gentle kick on the shoulder and left the horse with him.

Inside, the smell of old ale and rancid food recalled Mag's ordinary, and the dirty bodies strewn about completed the resemblance. Inigo picked his way through the mess, both human and culinary, and grabbed a handful of scraggly hair from the lord's table. Simon Spry's red nose snored at him.

Shaking the head, Inigo cursed at the horse thief. "Where is he?"

"Aw . . ." Simon muttered.

"Where is he? Are the guards like this, too?"

Simon slapped Inigo's hands away and burped. "Nah."

"Speak up, you son of a whore."

"Nah, you know he doesn't 'low drink on duty. He just had them hide theirselves so's not to get underfoot."

Curling his lip, Inigo ground out his question again. "Where is he?"

"Couldn't sleep."

"What are you talking about?"

"The master, he couldn't sleep. Wandered the house all night. In a taking, he was, cursing and pacing, pacing and cursing. Kept me awake, he did. Round dawn he took himself off on foot."

"You let him go alone?" Inigo fastened a hand around Simon's neck.

"Piss on yourself, Inigo. He didn't want company, and I like my head on my shoulders and my cock between my legs, so I didn't follow, thank you."

Shoving the thief away, Inigo asked, "Which way did he go?"

"Into the forest, but—"

"He's back," Christian said.

Inigo whirled to face the young man standing in a pool of light and dust motes. He was studying the dead tree branch that dangled from his fingers.

"Kit," Inigo said.

Christian poked a cup on the table with the branch. "Did you find the gardener?"

"Hext did, but the simpleton doesn't know who gets the messages."

"You used sufficient persuasion to be sure?"

"Of course," Inigo said. "And we found out where he leaves the ciphers. At a printer's shop near the palace owned by a fat hedgehog named Hugo Paderborn. But Hugo's gone to visit his sister in Wales."

"Tedious."

Inigo nodded, eyeing his master.

Christian gave the cup a final poke, sighed, and dropped the tree branch. "Have the steward send word to Castle Montfort to make ready for my wife's arrival. I'll send her in a few days, and we will go back to London."

Inigo cast an inquiring glance at Simon, who shook his head and fell to studying the congealed fat in a trencher. The sound of a door slamming and the tap of booted feet forestalled questions. Blade raced into the hall with his fencer's stride and

grabbed Christian's shoulder. He twisted the older man around
to face him and shook a fist at him.

"What have you done to her now, you piss-sucking blight?"

"Not now," Christian said.

Blade grabbed Christian bodily, only to be hauled back by
Inigo. Blade threw Inigo off and went for Christian again. This
time Christian was ready and kicked the youth lightly in the
chest. Blade bounced, ending up in Inigo's grasp.

"Let go of me, whoreson," Blade said, struggling. "He's
done something to Nora, and I'm going to make him send for a
leach."

Snatching Blade from Inigo, Christian brought the youth's
face close to his. "What mean you? She has sickened?"

"You didn't know?"

"No," Christian said. He released Blade and left the hall
at a run.

Clearing the stairs to Nora's chamber three at a time, Christian
was in her room before the others mounted the staircase. She
was alone, a small anthill beneath the rough linens that covered
her bed. Her black hair, snarled and dull, lay strewn over the
pillows. She made no sign that she heard him enter. She hardly
moved at all, but as he neared the bed, he could see that she
was awake.

He paused at the bedside, staring at her in silence. A steady
flow of tears washed over Nora's cheeks and down her neck.
Silent tears. His hand inched toward her face, but he pulled back
as Blade and Inigo ran into the chamber.

Blade perched beside Nora and touched the back of her
hand where it lay on the covers. "She's ill."

"No, I'm not ill." Her faint voice made them all start. "It's
just that I can't stop crying. I've tried. You must believe me.
I've tried so hard to stop, but I can't, and I don't know what to
do." She closed her eyes.

Christian heard a sigh, a sigh that turned into a faint, long
moan, and dread snaked through his gut. He touched Nora's
arm, and she cringed. Snatching his hand back, he made his
voice steady.

"How long have you been like this?"

"I don't know," she said between sobs.

Without another word, Christian stalked out of the chamber and into Mag's. The woman was lying sprawled on her own bed, a wet cloth covering her eyes. Christian jerked the cloth from her face and hauled her upright by one arm.

"I told you to watch Nora," he snapped at her. "Why didn't you call me when she started crying?"

Mag patted his cheek. "Weren't her tears the whole purpose of last night's masque?"

"There's something amiss with her, and you know it."

"But you wanted to see her suffer. You said you wanted vengeance."

Christian swallowed and looked away from Mag's derision. "How long has she been this way?"

Mag shrugged. Snagging a handful of the woman's hair, Christian repeated his question slowly and with precise enunciation.

"How long has she been this way?"

"Since before I locked her in after you left, I suppose. Ow, Kit, my hair."

"Fetch wine. Tell the steward I want his best, and clean cloths and water." When Mag didn't move, Christian lifted his hand. The gesture was enough to send the woman scrambling for the door.

Returning to Nora's chamber, Christian noted that Inigo was gone and that Blade now held her hand.

"How haps it that you concern yourself with my wife?"

Blade scowled at him. "Even I can recognize true goodness when I see it. You married her and turned animal. If you don't want her, let me take her away."

"What did she do, swoon over your charms and admire your prowess at killing? Did she—" He bit off his torrent of viciousness at the sound of Nora's moan.

Blade muttered soothing words to her, but she turned her head away and cried softly. With a shaking hand she tried to stifle the sounds coming from her throat. Blade lifted hate-filled eyes to Christian.

"Get you gone, for mercy's sake. Can't you see what your presence does to her?"

Pressing his lips together, Christian nodded to the youth and quit the chamber. As he stepped onto the landing, he heard footsteps pounding up from below. A rapid clatter joined them, and immediately after, a small missile plowed into his stomach.

"Come back here, you little plague!" Inigo yelled from the floor below.

Christian pulled the golden-haired arrow from his middle and set it before him. "How did you get here?"

"On a horse." Arthur scraped a bow at Christian before sticking his chin out, staring up at the man above him. "We married you, but you left me behind. I asked the Earl if I could come to my lady again, and he gave his permission."

" 'We'?"

Arthur tugged on the surcoat of his livery and poked his head to the side to peer past Christian. "We haven't ever been married before, but the Earl explained that married folk like to be alone. But I—I haven't been away from my lady in a long time."

Inigo plunged up the stairs. "There you are, you little sneak."

"I'll take care of Arthur," Christian said. "You go to the kitchens and help Mag.

"Come with me." Christian took Arthur's hand. It disappeared in his, and he was reminded of Nora's. "Your lady isn't feeling well, and you must give her cheer."

"Is it the sweat?" Arthur asked.

"No. She's a bit unhappy. I think she misses you."

Christian led the boy to Nora, allowing him to approach alone while he held back. He beckoned to Blade, and Blade slipped off the bed so Arthur could take his place at Nora's side. Arthur clambered up on the bed on all fours and stuck his face in front of Nora's. Before he could speak, Nora gave a cry, sat up, and hugged the boy to her. Arthur laughed and wrapped his arms and legs around his mistress.

Watching Arthur bury his face in Nora's neck, Christian held his breath. Nora cupped the back of Arthur's head with one hand and rocked from side to side. The room filled with soft murmurs of nonsense as the two conversed. Christian began to breathe again when he saw Nora's tears ebb. Glancing at Blade, he abandoned the two friends, with the youth in his wake.

Blade closed the door and studied the shiny lock in silence. Christian let out an unsteady sigh, propped his back against the wall, and stared at the ceiling.

"Think you this is the cure?" Blade asked.

"How could I have forgotten?"

Blade looked at Christian. "Pardon?"

"It was the shock and the betrayal. They drove me into madness."

"Forgotten what?" Blade asked.

"The puppies, the stray and starving cats, that great big heart compassed in a mite's body."

"You make no sense."

"I know. I haven't been sane since my wedding. God's blood, I don't know what to believe anymore."

"Just leave her be."

Christian laughed. "I can't, my comfit. You've asked me to do the one thing I find beyond my power. If you were to skewer me on a turnspit I still couldn't leave her be."

"You're lying."

"Shut your mouth." Christian slipped his arm across Blade's shoulders and forced him to walk toward the stairs. "You and I are going to eat and drink, and drink some more, and then mayhap I'll find some release from my 'foul yoke of sensual bondage.' "

After four days of Arthur's company and none of Lord Montfort's, Nora decided that only part of her heart had died. The most part, it was true, but some spark of life in that stubborn organ refused to drown under the flood of cruelty to which her husband had subjected her. On the fifth day she left her chamber.

Morning-crisp air jostled her spirits further, and she managed a smile as Arthur danced ahead of her, leading the way to a surprise. He pranced through the kitchens and out into the yard to a gate. This he opened and dragged Nora through. He pointed to rows of greenery and flowers.

"A herb garden, my lady. Cook says she hasn't had time to tend it, what with all the company the master brought. Lord Montfort says it's ours for as long as we want it."

Pain stabbed her chest at the mention of her husband, but

Nora was careful not to show Arthur her discomfort. He was so excited at having found a way to cheer her, and was skipping up and down the rows of plants, pointing as he went. He stopped by an herb with thick dark green leaves.

"Look, my lady, rosemary. And there's mullein and hore-hound and valerian, and over there is some tansy. And in the corner there's mugwort. I remembered all of those just from helping you."

She followed Arthur and put her hand on his head, tangling her fingers in his hair. "Such a dear friend you are."

"You are my very own lady. Nobody wanted me until you came."

"And I shall always want you, my Arthur." She smiled at the boy and knelt beside a broad-leaved plant. "Do you know what this is?"

He shook his head.

"It's betony. Some call it wood, and one uses it as a coun-termagick. I've read that two serpents will fight and kill each other if placed in a ring of it. I use it for headaches and to calm nerves."

"Let's find two snakes," Arthur said.

"No, you will not, sirrah. I shouldn't have told you that story, I can see."

"Would it work on frogs, or crickets?"

"I don't know, but this garden needs weeding, and I'd like to collect a few herbs. Would you fetch a basket and my gloves please?"

"Yes, my lady."

"And, Arthur, no snakes."

"My lady," Arthur said with a groan.

Nora watched Arthur disappear in the direction of the work sheds beyond the kitchen yard. When he was gone, she fumbled at her girdle for a kerchief and wiped her eyes.

As had often happened in the past several days, she had to fight to stave off the sudden memory of Lord Montfort and that woman. To her surprise, though, the lewd images no longer slashed deep cuts into her soul. After so much weeping all that remained was a dragging weariness and a muted ache, and sad-ness. She was numb.

Arthur's shout penetrated her numbness, sending her sprinting for the work sheds. As she ran, she could hear cursing and bellowing, a common occurrence when her page was about. She burst upon a scene of chaos.

Two gardeners were prying Arthur and another lad apart. Nearby lay an overturned wheelbarrow and two discarded shovels. As Nora skidded to a stop, the gardener lad kicked his captor's shin. The man yelped and released the boy at the same time Arthur slithered free. Nora lunged at the two, for the gardener's boy was larger and heavier than Arthur. She was too late. Arthur butted the older lad in the stomach and ran. Dodging the gardeners, he scrambled up a wood pile and onto the stone wall that surrounded Falaise.

"Arthur," Nora shouted, "come down at once!"

Sporting a cut lip, sweating, and furious, Arthur grabbed a log and hurled it at his opponent's feet. The wood hit the boy on the toes, and the lad jumped, falling backward to land on his rump.

"He called you a name," Arthur said to Nora. "No one calls my lady names, you son of a weasel."

"Donkey's arse!" the gardener boy yelled. He shoved himself to his feet and hurled a stone at Arthur.

Nora cried out and hurtled for Arthur as the stone hit him on the side of the head. He crumpled, falling into her arms. Nora sank to the ground, oblivious to the crowd that had gathered in response to the din. Cradling Arthur, she brushed aside bloodied locks of hair to reveal a gash in his temple. She pressed her kerchief to the wound.

"What passes here?"

She heard the voice of her tormentor but didn't look up. "He fought with another lad and was hit by a stone," she said. "Help me take him to my chamber."

Gardeners and servants gave way before their lord, and Lord Montfort lifted Arthur into his arms. Heedless of those around her, Nora ran ahead, snapping out orders to maidservants as she went. Frantic, she could hardly contain her impatience as her husband lowered Arthur's body to her bed. She shoved Christian aside, commanding him as she did so.

"Bring me herbs from the garden, agrimony, rosemary, verbena, and basil, but first I'll need Saint-John's-wort. Hurry."

She bathed the wound, cursing inwardly at Arthur's pallor

and the bleeding. Mild head wounds could kill if not tended properly. At this thought, her hands shook and tears threatened. She bit her lip to keep calm, but an unwelcome truth assaulted her: Arthur had been injured in a fight about her. He'd been swallowed by the war between herself and Lord Montfort.

Dear God, if she had protested her husband's actions, fought him, demanded fair treatment, Arthur wouldn't have been injured. She pressed her kerchief to the boy's wound to stanch the bleeding while she castigated herself. She should have realized Arthur would defend her, and should have spoken to Lord Montfort. She should have sent Arthur back to the Earl. She could have done any number of things to prevent such a tragedy, but she'd been too caught up in her own misery, too busy playing the coward.

Lord Montfort arrived with leaves plucked from Saint-John's-wort. After crushing them between the table and the base of a cup, Nora applied the leaves to Arthur's wound. Anxiously she listened to the boy's breathing. It was shallow but steady.

"Will he be all right?" Lord Montfort asked.

Nora didn't take her eyes from Arthur's face. "I don't know. I think so, but I must watch over him until he wakes. Then I'll know more."

"What happened?"

Pursing her lips, she finally turned to her husband. His dark violet eyes met hers, but she could see no emotion in them.

"He fought that boy because of me. Because of me."

"I'll get rid of the lad."

"No. There is no need. And why would you, when you've taken so much trouble to see that everyone knows of your contempt for me?"

"I'll not have fighting among my servants."

Turning back to Arthur, she waved a hand. "I have no time to listen, my lord. I beg you to leave me to nurse the child."

"I'll bring the other herbs."

Taking no heed of him, Nora resumed her vigil beside Arthur. In the hour that passed before the boy roused, she remembered what it was to fear for a loved one—remembered the terror she'd felt when Bishop Bonner had threatened Lord Montfort.

She imagined Arthur waking blind or never waking at all, losing her memory as she'd heard sometimes happened, or suffering terrible pain. Whatever the outcome, Arthur was hurt because she'd been too much of a coward to stand up for herself.

In the end, Arthur woke in pain and suffered a day and a night. During that time Nora slept little and ran off everyone who tried to help. No one could care for Arthur as she could, and the boy grew fretful if she left his side for long. As she tended him, Nora realized how much they depended on each other, far more than either of them had realized.

As the hours passed and she held Arthur's hand while he tried not to cry, Nora lived through an agony of regret. Slowly, as the boy grew stronger, resolve sprang into being within her, and with it, determination. What she would not do for herself, she would do for Arthur. She would fight.

In a fortnight Arthur regained his health. During that time Nora saw little of her husband. He left her to the care of his longtime servants, those who belonged to Falaise and had been warned to avoid Nora upon her arrival. Mag and her bawds vanished, as did most of Lord Montfort's ruffians. In their place stepped forth honest folk who gave service with dignity and good spirit. Nora wondered at the changes in Lord Montfort's household, but wasn't curious enough to brave asking her husband about them.

As the days passed, Nora gradually recovered from the plague of the spirit that had infested her since her wedding. Now that she was calm, she perceived within herself a great dread of Lord Montfort, as well as an abiding hatred. In spite of her pleas for trust, he had used her love as an instrument of punishment. Because he had done this, she couldn't think of him without physical pain, and—during the long, sleepless hours after dark—she no longer recalled his touch without experiencing shame and terror.

While she underwent this clearheaded suffering, Arthur rose from his sickbed, and her fears for him renewed. Indomitable of will, stubborn and contentious when aroused, he was sure to get into trouble again. She was in her tower room, trying to entertain her restless page with a game of cards and worrying about this problem, when Lord Montfort entered. Forcing her hands not to shake, Nora placed her cards on a stool and rose.

Lord Montfort approached her slowly, smiling at Arthur as he did so. Nora's heart lurched, and she clamped her teeth together. Clasping her hands in front of her, she didn't bother to curtsy. He didn't deserve her respect, and she was tired of bowing her head only to have it knocked against a wall.

Lord Montfort sent Arthur to the kitchens for sweetmeats and waited for him to leave before speaking.

"Now that Arthur is well, I have arranged for you to go to Castle Montfort. You will leave in the morning, and I shall return to London to ask questions."

"Castle Montfort? But that's so far away."

"Indeed. It suits my purpose, for you'll be far from London and any mischief, and if I receive unhappy news about you, well, there is an old keep in the middle of the bailey."

She stiffened her legs to keep them from wobbling. "You will shut me up in some ancient keep? For how long?"

"I don't know. But don't look so frightened. I've not decided upon the matter yet, and it may not come to that. Unless, of course, you turn out to be the most accomplished player I've ever known. In that case, you will deserve far worse than being shut up in stone."

"But I haven't done anything."

Cocking his head to one side, Lord Montfort reached out to touch her cheek with his fingertips. Nora jerked her head away as she felt the warmth of his flesh brush her skin. His hand paused in midair, and he frowned.

"I won't hurt you," he said. "Even when I wanted to hit you, I couldn't, and now . . . now I would cry peace."

He put out his hand again, but she skittered to the window seat and grabbed a cushion. Clutching it to her chest, she shook her head. Her husband's frown deepened. He came toward her, and with each step Nora's heart pounded harder. All the moisture disappeared from her mouth and throat when he stopped mere inches away. The full sleeve of his doublet brushed her hand where it grasped the cushion, and she tried to back farther away. Her heels rammed into the window seat.

Thrown off balance, she teetered, and Montfort steadied her, grasping her upper arms. She hurled herself into the window seat with a cry.

"Please! Don't touch me!"

Lifting his hands, Lord Montfort held them up as if to reassure her. "I said I wouldn't hurt you."

"Don't."

"Have you another touch of melancholy? I'll fetch some wine."

She buried her chin and nose in the cushion she held like a shield and spoke into it. "No."

He put his hands on his hips and glared at her. "Explain then."

Peering at him over the cushion, Nora forced herself to speak. If she didn't he would keep at her, keep touching her until she went mad.

"It is your touch that causes pain." At his look of confusion, she gritted her teeth and continued. "When you touch me, I hurt."

"Damnation. I never raised my hand to you." He reached out again.

Cringing, Nora blurted out the truth. "I can't! When you touch me, I remember the—the night. The wedding night. The love and then the hurt. No, don't touch me, please."

"God's blood," Montfort said. He took a step back and once more held his hands out so she could see them. "Calm yourself, or you'll take a fit. Look, you. I give my promise that I won't touch you unless you allow it."

Nora had buried her face in her cushion, but as he moved away, she lifted her head to survey him with one eye. He was staring at her, brows raised in alarm. He thought she was going to collapse into a weeping fit again, she realized. She'd done with useless weeping, though. Mayhap she did tremble and cower a bit, but she could face him. Not long ago she couldn't have done so much.

Watching as he lowered his hands to his sides, she perceived a change in his mood. The alarm gradually faded, but as it did, his eyes narrowed, then closed. He hardly moved except to lower his head.

"God forgive me," he said. "I don't know what I want anymore."

To Nora his words made no sense. It was plain to her he wanted to make her more miserable than the meanest criminal in gaol.

"You want to hate me," she said. "It's what you do best, my lord. You learned young and have practiced for years." She couldn't believe she was saying such things to him. He would kill her for it.

"I . . ."

He turned from her and folded his arms over his chest. His face was in profile to her, and she could see the muscles of his jaw clench.

"I don't want to hate you," he said. "It seems I have no choice, and I have no choice in something else as well."

"What?"

"I've changed my mind about sending you away."

"My lord, you make no sense."

Spinning to face her, he stepped toward her, then stopped abruptly, as if he'd remembered that she couldn't abide his nearness.

"It was a mistake to bargain with my body. A habit gained in my childhood, I fear. It seems I have lied to myself, for in truth, I offered the bargain only to get back in your bed, and only in part to get a confession from you."

She lunged up and past him, thrusting the cushion at him as she fled. Lord Montfort batted the cushion aside but made no effort to chase her. She paused at the door, her hand on the latch, her body tense and ready to spring.

"Running won't do any good, sweeting," he said.

"If you touch me, I'll go mad."

"I don't think so."

He walked toward her, and she flung the door open.

"Don't run," he said. "I give you my word that I'm not going to chase you down and take you in the hall."

As her husband continued to approach, Nora matched his every step with one that took her farther away. Unfortunately, she'd moved into the chamber next to hers and had her back to the bed. Montfort halted when they stood a bare foot apart. As he looked at her, Nora caught the telltale flicker in his gaze, the slight quickening in the rhythm of his breathing. The monster wanted her.

Whisperings of sweetness, murmurings from a low voice suffused with rough desire haunted her memory, and she felt again the pinpricks of arousal. Those fine stabs woke her fears of the ugliness that followed the pleasure, and she pressed her hands to her mouth to keep from screaming.

Her fear was so great, she didn't notice Montfort's response until he'd strode back across the room to the door. Hesitating on the threshold, he stroked the polished wood of the frame with a sun-browned hand, then threw a furious glance at her over his shoulder. She realized his anger was directed at himself, and perhaps at being thwarted by her aversion.

"You have this night to accustom yourself to the idea," he said, "but remember now that I've admitted to myself my true desire, I will have it—wife."

She jumped when the door slammed shut, then stood there gawking at it.

He was going to make her do it, she was certain of it. He was going to touch her, make love to her. No, not make love. He was going to couple with her for his own pleasure. In spite of his hate, or mayhap because of it. If he tried to use her she would fight him, and lose, and go mad. Mad. Then he could shut her up in his keep forever and no one would care. Was that his plan? To drive her mad?

Hugging her stomach to stifle the frogs that leaped about inside it, Nora paced the chamber and strove for calm. He would come for her tomorrow. He wouldn't wait for sunset, either. Tomorrow she would go mad, and when she did, Arthur would be left alone and unprotected. The boy would know Montfort was responsible. Dear Lord, Arthur would attack Montfort. But she couldn't allow that to happen. She had to protect Arthur, and therefore . . . therefore . . .

She had to protect herself.

Chapter
XVIII

Either he had crushed a baby chick beneath the heel of his boot, or he'd foiled the machinations of a devil in voluptuous form. To Christian's torment, he couldn't decide which was the case. The dilemma kept him up all that night, along with his body's anticipation of the relief he'd promised himself on the morrow.

He was up with the first light, rousing his body servant and harassing Cook and the poor steward. All of them were wroth with him already for descending on Falaise without proper warning, so they could prepare the house for his arrival. The steward, Master Nicholas Tideman, had know him from a babe, and when Christian had first arrived at Falaise, Tideman had made his displeasure clear at the intrusion of Christian's less respectable companions.

"Young viscounts do not invite such persons to give company to their ladies," Tideman had said, his lip curled in disgust as he examined Simon Spry and Odo Twitch.

As soon as he was dressed, Christian sought out Tideman. The older man was in the kitchen yard supervising the delivery of a new work table. Christian marched out to him, barely acknowledging the steward's salute.

"Tideman, I need a kitten."

"My lord?"

"Or a puppy, or mayhap both, or several of each."

"Master Christian, have you an imbalance of humors?"

"Even young weasels or hedgehogs will do if we've no kittens or puppies."

Tideman stuck his thumbs in the belt that circled his globular belly and lifted his nose. "Young viscounts do not play the jester to their retainers, Master Christian."

"I'm not playing the jester. I need a puppy, or a weasel, or a hedgehog. Something."

"And I am not in the habit of keeping weasels or infant hedgehogs, my lord."

Christian glanced over his shoulder at the men hauling the work table through the kitchen door and stepped closer to Tideman. "It's for my lady. Are you sure we've not got a wounded lamb or a starving fawn on the grounds?"

"Ah." Tideman nodded and chuckled.

"Amused, Tideman?"

"Your lady wife found no favor in the rude company you kept these several weeks past, and you seek her goodwill. It is well that you sent those lewd fellows away, Master Christian, and it is true that Lady Nora isn't wont to yearn for jewels and the like. Favors animals, does she?"

"I have no need to seek my wife's goodwill," Christian said stiffly while meeting Tideman's amused gaze.

"No, Master Christian."

"I am capable of thinking of another's pleasure, you know."

"Of a certainty."

"Then find me a puppy, Tideman."

Tideman responded with a tightness in his voice that meant he was trying not to laugh. "I believe there are some in the stables, Master Christian."

Christian chose the smallest and least fat of the puppies. To his disgust, they all possessed downy, bulging middles gurgling with a surfeit of their mother's milk. So much for finding a starving or abused creature for Nora to comfort. Wrapping the sleeping puppy in a fragment of a blanket, Christian returned to the manor house. On his way through the kitchens he met Blade, lounging on a bench beside a table.

"Found something else to torture?" the youth asked.

"If I wanted that kind of sport, I'd take you to the cellar for a few hours of entertainment," Christian said.

Blade took a hefty bite of a fruit tart, then turned sideways on the bench, bending a knee so that his foot rested on it. "It won't do any good. The puppy, I mean. She hates you as much as the disciples hated Judas."

"She needn't love me. She needs only to yield with grace and obedience."

Blade tossed his fruit tart on the table and scowled at Christian. "She told me what you want. Why don't you kill her and make an end to it?"

Christian shifted the puppy to the crook of his left arm and lifted Blade's chin with his fingertips.

"Have you been comforting my wife, marchpane?"

"Get your hands off me, Montfort. She invited me to play cards with her and Arthur."

"There will be no cards tonight." Christian left Blade cursing and ripping a loaf of bread into ribbons.

When he gained the landing outside Nora's chamber, he bethought himself to knock instead of invading, as was his habit. One couldn't woo a shy maid into bed by playing the infidel.

He shifted the puppy to rest on his shoulder. He could feel its nose snuffling at his neck and smiled.

Tap tap.

Silence.

Tap tap.

The puppy grunted and licked Christian's neck before subsiding with a snore.

Tap tap tap.

No response. She was asleep. Thinking to deposit the puppy in bed with her, Christian eased the door open and slipped inside.

The hangings had never been drawn about the bed. The trundle bed on which Arthur slept was still slid beneath Nora's larger one. Christian walked slowly to the empty bed, cradling his furry burden. Coming to a halt, he stared down at the spot where Nora's head should have been. With care he lowered the puppy to the mattress and stroked its small head, then bellowed for Nora's maid.

After three bellows, the girl appeared, flustered and fearful.

"Where is my lady?"

"Where—where—where—"

"God's blood, stop that chattering and tell me where my lady and her page have gone."

"I thought her abed, my lord. It is early, and she hadn't called." The girl squealed when Christian let out another bellow.

"Tideman!"

"I'll fetch him, my lord." The girl ran.

"Tideman!" Christian followed the maid, taking the stairs three at a time. He was barreling through the hall when he almost ran into the steward. "Where is my lady, Tideman?"

"Is she missing, Master Christian?"

Fury burned away his confusion. "Call all the servants to the hall, and the guards."

In a short time, Christian was standing before the fireplace in the hall, facing his household staff. Blade lounged on the steps that led down from the fireplace. Sunlight poured cheerily into the hall from the windows that reached almost to the ceiling, mocking Christian's anxiety.

"No one has seen her since last night, my lord," Tideman said. "Or the page, either."

"And a mare is missing from the stables?"

"The head groom was reporting so when you called, my lord."

Christian raced down the stairs and headed for his chambers. "Call my men to horse and set the household to searching again. I want to make sure she's not here before I leave. Blade, you're coming with me."

"But I like it here."

"I want you to be there when I catch her. I'm not fool enough to think she got away on her own. She's most likely gone back to London, and when I find her, I'll take a whip to her. Even Nora should know better than to prance about the highways of England with no more protection than that angelic pestilence."

Christian was dressed in riding clothes and mounting his stallion before all of his men were assembled. Cursing their slowness, he rode out with Blade and two sergeants at his heels,

anxious to pick up any signs of her passage before weather or
traffic destroyed them. He willed himself to go carefully, for
tracking demanded attention to detail and calm persistence. It
took the whole of his will to imprison his worry and his rage.
As it was, if the dangers of the road didn't kill Nora, he was
like to when he got his hands on her again.

She'd run from him. Was it because she was a traitor, or
was it because she couldn't bear for him to touch her? In all
likelihood it was both. He walked along the road from Falaise
to London leading his mount, his gaze raking the ground for
signs of her passage. As the hours passed and he found no trace
of her, his wrath grew and settled into his heart.

What a fool he must have looked, toting a puppy about his
own house and running after a woman who had fled his presence. She didn't want his hand on her, but that was exactly what
she was going to get. When he caught her, he would put his
hands on her any way he wished, for as long as he wished, and
he would watch her squirm.

Nora peeped through the screen of overgrown witch hazel to
survey the herb garden. It was deserted and bathed in the golden
light of the setting sun. They'd given up searching the house and
grounds long ago, and her husband was gone.

It had been her idea to remain at Falaise, and Blade had
been against it when she took the chance of confiding in him.
After an hour of her pleading he had agreed to distract her husband and direct the search for her to London. Lord Montfort
would expect her to flee witlessly into the forest or gallop off to
the city with no thought for the danger. She wasn't as stupid as
he thought, but she counted on him underestimating her. He
had, and now he was well on his way, searching and cursing,
no doubt. With any luck he would spend weeks ferreting around
in the city while she conceived of a plan for her and Arthur's
future.

The boy knelt beside her, impatient to be free of the witch
hazel vines that had overgrown this corner of the herb garden.
Flanked by two stone walls that formed the corner, the plants
encroached on verbena and a bed of petunias, reaching over

three feet high. They'd hidden there all day, feasting on the supply of food and drink provided by Blade.

As Nora had expected, once the search ended, Tideman set the household to work tidying Falaise. Satisfied that no one was about, she took the basket of leftover food from Arthur and stood. Her bottom was numb from sitting so long, and she watched Arthur's lithe movements with envy as he plunged ahead over her, shoving aside stalks of witch hazel. Once they were free of the vegetation, she shook her skirts into place and ran a hand through Arthur's rumpled curls. Handing him the basket, she walked behind him as he marched into the house, whistling.

In the kitchen Cook was bent over a pot of stew. As Arthur tramped into the room, the woman let out a squawk and dropped her ladle into the pot.

"My lady!"

"Good even, Cook," Nora said.

Potboys and Cook's assistants stared.

"My lady!" Cook repeated.

"A wonderful day for walking and feasting by the river, was it not?"

Cook rubbed her hands on her apron and worked her mouth open and closed. "My lady."

"Is something wrong?"

"We thought you'd run away."

Nora frowned. "Run away? What a foolish notion. Did you not consult your master? He knew I was going on a long walk today."

"But . . . but . . ."

"And where is everyone? The house is so quiet."

"God save us, my lady. The lord has gone off looking for you. Gone in the direction of the city."

"Looking for me? But he gave his permission for my walk days ago. Oh, my."

"My lady!"

Nora turned to see the steward gawking at her.

"Oh, Master Tideman," Cook said, "our lady hadn't run off at all."

Nora clasped her hands and inclined her head to Tideman. Here was the test, she knew. If Tideman could be fooled, she would be safe for a few weeks.

"It seems that there has been a confusion," she said.

"Your lord husband thought you vanished, my lady."

"So I understand," she said, and told her story again.

As she talked she eyed the steward, alert for any sign that he suspected her of mendacity. There was none. He frowned a good bit, and sputtered when she put forth the surmise that Lord Montfort had forgotten he'd given his permission for her outing. Nora felt a jolt of fear when the steward shook his head.

"Unbelievable," Tideman said.

"You question my words?" Nora did her best to look aghast.

"Oh, no, my lady. I meant that Lord Montfort's forgetfulness is unbelievable. So unlike him. He remembers the most inconvenient things most of the time, but since you came . . . And, of course, there was all that raving about hedgehogs and weasels."

"You must explain," Nora said.

"I fear my lord has been distracted of late." Tideman gave her a knowing look. "He has been melancholy and remote and this morning he asked me for a puppy or some such creature. I believe he wished to present one to you, my lady. Indeed, love has changed my lord in ways I had not thought possible."

"Love." Nora's wits refused to stir. "Ah, yes, you speak of our—our love. Of course you do. Our love. Mayhap you're right. My lord has been addled by it, as I have." She shook her head and smiled ruefully. "And to think I was only a short distance away, at the river."

"But we searched everywhere," Tideman said. He glanced at Arthur, who rocked on his heels and gave the man a wide-eyed look.

As Nora listened to Tideman voice his confusion, she counted the minutes that passed. The time approached for Blade's message to arrive, and her whole scheme depended on it. Blade had said he would bribe one of the grooms to pretend to receive a message. Where was the groom?

"We should send word to Lord Montfort anon, my lady," Tideman finally said.

"Oh, there's time aplenty for that," Nora said.

"But my lady—"

"I'm famished."

"The message—"

"I crave some venison, and perhaps a bread pudding."

As she piled up her list of cravings, a stableboy entered with a note in his hand and gave it to Tideman. Nora tried not to look relieved as Tideman glanced at the note, then at her.

"It is for you, my lady."

Taking the paper, Nora opened it, making sure she held it so the steward couldn't see the script. She popped her eyes open wide and giggled.

"Oh, Tideman. My lord indeed misremembered our conversation. He got halfway to London before he recollected where I was." She crumpled the note in her fist and smiled at the bewildered steward. "He sends his regrets and says he'll continue to the city to visit the Earl before returning. What a fine jest. We shall tease him without mercy when he comes home."

"As I said, my lady, Lord Montfort has been muzzywitted since he wed."

"I believe you, and thank you for your concern. And now I need rest, I think. I will be in my room until time to dine." Nora was about to leave when the steward put up a hand.

"My lord said that you would be moving to the master's chambers, my lady."

"There is no need since my husband isn't here." Nora hoped she wasn't blushing. "Has my lord said anything else?"

It was Tideman's turn to blush. "Forgive me, Lady Montfort. The master confided to me that you wished to become more acquainted with him before occupying the same chambers. I hope you understand that I have known Lord Montfort since he was in swaddling clothes, and he oftentimes entrusts me with his confidence. It is unfortunate that this snarl occurred upon the eve of your closer union."

"Yes, yes, unfortunate," she babbled. She would say anything to get away. "And I do understand."

Catching Arthur by the hand, Nora fled the kitchen before Tideman could embarrass her further. The man was so concerned for her, and she had to lie to him.

"Lady," Arthur said when they entered her chamber, "the monster might come back."

Arthur had taken to calling Lord Montfort the monster after Nora had told him as much as she felt he was able to understand about her husband's treatment of her.

"He's going to be so busy hunting for me," she said, "he won't have time to return. Blade will see to it by laying a false trail. You'll see."

And so she and Arthur established themselves as the sole occupants of Falaise, though several days passed before Nora could feel secure in her ruse. She even moved herself to a better chamber, larger and with windows that looked out over the front courtyard. Her security lasted a day. On the eve of the fifth day, she and Arthur were spinning tops in front of the fireplace in the hall when one of the lower sections of a window burst open.

"Kit, you pretty piece of manflesh, where are you?"

Tops skittered and smacked against the fireplace. Arthur gave a startled cry and Nora whirled in a flurry of skirts to face the intruder. A painted, leering face goggled at them. A bleary-eyed gaze roamed over Nora and Arthur, dismissing them. The head wagged back and forth, bobbing a tangle of false blond curls, and the smell of ale wafted toward Nora.

The painted mouth opened, and the intruder bawled, "Kiiiiiiiit. It's Sybille. Kiiiiiiiiiiiiiit."

Nora covered her ears, and Arthur giggled. As the woman continued to bawl for Lord Montfort, Nora heard Tideman's running steps. The steward rushed into the hall, then halted abruptly at the sight of the woman. Nora cringed at Sybille's high screech, and her temper gave way. How dare this bawd stick her head into Nora's house and bellow for the man who was her husband? Marching up to Sybille, Nora made a fist and pounded the top of the woman's head three times.

"Be quiet."

"Ouch. Here, love, there's no call for blows. I know I'm late, but I didn't get word of Kit's invitation till yesterday. Where is that man? I haven't had a taste in months."

Nora decided she didn't like Sybille. "He isn't here."

"Ow. My head hurts."

"You're drunk," Tideman said. "Get you from this house, woman. How did you get in?"

"I've been getting into houses of gentry morts since I was a dell."

Nora stepped closer to the window and found that Sybille not only smelled of ale but also was drenched. Her curly hair was wet, and her soggy clothes gave off a musty odor.

"You swam the moat," Nora said in disbelief.

"Can I swim the moat, too?" Arthur asked as he trotted up behind her.

Nora groaned. "No."

"Get you gone, woman," Tideman repeated.

His reply was a snore as Sybille's head dropped to the windowsill.

"I'll remove her, my lady."

"No," Nora said. "Give her the room next to mine."

"But my lady—"

"She's soaked and in a stupor. If we cast her out, she could die of exposure or be set upon. Put her upstairs, please."

"Yes, my lady."

The following afternoon Nora entered the room she had assigned to the bawd Sybille, with Arthur marching behind her, laden with a pile of clothing. Nora carried a tray, which she placed on a stool beside the bed where Sybille lay curled in a ball. THe woman pressed her hands to her forehead and groaned.

"Who's making all that noise? Ooooh."

"Mistress Sybille, you've swilled yourself into a stupor, and I've come to help you."

"Leave me alone." Sybille hunched her body so that her bottom stuck up in the air and her head burrowed into the mattress. "Tell Kit not to worry, I'll be ready to tup in a day or two. Oh, my head."

"Tup?"

Nora's benevolence expired in flames. She yanked the covers from Sybille and smacked the waving bottom. Sybille howled and scrambled away while Arthur clapped his hands and laughed.

"Arthur, this woman isn't fit company for you. Go help Tideman."

"Yes, my lady."

His disappointment marked by his slow steps, Arthur left them reluctantly after depositing his burden of clothing on the bed.

Nora put her hands on her hips and studied Sybille. The woman crouched as far away from her as she could get and peered at Nora through a tangle of snarled and matted hair. Pointing to the tray, Nora ground out her words.

"Drink that."

"What is it?"

"A brew of camomile and other herbs."

"Ech. No thanks, my lady. Where's Kit?"

Nora flew at the woman, grabbed a handful of tangles, and yanked her over to the edge of the bed.

"Ooooow! You pissing bitch. Oooow!"

Shaking her victim by the hair, Nora shouted above Sybille's protests, "Be quiet or I'll dunk you in the moat!"

Sybille was in no condition to fight. Clapping both hands over her mouth, she groaned and subsided. Nora released her hair and poured a cup of the herbal tea.

"Drink."

"Naaah."

"Remember the moat," Nora said.

Sybille took the cup in shaking hands and sipped. "Blehh."

Not waiting for another refusal, Nora shoved the cup to Sybille's lips and held it there until the woman had drained it. When released, the bawd gagged and spat, but Nora was back quickly with more tea. Four cups later, Nora allowed her patient to collapse.

"Eeeeewww. I'm dying."

"You won't be in an hour or so. I'll send up a tub at that time, and I want you to scrub and put those clothes on. And Mistress Sybille, don't go looking for my husband. He's not here."

"Bloody witch."

"I'll see you anon, Mistress Sybille."

Several hours later, Nora sat opposite a transformed Sybille. She eyed the woman's wildly curling hair and generous figure and began to doubt the wisdom of the plan she'd conceived during the night.

"God's bloody arse," Sybille said, "I feel wonderful, and I'm obliged to you, lady." She stuffed a meat pasty in her mouth and spoke at the same time. "Too baa Ah missed Kit." Swallow. "Might as well go back to town."

"Don't go."

Sybille wiped her mouth with the back of her hand, took a gulp of ale, and burped. "Why?"

"You're a thief and a . . . a . . ."

"Whore, lady, a damned good whore. Ask your lord husband."

"How would you like to spend the evening in the pigpen?"

"You just try it." Sybille began to rise from the table.

Nora sighed. "Enough of this arguing. If you'll listen, I've a bargain to strike with you."

"Well, hurry up, I want to get out of this place. That steward gives me the runs."

"Please, Mistress Sybille."

With little grace, the bawd plopped back down on the bench opposite Nora.

"As I said, you're a thief, and you seem to know how to—to get your way and to take care of yourself. The way my husband does, and I would like you to teach me."

"Why?"

"I need to know."

Sybille stared at Nora, and Nora stared back, but she couldn't keep a flush from stealing up her neck to her face.

"Well, stick me in a roomful of new-landed sailors."

"What?"

"Our Kit's too much for the likes of you, is he?" Sybille threw back her head and crowed. "I'm not surprised, love. He plies the whip like a slavemaster. Trouble is, he makes you like it."

Nora bit her lip to keep it still and to forestall tears. "I don't like it."

Sybille was quiet. She stuck her face close to Nora's and remained there for long moments, staring. "No, I can see that." Sybille backed off and leaned her elbows on the table. "Word in the stews is that Kit's gone and lost his heart to a shy little dove with blue blood and no stomach."

"I don't know," Nora said. "But he grinds me under his heel, and I can't have that. Not anymore."

Sybille tossed her head. "Do you mean to tell me you're still afraid of him? Silly chuck."

"I need to learn how to take care of myself and Arthur."

"What you mean is you want to snatch the whip from Kit's pretty hands and make him feel its kiss for once."

"Something like that."

"It will take some doing."

"I know."

"God's blood, I'd love to see Kit at the mercy of a woman, just once. There's a lot of us that would."

"Then you'll teach me?"

Sybille picked up another meat pasty and bit into it. Smiling through bits of crust, she nodded.

"For my room and board and a little extra, I'll show you enough to pit yourself against any coney catcher in the kingdom. Maybe a few tricks of the flesh as well."

Sybille swallowed and wiped her moth. " 'Course, we're going to need a few things. Got a nice sharp dagger about you, love?"

Chapter
XIX

Christian watched his father stroke the muzzle of the destrier that had carried him to victory in tournaments before the great King Harry, and felt as small and distasteful as the flies that buzzed around the creature's tail. The Earl had discovered Christian's treatment of Nora, and there was no reasoning with him. Fathers could be most stubborn. Sebastian glanced at Christian, and Christian felt an unaccustomed heat spread over his cheeks.

"This sinful lusting after revenge has gone too far," Sebastian said.

Christian settled back against an adjoining stable door, set his jaw, and twitched a pile of straw with the end of his riding whip. His father knew nothing of his most sinful acts against Nora.

"You should have thought before you acted. Nora is no dissembler."

"I had no time for reflection," Christian said. "I learned the truth moments before the wedding."

"It matters not. That young woman couldn't ally herself with anyone like Bonner or King Philip, and she'd choose death before she would hurt me."

"I have the cipher."

Sebastian offered his horse a handful of grain while he studied Christian. "Did you ever think she might be sending messages to someone who isn't our enemy?"

Resting the heel of one boot on the toe of the other, Christian gouged at the leather with the handle of the whip. He kept his mouth shut. His father snapped out one word:

"Christian!"

The whip flew across the stable, smacking against a wall, as Christian sprang erect and turned his back on the Earl. "You don't understand. All I could think of was you lying in your own blood, dying, and her being the cause. She betrayed us."

"You don't know that, my headstrong."

"I'll be certain by this evening."

"And when you're proved wrong?"

"It isn't possible, and in any case, I have yet to find the little mouse. It's been six days and she hasn't appeared. I've set watches at Becket's house, and Flegge's, and about the palace. I even sent men to follow the Queen, but they're not back, and I don't think Nora would have gone to Mary."

Sebastian brushed grain dust from his hands and approached Christian. Laying a hand on the younger man's shoulder, he shook his head.

"You must find her soon."

"I know. I can't sleep for imagining what could happen to her. God's blood, I think I'm in Hell."

"No," Sebastian said. "In love, mayhap, but not in Hell."

Christian turned his face away. "I can't love a traitor."

"You don't. Now come with me to the kitchens. You're not hieing off on one of your skulkings until I see you put meat in your stomach. You haven't eaten more than a few mouthfuls in two days."

Under his father's eye, Christian forced himslf to down a meal half the size of his usual serving. Late that night, after the Earl had retired, he slipped away through the concealed passage beneath the chapel and into the city, where he met Inigo and Hext. Near the shop of Unthank, Christian donned a black mask with slits to accommodate his eyes, nose, and mouth, and they took to the roofs. Slithering, leaping, and clambering, they capered from rooftop to rooftop until they reached that of Unthank and dropped through a window in the attic.

Christian shoved open the door that led to the third floor and listened. He heard nothing but the snores of Unthank's servants. He took a step, but Hext barred his way with one arm and took the lead, drawing his sword. Resigned, Christian cast an irritated look at Inigo, who grinned and bowed Christian on.

They floated through the dark house to the shop below, and paused at a panel in the wall of the stairwell. Christian felt along the seam, pressed with three fingers, and heard a click. The panel swung back to reveal emptiness lit by a vague glow. Down a flight of stairs, voices rumbled. With Hext in the vanguard, they descended the stairs silently, but once they gained the shadows at the end, Christian stepped in front. He waited in the darkness just beyond a pool of light where four men stood about a fifth tied to a chair.

The prisoner was a corpulent man of about thirty, dressed in a merchant's gown, his mouth stopped with a leather gag. Christian stepped into the light, and four pairs of eyes snapped to him. Unthank sighed and dropped his hand from his sword hilt, as did Simon Spry and two apprentices. The prisoner's eyes bulged.

"Hugo Paderborn," Christian said. He breathed the name softly, and Hugo's eyes nearly popped out of his head. Christian smiled a slow, lazy smile. "A fat goose ready to be gutted and basted. Remove the gag."

Unthank sniffed. "You'll regret it, my lord."

Upon hearing this form of address, the prisoner whimpered. Christian flicked his hand, and an apprentice slit the gag with a knife. Immediately the room filled with an unnaturally high whine, an octave above the range of a howling dog and several times more annoying.

"O God, don't kill me, don't kill me, please don't kill me. O God O God O God help me. Jesu deliver me, Christ the Savior deliver me, O Christ O God help me O God help me O God."

Christian gritted his teeth and clamped his hand around his sword hilt to keep from slapping Hugo. "Cease this blubbering at once."

"O God O God O God help me. Jesu deliver me, Christ

the Savior deliver me, O Christ O God help me O God help me
O God.''

On and on Hugo whined, his pleas interspersed with whimpers
and grunts. Christian lost what little patience was left to him after
days of worry and frustration. Swooping down on Hugo, he slapped
the man's flaccid cheek once, then again. Hugo's little red mouth
formed an O, and he burst into tears.

Christian threw up his hands. ''God's blood.''

Pacing back and forth in front of Paderborn, he waited for
the man to stop sniffling. A minute passed, but the prisoner only
redoubled his efforts by raising his voice to a wail. Christian
whipped out his dagger and leveled the point at one of the bulges
on Hugo's neck.

''Shut your mouth or I'll stick you.''

Hugo caught his lower lip between his teeth and stopped at
once, wriggling to avoid the metal tip that nicked his skin.
Christian sheathed the dagger, then rested a boot on a low stool,
propped his forearms on his thigh, and subjected Paderborn to
a silent examination. The longer he watched the man, the more
whimpers escaped Hugo's tightly shut mouth.

''I have but one question for you,'' Christian said at last.
''Who is your master?''

''O God O God O God.''

Christian laughed and addressed Unthank. ''Where is that
toy of yours?''

Unthank signaled his apprentices, and the two brought out
a metal object slightly larger than a man's head. Made of iron,
it consisted of four bars joined into a rectangle. The top bar was
pierced by a thick screw, which in turn clamped onto what looked
like a skullcap that hung in the middle of the rectangle. Christian
patted the instrument.

''Now, Paderborn, my jolly whale, you have less than a
minute to tell me who your master is before you don this pretty
cap. If I don't have my answer, these two lads are going to turn
that screw until your head pops like a dropped melon. I, of
course, will stand clear so that your brains don't soil my raiment.''

''O God O God O God O God O God.''

Glancing at the apprentices, Christian lifted a brow.
''Lads?''

The apprentices hoisted their instrument, and Hugo wailed. Everyone froze, though, as the door at the top of the stairs opened and a voice called down, ''I know that whine.''

Christian whirled about, drawing his sword. Hext and Inigo stepped between the stairs and Christian while the apprentices backed away from the prisoner and felt for their own weapons. A slight man came down the steps, unperturbed by the weapons. Masked similarly to Christian, the newcomer walked calmly into the midst of the armed men and stopped before Christian. As the man stepped into the light, Christian cursed and sheathed his sword. Everyone followed his lead, and Hugo started crying.

''What are you doing to my printer, Misrule?'' the newcomer asked.

''You're supposed to be in France.''

''I'm not in France,'' came the bland reply.

''Have you heard of the recent difficulties?''

''Yes, and I thank God the one dear to you was spared. I called upon him, and he sent me after you with a few words of ire that I won't repeat.''

Christian folded his arms over his chest. ''I but seek to protect those close to me and those I revere.'' Without taking his eyes from the visitor, he added, ''Show our fat goose the novelties of wearing your toy, Unthank.''

''Ohhhhhh.''

''Misrule, I know you're angry, but I can't let you squeeze the brains out of one of my best servants.''

Christian went still. The only movement visible was a vein pulsing at his temple. Slowly he lifted a hand, and Unthank began untying the prisoner. Christian turned his back to the room and contemplated the bricks on the wall and his new Hell.

Paderborn was escorted out, and soon Christian was alone with the visitor. When the door above shut, Christian walked to the chair vacated by Paderborn, lifted it above his head, and hurled it against the far wall. Splintered wood and chunks of brick went flying, but the noise was nothing compared to the obscenities that erupted from Christian's mouth.

The visitor made no sign of alarm. He removed his mask to reveal thinning hair and heavy-lidded, sensual eyes, then calmly folded the mask into a square.

''Both you and the Princess,'' he said, ''have the habit of

throwing things when aroused. Do you think she will continue after becoming Queen?''

Christian turned on the man, breathing hard, his body taut with the effort to contain the hatred he felt for himself. ''Cecil, do you understand what has happened?''

''Someone is trying to expose you.''

''Or kill me and my father, and I blamed Nora. May God forgive me.''

''Yes,'' Cecil said.

''But Paderborn serves you.''

Cecil nodded.

''And Nora was sending messages to Paderborn.''

''I know.''

Covering his face with his hand, Christian sank back against the wall. ''Merciful God, Cecil, you don't know what I've done.''

''I shudder to imagine it, considering your willful nature and your lust for vengeance. Nora but assuages her pain at seeing so many suffer by giving me what news she gathers at court.'' Cecil put a hand on Christian's shoulder. ''Lad, you're still in danger. Retire with your family to the country while I make inquiries. You'll be safer away from the city, and you've mistakes to correct.''

Christian lifted his face from his hands and stared up at the ceiling. ''But the Princess . . .''

''Balances between the Spanish and the French, keeping both guessing which she favors while she courts allies at home. It is my task to multiply the numbers of subjects about the Queen who clamor for Mary to name Elizabeth her heir. You can't serve our lady if you're dead. Go to the country.''

''I must find my wife.'' Christian eyed a stool, the only other piece of furniture in the room.

''Do so, and then leave London. The Princess wills it.'' Cecil glanced at the stool, too, and put his body between it and Christian.

Thwarted from giving further vent to his fury, Christian snapped at Cecil, ''You could have told me she was a friend.''

''What kind of spymaster reveals the identities of his intelligencers to all and sundry?''

''God's breath, what a miserable mishap,'' Christian said.

"Unfortunate, but not without remedy."

When his comment was met with silence, William Cecil departed as silently as he had come.

Christian heard the panel above his head snap shut. Bracing himself against the wall with both hands, he allowed his head to droop while he thought. Nora, cowering, shy little Nora, braved death to aid Princess Elizabeth. He reeled under the strain of fitting this picture to the one he had formed of the girl. His most vivid and recent memory of her was of her wide, frightened eyes. She was so small and so afraid. So courageous, too, it seemed, for how much more courage did it require to risk death when one was small and frightened and a woman, than when one was a man trained to defend himself.

Christian winced and his body cringed. "Everlasting damnation."

Images of what he had done penetrated his senses in flashes of memory. His mind reeled at the pictures—of himself standing over Nora in the bridal bed, taking her heart in his hands and tearing it in pieces; of Nora's face dissolving into horror as she realized it was he lying over Mag's naked body; of Nora huddled in her bed so hurt that she wept without stopping.

Christian grimaced, squeezing his eyes shut to block the pain and remorse. He whispered softly to himself, "No."

He remembered the last time he saw her. It was then that he'd noticed a change. Always before, even when she feared him, she'd followed him with her eyes, as if he were the only object of her interest. But that last time, though she had looked at him, that consuming interest had vanished.

As guilt flayed him, Christian considered for the first time the possibility that he might have killed the love of the only woman to whom he had ever considered surrendering himself. Close on this revelation came fear. Sailing in on bat's wings, putrid and festering, it settled over his spirit like the cloak of a leper.

Reeling under the onslaught of remorse and fear, Christian slid to the floor. Guilt fed his fear, stoking it into a bonfire of terror as great as that he'd experienced at nearly losing his father. He'd almost killed her body with his cruelty, and there was a good chance he had killed her love. Nora, great of heart, cou-

rageous for anyone but herself, quick of wit, and elegant of mind
. . . and full of secret sensuality until he had made her fear love.

Shaking his head, Christian gazed at a wall sconce without
seeing it. *"Christ."*

He couldn't find her. She might be dead because of him. If
she'd been hurt from his blindness . . . He covered his face with
his hands and willed the moisture in his eyes to disappear. For
once, he couldn't accomplish the feat. The phrases of an old
song thrummed in his head.

> Shall she never out of my mind,
> Nor shall I never out of this pain?
> Alas, here she doth me so bind
> Except her help I am near slain.

Had he killed her love? Christian shivered and rose to his feet.
He would search her out and ask her. It would be the most
difficult task he'd ever set himself, but he would fight to gain
absolution from her.

It was a hard thing, this guilt, a carrion thing, a punishment
worthy of his crime. Christian almost laughed at himself as he
headed for the stairs. Never had he imagined that one day he
would crave a woman's love more than he craved revenge on
Jack Midnight—and never had he thought to fear his fate at the
hands of a dainty mite like Nora Becket.

By the next morning Christian had successfully concealed his
remorse. The Earl summoned him to his study, only to be interrupted by Simon Spry. The thief barely got out three sentences of his report when Christian leaped on him. Propelled by
a boot to his buttocks, Spry flew out of the room to land in the
hall. Christian swooped after him, pausing in the threshold, arms
and legs braced to attack.

"Don't tell me you can't find her, you pig-sticking runt.
You're going to search London from one end to the other if I
have to kick you every inch of the way."

Christian moved, but Simon was on his feet and running.
Racing lightly down the stairs after his quarry, Christan slowed
as the thief vanished in the direction of the kitchens.

The creak of strained floorboards caught his attention, and he saw Anthony Now-Now lumber into view, trailing Blade. Blade scowled at Christian. "You can't expect me to make progress finding Nora or cozening de Ateca with this great anvil chained to my leg."

"Ah, it's the fruit sucket, all done up tastily and fit for devouring."

For once Blade laughed instead of bristling. "You don't fool me anymore. Your guts are braided into knots, and the longer she's gone, the more they twist."

Christian opened his mouth, but his father called down to them.

"I forbid this public quarreling. Both of you come up at once."

Blade walked past him, swaggering and smirking. As the youth passed, Christian whispered to him, "Be careful, my comfit, or I really will feed you to the Spaniard."

"Piss in your boot." Blade ran up the stairs before Christian could grab him.

Catching up with the boy in the Earl's study, Christian fixed him with a vulture's stare. Blade greeted Sebastian, falling to one knee and giving the Earl a humble and admiring obeisance that aroused Christian's suspicions. His father's voice distracted him.

"It isn't possible, my headstrong. Nora is too innocent and unwise in street ways to be able to hide this long in the city."

"I know," Christian said as he watched Blade handle a book of Greek poetry with apparent unconcern for their dilemma. "And I've been pondering the whole idea. When we set out from Falaise, I couldn't find a trace of her. There were tracks of a mare that had been taken from the stables, but those disappeared."

Easing his way toward Blade, Christian fell silent.

"And she was heading toward London when you lost her," Sebastian said as he studied a map.

Christian rested a hip on the table next to Blade's book. "Yes . . . headed toward London, but when the trail vanished, I was about to turn back to find it again, when our sweet comfit here found my wife's kerchief lying beside the road." Brutal in its swiftness, Christian's hand dove to pin Blade's arm to the table.

"Ow! Let go!"

As Blade protested, Christian sprang up and twisted the arm behind his back. "How convenient that I was diverted from my purpose by our reluctant guest." He yanked Blade's arm up, and the youth cried out. "Where is she?"

"Go tup yourself, you frigging arse."

"I'll show you frigging, you—"

"Enough!"

The Earl's command silenced them both. Sebastian was at Christian's side, his hand on his son's shoulder.

"Chris, this is not the way."

"He knows where she is."

"I will handle this. Release him, my son. I wish it."

Christian ground his teeth together, longing to twist Blade in half to get what he wanted, but the hand on his shoulder and his father's gentle command did what all the force in the kingdom could not. Christian yielded.

Sebastian stepped between his son and Blade and helped the youth bring his arm down. Blade was gasping with pain, and the Earl rubbed the tormented arm as he spoke.

"I've been searching for your family."

Blade cursed and dug his fingers into the flesh at his elbow.

"Christian has also," Sebastian went on, "but we've found no one. Of course, there hasn't been time to search all the northern counties. It will take some weeks, possibly months. Perhaps by winter—"

"It's useless," Blade said.

"No, it isn't, but I wonder if you understand what has happened." Blade shook his head. "My tempest of a son has dangled you from puppet strings and pricked you with his sharpest knives, but you're still alive."

"Ha!"

"You're still alive, and all the while he searches for your family."

"He uses me."

"Mayhap, but you must mark how he has changed."

Christian's voice rose. "Sire, don't."

"He loves that girl." The Earl sliced his hand in a warning

gesture as Christian growled. "He is suffering for his sins and wishes to atone. And I wish you to help him do that."

"He'll hurt her again."

"Blade, trust me if you can't trust Christian. I would never do anything to endanger Nora. I've seen them together, and the vision of each is filled with the other. Put them in the same room and no power in Heaven or Hell can keep them from touching each other."

"You mean he wants to debauch her."

"You keep your filthy thoughts off Nora," Christian said. He stepped toward Blade, but his father blocked his way.

Sebastian warded his son off with one hand while buffeting Blade with his other. "Tell me where Nora hides. If you can't feel pity for Christian, have mercy upon me. My son hasn't eaten in days and hasn't slept either. He's losing weight, and if his pain isn't eased soon, he will vanish before my eyes. Difficult as he is, I couldn't bear to lose him."

"He's too perverse to die," Blade said. "Oh, God curse it, all right. If I have your word that he won't hurt her again, I'll speak."

"Better," Sebastian said. "You will have Christian's word."

Christian rounded on Blade, his mouth a straight slash and his face expressionless. Blade glanced at the Earl with apprehension.

In a thrice Sebastian slapped Christian lightly across the cheek. Christian's head snapped to the side and his eyes rounded. He stared at his father as he touched the reddened skin of his jaw.

"Mulish child, this is no time to threaten. Haven't your aggressions wrecked your life enough?"

Meeting his father's glare, Christian beheld both condemnation and understanding. He sighed, muttered an apology, and forced himself to turn to Blade and draw his sword. Holding it in front of his body, hilt up, he spoke.

"I give you my oath upon this cross, I won't harm Nora."

Blade grasped the sword at the hilt. "Do you swear that you love her?"

"I am going to lash you at the whipping post."

"Christian," Sebastian said.

Scowling, Christian barked out his word. "I swear that I love her, you little blight."

Blade chuckled. "I suspected, but with you, it's impossible to be sure." Christian hurled an obscenity at him, and Blade danced out of sword's reach. "Don't try to kill me before I tell you where she is."

"Out with it, lad," Sebastian said, his mouth twitching. "Else he'll take a fit before your eyes."

Blade grinned. "Forgive me, my lord, but I've longed for a chance to make him dance for my entertainment." Bowing, the youth chuckled as he watched Christian fume. "Very well, I suppose I'll enjoy your fury when I tell you that she never left Falaise."

There was silence, and Blade's grin widened as he watched Christian take in the news.

"Never left Falaise?" Christian sheathed his sword, the metal singing with the violence of his movements. He grasped the edge of the table and tried to dig his fingers into the wood. "Bloody, everlasting, fucking Hell."

Blade's chortles were like dagger pricks, and Christian flexed his muscles, lifting the table off the floor. His father quickly intervened. Shoving his weight across the table, he slammed it back down on its legs.

Christian appeared not to notice. He darted a vicious look at Blade and stomped away, muttering again, "Bloody, everlasting, fucking Hell."

"My headstrong," the Earl called after his son. "I'm sending some of my own men with you this time. And Blade. In your present state you couldn't find your own toes, much less your wife."

Chapter
XX

Nora held her wooden knife at waist level, blade up, and pointed her forefinger. Trying to remember not to clamp her fingers around the hilt, she circled with Sybille in the kitchen yard while Arthur shouted encouragement. Around and around they went, each trying to make the other face the sun. Suddenly Sybille dove at her, and Nora saw the woman's blade strike downward. She sank in a rapid lunge and cut under, blocking the strike with her left hand while she lashed out with her right, hitting Sybille in the ribs.

Sybille grunted and then shouted at Nora, "Don't stop. Keeping moving, and don't give me time to recover. Jump back if you don't make a clean finish. You're too little to stay within reach and not lose."

Wiping sweat from her brow and chin, Nora backed away, circling again. She'd donned a maid's rough gown, pulling the back skirt up between her legs and tucking it in the waistband. The clothing gave her the freedom she needed to leap and dance about. And she did need it, for Sybille never let her rest when they practiced. Nora dodged Sybille's knife, blocked it to the outside, and swiped at the woman's throat with her own blade. The wood hit skin, and Sybille yelped.

Nora dropped her knife and rushed to the older woman. Sybille was holding her throat, and when Nora moved her hand, it came away smeared with blood.

"Oh, no. Oh, I'm so sorry." Nora dabbed at the wound with a piece of her skirt.

Sybille gave a snort and then chuckled. "Don't be sorry, love. You just killed me. I'd say I earned my wages."

Arthur ran up to them, laughing and clapping. "My lady won. Now it's my turn."

"Not now, you little beggar. Can't you see I've been sore wounded?" Sybille clapped the boy on the head and tickled his ribs.

"Then may I go to the ruins, my lady?"

"As long as you don't try to swim," Nora said.

As Arthur scampered off, Nora walked back to the house with Sybille.

"What ruins?" Sybille asked as she mopped the nick at her throat.

"An old tower. It's all crumbled and fallen down. It's by the river, and Arthur pretends to besiege it."

"Men, they're born ready to fight. That's why the likes of us have to know how to defend ourselves."

"But it's hard," Nora said as they entered the house.

"You're learning. It wasn't long ago that you whimpered like a tupped nun if I even gave you a mean look."

"Sybille!"

"Quick: What's the art of using false dice to cheat a co-ney?"

"Cheating Law."

"What's a nip?"

"He cuts purses with a knife and a horn thumb. And a foist picks a purse with his fingers."

"And what's cozenage with whores?"

Nora blushed but said, "Crossbiting Law. A bawd entices a gull into her room, and then a roystering boy pretends to be her husband or brother. He bursts in on them and threatens a duel to make the gull pay to save his life or his reputation."

"I'm good at crossbiting," Sybille said.

Nora lifted her skirt as they mounted the stairs to her chambers. "Oh. Um . . . how—how clever of you."

"You get more money from crossbiting than plain whoring," Sybille went on. "I remember one time last year, this new married son of a wool merchant couldn't even wait to get his clothes off before he started. It's better if they're caught naked, you know. Anyway, he was grinding away when Ham—that's my roysterer—when Ham comes charging in. That wool merchant bleated like one of his own sheep and paid us enough to last till spring."

"How fortunate," Nora said. Desperate to stanch the flow of lurid reminiscences, she reminded Sybille that she'd promised to bathe.

A long groan was the response.

"I'll give you one of my dresses if you bathe."

Sybille chewed her lip while she considered. "The blue one with the silver embroidery?"

"If you like."

"It's a bargain. Only I hope I don't catch an ague from bathing and die before I can wear the dress for Ham."

It wasn't long before Nora was arranging the skirt of her blue gown over the farthingale attached to Sybille's hips. The woman kept twisting out of her grasp in an effort to see herself in the long mirror in Nora's chamber.

"Hold still," Nora said.

"But I want to see."

Nora chuckled and sat back on her heels while Sybille whirled about.

"Bloody heaven and hell," Sybille said. "It fits, all except the top. It's squeezing my tits something terrible."

Nora eyed the woman's breasts. The bodice pressed them up until they bulged over the low, square neckline, which bit into Sybille's skin.

"We'll have to let the seams out. I can do that."

"Oh, look." Sybille pointed in the mirror. "I look like you."

Nora rose to stand beside the woman, and indeed, they were of similar height and build—discounting the chest, of course.

"Wait," Nora said.

She grabbed the matching French hood from the bed and fitted it onto Sybille. The headdress covered the top of her head while the veil concealed her hair. Nora stood next to Sybille again. Now each wore a gown and hood, and they struck the same pose.

"I could be a lady," Sybille said in a breathy voice. "I could be as pretty as you."

"I'm not pretty."

"Who says?"

Nora looked away from Sybille's skeptical glance. "Lots of people. My husband."

"Kit?" Sybille snorted. "He must have been furious. He's usually much better at concocting insults that will shrivel your skin. Nah, he's hot for you, or it wouldn't be all over the stews that the snow prince has melted."

"I don't think so."

Sybille suddenly looked toward the window.

"What's all that clatter?"

Nora opened the window and peered down into the courtyard. Across the lowered drawbridge trotted several men in Montfort livery. She didn't wait to see who they escorted, but quickly stepped back.

"Dear Lord, my husband."

"Where?" Sybille shoved her face out the window and opened her mouth, but Nora clamped a hand over her lips.

"Shhh! You'll warn him."

Sybille came back inside and shoved Nora's hand away. "So?"

"God's mercy, Sybille. You've got to help me get away."

"Kit won't like it."

"If you help me, I'll give you two more dresses."

"It's a bargain. You slip out the kitchen yard, and I'll meet Kit. If I stay at the top of the stairs when he comes in, I'll be in the shadows and he won't see me clearly."

Nora was already gathering a bundle of her clothing and some coins she'd found in Christian's chamber. "Make him chase you all over the house. Keep him busy for as long as you can. The dresses are in my old room."

"Don't worry, love. Quicker than a hind, I am."

Nora ran out of the chamber, calling behind her, "Thank you, Sybille. I won't forget."

As she hurried downstairs, Nora heard shouts in the courtyard. Darting through a door that would take her to the rear of the house, she paused on the other side to look back into the hall. The double doors at the other end crashed open, and she heard her husband bellow her name. Nora gave a peep of alarm and bolted. Racing past surprised Cook, Nora fled the manor through a sally port set in the rear wall. She crossed the one-man bridge over the moat and flew down the slope toward the forest that marched close on the back of Falaise.

She had to find Arthur and put as much distance as she could between them and Lord Montfort. The river wasn't far, and she soon burst into a clearing at its banks.

She stopped to catch her breath. "Arthur!" She had to call three more times before she got an answer.

"Over here, my lady."

Nora swerved to the right, plunged into a wall of shrubs, and stumbled on a fallen slab of hewn stone.

"Up here, lady."

Arthur's shining curls appeared above a chunk of stone high in the old tower. Not much more than a pile of rubble, the Norman structure was more ivy and crumbling mortar than anything else.

"Come quickly," Nora said. "Lord Montfort has returned, and we must flee."

As she finished speaking, someone roared her name. Nora turned toward Falaise and heard the sounds of someone thrashing about in the forest. Arthur was climbing down.

"No," Nora said. She threw her bundle over her shoulder and scrambled up the spray of stones at the foot of the tower. Reaching Arthur, she led him back to the top where they crouched, noses level with the highest stone. From this vantage, Nora could see Christian as he burst into the clearing. He stopped, head tilted to one side, and listened. Beside her, Arthur fumbled among the rubble at his feet until she stilled him with one hand.

Christian paced the clearing, looking like a tall, catlike animal who'd caught a scent. He slowed as he approached the tower, then knelt to touch the bent branches of a shrub. At once he was up and racing lightly toward them.

"Damnation," Nora said, her fear growing with each graceful stride he took.

Arthur shoved a rock in her hand, and she looked down at

him. The boy grinned at her, hefting a boulder in two hands. Nora peeked down at her husband. He had stopped a few yards from the tower and was looking up, scoring the ruin with his gaze.

"You might as well come down, chuck," he called. "I know you're there."

Nora hunched back down, shivering at the sound of the caress in his voice. He was in that strange mood again. He wanted to play with her. Her hand clamped around her rock and she bit her lip. He wasn't going to toy with her again, and she would kill him before she allowed him to hurt Arthur.

"Come, Nora, you're being irksome, and I've things to tell you."

As he spoke, Christian's voice grew louder, and Nora realized he was going to climb up after her.

"Now, Arthur."

She rose, bent over the top of the tower, and hurled the rock. Arthur did the same. Hers bounced off the side of the tower and sailed past Christian's ear. Arthur's missile hit the ground and ricocheted off Christian's boot.

"God's blood!"

Christian hopped backward holding his foot while Arthur laughed. Nora wasted no time in gloating. She rummaged about for more ammunition, straightening just as Christian stalked up to the tower again.

"Don't you dare throw that," he said. He put his hands on his hips and fixed her with a look of combined ire and dominance.

She cocked her arm and hurled the rock at his face. He dove to the side, but Arthur was ready with another stone, which hit him squarely in the back.

"Hell's demons!" Christian rolled to the base of the tower under a barrage and slithered up the pile, dodging bits of mortar and rock as he came.

"Run, Arthur!" Nora shouted when she saw her husband's head clear the last stone between him and them. "Run, and I'll catch up!"

Arthur hesitated, but she shoved him to the side and hurled a stone at Christian with both hands. He ducked, cursing, and Arthur slipped past him as he dove at Nora. Nora had another rock in her hands and was raising it over her head when Christian's shoulder hit her stomach. She flew backward under his weight, dropping the stone. They fell on the top ledge of the tower, with their upper bodies hanging over the edge.

Then Nora remembered her lessons with Sybille. Squirming for the right position, she jerked her knee up between Christian's legs. All she got for her trouble was a grunt, for her skirts padded the blow.

"You little wolf cub, stop that."

Christian wrapped his arms around her torso and rolled to haul her on top of his body. Frantic to escape and reach Arthur, she bit his neck. Her husband yelped and thrust her away. She regained her balance and launched herself down the spray of stones after her page. In moments a hand caught her arm and she was yanked back against Christian's chest. As she sailed toward him Nora doubled her fist and smashed it into his jaw. Christian yelped with pain and captured her fist.

"God's teeth, woman, you've transformed into a harpy."

She bent over his arm, ready to sink her teeth into the back of his hand.

"Oh, no, you don't." Christian grabbed her wrists and held her at arm's length. "Will you listen to me?"

"If you hurt Arthur, I'll kill you."

"Hurt Arthur?" Christian shook his head, then pursed his lips and whistled. Hext appeared with a struggling Arthur slung over his hip.

"Devil!" Arthur screamed. "Fiend! Let me go!"

Nora kicked at Christian's shins. "Let him go."

Christian dodged her foot and shook his head. "Stop fighting me. I won't hurt him, I promise."

Nora's foot was in midair, ready for another kick. She set it back on the ground and warily watched her husband while she caught her breath. Hair in a wild tangle about her face, she stood with her wrists imprisoned and drops of perspiration gathering on her upper lip. Christian was staring at her in an odd, startled way that puzzled her. Without looking away from her, he spoke to Hext.

"Take the boy back to the house and see that he's tended. Lock him in a room or we'll end up chasing him across the county."

Nora watched Hext disappear with Arthur still slung over his hip. When he was gone, she had no excuse to ignore her own fear, and her knees began to turn to melted cheese. She licked her dry lips and met her husband's gaze. He was staring at her still, as he had since she'd stopped fighting. Curiosity, confusion, hot arousal, and other unidentifiable emotions jumbled together in his eyes, exposing an agitation she'd rarely seen him reveal. She tried to shrink away from him, but he only tightened his hold on her wrists.

"I'm not going to hurt you either, Nora. Even though you've just tried to stone me to death. God's teeth, you've turned into a warrior."

She tugged at her wrists in vain. "How do I know you're not lying?"

"Beshrew you, woman, stop wriggling."

Nora twisted her arms and pulled at the same time. Christian muttered an obscenity and hauled her to his body so that her arms were trapped between them. Immediately she drew back her foot.

"If you kick me again, I'll throw you in the river."

Lowering her foot, she glared up into her husband's face. She was startled when he sighed with relief and smiled at her. She didn't return his smile.

"How do I know you aren't lying?" she asked.

His smile vanished, and he closed his eyes for a moment. When he opened them, Nora beheld something she'd never seen in Christian. Fear.

"I didn't want to begin it like this," he said, "but you give me no choice. I—Paderborn is a fool, you know."

"Who?"

"How was I to know?"

"Know what?"

"And you wouldn't tell me, and he was in France."

"Who was in France?" Nora shoved at Christian, who appeared to be suffering from all the evil humors at once.

"I should have listened to you."

"My lord, you've made no sense at all, and I still don't believe you mean no harm."

"But I don't," Christian said. He searched Nora's face before looking down at the ground. A flush stole over his cheeks and he lowered his voice. "I spoke with William Cecil."

It took Nora a full minute to realize what he meant. "Oh." She drew in a deep breath and let it out. "You can release me."

He loosened his grip and stepped away, only to fall to his knees at her feet. She gaped at him when he snatched her hand and kissed it. Turning it over, he kissed her palm, but she shook off his grip and put both hands behind her back.

"I was wrong," he said. He touched the hem of her skirt. "And I was cruel. A monster. Arthur is right to name me one, and I beg you to forgive me."

Nora looked down at Christian de Rivers, looked at him on his knees begging for her charity as she'd once dreamed of him doing.

"It doesn't matter," she said.

He leaned toward her. "Of course it matters," he whispered violently. "I can never make up for what I've done. It matters."

"No," she said as if she were speaking to a lackwit. "You see, it would matter if I cared, but I don't care anymore. I don't care if you believe me. I don't care if you love me. I don't care if I see you. I just don't care. So you see, it's not important to me that you know you were wrong and that you're contrite."

He rose, his hand strangling the hilt of his dagger. "Please, Nora, you must give me a chance to mend what I've broken."

Saying nothing, Nora watched as he reached out to her with one hand. It was a strong, clean hand, its skin smooth and brown and warm, and once she would have given all she possessed for it to stretch out to her so beseechingly. Now she didn't care.

"I have changed," she said.

"I'm beginning to see." He let his hand drop and tilted his head, his manner grave. "Mayhap we should begin anew, write a new Genesis."

She shook her head. "I've had time to think. I want to go back to my country house and live there with Arthur and my old servants."

"No."

"I don't want to be your wife."

She turned toward Falaise, but he blocked her way in two strides.

"No power on earth can undo our marriage," he said.

"I'm not a fool. Not all husbands and wives live together. You may live as you please, and so will I."

As she spoke, Nora saw Christian's expression harden. Contrition vanished, and he coolly examined her from head to foot.

"Who has taken my place?"

"What mean you?" She backed away as he began to stalk her.

"Did you seek comfort from some other man?"

Christian asked the question calmly, but his chest rose and fell heavily, as if he couldn't get enough air in his lungs. Nora kept backing away, and he kept coming.

"I think your wits have turned to mud," she said as she tried to avoid him.

"No one else will ever touch you."

"I want no one else."

"Ah!"

He swooped at her. She jumped back only to fall against a tree, and he was on her in a moment. He braced his arms on either side of her and pressed her between his body and the tree.

"There is hope if you want no one but me," he said.

She stomped on his foot. He grunted, and she smiled her satisfaction. "I didn't say that. I said I didn't want anyone."

"Else. You said you didn't want anyone else."

"Quibbler." She shoved at the velvet-covered chest that pressed against her own. "Get away from me, sirrah."

He nuzzled her cheek and whispered in her ear. "Too late. You're caught, my chuck, trapped between my body and a tree, and just pushing against you has made me as hard as this trunk. Don't you feel anything?"

He was doing it again, Nora thought. Trying to cozen her with his body. Moving it in that lascivious fashion that had once driven her frantic with desire. She gasped as he fitted his hips to hers and thrust. Feelings she'd thought impossible to resurrect burst to life again, and with them came the memory of her wedding night.

Fear clawed at her, the fear of being humiliated and hurt again, but this time Nora refused to give in to it. She wouldn't let him use her again. Wrath burgeoned, searing through her desire and her fear. It gave her the urge and the will to free one of her hands as Christian kissed her neck.

Reaching behind him, she grabbed a fistful of his hair and tried to tear it from his head. His upper body jerked back as he cried out, and she slid from beneath him while keeping her hold on his hair. She pulled hard, and Christian overbalanced, falling onto his back. Nora ran.

Too soon she heard him behind her. Casting a glance over her shoulder, she saw him leap, his face contorted with anger. She sprang forward, but he caught her anyway. They crashed to the ground, but Christian twisted at the last moment so that they landed side by side. Before she could recover, he rolled so that she was beneath him.

"By God, don't you ever do that again." He glared at her. She glared right back, and he blinked. "Beshrew me if you aren't more dragon than mouse now." He paused and wet his lips. "I've a craving for dragons."

He closed his eyes and thrust his groin between her legs. "God, Nora, I know you wanted me once. I can give you pleasure again."

Lowering his head, he pressed his open mouth upon her lips. Nora had thought herself incapable of greater anger, but she was wrong. As Christian succumbed to lust and cast aside his penitence, she writhed with fury. When he covered her mouth, she bit his lower lip. He cried out and pulled free. Grasping her shoulders, he shook her until her head wobbled.

"You—little—harpy!" he shouted. "You'll pay for that, damn you."

He stopped shaking her, but Nora's head still spun. Sharp pains arced up and down her neck, and her gorge rose. Falling limp, she would have hit her head if Christian hadn't supported her. Weak and disoriented, she kept her eyes closed, for the world whirled around her if she didn't. Suddenly Christian wrapped her in his arms, and the world stopped its dance. When he pressed her cheek against his chest and murmured an endearment, her nausea subsided.

"I've done it again," he said. "I'm sorry. But you must give me time to accustom myself to your defiance. After all, I was much enamored of Nora the mouse."

She spoke against the soft material of his doublet. "Let me go."

"Don't ask me that again."

Belying his words, he released her and got up. He pulled her to her feet, then swept them out from under her and lifted her into his arms. She kicked, but he clamped an arm tight around her thighs. As she began to struggle, he squeezed until she gave a cry of pain.

"Be still. You can't win, and I don't want to hurt you anymore."

"What are you going to do?" The fear was back.

"I told you. We will begin again. This is a week for beginning over, for I must win you back and find the true culprit, the engineer of my near destruction."

"Go look for your traitor and leave me alone."

He didn't answer. Nora wriggled ineffectively as he crossed the bridge to the sally port. She was still struggling when he dumped her in his bed in the master's chambers.

The bed was her undoing. She hissed a denial and scrambled to her hands and knees while he stood glaring down at her. His tension, the set hardness of his face all spoke of one intent.

"No," she said.

He nodded, not speaking, then put one knee on the bed. When his gaze strayed to her breast, she sprang at him. Taking advantage of his surprise, she yanked at his belt and swung off the bed in one movement, coming away with his dagger. As the hilt fit into her hand palm, an exultant sense of power flooded her, and she smiled. Turning on her husband, she gloried in watching his lust ebb, but a condescending smile soon curled his lips.

"Now, chuck, you don't want to play with that."

"I'm not playing."

He slipped off the bed and began to circle, and she moved with him. He stopped, surprised that she matched his pace. Then he started again, this time using a fighter's crouched stance. Nora bent at the waist and held her weapon level. Understanding came over Christian's features, and he whistled.

"You're making me drunk with enticement."

His arm shot out to snatch the dagger. Nora dodged and

brought her free arm around to knock his hand away. Keeping her distance, she worked her way toward the door.

"Very good," Christian said.

He came at her again, forcing her to circle away from the door. She adjusted by putting her back to the windows and making him face the light that streamed through them.

"It was Sybille who taught you this, wasn't it?"

"Yes."

"I'll have to turn her over my knee for it."

"What have you done with her?"

"When I caught her, I tossed her aside. I don't think she stayed any longer. She knows how I repay ill favors." He stopped and shaded his eyes against the window light. "Come, enough of this dancing about. You wanted me once."

"I don't want you anymore."

Smirking, he lowered his voice and caressed her with his eyes. "Oh, sweeting, if I made you want me once, I can do it again. And when I've delved between your thighs and taken my pleasure, you'll forget my trespass. I'll thrust it from your mind as I thrust my seed into your body."

Fury burned in Nora's heart, making her slow to react when Christian dropped, rolled, and struck her arm with his foot. It was a light blow, tempered by his consideration, and she remembered her instruction. Giving in to the force of the impact, she allowed her dagger arm to swing back, her body following in a circle. She avoided Christian's leap at her and faced him again.

He laughed at her cleverness, and that laugh shoved her over the edge. With a strength born of weeks of humiliation, she lashed out, cutting through the velvet and silk of his doublet. She felt the material rip, feel the blade slice through flesh. The shock of penetration stayed her hand, and she cried out, withdrawing the weapon from his shoulder even as he pulled away. Nora sprang back, panting and shivering as her husband clutched at the wound high on his shoulder. It hadn't been a deep cut, but it was her first, and she recoiled from the experience.

Expecting Christian's wrath, she raced for the door. He was there before her, hand still pressing against his wound. She backed away from him, dagger held at ready. Her jaw dropped when he began to chuckle.

"So this is what I get for pestering you to be brave," he said.

"It's what you get for presuming that all you have to do to make me fall at your feet is—is tup me."

"It is."

She tossed her head and gave him a look of scorn. "If what you say were true, I would be lying on that bed this moment. Shall I explain again, my lord?" She raised her voice to a shout that had the full force of her lungs behind it. "I don't love you. Do you hear me? I don't love you." She paused, then lowered her voice while her fury drained away. "In truth, my lord, I find that I don't even like you. But most of all, I cannot summon enough interest in you to find you worthy of my hate."

Silence filled the room as Christian took in her words. He grimaced once, then concealed his reaction behind a blank stare. They regarded each other warily while he held his wound and blood trickled between his fingers. Finally, he spoke.

"It seems we're to have a contest of wills. Take heed, my chuck, for mine is the greater, the stronger. God made woman to submit, and after all I am a loving master."

"You're not fit to be a dog's master."

He opened the door. "Since you've changed so much, I'll remind you of the words in the Bible. He quoted to her in latin, and the passage was well known to her, so she had no difficulty translating. 'Wives, submit yourselves unto your own husbands, as unto the Lord. For the husband is the head of the wife, even as Christ is the head of the church: and he is the savior of the body. Therefore as the church is subject unto Christ so let the wives be to their own husbands in every thing.' " He grinned at her. "So you see, I'm the savior of your body."

"Somehow, my lord, I don't think God had you in mind when he inspired Paul to write those words." Nora sprang at him, shoved him out the door, and slammed it shut.

Folding her arms over her chest, she scowled at the panel. She heard a a click as Christian turned a key in the lock.

"Monster!"

She could barely hear his chuckle through the door. She shrieked, launched herself away from the door, then turned and hurled the dagger. It stabbed into the oak and remained there, quivering, as she sank to her knees. She was hot and cold at the same time, and weak. She could hardly understand herself anymore.

She wasn't a termagant, a brawler, yet she'd bitten and kicked her husband and given him a taste of steel. She'd actually made him dizzy with her aggression. Was he right? Had she changed so much?

Nora sat on the floor and contemplated her own temerity. She had stood up to the frightening and beautiful and vicious creature she'd married. The question was, what was he going to do about it?

Chapter
XXI

Hurtling downstairs, hand still pressed to his wound, Christian almost collided with Blade and his escort of guards. He sidestepped the three and plunged into the bowels of the house as the guards fell back. In the kitchen he scowled at Cook, who fled along with her staff. Christian grabbed a cloth and dipped it in a bucket of water.

"Hell," he said. "Hell, hell, hell, hell, hell."

Evil humors must have invaded his brain for him to have behaved so to Nora.

"Hell, hell, hell."

A nasty-sweet voice interrupted him. "I hope it isn't my presence that has upset you, since my coming was your idea."

He turned to find Blade smiling at him. The younger man's guards hovered near the kitchen door, well aware of their master's mood. Christian waved them away, and they bumped into each other trying to get out of the room.

Pointing to a cauldron hanging in the fireplace, Christian matched Blade's treaclelike voice. "How would you like to join the vegetables in that stock?"

"I wouldn't like it," Blade said. "For then I couldn't watch

you suffer. You can't know how much pleasure I've gotten from seeing you writhe. You don't eat, you hardly sleep, and now your true pain is about to begin. You don't have to keep guards on me. I'll stay gladly.''

Christian wrung his cloth and laid it on the table, then ripped his doublet and shirt to the waist to expose his cut. "How obliging of you."

"Your hand is shaking."

Tightly gripping the cloth, Christian began wiping the blood from the cut. "Get out."

"I can see your fear." Blade came closer and pulled the cloth from Christian's hand. He dabbed at the wound, refusing to relinquish the cloth when Christian reached for it. "It has taken me a long time, but I finally understand. You tried to convince yourself that what you felt for Nora was lust and pity. But now that she hates you, you have to face the truth." Blade held the cloth over the wound and grinned. "It wasn't pity that made you marry her, and you know it. You love her, so much that it frightens you."

"You really are a little bitch."

Blade chuckled. He took Christian's hand and placed it over the cloth on the wound while he tore another cloth into strips and folded a third into a pad. "Whoreson, mayhap."

"No, bitch is the right word."

"You're just angry because for once someone is dangling you over the fire instead of the other way around." Blade shoved Christian's hand from the wound and pressed the bandage to it. "Shall I tell you what happened? You found her, begged forgiveness, and she spurned you. And you, who are so accustomed to ladies worshipping at the altar of your beauty, who cannot abide having your will thwarted, you tried to subdue her."

"Have you remembered who you are yet?"

Wrapping a strip of cloth around Christian's shoulder, Blade continued. "Poor Nora, you'll drive her to madness. While I will enjoy your anguish when you lose her, I grieve for the lady."

"Ha! Don't drag out your mourning rags so soon." Christian pushed Blade away and hopped off the table where he'd been sitting. "She's changed. Transformed herself into a dueler and harpy all at once. Nearly cut my arm off."

Blade's mouth dropped open as he looked at the bandage. "She did that?"

"Another ill happening that should make you rejoice. Now get out before I decide you'd benefit from a few nights in the cellar."

Christian placed his hands on the rim of the bucket of water, gripping it tightly as Blade began to chuckle again.

"You're even more frightened than I thought. What ails you, my lord? Don't tell me you thought seduction would work. Why do you think she ran away?"

Blade had taken no more than a step away before Christian was after him. Sliding around the youth, he blocked his path.

"What are you talking about?"

Frowning, Blade stuck his thumbs in his belt. "You haven't guessed, I see."

"Explain."

"You really don't look well." Blade pulled a stool toward Christian, who ignored it. "It's the ride and not eating. You're going to drop at my feet."

"I want an explanation."

"Before she disappeared, Nora told me that she couldn't bear for you to touch her, you know, as a man does when he wants to arouse a woman. Since the wedding night, she said. Christian!"

Lightness in his head kept Christian from protesting when Blade caught hold of him and lowered him to the stool. He pressed his lips together and gripped Blade's arm as he closed his eyes against dizziness.

"Am I entertaining you?" he asked.

"I'll call for help," Blade said.

"No, it will pass." Christian tried to open his eyes, but the room was still whirling, and he shut them again. "Does it give you good cheer to know that I've lost her?"

"What you did, was it so terrible?"

"Unforgivable."

"Are you sure?"

Christian almost smiled. "It was far worse than anything I've done to you, my comfit."

There was a long silence.

"I wish you would eat," Blade said at last. "There's no challenge in fencing with you if you can't even stand."

"I'm not hungry."

Forcing his eyes open, Christian noted that the table in front of him stayed in one place. Grateful, he pushed Blade from him and stood. The table wavered, and he reached out. His hands hit the edge, and he clutched it for support.

"Go now," he said. "I promise to fight with you later."

Blade hesitated before walking way. "I'll leave a man outside the door."

Inclining his head, Christian listened to the young man's footsteps fade. The little beast was right, he thought. He was afraid, afraid of meek Nora Becket. What Blade couldn't know, but had made Christian see, was that his fear angered him. The greater the fear, the greater the anger. Anger had been his comfort and his disguise for so long.

When he was small and a slave to Jack Midnight, he survived by turning fear into anger. Only now, the anger worked against him instead of helping. It made him lash out at Nora and drive her farther and farther away.

What could he do? She said she didn't care, and that frightened him. He could hardly bear to think of her indifference. He'd rather have her hate.

What he really wanted was forgiveness and love. God, he hadn't known what he possessed when he had her love. She used to look at him with such wonder, as if he were a treasure and feast all in one. And her mind, it was so unique. He could share the most complex philosophies with her, then arouse in her a lust that drove them both wild with the itch to sate it.

Christian sucked in his breath as his thoughts turned carnal. He held his hand up before his face. It trembled with the maelstrom of conflicting emotions within him. He'd made a mistake in giving in to lust, fear, and anger. He would correct the mistake. But how?

Curling the shaking hand into a fist, he grasped it with his other hand. "Please, God, help me."

Sitting on that stool in the kitchen, he spoke with God and set his wits to work. The hour of the evening meal approached by the time he'd settled on a plan. Meanwhile he had sent a maid to unlock Nora's door and give her a note promising good behavior in return for her word not to flee during the night. Nora sent back her agreement, and a truce prevailed.

Not with Arthur, however. Christian watched the boy ram a hunk of venison into his mouth and chew as if he wished it were his captor's flesh instead of a deer's.

"We hay yoo."

"Swallow your food," Christian said.

Arthur gulped. "We hate you. You're a monster."

"I said I was sorry."

"We don't believe you and we don't care if you are sorry. We hate you."

Knowing it was useless to argue with the boy, Christian left the kitchen. Outside Nora's chambers, he met Tideman. The steward's features were set in formality, and he held the same puppy Christian had picked for his wife all those days ago.

Holding out the grunting and wriggling bundle, Tideman murmured, "My lord, your pet."

"It's not mine." Christian tried to contain the creature in its blanket as it decided to climb his chest. "You're still angry."

"Young viscounts who discard chivalry and their sacred obligations of marriage—"

"I know, I know, I know."

"Causing a lady such distress."

"I'm trying to do penance, if you'll step aside."

Tideman shut his mouth and stalked away. His heavy tread on the stairs gave evidence of how unappeased he was. Slipping inside the master's chambers, Christian came upon Nora as she was holding a wardrobe door open for a maid. Inside he could see the gowns he'd kept from her, all hung or laid out, and he almost sighed. Another source of guilt. He'd ordered those gowns made a few days before their wedding. They'd been ready soon after she'd arrived at Falaise, and he'd kept them from her.

The puppy yipped, and Nora looked up. She saw the puppy, gasped, and started toward him, but when Christian smiled and held it out, she stopped. Christian lowered his arms, calming his burden, and dismissed the maid. Nora sat down in the window seat and gazed outside. He could see the outline of her breasts as she turned to the side, and pain snaked through his groin. Setting his jaw, he willed himself to ignore his swelling flesh. He approached and laid the puppy in her lap.

Nora instantly cuddled the animal, and she brought its nose level with her own. As she nuzzled the puppy, Christian curled his hands into fists to keep from shoving his way between the two and taking the animal's place. He was so caught in his lust that her voice startled him.

"You see, I knew in my heart that it was a foolish thing to hope you loved me." She held up her hand to silence him when he would have spoken. "Think you I don't know how unremarkable my person is? I have the fascination of a shoe buckle, and the ordinariness. So when you actually married me, I thought, how good he is, how kind and wise, to see my heart and accept what I have to give."

"Nora . . ."

"No, you must listen, for I won't say this again." She stood up, holding the puppy to her breast. "Before the wedding I promised God that I would be the most perfect and obedient wife in the kingdom in return for His gift. I believed He gave you to me as a gift, a wondrous, beautiful gift, a reward for all the years I tried so hard to make myself worthy of someone's love."

She stroked the puppy's head with her cheek, and Christian could see that her eyes were dry, as dry as her tone. A poisonous fog of dread seeped into his bones.

"But you cast me aside," she said. "Condemned me in your own Star Chamber without inquiry, and showed at last your true feelings for me."

"Can't you see that it was a mistake?"

"Of a certainty. I know it was all based on a misunderstanding, but you will never convince me that the misunderstanding didn't bring out your true feelings for me."

"All it brought out was my own weakness and stupidity," he said. "I want you to let me make amends."

"Unnecessary. If you want to do something for me, allow me to go to my country house."

"No."

Again Christian beheld Nora's anger. It flared in her eyes and seared his gut, this wrath his cruelty had set loose. A few week ago, she wouldn't have dared show it to him. It was quickly gone, however. She thrust the puppy at him and resumed her seat at the window. Turning her face from him, she stared out into the growing darkness.

"I gave this damnable creature to you," he said, holding out the dog.

"I'm waiting."

"For what."

"For you to leave."

He set the puppy on the floor and crossed his arms. "I'm not leaving."

"I don't think you perceive my meaning." She fixed cold eyes on him. "It will happen whenever you come near. Whatever you say, whatever you do, I will simply wait for you to go away. Rail at me, implore, threaten, scream. It matters not, for deep inside all I am doing is waiting for you to leave. And when you do, I will go about my own life—as if you'd never come into it."

Remorse vanished. Stalking to the window seat, Christian growled out his words. "You can't do that."

"I have been doing it since you entered this chamber."

"I won't allow it." He heard his voice rise and stopped. Swallowing the urge to roar at her, he said, "Beshrew you, woman, I am your husband, and you owe me obedience before God."

"I've been thinking about that for a while. God's word was written down by fallible men. I'm sure He meant for women to be equal, but men perverted His truth."

"Blasphemy!"

She turned to face him again, a distant smile of amusement on her lips. Christian longed to fling himself on her and show her how impossible it would be for her to remain cold to him with his body on hers. He couldn't. Not now. He would destroy even her tolerance of his presence.

"As I said, I'm waiting for you to leave."

"God's blood." He took a step toward her, but managed to keep himself from taking another. She made no sign that she cared that she'd roused his ire. The little dragon's heart was encased in ice.

A sly thought popped into his head, and he sighed dramatically. Nora gave him a suspicious glance, but he was too busy dropping his pretense of confidence and letting his sadness show to notice. He sighed again, louder, then recited.

> Shall she never out of my mind,
> Nor shall I never out of this pain?
> Alas, here she doth me so bind
> Except her help I am near slain.
>
> I never told her of my mind,
> What pain I suffer for her sake.
> Alas, what means might I now find
> That no displeasure with me she take?

Nora gave a little snort, and he frowned at her. He walked up and down before her, then halted.

"You don't believe me." Even to himself he sounded like an outraged child.

"A quick tongue and beguiling looks I have come to expect of you."

"I was telling the truth."

"Marry, sirrah, I trow you wouldn't recognize it if it sat on your lap."

Christian's control shattered as Nora glared at him. He slid over to her and touched her neck with his fingertips. She started and burrowed deeper into the window seat.

"Sit on my lap," he whispered, "and let us test the matter."

A sharp elbow jabbed into his chest, and he stumbled backward, falling on his rump. He sat up, cursing, but stopped when he saw the crimson flush that spread over Nora's face and neck and down to her breasts. He'd shattered the ice, by God's teeth.

Not wanting to do anything that would bring back that ice, he rose and made himself leave. As he quit the chamber, he caught a glimpse of Nora's face, still red, and couldn't help chuckling.

Nora heard and shouted at him, "Go cozen one of your bawds, my lord. Surely Mag is about somewhere ready to give you what I will not."

Christian's amusement vanished. He had forgotten how great was his sin, how cruel were the deeds for which he must atone.

No fuzzy, fat puppy was going to make up for his transgressions. No, it would take a long time, this atonement. A long time indeed.

Several weeks later Christian was well settled into Failaise but was not a feather's length closer to earning the forgiveness he desired more than he ever imagined. Pacing in his study late one afternoon while his clerk deciphered a message from Inigo, he crossed the path of a golden ray of sunlight. The haze of light struck the silver clasps of his coat, and he stopped, studying the flashing sparkle of his signet ring. It reminded him of the disaster of Nora's jewels.

Those jewels. Three days ago they'd arrived from the city in a silver-embossed casket. Pendants, rings, pearls in great ropes, and golden chains. Rubies and diamonds, yellow and red gold, more diamonds. He'd been glad of their arrival, for that morning he'd transgressed yet again by telling her she could not walk in the forest with Arthur.

She hadn't wanted his company and had said so. Her refusal had stung his already wounded pride, and he'd forbidden her the walk. Why should she enjoy herself, he'd told himself, when he longed for her so much, he would have followed in her wake like that puppy he'd given her, trotting at her heels, yearning for a pat on the head?

Thinking the jewels would soothe her ire, he'd brought them to her soon after she'd stomped into her chamber and slammed the door. At first, when he'd handed her the casket, she'd merely stared at it. He'd opened the lid for her, and his heart had thumped painfully as he watched her eyes widen in shock.

"What means this?" she asked.

"They are yours," he said. "You don't seem to want my words of apology, so I thought mayhap you would desire—"

"To be bought?"

He shook his head. He had been about to say that the jewels were as bright as her mind and soul, but she'd fixed her thoughts on bribery. She muttered something he couldn't hear and ran to the window, throwing it open. Digging a hand into the casket, she threw its contents out into the air. Unable to believe what he saw, Christian was slow to react. He watched a necklace with pearls as big as the tip of his thumb sail out the window before he cursed and hurled himself at his wife.

Snatching the casket back, he shoved her aside and peered out the window. The gravel path and lawn were sprinkled with jewels. A stableboy and gardener were standing on the path, gawking up at him. The rope of pearls hung like a white garland from the ivy on the wall below the window.

"Damnation," Christian said. "Don't leer at me," he shouted at the bewildered servants. "Pick them up." The stableboy blinked up at him and pointed to a chain of rubies and diamonds hanging from a tree branch. "Oh, God's blood, I'll be down anon."

Drawing inside, he turned on Nora. "Ungrateful scold, I was trying to please you." He snapped the lid of the casket closed.

"You dare tell me when I may and may not walk and then expect me to welcome gifts?" Nora curled her lip. "I suppose you think that because I am a woman, I have the moral character of a child, and that mere trinkets can appease me when I've been treated like possession."

Confused, Christian tried to decipher her reasoning. "You make no sense."

"You're expecting me to behave like a child. Only a babe can be spanked and then comforted with a fruit sucket."

"I wouldn't spank you," he said, trying not to show his bewilderment. She'd refused to speak to him further, though, and he'd had no choice but to leave her.

Shaking his head in disgust, Christian brought himself back to the present and resumed his trek across the study. He still didn't understand why she'd thrown that embroidery box at him as he'd stepped out of her chamber.

"My lord, the cipher. My lord?"

Christian held out his hand for the paper. The clerk stood by as he read the message, constantly wiping his hands on his black robe. Christian finished reading, then rolled the paper into a cylinder and touched it to a candle flame.

"Leave me, Thomas."

"My lord, it's too dangerous."

"At once."

Thomas left, and Christian walked to a book stand and

placed both hands flat on a translation of Plato. The cool leather of the binding failed to soothe him. He closed his eyes, searching for the will to command his rage. With Inigo's help, his father had taken over the search for their attackers. Not two days ago, Inigo had discovered that one of the murderers belonged to the household guard of Bishop Bonner. The Earl remained wary, Inigo had written, for if Nora had not betrayed them, someone else had.

Christian agreed. Bonner had been at the masque when the heretics had snuck out of the cellar against his orders. So had de Ateca. Jack Midnight had appeared out of nowhere to save them when they were attacked at the docks, and Christian had no faith that it was good fortune or Midnight's perversity alone that made for such a coincidence. His thoughts churned as he fondled the pages of the book. He would go to the city tomorrow. It shouldn't have been a heavy task to spy out the face of one of his attackers at Bonner's palace, yet he hadn't. However, the man could have been in hiding.

Someone pounded on the door, jarring Christian from thoughts of revenge upon Bonner. "Enter."

The door opened. Blade hovered at the threshold, but Nora appeared behind him and shoved him into the study. Surprised, Christian smiled at her. She returned his greeting with a scowl.

"The only reason I'm here is to protect Blade," she said, then punched the young man on the arm. "Out with it."

"I thought you'd be pleased," Blade snapped at her, "or I wouldn't have confided in you."

"I don't like de Ateca," she said, "and it is beyond my imagining to think that Lord Montfort could set you to cozening him. The man eats boys for dinner."

Christian rounded the library table and approached the youth. "What have you done?"

"Naught," Blade said.

Laying a hand on Blade's arm, Christian said, "Come now, marchpane, tell me a tale."

Blade stared at Christian, silent.

"You know what happens when he speaks like a lovestruck gallant," Nora said. "Better confess."

Edging away from Christian, Blade slipped behind Nora

before the older man could stop him. "As your dear cousin, I invited de Ateca to Falaise."

"Why?" Christian lifted Nora out of the way and headed for Blade. "Why, sweeting? Tell your loving cousin." He reached for the youth.

Blade danced out of Christian's way. "To provide you with a more cunning adversary than Nora."

"You're still angry for your own grievances, not Nora's."

"Both." Blade scuttled behind Nora again.

Christian stopped tracking him and put his hands on his hips. "You're mad. This day I've found nothing but vicious magpies in my house." At their pleased looks, he cursed. "When will the *conde* arrive?"

Blade wandered to a window and glanced out. "Oh, now, I think."

"God rot your hide." Christian sprang to Blade's side in time to see grooms leading several horses toward the stables. Sliding a look at Blade, Christian said, "You'll pay for this mischief. De Ateca may have the appetites of a Greek, but he has the twisted complexity of a Medici, and you've brought him near my wife."

As he finished, he noticed the quiet of the chamber. He and Blade looked up to find Nora gone.

"God's toes, she's gone to meet him."

Christian hurled himself out of the room with Blade close on his heels. One wrong word from Nora, and de Ateca would have the means to send all of them to their deaths. Nora was clever but innocent, and no match for the Spaniard. Praying that he reached them in time, Christian hurtled downstairs after his enemy and his love.

Chapter
XXII

Nora was approaching the gallery when she heard thunder on the staircase. His eyes smoldering, Christian swept down on her. She forestalled him.

"I'll rid us of de Ateca," she said.

"You can't."

"I got rid of you, did I not?"

She almost grinned when she saw Christian's neck and face flush.

"Listen behind the arras if you must," she added, and entered the gallery before her husband could object.

Ignoring his furious whisper of her name, Nora glided into the sunlit room with a greeting for the *conde*. Slender as a whiplash, the Spaniard glittered as he bowed over her hand, the light catching the shine of his hair and the rich silver brocade of his cloak.

"I fear you've caught me alone, my lord," she said. "Blade and my husband have yet to return from hawking. And you must forgive our lack of proper greeting, for, you see, that flighty cousin of ours misremembered his invitation. I have ordered rooms prepared, but there will be delay."

De Ateca made light of the inconvenience, as Nora had expected he would, and she hastened to put her stratagem to work.

"I've sent for wine, my lord, and welcome this chance to converse with you alone, for I fear Blade has taken a liberty in inviting you to Falaise." She managed to conjure up a flush. "Being but newly married, I find I need solitude with my husband, and this is his wish as well. Indeed, my lord is sending Blade to Castle Montfort anon, so that we have privy time to learn of each other."

Nora watched de Ateca's face but could catch no hint of anger or irritation.

"Perhaps I will give company to the boy on his journey," the Spaniard said.

"Oh," Nora said. She hadn't thought the man would be so persistent. The arras that concealed Christian and Blade jiggled, and she took the movement as a sign of her husband's displeasure. "Of course, it will be as my lord decides."

Walking away from the arras so that de Ateca was forced to turn his back to it, Nora waved her hand to gesture to the whole long gallery. "What think you of Lord Montfort's changes to Falaise, my lord? We are quite modern here. Windows, look at the windows." She pointed to the mullioned panes that traveled the length of one wall of the gallery and reached to the ceiling. "No more dark and clammy castle rooms. And chimneys. No more soot on the roof beams. I've never lived in a house with so many chimneys and windows."

Enjoying herself now, Nora prattled on about wainscoting and oak panels as the *conde* fingered the braid on his cloak and almost yawned. He would flee the manor house in fear of having his wits turned to stone from boredom, she thought gleefully.

"Yes," de Ateca finally said. He removed his jeweled cap and twirled it with both hands. "Modern. However, Lord Montford seems altogether archaic in some of his tastes."

"My lord?"

"Musings, my dear Lady Nora. How is the Earl?"

"Much improved," she said. "All his humors are in balance again, and the wound heals quickly."

"My physician said that the Earl was lucky to live."

"Yes, and I find that certain herbs are most beneficent in healing sword wounds. Camomile—" Her mouth twitched with humor as de Ateca interrupted her hastily, before she could make him suffer through a lecture on herbs.

"Your skill is bruited far and wide since you cured the Earl," he said. He wandered away from her, along the wall of windows and headed back toward the arras. Nora hastily cleared her throat and began to blurt out something about herbs. Halting, de Ateca forestalled her again.

"Brigands and runagates abound in this kingdom, my lady. A disgrace it is, and King Philip would never allow so many thieves and murderers to run free in Spain, even on the docks."

"So many are displaced from their homes by enclosures," Nora said, her ire showing. "The nobility fence in land and toss tenants out in the road without any care for their livelihood. Why, even Jack Midnight was respectable before his lord cast him off his land and—"

The *conde* interrupted her yet again, and as she began to think, Nora allowed him to launch into a tirade on the shortcomings of the English nobility. Something de Ateca had said bothered her. *King Philip would never allow so many thieves and murderers to run free in Spain, even on the docks. Even on the docks . . .*

Christian had never mentioned that he and the Earl had been on the docks when they were attacked. He'd said they'd been on the southern bank, in the stews. She remembered because she'd been jealous of what he might have been doing in the lurid ordinaries and bawdyhouses of the area. Yet de Ateca said Christian had been on the docks.

"Merciful God," she whispered.

She wet her lips and looked at the arras. It hadn't moved. Had Christian left? Even as she wondered that, the hanging was swept aside. Her husband stood poised with one hand on the arras and the other caressing his sword hilt. Her body went cold, and Nora hastened to put herself between de Ateca and Christian.

"My lord, you've returned."

Christian paid her no attention. His eyes never left the Spaniard, and she almost shivered as the two stared at each other. Christian didn't say a word. He remained in the threshold, the fingers of his one hand caressing the ornate silver and gold embossing of his sword hilt.

Nora heard herself stuttering an explanation of the *conde*'s presence, but neither man responded. Finally de Ateca smiled and spoke Christian's name with a caress in his voice. Again Christian ignored the words. Nora twisted her hands together and stood on her toes in an attempt to see over Christian's shoulder if Blade was still there. The youth was nowhere in sight. She was left to deal with these two men by herself. If only she could get Christian away from de Ateca before he decided it was time to kill him. The wrath of the Queen would descend on all of them if Christian killed one of King Philip's noblemen.

She had no doubt that her husband was going to kill the Spaniard. She could tell from the way his eyes had lost all hint of feeling and from the way he held his body in that relaxed and lazy pose that had deceived her more than once. De Ateca hadn't realized it yet. He was still eyeing Christian hungrily, a thing he should not do, Nora realized, for she could see that the Spaniard's lust only added to Christian's rage.

The silent perusal had taken on the quality of a duel, with de Ateca participating in both amusement and ignorance of his danger. The longer Christian remained mute, the more fearful Nora became, until she was too scared even to shake. She remembered Christian fighting Jack Midnight and the bloodlust that had turned his magnificent body into an instrument of death. If he pursued Midnight with such exclusive purpose, how much more merciless would he be with de Ateca, who had blithely risked the Earl's life? In that moment Nora knew she couldn't stop Christian. He wouldn't allow it.

The silence ended at last when Christian stepped into the gallery and walked toward de Ateca. As he passed Nora, he whispered to her.

"Get you gone, love."

He passed her before she could shake her head, and she turned to follow his progress. He strode toward the Spaniard, coming closer and closer. De Ateca remained where he was, allowing Christian to alight within a sword's length of him. Nora crept as close as she dared and thus heard her husband's voice, soft, warm, and menacing.

" 'If a man come presumptuously upon his neighbor to slay

him with guile; thou shalt take him from mine altar, that he may die.' "

Christian paused and gave de Ateca a sensual, alluring smile that made the Spaniard take a step toward him. Then he drew his sword. De Ateca gawked at the flashing metal aimed at his heart, then recovered and fell back, drawing his own blade.

"You be far from the altar of God in my presence," Christian said. "And you will die, but not before I hack the truth from you."

Holding his sword at ready, de Ateca asked, "What truth? Are you annoyed about your cousin? I haven't touched him."

"Stop the pretense," Christian said. "Nora, get out at once."

She had thought herself forgotten. "No. De Ateca, he means to kill you."

Christian grinned and nodded, to Nora's great exasperation. Alarmed at last, de Ateca started to back away from his host.

"The docks," Nora said upon viewing the Spaniard's perplexity. "You mentioned docks, and I think you must know about the attack upon the Earl and my husband."

De Ateca stepped sideways in Nora's direction, but Christian cut him off.

"Leave, sweeting, or I promise I'll beat you for your disobedience."

Nora stuck out her chin, knowing from experience that Christian couldn't lift his hand to her. "I have a right to know the truth, for I've suffered as much as you have."

De Ateca's laughter made her look at him. He was moving again, trying to force Christian to face the windows. She scurried to the opposite wall and put her back to it so that she was out of the way and wouldn't distract Christian.

"So," de Ateca said. "I betrayed myself, and the beautiful viscount was present to hear it. But you don't know it all, and mayhap if I tell you, we won't have to fight. You see, it was a mistake."

Christian pointed his sword at de Ateca's eyes and wove a pattern in front of them. "How so?"

"I suspected your pretty cousin was but a distraction. He seemed to offer so much, but surrendered nothing."

"Spaniards have distrustful natures," Christian replied.

"We're also strong of purpose." De Ateca lunged and rammed his sword along Christian's blade until the two locked at the hilt. Grabbing his opponent's forearm, he held on and faced Christian over the crossed swords. "When you fed me your cousin, I realized my efforts to gain your interest were useless, so I decided on another method. If you were desperate for your life, you might come to me for help, and then I would have you."

"The heretics," Christian said.

"What heretics?" De Ateca whistled softly. "So all the fantasies I whispered to Bonner contained a measure of the truth."

Nora shoved away from the wall, but remembered Sybille's teachings in time to stop herself from rushing at de Ateca. "You set Bonner upon Christian."

"It was the challenge, I suppose." De Ateca smiled at Christian over their locked weapons. "No one I've hunted has ever led me so intriguing a chase. By the Virgin, you nearly cut out my heart when I—but your wife doesn't want to hear about that."

"Out with it," Christian said. "I want to know what you said to Bonner before I kill you."

De Ateca clucked his tongue and shook his head. "You needn't fluff your feathers so, my cock. All I did was hint to Bonner about the possibility that you were a heretic. I considered threatening you directly, but decided you would kill me if I tried. So I used Bonner."

Christian shoved de Ateca away. The two surveyed each other.

"I expected you to be thrown in the good bishop's dungeon," de Ateca said. He sighed and flicked a glance at Nora. "But she interfered, and then Bonner set spies around your town house. I didn't know his minions were following you until after it was too late."

"You whoreson—"

"It is hardly my fault," de Ateca said. "I planned to come to you in Bonner's dungeon. I was going to give him enough time to make you desperate, but not enough time to mar your pretty face or any of the rest of you."

"That is sufficient," Christian said. "Make your confession, de Ateca."

"Christian, no," Nora said. "You've found out what you need to know."

"He will get all of us killed, Nora."

De Ateca chuckled. "Not if you please me as I demand."

"It will be as I demand," Christian said. "For not only have you threatened my father, you also cost me the love of this lady, and for that alone I will kill you."

Nora felt a jolt pass through her body. In an instant she understood the reason for Christian's fury, unbelievable as she found it. Belatedly she sensed the leashed but unmovable resolve in him, and its cause. Christian's body vibrated with it like a church bell struck by its clapper. For the first time she understood his remorse and his grief, understood that—much as he loved his father—the loss of her regard had driven him beyond his ability to endure. He was helpless, and Christian de Rivers could not endure being helpless.

"My lord," she said, "No. Think of the King and Queen."

"Look away, sweeting."

Christian charged de Ateca, wielding his sword so quickly that Nora could only see a blur. Even as she protested, de Ateca's sword flew out of his hand, clattering onto the marble floor near her. She snatched the weapon as de Ateca drew his dagger. When she straightened, Christian cast aside his own sword, aiming it to land at her feet. To her horror, his own dagger appeared in his hand.

"I want to feel you die when I stick this into your heart, Spaniard."

"You can't," de Ateca said. "After all, your father isn't dead."

"I'm not a fool. How long will it be before you threaten him or Nora to get what you want?"

"Not long."

Christian backed de Ateca toward an alcove holding a bust of Plato. The *conde* sidestepped the pedestal and bust at the last moment and leaped past his opponent, heading for Nora. Christian swerved and charged after the man.

For a stunned moment Nora watched the two race toward her, then cried out and bolted. De Ateca caught her skirt and yanked, but she bashed at him with the hilt of his own sword. The delay gave Christian the chance to catch up, and he launched himself at de Ateca.

The Spaniard turned in time to fend off the sweep of Christian's dagger, and the two fell to the floor, wrestling. Nora circled them as they tumbled one way and then another, cringing each time de Ateca's blade jabbed. Suddenly de Ateca threw his whole weight behind a lunge that rolled Christian beneath him, almost at Nora's feet. She pulled her skirts away from the fighters and backpedaled, but she was too late.

Christian caught sight of her dress. Distracted, he looked up at her, and de Ateca pulled his dagger arm free of Christian's grip, aiming for the younger man's throat. The tip darted toward the exposed flesh of Christian's neck, and primordial fear took hold of Nora. She raised de Ateca's sword in both hands, point down, and rammed it into the Spaniard's back.

She felt the sword slice brocade, silk, and flesh. It lodged deep in the man's chest, and blood splashed on her skirt. De Ateca gagged, his body rigid, then collapsed on top of Christian. Christian, his hands fending off the Spaniard's dagger, grunted and hurled the body from him.

The sword jerked from Nora's cold hands. She stumbled back, gaping at the dead man. Christian swept her into his arms, crushing her to him.

"He didn't hurt you?" he asked.

She tilted her head back to stare up at him. "I just stabbed a man, and you ask if I am hurt. Of course I'm not hurt. He is the one who is hurt."

"But you're a woman and delicate of mind and body."

"There is no time for delicacy. We must hide de Ateca."

"Blade stands guard outside. No one will come. You aren't going to faint?"

"Don't waste time, my lord." Nora chewed her lip while she thought. Vaguely annoyed that Christian didn't realize their danger, she set her mind to solving the problem while he fussed over her. "I know," she said suddenly. "Change clothing with him."

"What?"

"Put on his clothes." She was already busy pulling de Ateca's cloak off his body. "Quickly, before any more blood gets on them. You will steal out of the manor with Blade. We'll hide the body in the window seat for now. You and Blade will ride out to the forest. When you're far away but still visible, I'll see to it that his men catch a glimpse of you. Once you see them, ride into the forest.''

Christian was standing over Nora, his brow furrowed. ''Where de Ateca and Blade will encounter brigands.''

''Indeed.'' She yanked at one of the dead man's boots.

''This is another punishment,'' he said as he knelt to help her, ''making me wear a dead man's bloody clothes.''

''It serves you right.''

Christian paused in removing de Ateca's doublet. He ducked his head so that he could see her eyes, and she blushed.

''You saved my life,'' he said. ''I thought you said you didn't care about me.''

''Put the clothes on.''

''Nora, you killed a man for me.''

''I would kill a man for a kitten, too.''

''So,'' he said with a smile, ''I at least merit the affection you give kittens and puppies.''

She avoided his eyes by pulling up her skirt and ripping a strip off her petticoat. She began wiping the blood on the floor.

''Sweeting.''

She scrubbed furiously.

''Nora.'' He drawled her name in a low, caressing tone. ''My little dragon.''

She threw the bloodied cloth on de Ateca's body and tore another piece of petticoat.

'' 'Behold,' '' he murmured in Latin, '' 'thou art fair, my love; behold, thou art fair; thou hast doves' eyes.' ''

''Will you hurry? Cozen me not when we have a dead man in our gallery.''

Christian began unlacing his doublet. ''As you command, sweeting. 'One gracious word that from thy lips proceedeth, I value more than others' dove-like kisses.' ''

''God deliver me from all men.''

Several days later Nora was sitting on the riverbank with her embroidery while Blade and Arthur fished. At the moment Blade was lying on his back, eyes closed, his fishing pole stuck in the ground beside him. Arthur, on the other hand, busied himself with the task of spearfishing, having found Blade's method too tame.

Nora snipped a piece of gold thread and whispered to Blade, "You should be at prayers begging God's forgiveness for causing that man's death."

"He deserved to die. How many poor peasants do you suppose he sent to their deaths for not knowing the doctrine of transubstantiation?"

"Weeping false tears in front of those Spanish noblemen when they came to fetch the body."

Blade stretched his arms and yawned. "We were supposed to have been close. I had to."

"Telling them what a godly and virtuous man the *conde* was. Saying what a loss to King Philip it was."

"That was Christian's idea. Good, wasn't it?"

Tossing her embroidery aside, Nora clasped her hands and stared at them. "God will never forgive me."

"Nonsense. If He forgives popes for all the things they've done, He'll forgive you for defending your husband. It was your Christian duty."

Heartened, she lifted her head. "Do you think so?"

"Verily."

"I hadn't thought about it in that way."

Nora contemplated this newfound justification while Blade and Arthur gathered their poles and fish and tramped off to the manor in search of food. After she had killed de Ateca, there had been no time to think, only time to conceal the act and survive. Since then she had suffered tormenting guilt, certain that she was doomed to Hell. Not all her husband's reassurances that the *conde* needed killing had assuaged her remorse. The knowledge that she would do the same thing again to save Christian's life had proved to her that she was beyond forgiveness. Now Blade had pointed out that she'd promised to honor her husband before God. One couldn't very well honor a person by letting him die. Mayhap she wasn't doomed.

"To let him die would have been the greater sin," she assured herself aloud.

Satisfied, she looked around for her discarded embroidery.

It was lying on top of her sewing basket. She reached for it, and a shadow fell across the material. Looking up, she beheld the cause of her sin. Christian met her gaze and smiled at her, picking up the embroidery and kneeling to hand it to her. As she took it, he placed his hand on hers, and she started.

Bleakness overcame Christian's smile, and she glanced away from him. Irritated with herself for regretting his unhappiness, she removed her hand from his grasp and took up her needle. It wasn't her fault, she thought. His nearness scattered her wits and sent small demons to torture her body with unwanted excitations.

Christian rose and strolled toward the riverbank, his head down. She watched him, fascinated by the way his thigh muscles moved as he walked. Encased in their second skin of black hose, they seemed at once hard and yet flexible. Once she had heard one of the maids at Falaise twittering in rapture over Lord Montfort's legs.

God's mercy, she thought. It was becoming more and more difficult to hate him. She couldn't not hate him, for if she let go of her hatred, he would dominate her, bully her, crush her under his boot. Wouldn't he? Of late he seemed more interested in kneeling at her feet than putting her beneath his.

He turned suddenly to look at her, and she dropped her gaze to her sewing. She tried to ignore him, but he came back to her and dropped to her side. Extending those disturbing, long legs out and crossing them at the ankles, he propped himself up on an elbow.

"What can I do to make you stop hating me?" he asked.

Disturbed by the similarity of their thoughts, she shifted slightly away from him so that she wouldn't have to feel the heat of his body. "I don't hate you."

"But you don't love me."

"No."

"All feeling for me is dead?"

He was looking deep into her eyes, and she flushed, changing the direction of her own gaze to the gold and crimson threads of a flower in her embroidery.

"I don't know. Don't touch me!"

Whipping his hand away from hers, Christian rolled onte

his stomach. The movement brought his body on top of Nora's skirt, but he was careful not to trespass by touching her body.

"You're not sure," he said. "Sweeting, if you waver, it must mean that you are considering forgiving me for my unforgivable doings."

She shook her head, confused by his gentleness. A contrite and sweet-natured Lord Montfort was a creature of fantasy.

"Please?"

"You hurt me," she said.

"I want to spend my life atoning for it."

"That would do no good."

Christian ducked his head to catch a glimpse of her averted face. "Mayhap you need courting, my flighty mistress. Shall I woo you?"

"Cozen me, you mean."

"Nay, little dragon."

Quick as a fly, he twisted his body and rose on his knees. Sinking onto his heels, he captured her hand. Nora tried to get it back, but he wouldn't release it.

"It is mine by rights," he said. "At least let me hold it for a moment. I promise to do naught else. This time."

"Hmmph."

"I promise. Know you the laws of courtly love?"

She shook her head, for her mouth was too dry to allow speech.

"There are twelve, and the last declares that practicing the solaces of love, thou shalt not exceed the desires of thy lover. I swear to abide by the laws."

"But I don't trust you."

"How could you after what I've done? I must earn your trust, although after I tried to kill that bastard whoreson Spaniard only a stubborn woman would—God's blood, you try my small store of virtue, woman."

"Small store indeed." She yanked at her hand again to no avail.

"Hold still. I'm trying to court you."

"I have no need of courting."

"Yes, you do, and you're going to be courted if I have to it here until nightfall."

"Oh, very well." She gave up trying to wrest her hand from

his possession. Glaring at him, she set her mouth in a straight line and waited.

Christian grinned at her. He stroked the back of her hand with his fingers, then squeezed it.

"Such a mite of a hand." He kissed that hand. "Listen to me, Nora.

> Noble lady, I ask nothing of you
> save that you should accept me
> as your servant. I will serve you
> as a good lord should be served,
> whatever the reward may be.
> Here I am, then, at your orders,
> sincere and humble, gay and courteous.
> You are not, after all, a bear or a
> lion,
> and you will not kill me, surely,
> if I put myself between your hands.

She pursed her lips as he finished. His warm voice soothed her skittishness, but not completely.

"You are at my orders, sincere and humble?" she asked. "Humble?"

"As contrite and penitent as a debauched nun."

"Christian!"

"Curse it, I'm doing my best."

"Prove yourself, sirrah. Release my hand."

"But I'm not finished wooing."

"Release my hand or be branded for the cozening runnagate you are."

He threw her hand from him with an exasperated growl and planted his fists on his belt. "You are cruel."

"You said you were at my orders." She was beginning to enjoy her superiority.

"I also said I would be gay. I shall prove myself."

Nora didn't like the sudden glint in Christian's eyes. He began to whistle a tune and then burst into song.

> A rustical rosebud
> arose with the sun,

> *took flock and took crook*
> *and some wool to be spun.*

> *Her little flock boasted*
> *a sheep and a she-goat,*
> *a heifer, a bullock,*
> *an ass and a he-goat.*

> *She spotted a scholar*
> *ensconced by a tree:*
> *"What are you doing, sir?—*
> *Come and do me!"*

Christian whistled another few notes before breaking off to chuckle at her. Nora frowned, annoyed at the way her cheeks burned.

"As I thought," she said. "You're a cozener, a twisty, tricky lizard."

"You wound me, sweeting."

"And you're trying to make me laugh in hopes that I will forget all the terrible things you said to me."

"I confess it. You have me there."

"Well, you won't succeed." She jumped to her feet, scooped up her embroidery and sewing basket, and thrust them at her husband. "There. If you're going to serve me as you would an overlord, you may carry my burdens."

She gathered her skirts in both hands and set off for the manor without waiting to see if Christian followed. He did, though, for she hadn't gone more than ten steps before she heard him close behind, voice lifted in song once more.

> *I wish I were a throstle-cock,*
> *A bunting or a laverock,*
> *Sweet birds of the air!*
> *Between her kirtle and her smock*
> *I'd hide, I swear.*

Chapter
XXIII

In the fortnight that followed, peace descended on Nora's life, a peace she hadn't known since the day Christian de Rivers galloped into her life quoting poetry and lusting for blood and the pleasure of her body.

She hadn't realized how racked with chaos her life had become until Christian set about trying to please her. She woke one morning to find the entire household transformed. Tideman suddenly handed the manor's keys over into her keeping. With no explanation he and his underlings began to look to her for the ordering of the house, whether it concerned the making of tallow candles or the need to replace the rushes on the floors or the settling of a claim of paternity by one of the milkmaids. It took Nora little time at all to realize that, overnight, her husband had abdicated. Falaise was hers.

Thus Nora acquired responsibilities and duties for which she had been trained by nurses, governesses, and tutors but that she'd never dared imagine as hers. With the work came a growing feeling of worthiness, and deep inside her heart she felt iron bands loosening. She had work to do. Before, she had served Queen and felt useless without knowing it. In his search for he

goodwill, Christian had stumbled on an irreplaceable gift. Nora blossomed with each new task, each decision made and proved wise.

While she went about the unending chore of managing a nobleman's large household, Christian shouldered the duties Tideman so often chided him for neglecting. He rode across his lands, taking stock of forest and pasture, consulted with the clerk of the estate, and judged disputes. Yet he would disappear without warning, often for more than a day, and return to throw himself at Nora's feet and present some jewel or rare perfume to her. Not fooled, Nora refused the gifts while taking him to task for continuing to hunt for Jack Midnight.

One morning after Christian had returned from one of his disappearances, Nora was in the still room with three maids preparing to make rose water. She was standing on a stool and reaching for a jar high on a shelf when an arm lifted past her head. Christian plucked the jar from her straining fingers and swept her off the stool with his free arm.

"Good morrow, fair wife." He planted a noisy kiss on her cheek before he set her on her feet.

Glancing at the snickering maids, Nora nodded to Christian and snatched the jar from him. Undaunted by her frown, he indicated the open door to the still room, and the maids scampered out.

"I'm going to make rose water, my lord."

"An easy task for one as beautiful as a rose."

Nora lifted her brows and sniffed. Beautiful as a rose. What cozening. She turned away and set the jar on the work table behind her. The room darkened as she heard the door close, and she whirled to see Christian leaning against the shut door while he lit a second candle from the flame of one resting in the pewter holder by the door.

Already wary, Nora edged toward the vat filled with fresh water as Christian crossed the room.

"Don't take fright," he said. "I only want to give you something."

"Again?"

"Someday I will find a gift worthy of your admiration. Until then I will content me with poorer offerings."

He withdrew a small object from his doublet. Holding out

his hand, he opened it, palm up, to reveal a miniature prayer book wrought to hang on a lady's girdle. Bound with gold enameled in brilliant shades of red, blue, white, and green, it rivaled any Nora had seen hanging from the gold chains that swung from the Queen's girdle.

Unable to resist, she touched the binding with her forefinger.

"Take it," Christian said, his low voice sending quivers down her spine.

She held out her hand, and he placed the book in it. She opened it, perusing the Latin words. "It's beautiful."

"Far less so than you."

Fear burned through Nora's pleasure. He had praised her once before and then ground her heart beneath his boot. She handed back the prayer book.

"I don't want it."

Christian's shoulders sagged. "Why, Nora? I thought to please you. It's been so long—"

"Cooking-pot plain."

"What?"

"That's what you called me." She tried to swallow, but her throat was dry. "I've known for a long time that I was plain, but no one ever said that before. It was so much worse coming from you."

He made a violent movement with one hand. "Stop! You must forget the things I said. I lied. Can't you understand? I was mad, torn in two by love and hate. I don't know how you could believe those things anyway."

"Because my father already told me the truth."

"Your father wouldn't know the truth about you if God Himself came to earth and told it to him. I don't know what demon entered Becket's brain all those years ago, but I do know he's wrong about you." Christian eased closer to her, close enough to touch her sleeve. "If you don't believe me, I can send for at least a baker's dozen of my friends to swear to your beauty and grace of mind."

"A baker's dozen?" She twisted her hands together and thought a moment before shaking her head. "It's no use. I'm afraid to trust you again."

He stepped nearer. She met his gaze, and detected a firmness of purpose that increased her edginess.

"I bethought me that you might not," he said. "And if I don't find a way to regain that trust, I may indeed finally go mad. I can't even touch you. Blade says I will fade into dust soon. But don't look at me with those shaming eyes. I'm not trying to arouse your pity. I've decided that the way to gain your trust is to give you mine."

Nora left off twisting her hands as Christian held up the prayer book. He undid the tiny clasp to open it, then twisted the small tongue of gold metal. She heard a click, and the binding snapped open to reveal a compartment. He held the book out to her, and she saw inside a folded piece of parchment. He removed the paper.

"Take it," he said.

She took the parchment, opened it, and read. *"I, Christian de Rivers, Viscount Montfort, deny the Pope and his supremacy, and declare myself a believer in the church as ordained by the late Henry VIII of England."* Below the words lay Christian's signature.

The veins at her temples throbbed as Nora stared at the miniature confession that could send Christian to the stake.

"You're a heretic?" she whispered.

He shrugged. "According to the papists I am. I happen to think God cares more about the truth of our hearts than the outward trappings of our worship."

"You're giving this confession to me?" She suddenly recovered herself at the realization of what Christian had done. Fear lanced through her vitals, and with it, anger. She crumpled the parchment in her fist and pounded his arm. "Have you lost your wits? What possessed you to write down such a thing?"

Rushing around the vat, she stuck the parchment in the flame of one of the candles, then thrust the burning paper in the well of the candleholder. She watched it until she was sure the whole of it was burned. Turning on Christian, she shook a finger at him.

"You are never to do such a thing again, Christian de Rivers."

"You don't understand."

"I seldom understand the madness of fools."

"Listen to me."

"Writing it down, may God protect us."

He swooped down on her, catching her hand and pressing his lips to the backs of her fingers to silence her.

"You miss my point," he said. "I have placed my life in your hands." He turned her hand over and brushed his lips to her palm.

She gaped at his bent head. "Placed your life in my hands?"

"I trust you to keep it safe."

"But I wouldn't want you hurt."

Her shock had slowed her reasoning. It was beyond her to conceive of wanting to endanger Christian's life. It was also hard to believe that he would calmly hand her the means to do so.

"Mayhap I was too dramatic," he said. "I thought you would fancy the idea of holding my life suspended from your girdle."

Eyes widening, she cried out, "That's unconscionable! I could never do such a thing. The idea disgusts me."

Chuckling, he bowed to her. "I beg your pardon."

She reached out and boxed her husband's ear.

"Ouch!"

"Serves you right, addlepated fool. Have you written anything else like that?"

"No."

"Don't."

"Yes, little dragon."

"Give me the prayer book." She took it and placed it in the purse at her girdle. "So you don't take it into your head to make another madman's confession and put it in your hidey-place."

She opened the door to the still room, but Christian was after her in a trice. He stopped her by putting an arm across the threshold. She bumped into the arm, her breasts pressing against it. Throwing up her hands, she started to push him away, but he stooped to whisper in her ear.

"So if I want to hide something in the book, I will have to capture your girdle, my love."

She felt a hand on her waist. It slid down her skirt as if to search for the purse.

"Where is it?" Christian asked as he groped.

Her mouth fell open, and she gasped as his hand slid between her legs. Knocking his arm away, she scurried out of the still room.

"Come back here, wife. I've not done searching for my prayer book, and I've a sudden urge. To pray, that is."

For the first time in weeks, Nora found herself smiling. She quickened her steps as she heard the still room door slam and Christian call her name.

"Nora, you thieving shrew, come back here with my prayer book."

Lifting her skirts, she dashed through the house and on to the herb garden, where she hid behind a thick stand of foxglove. Christian raced past on his way to the river. When he was out of sight, she stood up and looked in the direction he had gone. Strange it was, she mused, that she felt a thrill at being chased by him.

During the next two weeks Nora's fear of her husband lessened. Mayhap it was because he tried to bury her in costly gifts, each of which she refused. It could have been his habit of launching into bawdy song whenever she grew pensive, or the way he would forget what he was saying if he caught her looking at him.

She found herself looking at him often. It had been a long time since she had wanted to gaze at him, but lately she couldn't help secretly studying his lips. They were a dusky rose color. She knew they were warm and pliant, and she remembered the way they seemed to tug at some hidden knot between her legs when he kissed her. More and more she caught herself thinking such thoughts, and others equally as carnal. She decided Christian had deliberately invoked them with his songs and his preening.

Like a cock in a henhouse, he had taken to parading before her. Only he kept shedding his finery instead of displaying it. Why else would he breakfast in nothing but a shirt, hose, and boots? Those shirts, they were of the thinnest silk or cambric. Though cut full, they clung to his shoulders and arms, outlining long expanses of brown flesh and arousing in Nora the urge to tear the white material and expose the flesh to her touch. If only she weren't afraid.

That was the trouble. She was still the same Nora—timid, and sheltering in her heart a fear that Christian would suddenly turn monster again. She could be brave for Arthur, and she would continue to be, but to be brave for herself alone . . . that was another matter altogether.

So she dithered and stewed, longing to cast aside her wariness, yet afraid that in doing so she would be hurt beyond bearing. While she dithered, she could see that Christian suffered. Blade had been right when he told her Christian didn't eat.

He also prowled the manor at night, unable to sleep, and Nora began to feel guilty that she was the cause of his pain. When he had first returned, she'd been too concerned with her own fears to care about what he felt or said. Nothing he did touched her heart, and all she'd had left for him was distaste. Gifts were insults, compliments mere deceptions. Until de Ateca came and threatened Christian's life, arousing within Nora a violence she had never suspected herself of owning. Once stirred from her indifference, she found it impossible to recover it.

She couldn't ignore him anymore, and as she began to truly look at Christian, she beheld a man in agony. The evening after de Ateca's body had been removed to London, she'd been an unwilling and secret witness to that agony. Still racked with her own guilt at having killed a man, she had ignored her husband all day. After the evening meal, he'd given up beseeching her goodwill and said he would take a walk. Later, Nora went outside herself to the herb garden, thinking he would avoid that place that was so much hers. She was wrong. He was there contemplating the rosemary, and Blade was contemplating him.

"You're going to cheat me of my entertainment if you die of starvation," Blade was saying.

"Go away."

"Here."

Blade thrust half a loaf of bread at Christian. Christian glanced at it with no interest, then shifted so that Nora could see his face in the light of the moon. The beam illuminated his beautiful features with silver and emphasized the shadows under his eyes.

"What is it you want, comfit?" he asked Blade. "To feed me so that I'll have the strength to suffer?"

"If you wish."

He turned on Blade without warning. "I'll strike a bargain." His voice broke, and he snatched Blade's collar, shoving his face near the youth's. "Look, damn you. Look at me. Can you see Hell in my eyes? It's there. I'm tied to the stake and burning in the fire I set myself. Does it please you? It should, for by God I'd rather be broken on the rack than suffer this agony." He released Blade. "Begone, young vulture, and if you tell her what I've said, I'll give you the lie."

Blade fled, but Nora stayed to see Christian drop to his knees and cover his face with his hands. As she watched, she began to ache—ache for Christian. Furious at the resurgence of sympathy, she ran from the garden and locked herself in her chamber.

Unfortunately, all these weeks later, she was still unable to regain her indifference. As she watched Christian grow thinner, she felt shame, for part of her gloated over the fact that this man who had hurt her was now hurting as well. She prayed for forgiveness for this sin, and tried to get her husband to eat.

In the end, the only way she convinced Christian to take much food was to eat with him, and so began their daily meals together. Served by a smiling Arthur, at first they were both wary. Blade's presence helped, for the youth taunted Christian, teasing him that he was too lovesick to eat and that the tale was going to spread to the whole court. Soon the two were sparring, and Christian would stuff his mouth full to forestall more jests. As the days passed in this manner, Nora began to feel as if she had a family, even if it did include a few bawds and vagabonds who appeared at odd times.

Late one night when the household was abed, Nora was drifting between waking and dreaming. She was having trouble falling asleep because Christian had approached her that evening, cornering her in an alcove of the hall and pressing his body to hers. He had run his tongue over her mouth, then kissed her with an erotic sucking motion that sent waves of titillation directly to her breasts. Her hesitation turned to response, only to be stifled by her fear once more. She fled, and Christian hadn't eaten a morsel at dinner.

He was probably still up, she thought, unable to sleep again. She remembered the purple stains beneath his eyes, marks of his strain. If he didn't find peace, he was likely to weaken himself until he fell victim to the sweat or a killing ague. As she worried over this danger, she heard the tiny grunts and whines of her puppy. He slept in a basket in her outer chamber, and she'd named him Catullus, Cat for short. The whines cut off abruptly, and she sat up in bed. She listened but heard nothing. Usually Cat's noises continued for a space while he rooted around in his bed, pawing at his blanket.

Curious, Nora got out of bed, donning slippers and a robe. In the antechamber she crouched beside Cat's empty bed. The little beast was prowling again, she thought, and someone had left the outer door ajar. She scurried after the puppy, but he wasn't to be seen. She heard a boot scuff on the stairs, and Cat yipped. The yip was silenced, and she heard Christian's voice soothing the puppy.

Even more curious than before, she followed the sound of her husband's voice, catching up with him as he stole past the herb garden. Clutching the squirming Cat to his chest and carrying a lumpy sack, he sped out of the sally port with a word to the guard on duty. Puzzled, Nora waited until her husband was through the port before sailing past the bewildered guard herself.

Outside, she spotted Christian racing across the meadow toward the tree-lined bank of the river. She hastened to follow, finally arriving at the clearing beside the tower ruins as Christian was dragging a flat rock into a pool of light cast by a newly made fire and moonbeams. Cat was gnawing at the discarded sack. Nora approached, concealing herself behind an oak tree.

As she watched, Christian snatched Cat up and fished around in the sack, producing a ceramic pot and jug. He placed the pot on the fire and poured liquid into it from the jug. Turning back to the sack, he withdrew what looked like a tangled rope and attached it to Cat's wriggling body like a harness. To Nora's consternation, he then began digging, loosening soil around a plant near the fire. This done, Christian tied a length of string to the base of the plant and attached the other end to Cat's harness. Then he crouched in front of the puppy and held out something. Nora heard his hushed voice.

"Here's some nice meat, Cat. Come get the goody. Come, Cat."

Cat stuck his nose in the disturbed earth and snuffled.

Thwarted, Christian stuck the meat in Cat's face; Cat chewed at one of his paws. Nora almost giggled at Christian's curse. He tapped Cat's nose with the meat, and this annoyance got the puppy's attention at last.

Short legs churning, Cat plunged after the retreating meat, dragging his harness and the string with him. Something popped out of the ground when Cat jumped on the meat. Christian laughed and snatched the object up in one hand while patting his assistant with the other.

By now Nora was almost certain that Christian's wits had snapped under the strain of their quarrels. He was digging for roots under the full moon. She could see the stalk of one in his hand. He placed it on the flat stone and began carving on it with his dagger. In a few moments he had a piece of the root separated. Rummaging in his sack again, he pulled out a gold chain. Nora watched him place the carved root in a locket suspended from the gold chain, then hang the chain around his neck.

Spreading his arms wide, he murmured something and lifted his face to the full moon. A black spider of suspicion crawled through Nora's thoughts. Witchcraft. She shut her eyes as the idea came to her, and by the time she opened them, Christian had moved. He withdrew from the sack six little pots and set them on the flat stone. Removing the pot from the fire with the aid of gloves, he set that on the stone as well. He pulled the cork stoppers from each of the six little pots, then took a pinch of something from one of them and dropped it in the hot liquid. Suddenly Nora heard his voice clearly, and she realized he was talking to Cat. The puppy climbed into his lap as he knelt behind the stone.

Christian held the snuffling puppy in one arm and stirred the brew with a stick. "Old goodwife Winnie said to put the vervain in first, Cat. I wonder if one pinch is enough. I don't want to wait. Waiting is killing me." Cat strained, trying to stick his nose in the pot. "No, you don't. That's not for you."

Nora smiled, certain that Christian couldn't be trying to work black magic with a puppy as a familiar.

"Five rose petals," he went on. "Here, Cat, you can have the sixth." Christian wiggled a rose petal in front of the puppy, and a small tongue lapped out to catch it. "Cloves, nutmeg, lavender.'' Christian dropped pinches of the contents of the other pots into his brew. "And ginger.''

Cat struggled out of Christian's grasp and watched intently as Christian stirred the contents in the pot with a stick. Murmuring softly as he stirred, he bent over the pot and sniffed. He sneezed. Cat sniffed at the vapors arising from the pot. He sneezed.

"Oh, no," Christian said as he tried to stir again. He sneezed a second time, and the puppy crawled onto the stone, sniffed, and sneezed just as Christian's own erupted once more.

Nora covered her mouth with both hands to keep her giggles from escaping. Christian sneezed; Cat sneezed. Christian sneezed, dropped his stirring stick, and waved his hands to disperse the fumes wafting up from the pot. While he was gasping for breath, Cat stuck his face over the rim of the vessel and lapped at the contents.

A muffled yip made Christian look down and snatch the puppy back. "No! See what you've done? You burned your nose, and it serves you right.'' He held Cat up in the air with both hands, sneezed, then growled in annoyance. Shaking the puppy, he said, "You probably ruined the spell, you greedy piglet.''

Cat squealed happily as his fat little belly swung in the air and his legs flailed.

"With my luck,'' Christian continued scolding, "it will be you who becomes enamored of me. I'll have a fat piglet for a lover.''

This last was too much for Nora, and she let out a hoot of laughter that startled Christian and his furry assistant. Leaning against the tree, Nora giggled while Christian thrust Cat from him and stood. As her husband stalked toward her, she tried to regain control, but the sight of him marching toward her with Cat at his heels only made her laugh harder. When he drew near, she managed to get a few words out.

"What are you doing?''

Christian frowned, toying with the chain around his neck. Then a crow of laughter burst from him and he caught her by the waist and swung her around in circles.

"It works!''

Nora felt her legs being swept out from under her as Christian picked her up and stopped circling. Cat yipped at them, then dashed off into the trees where he could be heard rooting around the leaf-strewn ground. Nora regained her breath, but lost it again when Christian squeezed her tightly. Before she could draw in enough air to protest, he swept off his cloak, threw it beside the fire, and plopped her down on it.

Landing on her bottom, Nora fell backward as Christian dropped on top of her. His body blocked out all light for a moment, then she felt his weight settle on top of her while he laughed like a boy with a new box of comfits. The chain around his neck hit her cheek. He stuffed the chain in his doublet, then lowered his head until his face was but a few inches from hers.

Startled at her own calm, Nora grinned up at his eyes crinkled in merriment. "I think your wits are addled by too much moonlight. What do you out in the dark, my lord? And how long have you been confiding your heart's wishes to puppies?"

Her answer came in a kiss. He said nothing, but covered her lips with his. Warm and quick, his tongue snaked into her mouth, teasing while he sucked. Nora forgot her questions, but the feeling of benevolence and merriment remained to be joined by a new and teasing tension. He lifted his head and began to lick and nip at her neck. She shivered.

"Christian?"

"I love you."

Not giving her a chance to reply, he kissed her again, all the while tugging at her robe. She felt the material give; then his body pressed against hers through the lawn of her nightgown. She tried to speak, but he kept her mouth too busy. Alarmed, she shoved at his chest. He lifted his head. His arm reached over her to the stone where the brewing pot rested. He grasped the vessel, lifted her head, and put it to her lips.

"Drink."

"But Christian, these herbs do nothing."

"Drink anyway."

He tilted the pot, and she took a sip to appease him. He got rid of the pot then and kissed her again. This time he pulled at the neck of her nightgown, ripping it to expose her breast. Pinching the nipple, he sucked rhythmically at her mouth before lowering his head to her breast. Nora gritted her teeth as pleasure flooded her breast and shot down her body to her groin. Breathing rapidly with each drawing motion of his mouth, she

complied when he pulled up her skirt and thrust his leg between
hers.

His hips nestled against hers, moving with the rhythm of
his sucking mouth, and Nora began to writhe. Christian yanked
her gown down around her waist and kissed a trail across her
ribs, over each breast, and up her neck to her mouth. His lips
barely touched hers.

"This is the food I need, my love. Feed me, feed me."

She opened her mouth, and he slipped his tongue inside.
She could hear him murmuring, urgent, demanding words of
hunger. They fed her own arousal as his hands fed the fire of
her body by stroking her bare legs. Skittering his nails over her
flesh, he tickled his way up to the juncture of her thighs. Nora
sucked in her breath as his fingers barely touched the warmth
between her legs. She gasped, almost spoke, but, as if he sensed
her protest, Christian took a nipple between his teeth and bit,
lightly. Nora shrieked at the jolt of agonizing pleasure that seared
her. Her legs parted, and he took advantage, covering her flesh
with his hand and stroking.

She wasn't given a chance to recover. She felt him tug at
her breast while he rubbed her wet and swollen flesh at the same
time. On and on he continued, stoking the fire of arousal until
her hips thrust upward. At their movement, he slid down her
body to press his lips to her groin. His tongue caressed and
stroked while his hands teased her breasts. When he fastened
his mouth over her and sucked, she arched her body off the
ground. Near mad with her frustration, she sobbed. Christian
lifted his mouth from her flesh, and she thought she might kill
him. He rose over her, holding his body away, his hands busy
with the laces at his hips. Nora lost all reticence then and ripped
at the ties that held his groin prisoner. His penis sprang free,
and she felt its heat on her hands. Christian whispered to her.

"Open to me, sweeting."

She hesitated, her gaze on his engorged flesh, and he swore.
Pressing her thighs apart, he shoved his swollen sex against hers
and flexed his hips. His sex teased her, and she grabbed franti-
cally at his waist, pulling him closer. The madness seized her
again as pleasure swelled in her groin, and she slipped her hand
between them to grasp his penis and squeeze. Christian arched

his back and let out a helpless cry. In one movement he shifted his organ and delved, slipping into her.

Nora felt her flesh part as he invaded, pressing his penis against the walls of her womb until they could spread no more. She lifted her hips, and he thrust fully into her, ramming against the base of her womb. She strained with her whole body, unsatisfied, until he grasped her breasts and pulled back. Pumping rapidly, he matched the thrusts of his hips with squeezes to her breasts, while Nora urged him on with violent writhings. Together they sank into a dark pool of sensation that fed arousal and admitted no other perception.

Nora gasped as Christian thrust deep into her, striving for the ultimate pleasure. She could feel it building to release, and she spread her legs wider as she arched her back to meet his driving penetrations. The release burst upon her when he suddenly grasped her hips, rose to his knees so that her feet left the ground, and impaled her with quick, driving thrusts. She screamed out her pleasure, and he doubled the pace of his thrusts. While satisfaction flowed over her, she felt him swell and swell, pump and pump. He threw his head back and cried out, and his hot seed spewed into her body.

The night air filled with their gasps. Nora's weight rested on Christian's arms as he remained frozen between her thighs, his penis jerking in spasms inside her. She lay with her shoulders braced on the ground, her legs falling on either side of his taut thighs, and feasted on the sight of him.

His head was still thrown back. With his features contorted in a tortured expression of ecstasy, sweat running down his neck and chest and disappearing beneath his shirt, he was a delicious sight. Nora wallowed in the sensuality of his abandonment to the needs of his body. He moaned, turning his head to the side, and thrust his penis deeper. She smiled, for she suddenly realized just how much a slave he was at the moment. Then his eyes slowly opened, and she beheld the lazy possessiveness within them. Her own eyes widened as he lowered her to the ground without withdrawing.

"Now," he said in a low, exultant voice, "now I have you." He kissed her nipples, then lifted his head to stare into her eyes. "At last, I have you as you have had me."

She tried to attend to his words, but she found their shift in position distracting. She wiggled her hips, and Christian sucked in his breath. Fascinated, she slipped her hands into his hose and grasped his buttocks. Squeezing the muscles, she turned her attention to the feel of his penis inside her. As she did so, she found that she could move her inner muscles to increase the feeling of fullness. It was easy.

"God's mercy, Nora, stop!"

"No."

He cursed and braced his hands on either side of her, shoving to try to withdraw. She pulled him back with her hands on his buttocks and sucked him farther into her body with her newfound muscles. He fell on top of her with a cry, then arched his back, forcing himself even deeper.

"Please, no," he muttered, closing his eyes and flinging his head back. "I can't. Ahhh!"

Feeling the swell of his organ, Nora lifted her hips against him. His penis responded, growing and shuddering in spasms to fill her again. A cry of defeat burst from his lips, and he surrendered with a renewal of his practiced movements. Obediently he pumped his organ back and forth, unable to escape. Soon Nora burned anew and they succumbed to their own lust in a mindless explosion.

Nora welcomed Christian's burning flesh as he collapsed on top of her. His hot cheek rested against hers. His arms and legs lay spread and trembling. He was heavy, but after all, it was her fault he was so exhausted.

She thought about his attempts at love magic and smiled. Only a man deeply in love would risk making a fool of himself. If his friends ever found out he'd consulted goodwife Winnie, he would suffer from their amusement and derision. Goodwife Winnie was a village cunning woman, one of many renowned in rural England for her knowledge of benevolent magic.

She remembered Christian's opinions about love magic, voiced long ago. Secure in his own near-magical appeal to women, he'd scoffed at poor louts who resorted to trickery. What such buffoons needed, he'd declared, was lessons in how to use their bodies to pleasure women, not spells. Poor Christian had been desperate indeed to have fallen so low.

Poor Christian. She turned her face to nuzzle his cheek, and heard his voice, low and vibrant with satisfaction, as he sang to her once more.

> *I have a gentle cock,*
> *Croweth me day:*
> *He doth me risen erly*
> *My matins for to say.*
>
> *I have a gentle cock,*
> *Comen he is of gret:*
> *His comb is of red coral,*
> *His tail is of jet. . . .*
> *His eynen arn of cristal,*
> *Loken all in aumber:*
> *And every night he percheth him*
> *In mine ladye's chaumber.*

Nora hadn't thought it possible for her skin to grow hotter than it was already. She burrowed her head into Christian's neck as he chuckled at her.

Poor Christian indeed.

Chapter
XXIV

Dreams relinquish their mastery, yielding to drowsiness, and Christian's wits surfaced from oblivion. A curious and disturbing state was this peace, he mused. He lay on his back, unwilling to rouse further, for when he did he knew he would suffer all the agitation of a spider with a torn web. It was almost Greek in its tragedy, his inability to trust his conquest. As if to underscore his apprehension, one of his eyes popped open to search through the fading darkness for Nora.

He spied a curve, and beholding it was all that was necessary to evoke a twitch between his legs. The other eye flew open, and he snaked his body over the mattress to plant his hips against her buttocks. Burrowing beneath the covers, he found her neck. Nora snuggled into the curve of his body, and he grinned a foolish grin he would never have allowed Inigo or anyone else to see. She had forgiven him, and he was silly with the generosity of her trucemaking.

If only he could be sure it was Nora who willed their communion and not the spells of goodwife Winnie. Nora had laughed at him for following Winnie's instructions about the mandrake root. Even now he blushed to think he'd believed the old woman when she said he mustn't pull the root from the ground himself. Still, Nora had appeared so quickly that night, she could have been ensorcelled to submit to him. Would her love disappear with the magic?

Even as he rubbed his groin against her pliant flesh, Christian had to thrust this fear aside. She had giggled at the notion that she wanted him because he had bewitched her. With an endearing blush she'd adjured him, protesting that his own sweet body was magic enough, and then proving it by worshiping it with her mouth. After this proof, he had spirited Nora to his chamber and refused to let her out for two days.

The two days hadn't been long enough to ease his lust, born as it was of a release from the fear that he would never have her again in any way. Peace was his undeserved reward—peace that arose from the knowledge that he was loved in spite of his most grievous faults and transgressions, and in spite of his rutting and uncontrollable lust. He felt Nora's hand fish behind her to clasp his penis, and he smiled. Mayhap his lust was not a fault in the eyes of its object. He sucked in his breath when she squeezed him.

"No wonder Mag caviled at giving you up," she said.

He shoved himself into her grip and bit the back of her neck. "She's had me since I was a babe and thinks she owns me."

"Not now. I do." Nora turned to face him.

"No one owns—*God's blood!*"

Christian's entire body arched as Nora pinched him with one hand while bringing her other hand up to cup him and squeeze. Before he could recover, she dove beneath the cover, took him in her mouth, and sucked hard. Clawing at the sheets, he only succeeded in tangling his arms into immobility. He fought the covers, trying to pull free of Nora's mouth at the same time. He almost won, but she outwitted him by shoving his thighs apart and using her teeth.

Searing jabs of pleasure drove him past thought, and he lifted his hips from the bed, pumping into her mouth while he writhed and gasped with a loss of control beyond his experience. When she squeezed the pouch beneath his sex, he hurled himself up blindly, lunging for her. Trapping his giggling wife beneath him, he set about erasing her triumphant smirk.

Though it cost him, he held her motionless, legs apart, while he cast the covers from the bed. Placing his hand over her sex, he cupped her firmly, yet did nothing else. She tried to wiggle, but his only concession was to lick her breasts. For long minutes he devoted himself to sprinkling long kisses on her nipples while refusing to remove his hand. He could feel her swelling and moistening, yet he kept his hand still.

Knowing she was trying to guess when he would move, he kept her in suspense as he took a nipple between his teeth and tugged, first one way and then another. Stiff and wet when he released it, the nipple jiggled before his eyes, and Nora hissed at him. Chuckling, he molded his lips around the peak and sucked. Then he stopped.

Still holding her, he lay his head on her breast and waited, listening to her ragged breathing. When it was almost normal, he slowly pressed with his index finger, sliding between moist folds, drawing it up to the apex of her thighs. He repeated the act again before parting her and loving her with his mouth. He kept at it until her nails scored his back. At that sign he rose, lifted her legs, bracing her thighs on his arms, and shoved into her.

It was then that he misjudged. His penis already ripe and painfully swollen, it took only that plunge to vanquish his precarious control. He rammed hard, and Nora clawed at his back. Working his hips with raw fury, he pleasured himself while she tried to swallow him with her mouth and her womb.

To his awe, Nora grasped his thighs and manipulated him to her own satisfaction. She forced his hips up against hers, then released a crescendo of groans as she climaxed. Her moist flesh sucked at him, and he ground himself into her mindlessly until he burst, spewing his wet release into that demanding vessel.

As he quivered in the aftermath of his pleasure, awareness returned. He opened his eyes to find himself on all fours, embedded in his voluptuous tormentor. Bewildered, he looked about the chamber, unable to believe his surroundings were the same, for surely he was not.

Sated though he was, a feral possessiveness flooded him, and he briefly considered sweeping this woman away to Castle

Montfort and locking her in a tower where no man but he could touch her. Madness.

A whimper escaped him as he pulled free of Nora, then lowered himself on top of her. He sighed, and she stroked his hair. He smiled at her whispered words of admiration, vowing to himself not to let her know how near to submission she'd driven him. There was no imagining what she would do to him if he surrendered mastery. Intrigued by the thought, he drifted into slumber wrapped in the soft arms and legs of his love.

Christian woke some hours later to the sight of Nora lacing her overgown. A caul of silver rested on the back of her head, in no way containing the wild locks that curled around her face and shoulders. She tied a last bow and looked up to find him watching her. At his frown, she sidled away from the bed, then sprang for the door. He leapt after her and threw himself against the portal in time to block her way. She bumped into his chest.

Catching her by the shoulders, he set her away from him. "No, sweeting."

"This is the third day," she said, folding her arms across her chest.

"I don't care."

"I have work to do."

He pointed behind her. "In that bed."

"You're afraid."

He lifted one brow. "Not of you."

"Yes, of me."

"Get back in bed, wife. I've more bawd's tricks to teach you."

"Christian de Rivers, your subtleties and cozening fool me not." She stepped close and poked him in the chest with one finger. "When roused you're capable of all evil, but you've cast aside your devil's mask with me, and I won't allow you to don it again. You're afraid the past days have been but a spell. That's why you're acting like a bee with a plucked stinger."

Trying not to look as worried as he felt, Christian caught the hand that jabbed at him and pressed it flat on his chest. Grinning lasciviously, he drew the hand down to his groin and thrust against it.

"Come, love, I need you." Nuzzling his wife's cheek, he lowered his voice. "Ripe as a turnip, I am, and as hard. Don't leave me in such pain."

"Deceitful jackdaw."

Having worked himself into a fit of hot lust, Christian was slow to react when Nora wriggled free.

She pointed at him, breathing heavily. "Naughty, naughty cozener of innocent maids. Unsporting, that's what you are. I love you beyond all reason, but I can't—I mean . . . Bedevil you, Christian, I'm sore!"

"Oh." He blinked at her, then snatched her hand to kiss it. "Damn and curse me, sweeting, I'm a rutting, selfish monstrosity."

"Mayhap not so terrible as that."

Stroking the back of her hand, he kept his gaze fixed on the path of his fingers over that small expanse of white skin. "What if you change? All this time you've been near the amulet." He touched the locket suspended from its chain around his neck.

"Goodwife Winnie is even more of a charlatan than you, my lord." She snuggled up to him and whispered in his ear, "Tideman says she tricks ignorant village wives into paying for fertility spells before they discover they're with child."

"The love potion worked."

"I use those herbs and spices to cure bad digestion and coughs."

"Bad digestion?"

"I will swear on the Bible."

"Nay, I would never think you a liar, sweeting. I know better." Christian sighed, unable to quell his growing desolation.

"I know," Nora said. "You can watch me step out of the chamber, and at the least sign that I hate you, jump at me."

"You're laughing at me."

"Only a little."

"Verily, you are a cruel mistress."

He sighed again, but turned and opened the door. Holding her hand, he nodded, and she took a step over the threshold. Twisting, she faced him and began to walk backward, slowly, smiling at him. Not returning the smile, he eyed her, his arm outstretched until his fingers could no longer stretch to reach her. He stopped breathing when she gained the top step of the staircase, but Nora only waved and vanished down the steps.

Cursing, Christian slammed his fist into the door frame. He should never have risked separation. He would lose her again, and mayhap die from it. Something pattered on the stairs. He glanced up, and a black-haired arrow shot at him. He toppled back as Nora threw herself into his arms.

"Boo!"

"Nora?"

He fell against the door frame, his arms full of curves and velvet. He felt a wet mouth on his neck.

Between kisses, Nora giggled. "There's magic, but it never fades, you delicious piece." She touched her nose to his, and he began to smile. "It is I who should be afraid to leave you unguarded. Any woman free of her winding sheet would give her whole dowry to drag you behind a bush."

"I only yield to black-haired witches with rose-petal cheeks and heads stuffed with Greek and Roman poetry."

"Then yield now, before I must needs see to the pickling and the making of almond butter and violet syrup."

Christian allowed his wife to force him down to the floor, not caring if the door was thrown wide open. "I yield, mistress, but only if you promise not to pickle a certain ripe cucumber."

This time when he woke, Nora was gone and a tub of hot water sat near a newly laid fire. Weary, his muscles aching, Christian took his time in bathing and dressing. When he finally emerged downstairs, he could smell roasting meat that signaled the approach of the evening meal. Nora wasn't in the kitchens, though jars of syrup and pots of butter attested to her day's labor. When he stuck his finger in an open jar of violet syrup, Cook chased him away. A turnspit smirked at him and said that Lady Nora was in her drying shed.

He was so addled he offered amusement for kitchen boys, Christian thought, scowling. He marched out of the house and through the kitchen gardens to the shed where Nora kept her herbs, spices, and tools. She was likely brewing some noxious tea for a sick villager or making a poultice, he mused. Since she had taken up her duties, the peasants looked to her for succor, as they had to his mother in times past.

Christian reached for the door of the shed, which was ajar, but his hand paused as he heard a man's voice.

"The tincture was a miracle. I drank it as you instructed, and a marvelous peace overtook me."

"It was the strain of fighting Christian and your own confusion at once," Nora said. "In time your humors will balance and your soul will calm, and perhaps then—"

"It's happened already. That's what I wanted to tell you. I remembered. Dear Nora, I . . ."

Christian turned his head to catch the rapidly fading words. It was Blade. Why was he whispering? Christian's eyes narrowed as he perceived the quality of Blade's low voice. Like a tightly wound lute string it vibrated, as warm as sunlit honey. Christian had heard that intensity in his own voice when he was alone in Nora's arms.

Easing the door open, he slid inside the drying shed, his gaze seeking Nora. She was standing beneath bunches of flowers and herbs hung on a beam to dry, a bundle of cinquefoil in her hands. The leaves crackled as she leaned close to Blade, and a wisp of a smile brightened her face and seemed to light the shadows in the room.

Christian held his breath, his hand sliding to the hilt of his dagger while he watched Blade bend over his wife, all cynicism and hauteur banished from his expression. As he spoke, his hand stole to Nora's cheek. Surprise plain in her widened eyes, Nora looked up at him.

"My everlasting thanks," Blade murmured. He lowered his mouth and covered Nora's.

His own bellow of rage caught Christian off guard as he hurled himself at Blade. Tearing Nora from the youth's arms, he rammed his shoulder into Blade's stomach. They both plunged to the ground, knocking over a table and a box as they went. Blade collapsed beneath him and banged his head on the packed earth floor. While the boy flailed blindly, Christian grasped a handful of doublet and drew his dagger. Rage burned through his body, sending all else into nothingness. He stuck the tip of the dagger into the soft flesh at the base of his victim's throat.

"Christian, no!"

He cried out, for Nora had taken hold of his blade even as he placed it at Blade's flesh. The slightest movement on his part would cut her. He froze, his gaze fixed on her fist.

"Remove your hand," he said.

"You can't kill him."

He smiled and met Blade's eyes. The youth's pallor and the heaving of his chest were the only signs of his fear.

"You're mistaken. I would kill him for his thoughts alone, much less for daring to touch you. Now take your hand away so I can hack his head off."

"He was but thanking me for helping him remember."

Tossing his head, Christian threw a lock of hair back from his brow. "I know the difference between gratitude and desire." Jerking Blade closer, he snarled into his face, "Whoreson jade, you'll tup no more men's wives."

Christian got no further, for a mass of prickly brown leaves attacked his face. Dust flew, and he sneezed. As his head jerked in reaction, Blade grabbed his wrist and thrust his hand and dagger away. Off balance, Christian fell sideways, and Blade threw him off completely with a heave of his body.

Christian rolled and, supple as a willow switch, sprang to his feet. Drawing back his arm, he backhanded Blade. The youth fell again, but lunged to the side and clutched a work table for support. Nora shouted Christian's name and thrust herself between the two as Christian charged. Careening into his wife, Christian picked her up gently, intending to set her aside. She swung her legs instead and wrapped them around his waist while looping her arms about his neck.

"You stop this at once, Christian de Rivers."

He pawed at her arms and legs. They stuck fast, and he growled with frustration. "This is one puppy you won't save." He tried to lift Nora's hips from their nesting place too near his groin. "Loose me, woman. Think you I'll let him touch you and destroy us? That's what he yearns for."

"It is not," Blade said. He wiped blood from the corner of his mouth and glared at Christian.

Christian was still trying to pry Nora from his body. "Stay you there but a moment," he told Blade, "and I'll be free to kill—"

Nora stifled the rest of his threat by forcing a kiss on him.

Christian struggled against the invasion of her tongue and tried to wriggle free of her body, only to stumble and fall against one wall of the shed. Tearing his mouth away, he caught a glimpse of Blade's back as the youth vanished from the shed.

"He flies. Let me go, Normmmph."

Her tongue darted into his mouth, and he almost forgot his wrath as she sucked. When she began to rub herself against him, his arms pressed her to his rapidly swelling organ. The heat of his rage fought with the burgeoning inferno between his legs. His undoing came when Nora at last slid from his body, leaving him panting and propped against the wall like a dizzy tippler. Giving him no opportunity to recover, she knelt and released his sex from its cushioned prison.

Coming to his senses, Christian was too late to save himself, for Nora cradled him in one hand and guided his organ to her mouth with the other. His body jerked in a puppetlike response, and he was soon mindlessly thrusting. His anger drowned in passion, he sank to the floor on top of his wife and brought them both to a noisy, joyous climax.

Christian roused long minutes afterward, braced himself up on his elbows, and scowled down at his wife. "You did that apurpose."

She smiled.

"You said you were sore."

"I am, even more now."

Flushing, he pulled free as gently as he could and peeked at his wife's thighs. Spying reddened flesh, he cursed and stuffed his uncontrollable self back in his clothing. Jerking at laces, he was about to scold Nora and then take off after Blade, when someone outside the shed spoke loudly.

"Well now, Poll, it seems our Kit's forsaken stews for sheds."

Christian winced at the sound of Inigo's voice as he tied a lace.

"Haven't heard such squawking from a gentry mort since I tupped that hang-bellied priest," Poll said. "Must have been nigh twenty years ago."

Nora covered her mouth, but Christian could see her eyes crinkle and brighten and her body shake with stifled giggles. It was his own fault for burning away her shyness with his lust.

Near bursting with the effort to forestall his explosion of temper, he stood, wiped the sweat from his forehead, and yanked her to her feet.

"This is your fault," he said.

He turned his back and stalked out of the shed, blinking as he emerged into the light. Inigo and Poll were waiting, smirks mounted on their faces like royal standards.

"Ooo," Poll crooned. "Look at him, all disheveled like a maid what's been jumped by a lord behind a woodpile."

Christian tugged at his doublet and refastened his belt. "How would you like to spend a se'night in gaol with about thirty gulls, whipjacks, and cutpurses for entertainment?"

"Now, Kit," Inigo said, "we but followed the steward's guidance. We'd have left as he did, but we were worried when you didn't reply to our messages."

Nora appeared at his side and placed her hand on his arm. "My lord has been most busy these past few days casting spells on puppies and—"

"Nora!"

Inigo laughed. "The Earl's in the house. Ready to chew nails, he is. Says if Kit hasn't thrown himself at Lady Nora's feet, he's going to take a riding crop to him."

Ignoring his wife's smile, Christian unsheathed his dagger and smoothed a finger down the flat of the blade. "Noses can be chopped off if they're stuck in places they don't belong." Poll retreated, but Inigo only grinned. "Does the whole kingdom busy itself with my affairs?"

"Nay, Kit. Word of your antics only spread as far as the South Bank. Since the Queen isn't in the city, the court won't know for weeks."

"God's blood, I'll carve that smirk from your face and wear it as a tourney favor."

Inigo held up his hands in protest. "I give. Got no wish to kiss the back of your hand like poor old Blade."

"Blade!" Christian rounded on his startled wife. "You thought I'd give up, you corrupting tease." He snatched her to him with one hand, shoving his face close to hers. "No man touches you and lives."

Thrusting her from him, Christian bolted for the house. Inigo called after him.

"The lad rode out to the east. I thought you knew. Wait, Kit, you haven't heard why we came."

Christian changed direction and made for the stables, shouting at the grooms for his horse. He was kicking his mount into action by the time Nora chased him down. Oblivious to her cries and those of Inigo, he urged his horse into a gallop along the eastern trail that skirted fields of corn and led to the forest.

Anger flaming anew, Christian strained over the neck of his mount, eyes searching for signs of hoofprints and broken vegetation. Blade's trail was easy to follow, for his horse had a dented hind shoe. Christian plunged into the darkening forest, knowing he had less than an hour's light to find his quarry. On and on he rode, his task made easy by Blade's failure to conceal his passage. Odd. It was as if the boy didn't fear Christian's pursuit. Mayhap the little traitor counted on Nora subjugating him entirely. The fool.

Christian pulled his mount up short when he heard a noise. Hardly daring to breathe, he waited while he sorted out the sounds of wind-tossed leaves and the swish of his horse's tail. There it was, the periodic *plop* of pebbles being tossed into water. He dismounted without a sound, then raced through the trees toward the *plops*.

Blade sat on a boulder at the edge of a pool, one knee bent, and tossed pebbles into the water from a collection in his hand. As Christian drew his dagger and crept up behind him, Blade sighed and held the handful of stones over the pool. One by one he rapidly dropped them into the water, then lowered his chin to his knee and studied the ringed waves that spread out from where the stones entered the water. Placing one hand on the boulder, Christian leaned toward the boy and laid the flat of the blade on his cheek.

"Coy little bitch, I've found you."

Blade dodged aside, whipping around to face Christian, and put his hand to his dagger hilt. Christian jumped, landing on top of Blade and squashing the youth's lighter body beneath his own. In a heart's beat his dagger was nicking the flesh at the side of Blade's throat. The youth went limp.

"Giving up so quickly?" Christian asked. "Unsporting of you, marchpane, for I lust after your suffering as much as for your blood."

Blade turned his head to the side as if to avoid the prick of the dagger. "I told you. I was grateful to Nora because I finally remembered who I was."

"How unfortunate that your discovery will do you no good."

"My father was dying when last I saw him."

"Be quiet."

"There is only me. I know that much. I'm his only child, spawned when he was already old. Think you he still lives, after grieving for my loss?"

"Keep silent, you whoreson infant cuckolder."

"Your father was quite young, but mine—"

"Damn your soul." Christian eased the dagger tip from Blade's throat. "Your name?"

"Nicholas. Nicholas Edward Fitzstephen. My home is on the Scottish border, a crumbling pile of stone and lichen, if I remember well. The Scots' raids have drained us, and Father likes not court or city life, so we kept to ourselves. You told me I sounded like an Oxford don. That's because my old tutor came from there. Father's mistake was to send me south to Oxford for more study. I never got there."

"You still might not."

"God's arse, Christian, I told you."

"Cease your protests." Christian shifted his weight, but still pinned Blade to the boulder. "Curse it, I could have killed you if you hadn't remembered."

From behind a tree a voice called, "Lies. If he was going to kill you, you'd be dead."

Christian sprang off the boulder, whirling to face the owner of that voice. Blade dropped to his side as Jack Midnight sauntered into view followed by a half dozen minions.

Chapter
XXV

Christian stared at his old enemy and cursed his own schoolboy jealousy for leading him into Jack Midnight's snare.

Midnight guffawed at Christian's expression and spoke to Blade. "He's wondering now. Wondering if you tricked him. His brain's bubbling and simmering with it, trying to decide if he can trust you. You were always quick, my treasure." Midnight held out a hand, palm up. "Come closer."

Christian held back, as did Blade.

"Don't make me send someone after you. So undignified for two lads of such noble lineage to be manhandled nd trussed up like geese."

Christian walked toward Midnight, halting at sword length. Blade followed to stand at his side. Midnight smiled at them, his gaze lingering to catch Christian's eye and hold it. Laughing softly, he walked in a circle, inspecting his two captives. He clucked his tongue against the roof of his mouth.

"For shame, rushing away without swords. Hot-blooded youth is your downfall."

Midnight stopped in front of Christian and drew his sword. His men closed in, weapons drawn. Christian dared not move.

"Throw the daggers in the pool," Midnight said.

Christian obeyed, and Blade also. As the daggers hit the water, Midnight raised his sword and touched Christian's cheek with the tip.

"I've been waiting a long time, love."

Mouth closed, Christian remained silent while he assessed his chances. He couldn't move until he knew whether Blade was an enemy or not. As if he sensed Christian's dilemma, Midnight chuckled.

Crooning softly, he said, "Ah, no, it's not what you think. One of my men spotted the boy. I thought to catch one pretty rooster and got two instead. Blade was always a bloodthirsty little cock, so I had to wait for more men. You see, it's a hard task to catch a beast rather than kill it, but I'm patient, and look at my reward."

"I'm not a child anymore," Christian said. "What do you want with me? Or with Blade?"

"That is my secret, love. And besides, you've hunted me from one end of this island to another for vengeance's sake, so you shouldn't be surprised."

"Where do you think I learned it?"

"Enough talk." Midnight traced a line down Christian's cheek with the sword and rested the point at the base of his captive's throat. "Now be a good boy and let Odo tie your hands."

"No. If you want me, you'll have to kill me."

Midnight hesitated. Christian tightened his leg muscles for a jump backward, but the highwayman's next words sucked the strength from his body.

"You don't want to die, Kit my love, for then you won't hear who it was who brought me out on this day of all days." Midnight paused to heighten Christian's interest. "Not Blade, love. Nora."

Christian shook his head.

"Oh, yes. The lady sent a message. Take him away, she begged. Kill him. A determined woman, your wife."

The world grew cold as Christian listened. He tried not to hear, but the words sank into his brain like arrows shot from a crossbow. Had he been fooled all along?

Blade jerked at his sleeve, rousing him. "It's another lie. Don't let him deceive you."

Shaking his head again, Christian said to Midnight, "You always did have a facile wit for a peasant, but you'll never convince me that Nora would—" He forgot what he was saying when Midnight held up a letter with a broken seal.

"An entreaty in your wife's own hand, love."

Christian slowly took the proffered letter. A few words crawled on black legs across the page. *Come to Falaise and he will be yours.* At the sight of Nora's name beneath the message, he shut his eyes. The letter was taken from him while he tried to stop the destruction of his very being.

Pitting all his will against it, he still lost, and hope died. It was if he were a castle and his foundation stones had turned to water. He could feel their massive support dissolve.

"You fool," Blade said. "That letter is false. She would no more betray you than light the faggots beneath a heretic at the stake."

"I hurt her so much," Christian said, not seeming to notice when Blade was pulled away from his side.

He stood motionless. With a ring of swords around him he couldn't dredge up the will to resist as Jack Midnight closed in on him.

"Christian!" Blade shouted, straining against the men who held him.

While Christian studied a dead log with blurred vision, Midnight grasped his arms and pulled them forward. With elaborate care the thief slipped a pair of manacles around Christian's wrists. Midnight's palm brushed his cheek, and Christian looked up to meet his enemy's bemused gaze.

"I expected fury and a fight."

Giving his head a slight shake, Christian tried to summon his old venom but found it drained along with his will.

"Have I your attention, love?" Midnight lifted Christian's chin. "Have I won at last, without having to put you to the scourge?"

"I would have preferred the scourge. Now I don't care what you do with me."

Christian watched without much interest as realization suffused his opponent. Midnight swore and yanked on the manacles.

"Bestir yourself. I want a fight."

His voice faint, Christian said, "There is no reason."

"There is reason!" Midnight shouted. "God's cock, your lineage is reason enough. And I want my final vengeance. I want you to fight and writhe when I break you to the saddle. There's no satisfaction in commanding a docile slave. Why do you think I chose you, and then Blade as your second?"

"I don't care."

Midnight sprang at Christian, slapping him across the cheek, then crashing his fist into his jaw. Christian reeled under the blows, his head near bursting. He sank to one knee, but two of Midnight's men hauled him upright to stand between them. Christian tried to pay attention, but the death of hope was smothering him.

He felt as if his wits were seeping from his body, trickling out on the ground and bleeding into the soil where they would be lost. He couldn't summon the will to protest, even when Midnight grabbed the chain between his wrists and dragged him to a tree. He heard Blade shouting, but it was too much of an effort to attend to the meaning of the words.

Vaguely surprised when someone unfastened his manacles, Christian's interest ebbed when they were replaced with his hands held behind him. Midnight tied a rope to the chain between the iron cuffs and tossed the other end of it over a branch overhead. He appeared at Christian's side, rope gathered in one hand.

"You need reminding of who is master," he said.

The highwayman began to tighten the rope, and Christian's arms inched backward until they were taut.

Blade hurled obscenities from where he had been tied to another tree. "Midnight, you son of a dog bitch, let him go!"

"Do be silent," Midnight said. "Your turn will come soon enough."

At this, Christian roused. "Midnight, release the boy. You have me."

"I want you both. Feel how much I want you."

Midnight yanked on the rope. With a snapping sound, it pulled tight, and pain stabbed through Christian's shoulders and arms. His body jerked. He bit back a cry as a burning sensation fired along his strained muscles and tendons. Midnight released the rope, and Christian's arms dropped.

The movement caused greater agony as the tension on his muscles was released. His jaw clamped shut to prevent a scream of pain. Sweat beaded his face, and his breath hissed through locked teeth. Midnight jerked the rope once more, and pain tore through his flesh again as the weight of his own body ripped at his chest and arms.

At last Christian cried out, then sank his teeth into his lower lip to prevent another lapse. Midnight loosened the rope, and waves of pain washed through Christian's arms, turning his leg muscles to water. He wobbled, but Midnight caught him around the waist. The thief shouted something at him, but Christian was deep in the anguish and couldn't hear.

As he felt himself losing the ability to control his responses, he decided that he didn't like pain any more than he had before Nora had made him want to die. A pity he'd not discovered this important truth a little sooner.

Christian chuckled at himself, and the chuckle fermented and frothed until it became laughter. Leaning against the highwayman, he shivered. Old memories of beatings came to him in red-tinged images of Midnight's face. Midnight's hand on a whip. Shivering again, Christian realized he hadn't stopped laughing.

Midnight cursed as Christian turned his head to look at him and chuckled. Pulling the rope taut once more, Midnight grabbed a handful of Christian's hair and forced his head back.

"Remembering old times, love?"

"May the heavenly Father rot your cock."

'That's my Kit,'' Midnight said. "You were made to prey on the innocent, not swoon over them." The thief gave the rope a jerk, and smiled when Christian's face drained of all color. "Join me of your own will, love. What else is left to you, now that you've had your fill of marriage? I'll help you get rid of your wife."

"Leave me be," Christian said between gasps.

Midnight shook his head. "I can't do that. Besides, one more tug on the rope and you'll beg me to do what I want with you as long as I stop the pain."

"No wonder your lord threw you off your land. Did you starve your own wife and child?"

The highwayman rammed his fist into Christian's stomach and pulled hard on the rope at the same time. Christian screamed this time, a scream that would have satisfied Jack Midnight's craving if it hadn't been for the mounted riders that charged at that moment.

In his pain, Christian was only aware of the sound of hooves and the clash of swords after Midnight had dropped the rope. The noise of battle pierced his senses as he fell. Midnight stopped his descent, hauling him to his feet. Christian stumbled forward over the arm that braced his body, and the thief grabbed his neck. Forcing Christian's head up, he put a knife to his captive's throat.

As his head came up, Christian beheld his father and three knights battling with Midnight's men. The Earl leaned to one side on his horse and slashed a man almost in two. Midnight bellowed at the Earl, and Sebastian looked at his son. There was a moment's pause during which the Earl stayed his sword. Christian tried to struggle against Midnight's hold, but his arms wouldn't move. Numb and useless, they were trapped between his body and that of the thief.

"Surrender, my lord," Midnight called, "or I'll kill your son."

Horror filled Christian's brain at the thought of his father in the hands of Midnight. "No!"

Writhing in Midnight's grip, Christian paid no attention to the blade that cut his skin as he fought. Sebastian shouted at Christian to stop, but he was past reason. Flinging his body to the side, he cursed as his small strength proved no match for his enemy.

"Hold still, love," Midnight said to him as he tightened his grasp, "for I want your head on your shoulders a bit longer."

Seeing his father dismount, Christian yelled a protest and renewed his struggle. Suddenly Jack Midnight yelped. The highwayman's body jolted, and Christian thrust a leg out to trip the man. Midnight lost his balance and fell to the ground with Christian beneath him.

Christian's head pounded the earth. Midnight's weight crushed his already tortured arms and chest, but he heaved violently anyway, throwing the man off him. The sounds of battle renewed as he scrambled to his knees.

Tossing hair away from his eyes and spitting dirt, Christian whirled, looking for Midnight. His jaw dropped when he saw Nora standing over the highwayman, a log in her hand. She bashed at Midnight's head as the thief lunged to the right. The wood caught him on the side of his head, and Midnight grunted and swayed.

While Christian watched, Nora darted forward and pulled her own knife from Jack Midnight's right buttock. The thief cried out and clamped a hand over the wound as he scrambled for safety. He crawled away, only to run into the braced legs of the Earl. Sebastian lifted a booted foot and jammed it into Midnight's shoulder, then pointed his sword at the man's nose and smiled.

"Well met, sirrah."

The skirmish subsided with the taking of Midnight, and still kneeling in the dirt, Christian looked up at Nora.

He met her eyes reluctantly. "Sweeting."

"What a crackbrained, goosewitted, addlepatted fool," she said. "You have the wits of a hobbyhorse."

Nora's fear for Christian brought tears to her eyes. She wanted to throw herself in his arms and spank him at the same time.

"You galloped off into the forest with no weapons and no escort," she scolded instead. "It's feverish mad you are."

"He said you brought him here."

"And you believed him? You faithless weathercock. You have a goose quill for a spine if you can't fortify yourself with trust in my love for you. Oh, beshrew that." She knelt beside him and touched his bruised cheek. "I would have your word, at once, that you will never frighten me so again."

"Stop him!"

They both turned at Blade's shout. Jack Midnight raced away from the Earl and bounded onto a horse. He yelped when his buttock met the saddle, but kicked the horse into motion.

"Midnight!" Christian yelled.

He struggled to his feet, but Nora grabbed him. "No, Christian."

"Let me go. He's getting away."

Desperate, Nora clutched at her husband, but Christian managed to throw her off. He took three bounding leaps in the direction of his horse. Blade ran up, holding out a key, and she watched the youth free her husband of his manacles.

Nora stretched out a hand to him, but he wasn't looking. He sprang for his horse, running lightly while holding his arms bent and close to his chest. As she beheld Christian succumbing once again to his obsession, she let her hand fall to her side.

"But what about me?"

She'd spoken to herself. He couldn't have heard her, for hopelessness had weakened her voice, yet his steps slowed. Hurt at his desertion when she wanted so desperately to hold him and be held, she dared not hope. Yet he stopped and turned back to her.

Midnight had already vanished with two knights in pursuit. She knew well that the thief was capable of escaping them, and that Christian knew it, too. Yet he had stopped.

She held her breath as he looked at her, then looked to where Midnight had disappeared. He stared in that direction for a long time and then turned his back to it. A thrill rippled through Nora's body as he took a step toward her, and another. He was coming back.

He stopped close to her and gazed into her eyes. His own were filled with pain. He didn't touch her, though he stood so near, his disheveled beauty a siren's call to her senses.

Nora's heart overflowed with love and longing, but she was uncertain. Her confidence in his love was too new, and he had proved his distrust of her twice in one day. All her old fears returned, gnawing at her faith in her worthiness. Mayhap he couldn't believe in her because there was so little in which to place his faith.

He touched her hand, and she gathered up enough courage to meet his gaze.

"If you can forgive me once again," he said, "I will devote the rest of my life to proving my love."

She hesitated, then said, "There is a thing I wish for."

Taking both her hands in his own, he stepped closer. "I will grant any wish."

"Wait before you promise," she said. "Will you give up

this mad vengeance? You feed it daily, and in doing so, starve our love. And Midnight could destroy us both.''

She waited, her fear held at bay only by her will. Christian lowered his head and kissed her hands before straightening to look into her eyes again.

''I was going to jump on my horse a moment ago and chase him until one of us dropped. I was almost there when I realized that my arms were too weak and I might not be able to get on the horse, much less ride. Then a strange thought occurred to me.'' He smiled and bent to kiss her cheek. ''I found that I was chasing Jack Midnight out of habit rather than need. I've lost interest in him.''

''You have?''

''Do you know what does consume my thoughts?''

She shook her head.

''The question of how my ferocious little dragon of a wife might punish me for my lack of faith.''

She threw herself at him, wrapping her arms around his neck, and burst into tears. Groaning as he lifted his arms to her waist, Christian murmured comforting words to her. Nora only cried harder.

''Y-you could have been ki-illed!''

''I'm sorry.''

''Never d-do that again.''

''Never.''

She bawled louder, and she felt his lips on her ear and her neck.

''Nora, don't. If you weep much more, I'm going to have to pick you up, and that will hurt my arms. You wouldn't want that.''

''Oh, your arms.'' She pulled back from him, wiping her cheeks. ''Do they hurt much?''

''They feel like they're stuffed with lead.''

''A well-deserved punishment,'' said his father.

Sebastian was seated on a nearby log, wiping his sword with a rag.

''Sire,'' Christian said.

''Hold your tongue, baggage. I'm all distempered because of you. I dislike having to save your life before dinner.''

Nora giggled, but covered her mouth with a hand whe

Christian tried to quell her with a threatening scowl. She placated him with a hand on his chest.

"Don't you want to know why I asked your father to give chase?" she asked.

"It would be a courtesy," Christian said.

"If you had listened to Inigo, you would have known that he got word that Jack Midnight had left the city. Poor Inigo came to warn you, but you wouldn't listen. And when you ran off, he told me instead. Marry, I near lost the beat of my heart with fear for you."

Christian started to lift a hand to his brow, but winced and lowered his arm. "I begin to think those spells I got from goodwife Winnie went awry and leached my brains."

Nora smiled at her husband. Even with his clothing torn, his face smudged with dirt, his body still called to hers, bewitching her as no spell could. His doublet was torn open, and the shirt beneath as well, revealing smooth skin that glistened with perspiration.

She hadn't yet had time to consider her response to his violence and jealousy. Now that he was calm, she found herself in awe. He was jealous. From the way he still eyed Blade, she could tell his anger at the youth hadn't faded completely. Poor Blade was helping the Earl's men tie their prisoners and kept a considerable distance from the viscount.

Nora was jolted out of her own thoughts by Sebastian's voice. It snapped with impatience as he castigated his son.

"If you had behaved yourself in the first place, she would have thrown herself at your feet, and you wouldn't have had cause to be jealous of an eighteen-year-old boy. God's blood, I've seen you charm jaded harlots and court matrons stuffed with virtue. How could you not win back the favor of so gentle a maid?"

Drawing closer to her husband, Nora watched shame and grief steal over his face. She took one of his hands in hers.

"Please, my lord," she said to the Earl, "he had won my favor and regained my love some days ago."

"You don't have to lie for me," Christian said.

"I'm not lying. It's only that I'm such a coward. I was afraid to trust again, until I saw you trying to cast a spell with Cat's aid. Before that, you were so . . . so . . . well, you're a frightening man, but there you were, in the middle of the night plotting to enslave me with a puppy and a magic spell.''

The Earl howled his laughter, almost falling off his log. Christian muttered something Nora couldn't hear, then bent down to whisper in her ear.

"Did you have to say that in his hearing? Beshrew you, woman, I'll not have my wife telling stories about me to my own father.''

Noting the rosiness that crept over her husband's face, Nora bit the inside of her cheek to keep from smiling. Newly burgeoning confidence flooded her. ''But Christian, you're so wondrous.''

He stopped his fuming and gaped at her. "Think you I am wondrous?''

She snuggled close, lifting his sore arms so that they rested on her waist. Raising her head, she looked directly into his eyes, letting him see all the worship and love she felt. She'd been afraid to reveal to him the whole of her enslavement, but now that she knew of his own captivity to her, she could be honest.

Christian was still frowning at her and didn't seem to know that he was rubbing his hip and thighs against hers. Her breasts tingled, and she stroked the soft flesh at the base of his throat. He murmured her name on a gasp and nuzzled her cheek.

"Wonderful,'' she whispered in his ear. ''Beautiful, wild. You heat my blood just by walking into a room.''

"I rejoice to hear it, for I plan to walk into rooms constantly.''

Standing on tiptoe, she kissed him. He remained quiescent while she explored his mouth, but soon rammed his tongue deep and thrust his hips against hers.

"Lewd baggage,'' the Earl said.

Christian lifted his head to smile into Nora's eyes. "We're lost to shame, sire.''

"Your pleasure will have to be delayed, Chris. You haven't noticed, but darkness is upon us, and I'm hungry. If you keep me waiting much longer, I'm going to throw you over my saddle and you can ride home like a sack of turnips.''

Nora giggled, and Christian released her.

"Please, sire. How can I teach my wife to respect me if you make such threats?"

Taking Christian's hand again, Nora said, "You may ponder that dilemma on the way home, my lord. And I will help you mount. A good wife would never risk having her husband look like a sack of turnips."

Chapter
XXVI

Two days after saving Christian's life again, Nora was overseeing the spinning of wool when Arthur burst into the spinning room, out of breath and flushed with agitation.

"Lady, they're fighting again, and I can't find the Earl." Arthur skidded on the flagstones as he tried to halt his flight. His foot knocked the leg of a spinning wheel, and the maid who was using it tried to cuff him. Arthur ducked and pranced out of reach. "Hurry, my lady!"

Nora lifted her skirts and dashed out of the chamber. Running behind Arthur, she only caught up with the boy at the door to the gallery. Though closed, she could hear Blade's angry tones through the panel.

"I won't do it."

Christian replied in his lilting minstrel's voice, which caused Nora and Arthur to exchange looks of dread.

"How foolish of me to expect you to be grateful."

Nora hastened to enter. Knowing that sweet tone marked the coiling of her husband's temper, she hurried to join him. He was sprawled in a chair in the bay of a window, long legs hanging over one of the arms. Dark hair gleaming in the sunlight and ruby earring flashing, he toyed with a sealed letter.

Christian glanced at Nora but returned to his lazy inspection of the seal on the letter. "The whelp summoned you to defend this ungrateful churl."

"How haps it that such defense is needful?" Nora asked. "I so enjoyed these brief days of peace."

Throwing up his hands, Blade snorted and jerked his head in Christian's direction. "I won't be herded like a sheep anymore. And I should be grateful for being prisoned in towers, beaten, and harried?"

Yawning, Christian suspended the letter between thumb and forefinger and began to swing it to and fro. Nora tried to read the name on it, but the parchment swung too quickly. She could see that, as intended, Christian's nonchalance dug into Blade's hide. The youth balled his fists and hissed curses under his breath. Before he could erupt into action, she darted her hand out and snatched the letter.

"This is for you," she said. She held it out to Blade, who put his hands behind his back.

Christian rose from his chair and slouched against the frame of the window. "He won't take it. Stubborn as a hired nag. My father sent emissaries to his father, all that way to the border and back, and now he sticks at reading the reply. I'm going to tie him to this chair and read the thing aloud to him."

"Whoreson pig-tupping ass."

Christian leapt from his slouched position to Blade's side, but Nora was ready for him. She dashed in front of her husband at the last moment and grasped his arms. Responding naturally, Christian enfolded her, then groaned as he realized his defeat. Over her head, he threatened Blade.

"If you don't clean your dockside tongue in Nora's presence I'll cut it out."

"Please, both of you," she said. "I'm weary of this bickering. Blade, why won't you read the letter from your father?"

Turning away, Blade said nothing.

"Come on, marchpane," Christian said. "Answer Nora, for it will be easier than answering me."

Quelling her husband with a look she'd learned from him, Nora went to Blade and put her hand on his shoulder. "You're afraid."

Blade nodded.

"Christian was afraid to face his father once, too."

Christian growled at her. "Nora!"

"He feared," she went on, "that the Earl wouldn't want him once his name and deeds were blazoned throughout the kingdom." Blade nodded again, and she squeezed his shoulder. "But the Earl cared naught for any of it. He loved Christian and wanted him back. Does your father love you?"

Blade's chin almost rested on his chest from his efforts to hide his face, but he managed another nod.

She held the letter out. "Then this can only be a message of love and rejoicing, and you need not fear to read it."

She waited patiently and at last heard a sigh. She edged the parchment nearer, and Blade took it. He stared at the seal, rubbing it with his thumb. Nora left him to take Christian's hand and urge him down the gallery.

"I don't want to go yet," Christian protested. "He might not read it, and I promised to send him north with an escort."

She jerked his hand, refusing to let it go as he hung back. "Heaven's mercy, I wish before God that someone had taught you that you can't govern the course of everyone's life."

A hand snaked around her waist, and Christian swept her up in his arms, carrying her out of the gallery. He kissed her as they passed a gaping Arthur.

"Beshrew Blade. I've found someone else who takes much more governance. And I've a yen to try my hand at it in bed."

"Christian, I was spinning." Nora kicked her feet as he climbed the stairs to their chamber two at a time.

"You can spin beneath me if you're able."

"You're a lewd man," she said as he paused at the head of the stairs to bury his face between her breasts.

"Yes." Christian's voice was muffled. "Remember to thank God in your prayers."

A se'night later, on a cool and misty morning, Nora stood at Christian's side and waved Godspeed to Blade as he rode across the drawbridge on his way north to his father. Blade's fears had receded, and she was only a little apprehensive about his safety, since the Earl accompanied him. Christian assured her that even

Jack Midnight wouldn't attack an earl and his party of soldiers and knights.

Rubbing drops of mist from the tip of her nose, she waved one last time. Christian took her hand abruptly and began pulling her into the manor house and up the stairs.

"What are you doing?" She still couldn't accustom herself to Christian's tempestuous behavior.

"Hurry. We must change and be gone quickly if we're to be in time."

She clutched the banister as he hauled her behind him. "Gone? Where are we going?"

"It's a surprise."

Minutes later Nora found herself dressed in a coarse wool petticoat and a gown that laced up the front. Her hair was covered with a white cloth, and she wore a cloak whose fabric sported shiny patches denoting its age. Christian matched her in his wool stockings, leather jerkin, and scuffed boots. He donned a plain soft cap, which he cocked at a jaunty tilt before grabbing her hand again.

"Come," he said.

Nora hung back, opening her cloak. "I can't. Look at the neck of this gown." She dodged Christian's groping hands. "No, sirrah. I've a caution of you when you turn that fierce wolf look on me."

"But sweeting, you're so—"

"Help me with these laces or I won't go with you. I think the petticoat is caught beneath." With Christian's assistance, Nora pulled the garment up until it covered more of her breasts. "Where did you get these clothes?"

"Marry, sweeting, I've forgotten, it's been so long, but it's clear that the lady who owned it before was boy-flat in the chest and wide as a galley at the hips. Are you sure you don't need more help?" He trailed his fingers down the cleft between her breasts, and she slapped them.

"You're the only nobleman I know who keeps chests full of clothes that belong to wool merchants and peddlers."

"We're going to be late."

He hurried her out of the manor, warning her to keep her cloak pulled over her gown. They set out with Inigo, Hext, and a dozen men, riding into the mist that still clung to the fields and forests that surrounded Falaise. They rode most of the day along little-used trails, with only short breaks for rest and food. The sky never cleared, and they traveled beneath a screen of unbroken gray.

As afternoon wore on, the mist thickened and the air chilled. Nora was riding beside Christian when he turned his mount and dropped back to speak to Hext. He returned quickly, and she noticed their escort left the track they were following and plunged into the trees. As they vanished, she turned an inquiring look on Christian.

"We'll go on alone from here," he said. "Hext will make camp for us."

"But what about thieves and Jack Midnight?" she asked.

"No thief travels these woods."

"Why?"

He stared into the thickening haze and smiled slightly. "These are special woods."

"You're being deliberately mysterious."

"Mayhap you're weary. We'll rest in a little while."

He guided them down into the woods. As they rode on, the mist thickened into a white sea of moisture, yet to Nora it seemed that Christian never faltered nor confused his way. No birds sang, and all the animals of the world seemed to sleep, for she could hear little but the thud of their horses' hooves on the padded forest floor, the clink of snaffles, and the creak of saddle leather.

When Nora's bottom was numb and her leg cramped from hugging the sidesaddle, Christian at last called a halt. After tethering the horses behind a screen of bushes, he gathered a blanket and a leather water bottle. He led Nora to a pile of blackened wood, the remains of a tree that had been struck by lightning. Behind it he spread the blanket and helped Nora sit. Groaning, she stretched her legs out in front of her while Christian dropped to her side.

"Now will you tell me where we're going?" she asked.

"No."

Fidgeting with the tassels on her cloak, she cleared her throat and tried to keep her voice from quavering. "You're—you're not angry with me?"

"Of course not."

She wet her lips and tried again. "Christian, you haven't decided to—to put me away?"

Shooting upright, he gaped at her, eyes wide. "By God's toes, you're afraid."

Letting out a sigh, she shook her head. "Not anymore. Not when you look so astonished. It's just that I hardly know you."

"It will take time for you to learn to trust me completely." He rested on his haunches and gave her a gentle kiss. "I understand, though it hurts to know that you fear me still. Don't be afraid."

He kissed her again, and her agitation vanished.

"I'm so glad you're not going to put me away," she said as he rubbed his cheek against hers. He murmured something she couldn't understand. "Because I would have to escape and fight you, for Arthur's sake."

Christian kissed her neck, then looked into her eyes. "I don't want to fight."

His stillness and the way he fixed his gaze on her finally snared Nora's attention.

"We're in the middle of a forest," she said, and put both hands on his chest.

He grasped her wrists, pulling her hands away as he bore her down beneath him. "I know."

"There's a mist."

"I know."

She wiggled as he grasped her ankle and slid his hand up her leg. "There could be bears and wolves."

"Not in this forest."

He pressed his palm against her inner thigh to spread her legs farther apart. When he slid between them, Nora tried to get up, but he pushed her back by the force of his lips on hers. She protested between kisses.

"We can't. Anyone might come along."

"Trust me. No one will come along."

She felt his fingertips teasing a path from her neck to her breasts. "Is this the surprise?"

"No. Now be quiet."

"But Christian—"

"Marry, woman, I shall have to make you be quiet."

Unfastening her cloak, he kissed her, and with his tongue

in her mouth she couldn't voice her objections. She tried to capture his hands, but he was too quick. Before she could stop him, he pulled the neck of her gown down to expose her breasts and stroked a nipple with the backs of his fingers. Tendrils of pleasure crept through her body, and she arched her back, forgetting bears and wolves.

They made love fiercely until at last they subsided together, weak and damp with sweat and mist. Christian sank down to her breast, and Nora could feel his sex buried within her, still swollen and alive with readiness. She lay in a daze and squeezed the taut mounds of his buttocks while he panted in her ear. After a moment he lifted his head and looked at her. She was shocked to find his eyes glassy with unshed tears.

"What's wrong?" she asked.

"Nothing. Everything is so right that I fear I'll lose it all, lose you somehow." He rested his forehead against hers. "Now do you see why I didn't want to need you, to love you? I'm afraid. It was like this when Father found me again. I was so afraid of loving someone, of being happy. If you love, you risk being hurt, and now I love you so cursed much, I think I would die if I lost you."

She hugged him to her, wrapping her legs around his and squeezing as hard as she could. "The only way you will lose me is if you stop loving me."

"You could die."

"Yes, but I would wait for you."

Lifting his head, he frowned at her. "Wait for me?"

"In Heaven," she said. "If I should die, I would wait for you in Heaven so that we can be together forever."

"I hadn't thought of that."

"Of course, you must promise to do the same, and no tupping any pretty angels while you're about it."

He started, then gave a bark of laughter. Holding her tight, he rolled, then withdrew from her and pulled her onto his lap. He chuckled and hugged her.

"You're a miracle. You have the wits of a scholar, the body of a—nay, I won't say it for fear of rousing the little dragon."

She kissed the top of his nose. "Can it be that the fearsome monster is cultivating discretion in his dealings with me?"

"It's not my fault that my schooling in the ways of the flesh took place in the stews." Christian straightened his clothing and helped Nora tie her laces before pulling her to her feet. "The time draws near, love. We should go if we're to make it back to Hext and the others before dark."

They mounted again, and Christian led the way through trees and mist until they reached a stream. As they rode along the stream, the landscape became more rocky, and the stream twisted and snaked through the uneven country. After less than a half hour's walk, Christian stopped. Nora pulled up beside him and saw that he was listening. She looked in the direction of his gaze and beheld an outcrop of rocks and fallen boulders behind which the stream disappeared.

In spite of the intensity of Christian's attention, Nora heard nothing unusual to merit the tension that gripped his body. His head craned forward, and she could see his thighs knot as he lifted his body in the saddle. Then she heard it. Faint it was at first, the voice of a woman pitched counter to those of several men. Low for a woman, the voice reminded her of someone she couldn't quite place.

Before she could pursue the memory, Christian dismounted and lifted her to the ground. He tied their horses and rounded on her, his jaw set and his eyes bright like jewels cast into fire. He looked at her without speaking, as if judging her worth, then smiled slightly and pulled the hood of his cloak over his head. He reached behind her and drew forth her hood too.

"Whatever happens," he said, "don't uncover. You must promise."

"You're frightening me again."

"Promise."

"I promise."

"Then come."

He took her hand and walked beside her to the rock outcrop. Stopping there, he took her other hand and waited, shaking his head when she asked what he was doing. The voices grew louder, and she realized that the strangers were coming toward them. As the newcomers rounded the outcrop, Christian dropped to his knees before her, kissed the backs of her hands, and giving her a swooning look, began to speak.

Since, love, our minds are one,
What of our doing?
Set now your arms on mine,
Joyous our wooing.
O Flower of all the world,
Love we in earnest!

Honey is sweet to sip
Out of the comb.
What mean I? That will I
Show, little one.
Not words but deeds shall be
Love's best explaining.

Nora's face burned, and she tried to pull her hands free as Christian recited to her before the approaching strangers, but her efforts were futile. He sighed and cooed at her, fawned and kissed her hands, until she thought he must have been struck by a wood faery's spell.

The strangers drew near, and Nora at last yanked her hands free. Christian stood, and she turned to face the newcomers. Her heart dropped to her toes. Walking toward them was a young woman with long, red-gold hair and pale skin. A tall woman who walked with the purpose of a military man and the grace of a queen. She was gowned in a riding habit of black velvet shot with gold. The lady's fingers were bedecked with rubies and emeralds, and a diamond perched in the crown of her hat.

Her gentlemen retainers, dressed almost as richly as their lady, had fanned out to the side and before the woman as soon as they heard Christian's besotted voice. One of them shook his riding crop at Christian.

"What do you here on royal lands? On your knees before the Lady Elizabeth's grace."

"Oh!" Christian said. He dropped to his knees again and jerked Nora down beside him. "Oh, oh, oh, we meant no harm, my lord. We're lost, my lord."

Stunned, Nora watched her husband's changeling performance while trying to take in what was happening. She hung her head and peeped around the edge of her hood to stare at Princess Elizabeth.

The Princess allowed her attendant to search Christian for weapons and belabor him with questions. Twitching her riding crop incessantly, she inspected Nora and Christian. Finally the lady appeared to lose patience with her zealous man.

"Enough, Alan. These are my good people. Good, honest folk who have lost their way. No doubt they are two lovers. I would speak with them a while, for it has been long since I've seen such happy faces about me. I will return to you anon."

Nora watched in awe as the Princess's words sent the five prepossessing noblemen away. They did not go out of sight, but far enough away that they couldn't hear their lady's conversation. When they'd gone, the princess drew near and held out her hand to Christian.

"Misrule, the tyrant has given way to the slave, I see."

"Not so, Your Grace."

Christian kissed Elizabeth's hand, and Nora was sure she saw the woman pinch his cheek before offering her hand to Nora.

"This is the young woman Cecil told me about?"

"Yes, Your Grace. My wife, Nora."

Nora took Elizabeth's hand. It was warm, and as she touched her lips to it, Elizabeth squeezed her hand. Nora felt something drop into her palm, but she had the wits not to acknowledge it or open her fist. She stuffed her hand inside her cloak. Elizabeth smiled at her, allaying some of Nora's apprehension.

"We hide, all of us, behind myriad disguisings," Elizabeth said. "But not for much longer, I pray."

"Fall draws nigh, Your Grace," Christian whispered, "and the physicians say the Queen can't last out the winter."

"Which do you favor?" Elizabeth asked Nora, indicating her riding skirt. "The French or the Spanish fashion?"

Nora's heart flip-flopped like a hooked fish. Elizabeth wasn't the kind of woman to ask frivolous questions.

"Neither, Your Grace. I like plain English best, whether it be fashion, food, or family."

Throwing back her head, Elizabeth laughed and slapped her crop against her thigh. "Yet you married this fanciful creature."

"My lord is indeed something of a—a phoenix, but he's an English phoenix."

"And what of Spanish and French birds?" Elizabeth asked. "Don't chew your lip, girl. Give me an honest answer."

"French and Spanish birds make noises like peace doves and conceal hearts full of deceit and malice, my lady."

Elizabeth glanced at Christian while Nora marveled at her own forwardness.

"Misrule, how haps it that you choose a wife so well when you spend most of your time cavorting with whipjacks and bawds?"

Christian bowed his head, then looked up at the Princess with a smile. "One who swims in mud oft appreciates a dip in clean water, Your Grace."

"Be off with you, insolence. And for the next few months play the enamored bridegroom. Keep you both in the country and avoid London. The ship of England is scuttled, and its crew is swimming to the nearest land. Some are drowning, and I would like it not should my dearest friends follow such unfortunates down to the depths."

"We will retire to Castle Montfort, Your Grace, and summon men to hold in readiness." Christian bowed his head again, and Nora ducked her own head as well. Elizabeth turned to go, but paused to whisper to Nora.

"If I were free, I would do as you have done. But then, I do so love glory, and each of us much act according to God's design. Farewell, Lady Misrule."

Nora clung to her husband's hand while they watched the Princess walk into the mist. When she could no longer see Elizabeth's black and gold figure, Nora shook her head.

"Merciful Heaven."

"I thought you would be pleased," Christian said.

"O merciful God."

Christian laughed at her, but Nora kept shaking her head from side to side.

"Merciful heaven."

"It's time to go," he said. "We must find Hext before nightfall."

"Merciful God." Nora was staring at her open hand.

"Nora, you're babbling."

"Look."

Holding out her open hand, Nora gazed at the object Elizabeth had dropped in it. It was a ring set with a cameo of ancient

Roman design depicting Venus and Cupid. On the back of the gold mount was engraved a Tudor rose.

Christian took the ring and slipped it on Nora's finger. "She's had to be brave for so long that when she hears of courage in others, she honors it."

"Courage? Me?"

Raising his eyes to the sky, Christian sighed loudly and began guiding Nora back to their horses. Still dazed, Nora said nothing until he gripped her waist and lifted her into the saddle. The feel of his strong hands on her body jolted her out of her shock. She placed her hands over his and feasted on the contrast between his violet eyes and the dark flush of his lips. She hadn't missed Elizabeth's flirting manner and concealed sexual appraisal of Christian. They were but a taste of what would happen when they emerged from seclusion.

Suddenly the dangers and troubles of the kingdom and Elizabeth's praise lost their primacy in her concern. Both could wait while she pondered the urgency of Christian's allure to other women. Then she remembered Christian's own professed weakness.

"Christian?"

Busy with Nora's saddle, he grunted at her. She bent down and put her palm to his cheek, and he glanced up at her. Her tongue darted out to trace her upper lip, back and forth, and his hands stilled on the girth straps. His lips parted as if he would speak, but he appeared to lose track of his thoughts as he stared at her lips. Her fingers skittered along his throat, delved beneath shirt and doublet, then retreated to play with his dark, soft hair. His lashes lifted, and she was drawn into the wildfire she'd aroused.

Christian grasped her hand and pulled it from his hair. "Careful, love, or you'll get what you're asking for."

"I wouldn't ask if I didn't want."

"Beshrew me, I think she means it."

He reached for her, but she knocked his hands away.

"Stay you, lecherous fiend. I've a yen to see you undress in a tent by candlelight."

Christian closed his eyes and moaned. "God has seen fit to punish me by enslaving me to a woman of cruelty and appetite." He ran to his horse, jumped on the poor beast, and kicked him into a trot. As he passed Nora, he pulled on her mare's bridle, urging her into motion. "Hurry, love. Hext has had plenty of time to put up our tent."

"I just had a thought," she said.

He pulled his horse near hers and urged the animal's shoulder into Nora's mare. Nora relented, kicked her mount, and they were off.

"What thought?" Christian asked.

"It occurred to me that I was indeed courageous, for it takes a woman of rare bravery to rule the Lord of Misrule."

"We'll see who does the ruling, woman."

She laughed, but cried out when Christian leaned over and plucked her from her horse. He set her in front of him and took her mouth in a long kiss.

"Mayhap we should share the ruling," she said when he released her.

"Mayhap." His gaze fastened on her lips. "And I will enjoy meeting your challenge."

Nora discovered that she wasn't afraid of his threat, so she smiled up at him, wrapping her arms around his waist. "And I find that I will enjoy the battle as long as you are the prize, my lord."

Don't miss Suzanne Robinson's next thrilling historical romance,

LADY HELLFIRE

on sale in February 1992 in the hardcover edition from Doubleday and in May 1992 in the paperback edition from FANFARE.

A lush, dramatic, and touching historical romance, LADY HELLFIRE is the captivating story of Alexis de Granville, Marquess of Richfield, a cold-blooded rogue whose dark secrets have hardened his heart to love—until he melts at the fiery touch of Kate Grey's sensual embrace. An American new to English high society, Kate is dazzled by Alexis's handsome looks, air of authority, and edge of danger. But he snubs her, and she vows never again to be so enthralled with a man. When she unexpectedly taps the vein of tenderness he conceals with bitter words, a blazing passion ignites between them. Still, he believes himself tainted by his tragic—and possibly violent past and resists her sweet temptation. Tormented by unfulfilled desires, Alexis and Kate must face a shadowy evil before they can surrender to the deepest pleasures of love. . . .

FANFARE
Now On Sale
CARNAL INNOCENCE
☐ (29597-7) $5.50/6.50 in Canada
by Nora Roberts
New York Times bestselling author

*A seductive new novel from the master of romantic suspense.
Strangers don't stay strangers for long in Innocence, Mississippi, and
secrets have no place to hide in the heat of a steamy summer night.*

A ROSE WITHOUT THORNS
☐ (28917-9) $4.99/5.99 in Canada
by Lucy Kidd

*Sent from the security of her Virginia home by her bankrupt father, young
Susannah Bry bemoans her life with relatives in 18th century England until
she falls in love with the dashing actor Nicholas Carrick.*

DESERT HEAT
☐ (28930-6) $4.99/5.99 in Canada
by Alexandra Thorne

*Under an endless midnight sky, lit by radiant stars, three women ripe with
yearning dared to seize their dreams -- but will they be strong enough to
keep from getting burned by . . . Desert Heat?*

LADY GALLANT
☐ (29430-X) $4.50/5.50 in Canada
by Suzanne Robinson

*A daring spy in Queen Mary's court, Eleanora Becket was williing to risk all
to rescue the innocent from evil, until she herself was swept out of harm's
way by Christian de Rivers, the glorious rogue who ruled her heart.*

☐ Please send me the books I have checked above. I am enclosing $_____ (please add $2.50 to cover
postage and handling). Send check or money order, no cash or C. O. D.'s please.

Mr./ Ms. _____

Address _____

City/ State/ Zip _____

Send order to: Bantam Books, Dept. FN, 414 East Golf Road, Des Plaines, IL 60016

Please allow four to six weeks for delivery.

Prices and availablity subject to change without notice.

THE SYMBOL OF GREAT WOMEN'S
FICTION FROM BANTAM
Ask for these books at your local bookstore or use this page to order.

FN 19 - 1/92

FANFARE

On Sale in January

LIGHTS ALONG THE SHORE

☐ (29331-1) $5.99/6.99 in Canada
by Diane Austell

*Marin Gentry would become a woman to be reckoned with -- but a
woman who must finally admit how she longs to be loved.
A completely involving and satisfying novel, and the
debut of a major storyteller.*

LAWLESS

☐ (29071-1) $4.99/5.99 in Canada
by Patricia Potter
author of RAINBOW

*Willow Taylor held within her heart a love of the open frontier -- and a
passion for a renegade gunman they called Lobo -- the lone wolf.
Their hearts ran free in a land that was LAWLESS . . .*

HIGHLAND REBEL

☐ (29836-5) $4.99/5.99 in Canada
by Stephanie Bartlett
author of HIGHLAND JADE

*Catriona Galbraith was a proud Highland beauty consumed with the
fight to save the lush rolling hills of her beloved home, the Isle of
Skye. Ian MacLeod was the bold American sworn to win her love.*

THE SYMBOL OF GREAT WOMEN'S
FICTION FROM BANTAM

Ask for these books at your local bookstore or use this page to order.

FANFARE

FANFARE

Sandra Brown

_____ 28951-9 TEXAS! LUCKY .... $4.50/5.50 in Canada
_____ 28990-X TEXAS! CHASE .... $4.99/5.99 in Canada

Amanda Quick

_____ 28932-2 SCANDAL .... $4.95/5.95 in Canada
_____ 28354-5 SEDUCTION .... $4.99/5.99 in Canada
_____ 28594-7 SURRENDER .... $4.50/5.50 in Canada

Nora Roberts

_____ 27283-7 BRAZEN VIRTUE .... $4.50/5.50 in Canada
_____ 29078-9 GENUINE LIES .... $4.99/5.99 in Canada
_____ 26461-3 HOT ICE .... $4.99/5.99 in Canada
_____ 28578-5 PUBLIC SECRETS .... $4.95/5.95 in Canada
_____ 26574-1 SACRED SINS .... $4.99/5.99 in Canada
_____ 27859-2 SWEET REVENGE .... $4.99/5.99 in Canada

Iris Johansen

_____ 28855-5 THE WIND DANCER .... $4.95/5.95 in Canada
_____ 29032-0 STORM WINDS .... $4.99/5.99 in Canada
_____ 29244-7 REAP THE WIND .... $4.99/5.99 in Canada

---

Ask for these titles at your bookstore or use this page to order.

Please send me the books I have checked above. I am enclosing $ _____ (please add $2.50 to cover postage and handling). Send check or money order, no cash or C. O. D.'s please.

Mr./ Ms. _____

Address _____

City/ State/ Zip _____

Send order to: Bantam Books, Dept. FN, 414 East Golf Road, Des Plaines, IL 60016
Please allow four to six weeks for delivery.
Prices and availablity subject to change without notice.   FN 16 - 12/91